A Nordic Knight
of the
Golden Fleece

Kris Tualla (signature)

Kris Tualla

*This book is dedicated to my husband,
who supports my efforts without fail,
and brags to everyone about my books,
even though
he won't read them.*

♥

Chapter One

November 19, 1518
Barcelona, Spain

Jakob Hansen sat astride his weary destrier, Warrior, and gazed down the steep hill at the city of Barcelona, nestled like a sleeping sea lion along the edge of the brilliantly blue Mediterranean Sea.

"Ah. At last." Sir Percival Bethington turned in his saddle to face Jakob. "After forty days of wandering through France, I feel a bit like the Israelites spying their promised land for the first time."

Jakob snorted. "Let's pray that we are not entering something far worse."

Bethington returned his regard to the city below. "True words, my brother."

Relief and trepidation warred within Jakob's gut. The journey through France took longer than they anticipated, mainly because Percival refused to travel on any day that looked as though it might rain.

Jakob rubbed his aching right thigh. If he were honest with himself, he suspected some of Percival's refusals were intended to allow him to rest his injured leg. Jakob did not want to ask the man outright—to do so might embarrass them both—but he never argued with the English knight when a day devoid of travel was declared.

Jakob smiled a little at the recollections.

Though he was attending the Order of the Golden Fleece to represent King Christian the Second of Denmark and Norway, he had spent the last several months in England serving King Henry the Eighth. As a result, Henry paid for Jakob's easy passage to Barcelona in the company of his own pampered representative, Sir Bethington.

Spending the two extra weeks elongating their journey at comfortable inns with fine food was in no way a hardship. Only his eagerness to reach Spain and begin his search for the Lady Avery Albergar of Toledo prompted his desire to move forward more quickly. His leg, on the other hand, greatly appreciated the respite.

Bethington glanced at the hazy sky, pale grey as a dove and hiding the sun, but offering no imminent threat of a downpour. A chilly breeze gusted up the hill, and he tightened his neck scarf.

"We ought to go on now. We still must find the house, and it is well past noon already."

Jakob nodded, and followed Percival's steed down the slope. Askel, his valet, and Denys, Bethington's man, came behind him, each leading a pair of heavily laden pack mules. The knights decided to forgo a wagon during this last part of their journey, due to the mountainous landscape.

Jakob had no idea what to expect of the Order, which was meeting in Barcelona's Cathedral de Eulalia for the second time in three years, and he had no idea how he would find Avery, who escaped four months ago from England and headed to somewhere in Spain. But he was greatly looking forward to sleeping in the same bed every night, and spending time in a seat that didn't rock and sway beneath him.

§ § §

Locating Barcelona Cathedral proved quite simple. The massive Gothic structure loomed over the city like a giant stone troll waiting to devour the disorderly and disobedient. Once inside its towering walls, Jakob made enquiries of the Spanish priests regarding the location of the leased house which he and Bethington would share while attending the Order's gathering.

Percival could have done so himself—as the men traveled these past weeks, they spent their mornings conversing in Spanish for the practice—but since losing the language competition to Jakob, and their shared tutor to unexplained circumstances, the Englishman's confidence was dashed.

Not only did the priest give Jakob directions to the house they were leasing, but the knights were presented with wrapped and tied bundles containing the robes they were required to wear when they attended the Order.

That was unexpected.

Jakob shot a questioning gaze at Bethington, who shook his head and gave a little shrug. The men accepted the packages, and Jakob wondered where they could tie them onto their over-laden mules. He blew an impatient sigh, resigned to carry the bulky thing on his lap.

"You may hesitate in Spanish, I haven't a care about that. But you will speak to me in Norsk," Jakob prodded in that language. The men and their entourage were once again winding through Barcelona's angled streets, following the directions given by the priest.

Percival smiled and nodded; their afternoon conversations in the Germanic Norsk flowed much more easily for him than the Romantic Spanish language did. "*Ja.*"

The men rode northeast along the Carrer de la Princesa, as they were instructed. The end of the narrow road called Carrer dels Assaonadors, where the leased house was located, was said to be less than half a mile from the Cathedral and would prove an easy walk, much to Jakob's relief.

The street they traversed now was lined with large limestone palazzos; clearly this was an area of the city where the wealthy had chosen to build their homes.

The huge houses were graced with an abundance of shuttered windows, many facing the sea in an attempt to catch the capricious breezes which chased each other through these manmade canyons of stone. Most of the houses had heavy, terracotta-tiled roofs, and inner courtyards—which could be glimpsed through an occasional wrought iron gate.

When the men reached the road called Carrer Montcada,

however, they were prevented from continuing their brief journey. A phalanx of men and women stood three and four deep along both sides of that prominent street, blocking their way.

All heads were turned to Jakob's right. Whatever held their communal interest was approaching from that side, and invisible to Jakob around the edge of the impressive palazzo on the corner.

"What is it?" Percival asked.

Jakob shrugged. "I can't see past this building. But I hear a drum."

A quartet of white horses moved slowly into view, their driver holding them back to match the pace of a stately human procession. Their black polished traces gleamed dully in the dim afternoon light, and their bridles' headpieces sported black-feathered plumes. The cool intermittent breeze caused the horses' tails to tickle their legs, and they whisked them in irritation.

The horses were held in check by a teamster dressed in black and wearing a wide-brimmed hat. He kept his head low.

"Funeral," Jakob murmured.

"Yes," Percival agreed.

An ornate, black-and-gilt wagon gradually moved into view. Stretched along its generous length was a very large casket. A few of the observers threw flowers onto the wagon; some made the sign of the cross and kissed their rosaries. Others merely watched in curious silence.

Judging by the outrageous size of the casket, and the plethora of gilded carvings covering its surface, the deceased was either very obese, or very wealthy.

Most likely both.

"Can you see how long the procession is?" Jakob leaned forward in his saddle, but he was too far behind the crowd to be able to see around the corner.

"No." Bethington pointed toward the procession. "But that must be the wife."

A woman, dressed all in black and carrying a bouquet of white flowers of a type Jakob didn't recognize, walked about five yards behind the hearse, as if to distance herself from the dead man.

She held her head high, nonetheless. Her back was stiff and straight, and she walked in a slow measured cadence with the drum beating behind her. Her bearing was almost defiant in nature, making Jakob wonder what sort of marriage this might have been. *Content* was not a word that leapt to the forefront of his consideration.

Though her face was covered by a veil of black lace, something about her deportment pinged in Jakob's mind. He leaned sideways toward Bethington, his eyes remaining fixed on the widow.

"Does she—" Before he could finish the question, a wet gust of sea air lifted the edge of the woman's veil.

"Good God!" Percival breathed. "Is that—?"

Jakob's heart tripled its own cadence in an instant. He stared hard at the widow, and mightily willed the breeze to blow again. To bless him with another glimpse.

An impulse prompted him to call out her name, before a hard slap of good sense closed his mouth. As she crossed his field of vision, passing between the rows of gathered bystanders, Jakob saw his chance fading.

Please, God. Let me see her.

The veil edged up again, higher this time on a stronger gust, and he saw the woman's aristocratic profile, pale skin, and neat black brows.

Percival grabbed Jakob's arm. "She looks like the Lady Avery."

Jakob nodded, unable to conjure a coherent sentence from the multitude of realizations bashing around in his head—until one thought bubbled to the top.

"*Perdóneme*," he called out to the well-dressed man standing closest to Warrior. "*Que ha muerto?*" Who has died?

The gentleman looked up, squinting in the pale afternoon glare. "*Señor Paolo Pacheco Mendoza, Vizconde de Catalonya.*"

A vizconde? Jakob imagined that would be a step down for a woman of Avery's status—if the widow proved to be her.

"*Y el nombre de su esposa?*" he pressed.

The man looked at him as if he was daft. Then with a shift of expression, which Jakob interpreted as extending grace for an obvious foreigner, he replied, "*Su nombre es Señora Averia Galaviz de Mendoza, Vizcondesa de Catalonya.*"

Averia. *Avery.* Vizcondesa of Catalonya.

Married. Now widowed. *Skitt.*

§ § §

Jakob sat in his saddle, stunned and unmoving, until the occupants of the crowd gradually returned to their previous occupations and their path was opened. Percival cleared his throat. Jakob lifted his eyes to meet the other knight's.

"I believe we continue this way." He nudged his horse forward.

Askel and Denys waited for Jakob to follow his fellow knight before they fell in behind him, leading the tethered pack mules.

Obviously now was not the time to discuss what they has just witnessed, and the glint in Bethington's eyes made that clear; but he had seen what Jakob saw. The set of the Englishman's jaw communicated that he had recognized the lady as well.

Averia Galaviz de Mendoza.

Avery had been married.

Is that why she turned his proposal aside and left England so suddenly—to be married to some *other* man?

If so, this union must have been arranged far in advance. Four months was barely enough time for her to travel the distance, take vows, and lose this husband. Her second husband.

Who was not him.

The idea taunted Jakob with vicious jabs, ridiculing him without mercy for daring to hope that he might yet, at the age of thirty-two, find a woman to share his life. Now that door was not only slammed shut, but wrapped in heavy iron chains and hung with an enormous lock.

How could he have misjudged her affections so completely, he wondered. When he held her in his arms... He could still feel the curves of her frame pressed against his, and smell the soft aroma of her perfume. Jakob gave his head a quick shake to dispel the excruciating memory.

Perhaps it was a monetary decision. Perhaps she did not have the income which he assumed that her status as the noble childhood friend of King Henry's wife, Queen Catherine of Aragon, and her position as the queen's chief lady-in-waiting would provide.

Even if that were true, there was no reason to believe she might be tossed from the Tudor court and be left to her own devices. She could remain safely at court throughout Catherine's lifetime.

Averia Galaviz de Mendoza.

Bethington rode in front of him. Wisps of his dark brown hair were loosened from its ties by the brisk breezes and flailed airily about his head. He cast a worried glance back at Jakob now and again, his clear green eyes bright in the dimming day.

During their six-week journey, Jakob eventually told the Englishman—who had, himself, courted Avery unsuccessfully for a year before Jakob arrived in London—the whole of what transpired between him and the beautiful Spanish lady. Including, of course, Jakob's spurned offer of marriage to the woman known in the Tudor court as the Ice Maiden, made just three days before Avery disappeared from England without explanation.

Percival offered all the appropriate sounds of understanding and co-misery and then, at his urging, the pair of knights commiserated in the tavern until morning. That was the one day that they did not travel even though the capricious French weather was unusually pleasant and accommodating.

Averia Galaviz de Mendoza.

Skitt.

Chapter Two

"This should be the right house."

Bethington's statement shook Jakob from his melancholy. He tilted his head back and looked up at the building, three stories tall and looking solid as the stone from which it was crafted.

Jakob nodded. He and Percival dismounted and approached the home. Percival lifted, and then dropped, the heavy iron knocker, summoning anyone from behind the dark wood-and-iron gate. "The leasing agent said that the house should be staffed…"

An unfriendly face appeared in a little square, and barred, opening.

"How may I help you?" the man asked in Spanish.

"I believe you expect us," Jakob answered in kind. "I am Sir Jakob Hansen of Norway and Denmark, and this is Sir Percival Bethington of England."

Jakob noted that the man's brow twitched when he heard the Old Testament name. His questioning eyes flickered over Jakob's tall frame, pausing on his golden hair and blue eyes.

Jakob wondered if, while he bided in Spain, he might be wise to call himself by his middle name Petter. Queen Catherine's parents, King Ferdinand and Queen Isabella, had driven all Jews out of Spain only a quarter of a century earlier. If he did so, that might ease his path in this determinedly Catholic land.

The man sniffed, deciding. "Yes. One moment." Then he disappeared.

Jakob cut his gaze to Percival, wondering if the Englishman was thinking about Lady Avery and their startling discovery—because in truth, he could think of nothing else.

Bethington flashed a rueful, tight-lipped smile, but said nothing.

With a loud clank, the bar was lifted from behind the gate. Then both of the wide paneled doors were pulled open from the inside, their hinges groaning in thirsty protest.

Jakob stepped back and took Warrior's reins. He led the big stallion through the opening into the cobbled courtyard inside, where the clop of his iron shoes reverberated off the house's white stone walls as if to announce the knights' awaited arrival.

The ground level of the structure was comprised of the palazzo's service areas—the workshops and enclosures which would be dispersed around the perimeter of the main house if this home was located in the countryside and not the center of a busy seaport city: stables, carriage house, storehouses, and kitchens, among others.

The men handed their mounts to a pair of young grooms, who led the four horses into the stable. The quartet of mules waited patiently, each with one leg cocked and head down, until their packs were unloaded by three house servants under the watchful eye of the majordomo.

"How many servants abide here?" Jakob asked.

"I believe there is a staff of about two dozen," Percival replied.

The majordomo, whose name was Señor Esparza, spoke to Askel and Denys, both of whom had been listening to a-month-and-a-half's worth of their employers' Spanish conversations.

Denys nodded and nudged Askel's arm.

Askel nodded as well, though his expression was far less confident.

The majordomo clapped his hands and barked a name, prompting the hurried appearance of a footman whose purpose was apparently to claim the knights' personal assistants and get them settled into the servants' quarters. After brief introductions, the valets followed the footman through one of the opened doors on the ground level.

Señor Esparza faced Jakob and Percival with the first smile he had yet deigned to bestow. "Please follow me, my lords."

He led the men up a beautiful painted-tile staircase, which curved to the second story of the building. A wrought-iron-and-pilaster railed balcony overlooked all four sides of the courtyard, and was littered with doorways leading to the public rooms of the palazzo: various drawing and sitting rooms, a library, a spacious ballroom, and a dining room large enough to accommodate four dozen guests.

Jakob paused to make a quick assessment of the best way to protect the inhabitants of the home. Though there was no imminent danger that he could determine at the moment, he and Bethington were strangers in a very strange land. Caution and preparation were indispensable tools for any knight.

Satisfied, he returned his attention to Señor Esparza's tour of his new abode, wondering all the while when he would have the opportunity for a private chat with the Englishman.

§ § §

The third floor, which held the private apartments, was accessible by a wide interior staircase off an enclosed hallway which ran behind the public rooms—presumably for use by servants, and by residents or guests in inclement weather.

Jakob's rooms on the third floor were very spacious and comfortable. Shuttered windows, which looked over the street on one side, and the courtyard on the other, offered sea breezes a chance to scuttle through. Though the day was quite cool—and the clouds thickening—Jakob opened them wide, needing the freshening air to help clear his mind.

As he did so, Askel arrived with the luggage. The younger man stepped around Jakob as he unpacked the satchels from the mules, as well the packets he and Jakob kept strapped behind their saddles.

"Where do you want your armor, my lord?"

Jakob turned away from the window. "Did you see her?"

Askel blinked, chainmail spilling heavily over his arms. "The Lady Avery?"

"It *was* her—was it not?" Jakob stepped toward him. "Tell me I was not mistaken."

Askel's arms sagged and the mail chinged softly. "The widow bore a striking likeness, to be sure."

Jakob looked down at Askel's burden, realizing what the man had asked him. "The armor? I do not care. Put things wherever you believe they should be put."

"Yes, my lord." Askel dumped the chainmail back into the waiting chest. "Might you give me a hand, my lord?"

Together, Jakob and Askel shoved the chest of armor into a corner too dark for any sort of useful industry.

Jakob could not postpone his conversation any longer; he felt questions gnawing on him in the manner of a hungry dog with a marrow bone. "I am going to speak with Sir Percival."

The valet nodded and wiped his brow, though the room was of a comfortably cool temperature. "Yes, my lord."

Jakob paused at the door. "I do not know the customs for meals here. Might you and Denys ferret that out before the supper bell?"

"Yes, my lord."

Jakob left Askel to his tasks and strode down the hall, making two turns before reaching Bethington's apartment on the opposite side of the square structure. Percival's rooms had the same configuration of windows as his own; clearly the assignment of quarters was intentional for the knights' comfort.

Jakob looked out the window which faced the courtyard. He could see Askel across the courtyard through the open shutters. "I suppose that if I have a message for you, I might send it across on an arrow."

Percival chuckled. "Give a shout of warning first, if you will." He walked to the window. "I assume that is your chamber?"

"Yes." Jakob leaned out and looked down at the balcony extending outward one floor below. "The drop is about sixteen feet onto hard tile."

"I would not recommend it." Percival grinned broadly. "Unless her husband is holding a breech-loader at close range, of course."

The Englishman's jovial personality—which Jakob had found annoying at first—soon showed an amusing and quick wit.

"Not to worry." Jakob's lips twisted. "Her husband is dead."

Percival motioned for Jakob to return to the outer room, leaving

Denys alone to echo Askel's assigned tasks.

The Englishman lifted a decanter. "Claret?"

Jakob had no idea how Percival procured the beverage, but was grateful for his ingenuity. "Yes. Thank you."

Bethington handed Jakob a full cup, and the men settled into two upholstered chairs amidst the detritus of the Englishman's still-scattered possessions.

Percival raised his glass. "First, to our new adventure. And our very comfortable surroundings."

Jakob could not argue with that—the house was large, beautifully appointed, and well-staffed. He nodded, and then took a healthy gulp of his wine, pausing a moment to appreciate the skill of the vintner.

"And second..." Percival pinned Jakob's gaze. "To discovering the mystery of the Ice Maiden."

Jakob snorted and drained his cup, then held his glass out in front of him, his unspoken request understood by his companion.

Percival pushed himself to stand and brought the decanter to Jakob, who promptly refilled his own glass, and then set the decanter on the floor beside him.

With a huff of appreciation, Percy returned to his own seat. "Let the discovery begin, then. We shall compare facts. What do you know about the lady—for certain, that is?"

"For certain?" The question stung like lemon juice on a deep cut. "Nothing, as it appears."

Bethington's gaze shifted to the window. "You do know her name."

"She is called *Señora Averia Galaviz de Mendoza, Vizcondesa de Catalonya.*" Jakob wagged his head. "She never was the Lady Avery Albergar of Toledo."

"She has known Catherine all her life—I can attest to that." Percival sipped his wine. "So the queen was aware of the deception."

Jakob stared at the other knight. "And what was the point of such trickery?"

"That depends on the circumstances." Percy's green eyes met his. "Why would a noble woman wish to hide her identity?"

"Why would a noble woman wish to *hide?*" Jakob countered.

"If she walks the street openly, she is not hiding because of the commission of any sort of crime."

Bethington's brows pulled together. "Avery is not the sort of woman to commit a crime. She is far too pious."

Jakob dipped his chin. "Agreed. Perhaps there was something connected to her first husband."

Percival nearly dropped his cup. "She was married before?" That was surprising. "Did you not know?"

"No one at court knew!" Percival set his wine down before he spilled it, his hand twitching with surprise. "Everyone assumed she was a spinster."

Jakob fell back in his chair. The idea that such a beautiful and refined noblewoman had never been married to anyone was incomprehensible to him. He was certainly not surprised when she told him—she was thirty-four years old, after all, and not in any way naïve.

"So why would a woman change her name to hide the fact she was married?" he probed.

"Well, if it was not a crime, the next thing that comes to mind is debt." Percy rubbed his chin. "Perhaps she did so to protect her own income."

"Her husband ran up so many accounts before he died, that she would have been left destitute?" Jakob narrowed his eyes. "So she escapes to the safety—and anonymity—of the Tudor court, with her finances intact."

"That is very possible," Bethington confirmed.

Jakob took another gulp of his wine, pondering the plausible likelihood of that scenario. "She most likely never lived in Toledo."

Percy lifted his wine glass and watched it to assure that hand was steady once again. "That would my guess."

Jakob slapped a palm against his forehead. "My Lord—I only now realized!"

Bethington startled and turned rounded eyes to Jakob. "What?"

"*Albergar.*"

"Yes?"

"The word is Spanish for 'harbor' or 'shelter'..." Jakob pinned Percy's gaze. "To offer refuge."

The Englishman coughed a laugh. "The clue was there all

along, was it not? Only no one put it together."

"No. They did not." Jakob finished his wine and refilled his glass once again.

"And so our best guess is that the Lady Avery—I still want to call her that," he interjected apologetically.

Jakob nodded; he would never call her anything else.

Percy continued, "The Lady Avery was hiding under an adopted identity in Catherine's service, because of some unsavory circumstance in her past."

"And the queen knew it." Jakob pointed at Bethington with his filled glass. "And Catherine supported her in that endeavor, because the lady was innocent." *I hope.*

"At least she was a victim, if not entirely inculpable herself," Percy qualified. "And if her troubles were financial in nature, perhaps she married this time purely for wealth."

Jakob made an agreeable gesture, then returned to his wine. The question buzzing in his head was: what would he do now?

"She did not see us today, I do not believe." Bethington's mouth quirked. "If she had, I do believe she would have reacted in some noticeable way."

"No. Her thoughts were otherwise occupied." Jakob sucked a breath, punched by another obvious realization. "She knows well, however, that we will be residing in Barcelona for the duration of the Order."

Percy pulled his own gasp. "Do you believe she fears us finding her out?"

Absolutely.

And she will run again, as soon as she is able.

Jakob emptied his glass and stood. "I am going to enquire as to her current residence."

Bethington stared up at him. "What will you do then?"

Jakob straightened his travel-weary tunic. "For now, I will find the house, and see what sorts of occurrences are taking place there."

The Englishman watched him carefully.

"And then on the morrow I shall pay the lady a visit, and find out for myself what sort of ruse she might be hiding behind now—and why."

§ § §

The address of the newly-deceased Count Mendoza's palazzo was easily discovered. The regal home was located very nearby, in a slightly more elegant section of the same general neighborhood as their leased house. Jakob, a wide-brimmed hat pulled low and his golden hair tucked out of sight, strolled past the house, hoping to surreptitiously discover whatever he could from a safe distance.

The gates to the courtyard were open. Well-dressed noblemen and noblewomen entered and departed in a steady stream of mourners, presumably offering their condolences over a rich buffet, which Jakob could smell from the street. By common tradition, the somber reception would continue all evening. His belly rumbled the reminder that he had not yet eaten.

Jakob was sorely tempted to walk in straightaway and observe the look on Avery's face when he did so; but he resolutely shoved the lure aside. He had a better plan in mind.

On the morrow, he would bathe, shave, and don his finest tunic. Riding into her courtyard on Warrior—unnecessary for the distance, but very necessary for the appropriate impact—he would demand to see the Lady Averia Galaviz de Mendoza. And he would not leave until he did so.

Jakob remained on the street until darkness made the faces of the guests incomprehensible. Then he sauntered back to his new home, and his own supper.

Chapter Three

November 20, 1518

Avery suffered through three exceptionally horrible days. Considering the unpleasantness of which these last four months had been comprised, the unflattering designation was indeed impressive.

Thankfully this one was nearing its end.

She rubbed her forehead, trying to ease the invisible iron band squeezing her skull and making it harder by the minute for her to remain coherent, much less gracious, to the stream of visitors offering condolences with one hand, and asking for payment or favors with the other.

Though the possibility had niggled in the back of her mind—how could it not, once she saw Paolo's condition?—she truly had no idea how bad her financial situation had become until this very week, when her husband's death was mere days away, and his accountant and lawyer appeared at her door.

During the nine years she spent hiding in the Tudor court as chief lady-in-waiting for Queen Catherine, Avery knew she would someday be summoned to return to Barcelona and deal with her husband's death.

Since Paolo had no heirs, she expected the process to be a simple one—and one which left her as a titled lady of means, able to fully claim independence for herself; independence which she had enjoyed in part at Catherine's court in London.

The nights she dressed as a man and snuck out of the Tower to gather information on Catherine's behalf were exhilarating. To be freed from all constraints was a heady experience. Avery hoped Paolo's wealth would free her permanently.

That hope was dimming, and quickly, in the situation which was making itself depressingly clear.

To compound her discomfiture, her elder brother arrived the day before Paolo died, come to ostensibly support her through this difficult time. Though Avery initially greeted him with gratitude, his pointed questions about her finances betrayed a deeper and more insidious motive.

While Reynaldo had inherited the Galaviz fortune and estate, he also married a woman with extravagant tastes. Carlotta Engracia Federico was an exceptionally beautifully woman, and she knew it. Avery always believed the woman chose her brother Reynaldo for a husband because he was never confident that she truly loved him.

Men are easier to control if they are desperate. And they give expensive gifts—lots of them.

"If he was sincerely concerned for my welfare, he would have left that grasping hornet at home in Segovia," Avery muttered.

Avery could not wait until Carlotta discovered what a horrid mess dear Paolo left behind, and wondered how quickly her sister-in-law would leave Barcelona once she did. Chances were also quite good that Reynaldo would head up the exodus.

Avery made a spitting sound, and then crossed herself. *I'll not be praying* you *out of purgatory, husband.*

"My lady?" Paolo's—now Avery's—majordomo, Esteban, stood in the doorway, hands clasped respectfully across his waist. A darkly handsome man, he had been with the Mendoza family for the past fifteen years.

Avery massaged her throbbing temples. "Yes?"

"There is one more... gentleman... who wishes to speak to you."

She noted the hesitation in Esteban's declaration. "What is his name?"

Esteban shook his head. "He refuses to give it."

Avery waved an exhausted hand. "Please tell him to leave. And then serve my supper in my chambers."

The majordomo shifted uncomfortably. "I *have* asked him to leave. Repeatedly. And yet he remains."

Avery frowned. "How long has he been here?"

"Since the ninth hour this morning."

"He has been waiting these past eight hours?" Avery shook her head, hoping to rattle a clear thought to the forefront. "How is his demeanor?"

"Polite. Patient," Esteban begrudgingly admitted. "And, staunchly determined."

"Determined?" Avery heaved a heavy sigh. The pounding in her head was growing worse, and now her stomach was beginning to protest as well. "What shall I do, Esteban?"

The man's black brows pulled together. "If you do not see him today, he promises to return on the morrow, I am afraid."

"Oh, very well then." Avery waved a limp hand toward her empty chalice. "Might you pour me some wine before you escort him in?"

"Is it your head, my lady?" Esteban moved to fill the cup.

"Head, neck, stomach, back. I feel as if I have been severely beaten and left for dead." Avery accepted the cup and took a healthy draught of the sweetened red wine, flavored with slices of fruit. She felt it warm and sooth her belly, though the pain in her head banged on.

"Bring in our mysterious man," she instructed Esteban. "But do stay with me until I dismiss you, in the event he is neither as polite nor patient as he seems."

The majordomo bowed. "Very good, my lady."

§ § §

Jakob sat alone in the hall, the last remainder of the day's many visitors. One sympathetic caller after another had arrived and been promptly escorted into the drawing room for an audience with the newly widowed Vizcondesa Averia Galaviz de Mendoza—while he sat and waited.

He was not surprised by this, since he refused to give either his name or the nature of his business with the vizcondesa. Jakob was afraid that if Avery knew it was he who waited to see her, she would have him thrown out of the house.

That situation which would have necessitated brute force and, determined as he might be, he did not wish to make any sort of unpleasant public scene.

She might have guessed it was he in any case. But until he saw her, he would not leave willingly.

The majordomo appeared in front of him. "The Vizcondesa will see you now."

Jakob rose to his feet, his right thigh gone painfully stiff and strongly objecting to the movement. He straightened and refused to rub the aching limb. "Thank you."

After a staunched flicker of surprise at the Norseman's height, the majordomo's regard of Jakob intensified. "I am to remain with her for her protection, at her request."

Jakob dipped his chin. "I understand."

As he followed the servant, Jakob reminded himself to remain calm. His pride was riled up and stoked by impatience, and he was keenly aware of it. Though he was here to air his grievances with the way Avery had comported herself, he knew that he must not attack her with his words. Even so, he wanted answers.

Needed them.

The door stood open, and the majordomo entered the room first. Jakob followed, his heart pounding and his palms sweating.

When Avery saw him, her normally pale skin whitened alarmingly. Her jaw fell slack, and her eyes grew round as platters under the black plunging knives of her brows.

"You!"

§ § §

Avery watched the walls of the room begin to swirl and melt. She slipped into a dark cloud, first falling, and then rising, before settling on a cushion. Though the relaxing oblivion was enticing, she drew a deep breath and opened her eyes. Bits of her body slowly returned to their appropriate places from wherever they had flown.

A Nordic Knight of the Golden Fleece

Jakob Petter Hansen hovered over her, his reddish-golden hair resembling a halo and his blue eyes dark with concern.

"A wet cloth!" he barked. "Now!"

Avery started to sit up, but he pushed her back down on the couch.

"Be still a moment."

She did not argue with him.

Esteban started to lay the cloth on Avery's forehead, but Jakob took it from the majordomo. He refolded it needlessly to make some esoteric point, and then gently placed the soothing linen across her brow.

"When did you eat last?"

Avery looked at Esteban for confirmation. "I have not eaten since I broke my fast this morning."

Jakob rounded on the man. "Please bring food for both of us. I, too, have not eaten since the morning. And a pitcher of cool ale, if you have it."

The majordomo pulled himself up to his full height—considerably less than Jakob's—and glared at the knight. "I take my instructions from the Vizcondesa."

Avery lifted her hand, surprised by the amount of effort that simple movement required. "It is fine, Esteban. Please do as Sir Hansen requests."

"You are acquainted with this man?" Esteban's nose twitched his surprised displeasure. "Are you quite certain you do not wish me to stay, my lady?"

Avery huffed a sigh of defeat. "Yes, I am acquainted with him. And I assure you that I am quite safe." Her gaze cut to Jakob's stern expression; her assumption was clearly correct. "I believe the knight and I have much to discuss."

With a lingering scowl of warning aimed at Jakob, the majordomo left the room.

Avery did sit up then; lying on her back made her feel far too vulnerable. She wondered if she had regained enough control of her body to move to a chair.

"Would you prefer a chair?" Jakob offered. Her glance must have revealed the direction of her thoughts.

"Yes, I would. Thank you."

Jakob pulled the largest upholstered chair toward the couch and offered his arm.

As wobbly as she felt, Avery could not accept his assistance. She was already at enough of a disadvantage in this awkward reunion. Not only was she surprised by the Norseman's sudden appearance, she had fainted from hunger and headache when she saw him.

And none of that even began to touch on her unexplained flight from England following his declaration of love and proposal of marriage, nor the truth of her situation here.

There was indeed much to discuss.

Avery stood, stepped to the chair, and sank gratefully into its supportive embrace. Jakob's jaw clenched, displaying his irritation. He pulled another chair close to face hers.

"How did you find me?" she began, her voice sounding much weaker than she hoped.

Jakob cut her an angry gaze. "You were kind enough to march down one of Barcelona's main thoroughfares upon my arrival."

She cleared her throat, hoping that would help. "You—and Percival, I assume—arrived yesterday, then."

"Yes. And it seems condolences are in order on the death of your new husband," he growled.

Avery rubbed her forehead. *Did he say new?*

"When was the marriage arranged?" he continued. "You clearly wasted no time entering into it once you left England."

She dropped her hand and stared at him, confused. "What are you talking about?"

"I only have one question." Jakob's fierce scowl reminded her of a snorting bull in the ring, about to charge his tormenters. She could feel the heat of his anger radiating off his body. "Did you love him?"

"Jakob—"

He cut off her explanation. "Yes or no."

"No. It was arranged." Avery shook her still-muzzy head. "What do you mean by *new* husband?"

That question clearly caught him off guard. "You said—when I told you about my marriage—you said you were a—a widow," he stammered.

Guilt wrapped bony fingers around Avery's chest and squeezed it. Hard. "No, I did not say I was a widow."

Confusion twisted his features. "Yes. You did."

"No," Avery said softly, heart pushing against the guilty constrictor. "I was not a widow. Not just yet."

Jakob's eye narrowed and a whoosh of understanding left his body. "You were still *married* to the Vizconde?"

She nodded.

"All the time I—we—you were *married?*" he bellowed.

"I am so sorry, Jakob," she croaked. "No one knew."

Jakob leapt to his feet and began to pace in long, limping strides around the room. He scuttled his hands through his hair, loosening the shoulder-length brassy locks from their leather thong. His countenance was as thunderous as an autumn tempest and his blue eyes darkened like storm clouds.

"Gud forbanner det til helvete!"

It wasn't until Jakob swore loudly in Norsk that she realized he had been speaking to her in Spanish. He whirled to face her.

"What do you mean no one knew?"

The door opened and a servant entered with a tray of food. The aromas of roasted pork, smoked fish, fresh bread, and garlic-infused olive oil made her belly rumble in relief. Esteban followed with a fresh decanter of sangria, and a pitcher of cooled ale.

Avery and Jakob waited in a silence as volatile as lightning. Esteban instructed the servant where to put the tray, and shot Avery an inquisitive glance.

She gave a little nod, indicating she was in no danger from the tall, sullen knight. Esteban tilted his head toward the bell pull, and both men exited the room. The heavy door shut with an iron clank.

"Are you hungry?" she ventured.

Jakob crossed the space between them in three quick strides. "What do you *mean* no one knew?"

She rose to her feet with care, having regained some small measure of her composure. She met his angry stare with one of her own.

"The tale is a lengthy one, and I am weak from hunger." She pushed past him and took a seat at the table holding the tray. "You may join me. Or not. That is your decision."

Kris Tualla

Avery poured out the olive oil and tore a chunk from the warm loaf of bread. She dipped it in the oil and took a bite. The garlic tickled her sinuses and began to soothe her headache.

After a tense moment, Jakob joined her.

He took the chair facing hers and forked a chunk of pork onto his pewter plate. He took a bite, and then imitated her actions with the bread and olive oil. A look of surprise eased his features.

"This is very good." He took another bite and his stomach gurgled loudly. "It is truly better that we do not talk with empty bellies."

Avery could not think of an answer more elaborate than, "Yes."

Jakob rose and poured two goblets of the ale. He set one in front of her, drank the other, and then refilled it.

He pointed at her cup. "Drink that. The ale will restore you better than wine."

Avery did as he bid—anything to calm his mood before she began her explanation.

The pair ate their supper without attempting conversation. Avery was the first one to set aside her utensils. Determined to control the coming exchange, she felt she should begin speaking while Jakob was still engaged with his meal.

"My story began fourteen years ago, when I was twenty years of age," she stated without preamble. "When my father arranged my marriage with a very wealthy merchant, Paolo Pacheco Mendoza."

Chapter Four

Jakob chewed slowly, watching Avery carefully for any signs of guile. The situation she described was quite common thus far, and he had no reason not to believe her.

Yet.

"Vizconde Paolo Pacheco Mendoza was twenty-one years my senior. And I was his third wife." Avery took another gulp of the pale ale.

Jakob wagged his head. "Because of your connection with Catherine, I would have thought your status higher than vizcondesa."

She nodded, the color in her cheeks heightening. "My father was an earl, and my mother a marquésa."

So arranging the marriage of a woman to a man below her station had already been accomplished in Avery's family. "Why did you marry a vizconde?"

"He offered my father money. Quite a lot of money, in fact." The color in her pale cheeks blazed. "He hoped I would give him children. More specifically, an heir."

"Neither one of his previous wives…" Jakob left the sentence hanging.

She lifted a curved eyebrow. "Nor any of his many mistresses, as it turned out."

Jakob hated to continue poking her bruises, but he needed to understand everything clearly. "What you told me about never having children—"

"Was absolutely true!" she interrupted.

A chill skated up Jakob's spine. "What happened to his first two wives?"

Avery looked away. "Dead."

"How?"

She shrugged. "I lived in Madrid, and Paolo lived here, in Barcelona. By the time I arrived in his home as his new bride, no one would tell me."

Jakob didn't have to ask if Avery found that suspicious; the stark alarm in her eyes, prompted by the telling, was obvious. An entire new array of realizations blossomed in Jakob's mind.

She would have feared for her own life.

"How did you come to be in Catherine's court?" he probed.

Avery sighed. "She was prevented from coming to my wedding, of course. Arthur was dead by then, and she was betrothed to Henry—though his father was fighting that arrangement."

Jakob nodded his understanding. "Then she did marry Henry. After his father died."

"Yes. Five years after I married Paolo, Catherine was finally able to marry Henry."

"Did she know you were so unhappy?"

Avery recoiled. "I did not say I was unhappy."

"No," Jakob conceded. "But you were miserable, were you not? And afraid for your life, if you did not produce an heir for the Vizconde?"

"How could you possibly…" She stared at him, stunned at his apparently accurate deconstruction of her life. Her entire frame slumped in acquiescence. "I—I was in hell."

Jakob understood, though he had not yet deigned to soften his demeanor. While the lady's pieces were falling neatly in place, he was still very angry with her. Her betrayal seared through his core.

"And so your dearest friend, Catherine, rescued you as soon as she was crowned queen, by inviting you to join her court as her chief lady-in-waiting."

She gave a little nod. "Yes."

And then the final candle lit in Jakob's mind. He narrowed his gaze. "Your husband had no idea where you had gone, had he."

"No." Her lips moved in a rueful twist. "I became the Lady Avery Albergar of Toledo. And my very life depended on that secret never being discovered or revealed."

Jakob rubbed a hand over his mouth, considering that information. "Did the 'Ice Maiden' truly never take a lover?" he pressed.

Avery recoiled again, this time in anger not surprise. "No! I shall not burn in hell for adultery, no matter what sort of man I was married to!"

Jakob leaned back in his chair and regarded the elegant woman across the small table from him. In spite of the purple smudges under her eyes, and her gaunt, pale face, the dark and vibrant beauty he which knew in England was not gone—merely dimmed by her unpleasant and burdensome circumstances.

"Why did you come back to Barcelona so suddenly?" he asked.

"My husband was dying." Avery rolled her eyes. "At the last."

"At the last?"

She took a fortifying sip of her ale and settled her shoulders before she spoke. "I received word five years ago from a priest who serves in the cathedral—the only person whom I could trust with my situation and my whereabouts, you understand. Because I told him in confidence. In the confessional."

He gave a little nod, encouraging her to continue.

"He wrote to tell me that Paolo was suffering the effects of syphilis. He was concerned for my health." Avery waved a hand before Jakob could speak. "I had been gone for four years at that point. I was, thankfully, not afflicted."

Jakob stood, stretching his stiff leg, and refilled his cup with the last of the ale. He lifted the decanter of wine in Avery's direction, his silent question obvious.

She shook her head and claimed the last piece of bread, tearing it into tiny pieces, and eating them one at a time.

Jakob recognized that anxious sort of action. It was the type of thing one does when anticipating something uncomfortable is about to happen.

She is correct.

He reclaimed his seat and faced her. He kept his tone calm, though a multitude of emotions surged and bubbled under his heart.

"I must assume the priest wrote to you once again, this time to inform you of your husband's approaching death?"

"I had to come back, Jakob." Her bottomless dark eyes pled for his understanding. "There was so much to do to prepare beforehand, and decide upon afterwards."

He shook his head slowly and stared down at the remnants of his meal on the gleaming pewter platter; he could not gaze into those entrancing eyes and remain stern.

His voice was low, and even he could recognize the pain it held. "Why did you not tell me?"

Jakob heard her breath catch in her throat. "I could not."

"Could not?" He lifted his eyes to hers, then. "Or would not?"

She stretched out her hand. "My heart was breaking, Jakob."

His fist hit the table so hard that his empty cup tipped over. "*Your* heart?" he shouted. "What about *mine?*"

Her hand jerked backward and landed on her throat.

Jakob pointed a stiff finger in her face. "I told you things—"

His Spanish failed him in the midst of his anger and anguish, so he continued in English. "Things that I never told anyone else. Ever! I trusted you. I laid bare my soul to you. Do you *remember* that?"

A sob escaped her, and her shoulders convulsed. She nodded, her distressed countenance sculpted by fear and uncertainty.

Jakob forced his fist open. "I did not know—and I *still* do not know—why you did not trust me in return!"

Avery's gaze dropped to the carpet. Her hands were clasped so tightly in her lap that her knuckles stood out like sun-bleached pebbles on a worn beach.

He loosed an arrow into her defense. "You knew exactly what Henry was compelling me to do."

She coughed a sob, and clapped her hand over her mouth. His shot had hit its target.

"I trusted you with that as well, did I not?" The second arrow landed true. Avery flinched visibly and cowered under his verbal attack.

He stood now, and put his hands on the table, leaning forward to send the mortal arrow. He wanted her to feel the same sort of piercing pain that he felt when she abandoned him without word or warning.

He spoke the next words quietly, their misleading gentleness enhancing their impact. "I had mistakenly believed that we were friends."

§ § §

A keening wail emanated from the depths Avery's chest.

The doors to the drawing room flew open. Esteban was on Jakob before Avery was aware of him; and he had the knight in a sort of locking grip.

"Let go of me!" Jakob shouted. "I am leaving!"

Avery jumped up too quickly, and a hoard of black gnats danced in her vision.

"Leave him be, Esteban!" she croaked.

The majordomo wrestled with the Norseman for a moment, unsure of what to do. Avery rounded the table on alarmingly unsteady limbs and grabbed his elbow.

"Sir Hansen is lea—leaving. Le—let him go!"

Esteban pulled his arms away from Jakob's body suddenly and with a menacing flourish. But he remained close by, panting.

Jakob straightened his body and his clothes without a word. Turning on his heel, he walked in a slow and dignified manner to the doorway. Avery knew what it cost him to hide his limp, but hide it he did.

He paused there, and looked back at her.

Her world froze. She waited for him to speak as long as her nerves would allow. "Jakob—"

"No." He wagged his head sadly. "I'll not be so foolish as to love anyone else, ever again."

And then he was gone.

§ § §

When Jakob walked out on her, Avery couldn't breathe. She gasped for breath, unable to pull enough air into her lungs. She

Kris Tualla

flailed for the chair which Esteban shoved against the back of her knees. She fell into it, sobbing and incoherent, until her lady's maid was summoned.

Zurina took command and somehow managed to move Avery upstairs, place a hot cup of tea in her hand, and get her undressed and into this bath.

Her bath water was infused with lavender and eucalyptus, both intended to soothe her aching head, as was the tea made from chamomile and willow bark. Nothing could stop the constant flow of tears, however, and her eyes swelled and stung with them.

Her middle-aged maidservant moved quietly around the room, straightening random things, and generally just remaining in her lady's presence until Avery called on her services once again.

Avery closed her eyes and relaxed against the edge of the small copper-lined wooden tub, inhaling the soothing aromas and trying to shush her accusing thoughts.

I meant to be gone from Barcelona before he arrived.

Of course she knew Jakob was coming to Barcelona, but she didn't expect him to arrive before December. She planned to deal with Paolo's holdings and garner all that she could from them, before deciding where to spend the second half of her life—and with whom.

Returning to England to spend the rest of her days as a lady of influence in Catherine's court was as a possibility. The weather in Spain, however, was much preferable to the damp chill of England; remaining here as a titled widow also opened many doors.

Avery hoped to accomplish these tasks and make her decision quickly, because she firmly believed Jakob would come looking for her. And even with the wrong name and wrong location, he was intelligent enough to search out her royal connections and make enquiries.

But when she first arrived in Barcelona, optimistic about her soon-to-be unfettered future, Avery had no inkling of what an incomprehensible mess into which the sick man had allowed his empire to fall. She would not have believed anyone could spend so much money in such a short amount of time.

Now, rather than take up a peaceful and independently dignified existence, she was presented with bills and debts and demands, which she had not yet begun to sort out. She feared it would take weeks for her to make sense of it all—now that Paolo was dead, and the bankers and lawyers were at last forced to deal directly with her.

Depending on what she discovered, it might require months to recoup what was left, if anything.

Why didn't she simply leave? Return to London now, and make her appeal to Catherine? Avery drew a ragged sigh,

Though living as a servant in the Tudor court would assure she had plenty of food, clothing, and solid walls surrounding her, she would not have any say about her own life's situation ever again. The queen might even marry her off to a nobleman from whom she wished a favor.

Perhaps she should enter a convent, and dedicate the rest of her otherwise useless life to God's service. Again, she would be taken care of, and no one would be able to reach in and destroy her further, no matter what Paolo had done. Perhaps that choice was preferable.

Fresh tears rolled hotly down her water-cooled cheeks. She could not bring herself to leave Barcelona now, and she knew it. Unwelcome as the realization was, Jakob Hansen's strong and solid presence was the reason.

But she had ruined everything with her mishandling of their admittedly more-than-friendship. And when Jakob left her today, he slammed a silent door, the impenetrable obstacle now standing between them. At that moment, Avery realized she had handled their relationship wrong, even from the very beginning.

I should have trusted him. He is right.

Was there any hope for restoring their friendship? Even if Jakob could never love her again, she realized with horrific clarity that the angry Norseman was her only true and trusted friend in Barcelona.

She slid a glance toward Zurina from under half-closed lids. The woman had come to the Mendoza household sometime after Avery abandoned it. She did not know where the woman's loyalties lay, and wondered how she might accurately determine that.

Esteban was Paolo's man to the core—which was fortuitous because, in the last few years, her husband's syphilitic mind was too far ravaged to attend to his business with any sort of lucidity. Without Esteban's help, there might not have been a home for her to return to, no matter the condition.

Avery shifted in the water, stirring it so it felt warm again and released more of the fragrant scents. To be completely honest with herself, it felt quite odd to be back home in Barcelona after spending so many years absent from this place...

No, not home.

Homes should be comforting places. Welcoming places. Places where one could relax, enfolded by safety and the love of others. Even though everything in this house was familiar to her, she had never felt any of those emotions while living in the grand palazzo.

She felt fear, that was certain. And revulsion for her husband, an unkind and demanding man, who used women harshly before discarding them like worn rags.

Whether he was married or not was never a concern for him—all that he desired was to plant his seed in someone's fertile ground, and extract the maximum amount of personal pleasure possible in the frequent attempts.

He received the reward he earned, she mused. *And now I am free of him.*

Was she, though?

The mountain of Paolo's finances was convoluted at best, as if the truth was to be obfuscated, not illuminated. His accountant spoke to her like he might to an imbecile, and his lawyer did little more than flash contracts in front of her and explain she had no choices, only obligations.

Avery needed an advocate of her own, someone whose intent was for her to emerge from this debacle in the best possible manner: with her dignity intact, and an income to sustain her. How might she find such a person?

She daren't ask Esteban, lest he think she either did not trust him, or that she was not grateful for his years of faithful service to her husband.

With the scheming leech Carlotta firmly attached to his side, her brother Reynaldo would be of no help. Besides, Avery noticed a distinct touch of shabbiness in his clothes. Though she initially attributed that to his journey here from their family's estate outside of Madrid—no one wore their best attire when traveling—she really had no idea how her family's estate was currently faring.

To complete the depressing scenario, today she had completely alienated the Nordic knight, the single person who might have been able to assist her, and had no economic stake in her situation.

Avery heaved another shuddering sigh, and waved for Zurina to help her from the bath. She rose on weak legs, accepted the maid's assistance in stepping over the rim of the tub, and waited while she was toweled dry.

The older woman clucked disapprovingly. "You have grown too thin, my lady."

"I have not had much of an appetite, I am afraid." She lifted her arms, and Zurina slipped her embroidered nightdress over her head.

"You have finally lost a burden, I think," the maid ventured. "But you will need your strength more than ever now."

Avery shot a look at the maid, wondering if Zurina had somehow read her mind.

"Get into bed and I will bring your supper." The maid collected the wet towels before she faced Avery again and spoke with authority. "And I will remain until you finish the tray."

Avery climbed into the big bed, the understanding of Zurina's words prompting a fresh wash of tears. Even her lady's maid knew that Avery was facing an adversary—probably more than one—and that no visible hero awaited outside the walls of the palazzo to save her.

I truly have no home.

Chapter Five

November 21, 1518

Avery sighed as Zurina combed and braided her hair the next day. "Obviously my absence for the last nine years has been noted by the residents of Barcelona."

The maid kept her eyes on her task and did not look into the silvered glass. "Yes. I would imagine so."

"And the cause of Paolo's lingering demise was no secret either, was it?"

The maid did shoot her an empathetic glance at that. "No my lady, it was not,"

Avery pinned the older woman's gaze. "You arrived here after I was gone. What did they say about me?"

Zurina's expression took on a hunted mien. "They?"

Avery turned around in her seat to face Zurina. "Let us begin with the household staff. What was their opinion of my sudden... desertion?"

The maid worried the comb with fingers swollen with arthritis. "You must understand that everything I know is hearsay—I was not here."

Avery nodded and removed the comb from Zurina's surprisingly strong grip before the maid broke it in half.

"Please sit. And be honest, I beg of you. Nothing you say will anger me, I promise you that."

Zurina turned a chair to face Avery, her movements hesitant. She lowered herself slowly and clasped her knobby hands in front of her.

"There were two differing opinions among the staff," she began. "The ones who were loyal to Señor Mendoza, of course, felt that you betrayed him and willingly denied him an heir."

"Of course." That was what Avery expected to hear.

"But not the others." Zurina allowed a hint of a smile, which deepened the creases by her eyes. "The ones who were loyal to you, my lady, talked among themselves, rather than risk the wrath of Señor Mendoza."

Avery straightened on her bench seat. "There were servants loyal to *me?*"

The maid's brows shot upward. Her forehead became a field of ridges. "Of course there were. Did you not know?"

Avery looked away and tried to remember the names of those men and women who served her nearly a decade ago. Only Maria came to mind, her lady's maid and Zurina's predecessor. She returned her regard to the older woman.

"Was Maria one of them?"

Zurina nodded. "And it would seem that is why she was let go from her position. Apparently, I was hired in her place."

Avery groaned at that. "I am so sorry to hear that." Then catching Zurina's expression, she hastened to add, "But you have been wonderful to me since I arrived. I truly do appreciate your service more than I can say."

She did smile then. "I am honored, my lady."

Avery leaned forward. "After hearing all the talk, what conclusion did you arrive at?"

"It is not my place," the maid demurred.

"It is your place if I ask you," Avery prodded. "Please. There will be no repercussions, I promise you."

Zurina swallowed audibly. "Well, from the beginning I agreed that you should not have left your marriage. You took sacred vows before God, and it was your duty to uphold those vows. I took the side of those loyal the Vizconde."

Avery nodded, her lower lip caught in her teeth. She should not be surprised, considering that she had not been present to defend her own actions.

Zurina sucked a small breath and held it for a pace. Her eyes narrowed as she considered what to say next.

"Go on," Avery whispered.

"Forgive me."

Avery wagged her head. "There is nothing to forgive."

"Not as yet, but…"

"Please. Go on," Avery urged, her curiosity piqued.

"I came to realize that—" She faltered, and tried again. Her voice was soft, as if she was afraid she might be overheard. "I came to realize that Señor Mendoza was a horrible man."

A breathy sob escaped Avery's mouth as a flush of relief washed through her veins. She pressed her fingers against her cheeks and closed her eyes.

"Thank you."

"He did not keep his vows to you. Nor had he kept them to his first two wives." Now that the precarious damn was breeched, Zurina's words poured out in a rush. "The women he brought here—sometimes two at a time—I had never seen such lewd behavior."

Avery opened her eyes. "So why did you stay?"

A violent blush crept up from Zurina's neck. "I needed the position. He paid us very well, and my mother was ill."

Then she gave an apologetic shrug. "I knew I should *not* stay, that God was not pleased with the things happening in this house, but I turned a blind eye. Medicines are expensive, you see."

Avery risked the obvious question. "And how is your mother now?"

"She went to Heaven almost a year ago. She was eighty-two." Zurina made the sign of the cross. "But by that time, the Vizconde was near to dying himself. And all of the servants assumed you would return when he passed."

Avery gave her a puzzled look. "Did you know where I was?"

"No, my lady. But we knew the priest who visited the Señor to pray over him knew. He told us that he had written to you and asked that you return."

That explained why her chambers were ready when she arrived, and why no one asked her too many questions when she suddenly appeared outside the gate two months ago.

"So you waited for me? Before you even knew me?" Avery was deeply moved by the idea.

Zurina straightened and shot her a determined look. "I wanted to decide for myself."

Avery's chin quivered. "And you are still here."

The maid gave a little shrug. "At first, I stayed to make certain that nothing happened to you."

Ice skated up Avery's spine in a chilling path. "What do you mean by happened to me?"

"There was always quiet speculation, whispers in the dark that the two Vizcondesas before you might have been..." Zurina's voice trailed off.

Avery's throat tightened. Her voice sounded thin. "Murdered?"

Zurina nodded and crossed herself again. "But the Señor was too ill to consider this, I think. And you were safe, because now we all must depend on you for our livelihood."

Avery drew a deep breath. "We are all in trouble on that count, I am afraid."

Zurina's somber gaze fell to the floor. Avery's statement had not taken her by surprise.

"I have treacherous waters to negotiate in these next months," Avery said slowly. "I need to know which men and women are my allies, and of whom to be wary."

Zurina slid from her seat to kneel in front of Avery, her head bowed. "I pledge to you my full allegiance, Averia Galaviz de Mendoza, Vizcondesa de Catalonya. On pain of death."

Avery reached down and grasped the woman's hands. Zurina lifted her brown eyes, their edges displaying the beginnings of cataracts.

Tears threatened, yet again; these past months were a season for them, it seemed. "Thank you, Zurina. I accept your pledge."

The blush returned to Zurina's cheeks. "I prayed for you, my lady. Once I saw what he was."

Avery's words abandoned her then, even as tears began to dribble down her face. All she could do was nod and press Zurina's

Kris Tualla

hands tightly in her own.

Finally, she managed a thick, "Thank you."

Zurina climbed to her feet with a little grunt. "I am getting too old for this."

Avery turned to face the mirror again, examining the unhappy face that stared back at her. "And now, I shall have an audience with my brother. This should prove interesting."

Zurina quickly put a few final pins in Avery's hair. "I have finished with your hair, my lady. Let us get your skirt on."

Zurina lowered the brocade skirt of Avery's newest Spanish-styled gown over her head. Here in Barcelona, the front of her skirt was not split and pulled back to display an underskirt every bit as elaborate as the overskirt. The sleeves were narrower than in England, as well.

She twisted in front of a tall mirror in a standing cherry-wood frame. "My face looks appalling, but the gown is beautiful."

Zurina handed her a linen cloth, damp with cold water. "Your beauty cannot be dimmed by a few tears, my lady."

Avery washed her face, scrubbing hard to bring its color back. There had been more than just a few tears. In these last months, she had shed enough tears to fill a brace of buckets.

As she handed the cloth back to Zurina, a thought came to mind. "Do you know what happened to Maria once she was dismissed?"

"Yes, actually I do." Zurina rinsed out the linen. "She was taken on by a man who leases houses in Barcelona. The houses are fully staffed as part of the contract."

That was a relief. "I am glad to hear that she has not been left destitute."

"No, my lady."

Avery pulled one last steadying breath. "It is time to enter the fray once again."

§ § §

Avery sat in her favorite of the three ornate drawing rooms in the huge Mendoza palazzo, waiting for her brother Reynaldo, Earl of Segovia, and his witch of a wife, Carlotta Engracia Federico de

Galaviz, to join her. Nothing about the coming interview portended anything pleasant.

Carlotta entered the room first, a sweeping cloud of olive green velvet, embellished with gold embroidery and pearls of varying sizes. Reynaldo followed close behind. He, on the other hand, was wearing the same garments he wore on the day the couple arrived in Barcelona.

Avery rose slowly. "Good morning."

"Good morning, Sister." Carlotta's evaluative gaze took measure of Avery, even as she took Avery's hands and kissed her sister-in-law on the cheeks. "Is that a Spanish gown?"

Avery smoothed her skirt. "Yes. I felt that I should dress acceptably for the people of Barcelona."

Carlotta made a little moue, arched brown brows gathering over grey eyes. "I had hoped to see you in the English and Tudor styles. Henry the Eighth is so fascinating, is he not? I understand their fashions are more daring than this." She flicked a wave over Avery's body.

In truth, the Spanish styles were more conservative than either the French or the English, who often copied the French styles. The neckline of her gown's bodice reached to her throat, modestly covering her bosom, and the solid-fronted skirt did not reveal her ankles or slippers.

In her particular situation, Avery was glad about that. Enough of the men who came to pay their respects had hinted about their willingness to take her dead husband's place, and quickly. Avery had no wish to appear encouraging in that aspect.

"I am freshly a widow, Carlotta," Avery reminded the woman.

"You are not dressed like one," she challenged. "Where are your mourning clothes?"

"I said I am a widow, I did not say I am in mourning," Avery snipped.

Reynaldo stepped forward and kissed her cheeks as well. "You look tired, Averia."

"And you look ragged, Reynaldo." Avery launched her first salvo. There was no point in extending this audience longer than necessary.

Carlotta hit his chest with her fan. "I told you not to wear your traveling clothes."

Reynaldo appeared to struggle with his response. "Because of your extensive wardrobe, my darling, I was not able to pack as much of my own."

His wife rolled her eyes. "They have plenty of tailors in Barcelona. Better ones than in Segovia, I imagine. Order yourself some new pieces."

Reynaldo's jaw stiffened. "If our stay is extended, then I shall."

Avery interrupted the revealing exchange. "Please sit. I have ordered refreshments."

Reynaldo and Carlotta settled on the couch, side by side but not touching, as Avery reclaimed her upholstered chair. Carlotta's regard moved around the room as if calculating the worth of its remaining art pieces and expensive furnishings.

A pair of servants entered and set a tray of pastries on the low table between Avery and her guests. Their conversation did not resume until the trio was once again alone.

Reynaldo took a couple small sips of his tea before setting the cup down and leaning forward, a solicitous expression sculpting his features. "Do you find yourself overwhelmed, Averia?"

"Why should I be overwhelmed, Brother?" Avery snipped. She set her tea aside as well, gathering her words to answer the preposterous question. "I only have a lifetime of finances to make sense of, a household which is hanging by a thread, and enough debts to bury me."

Reynaldo recoiled, his face blooming scarlet.

Carlotta stepped into his void. "Whatever your current situation, my dear, I am certain Queen Catherine would come to your aid."

Avery glared at her sister-in-law. "You do not know, what you think you know."

"Even so," Carlotta affected a concerned expression. "If you are too embarrassed to do so, I would be willing to go to London and speak with her on your behalf."

Avery laughed out loud. "I have no doubt about that."

Carlotta bristled. "I am only thinking of you."

Like a spider thinks of a fly.

"And I do appreciate that." Avery strained to keep her amused skepticism from her tone. "But I can assure you, Carlotta, that if I find I must make use of Catherine's influence, I shall do so myself."

"And if you wish for a traveling companion, please think of me." Carlotta's voice held a clearly desperate quality. "I wish to help you in any way I can."

In that moment, Avery saw what her brother's wife had truly hoped for when making the journey here: a chance to escape her husband in exactly the same manner that Avery had escaped her own. Her shoulders fell under the weight of that sad epiphany.

She turned her attention to Reynaldo and wondered if he had any clue about his wife's expectations.

Apparently he did, because he fairly reeked of desperation as well. "I have come to help you, Averia. I can advise you on your investments. I am quite certain you merely misunderstood some of the information you were given, and with proper guidance all can be put right."

Avery wondered how best to make her brother comprehend her humiliating and diminished situation—which she had learned of in fits and starts over the past two months since she arrived.

At first, she lived in a haze of denial, refusing to face the truth head-on; but that was no longer possible. Since Paolo's death, it had been thrown in her face at every turn. Avery was in deep financial trouble. And at the moment, there was no visible way out.

She had nothing to lose by being blunt, so blunt she would be.

"Reynaldo, your shabby clothing, and lack of attending staff traveling with you, tell me that the Galaviz estate is on the brink of ruin itself."

Carlotta gasped. She snapped her lace fan open and put it to anxious use.

Avery glanced in her sister-in-law's direction, but continued to address her brother. "I am telling you the truth: Paolo was an ass. He was disabled by his disease, and others seem to have spent all of his money for him. All. Do you hear me?"

Reynaldo waved his hands dismissively. "This is only a minor setback."

"Yours? Or mine?" Avery pressed. "Because mine has no end in sight."

"Averia, women do not always understand—"

Avery was on her feet like a catapult had thrown her. She pointed an angry finger at her brother. "Do *not* tell me that I cannot understand money!"

"But investments are not exactly money—"

"No—investments are monies put to work on your behalf, am I correct?" she challenged. He flinched. "And if the investments are bad, the monies are gone. True?"

Reynaldo was still sitting on the cushions, looking up at her. "Yes, but—"

"And when monies are borrowed, there is interest charged. The borrower owes more than was taken, and that repayment grows over time." Avery leaned over Reynaldo and glowered. "Do I have that correct as well?"

"You do, my dear, but—"

"Stand *up*, damn you!" Avery cried, stomping one foot in explosive frustration. "Act the man!"

Reynaldo clambered to his feet, his features shifting from placating to thunderous. "You do *not* tell me how to act!"

Avery poked his chest, shocked at her own uncommon display of temerity but not backing away from it. "And *you* do not tell me that I do not understand my own circumstances!"

Carlotta rose and wedged her way between sister and brother. "Stop this! Stop this instant!"

Avery stepped back. Her body trembled with violent emotions. "I apologize to you both. This is no way for me to treat guests."

"We are not guests, we are *family*," Reynaldo growled. "Family who came to help."

Avery stared up at her brother, four inches taller and five years older. He was gray at the temples and squinted when he read.

"I cannot help you, Reynaldo."

"That is not what I said!"

"No, but that was what you hoped." Avery slumped back into her chair. "You had hoped that by managing the Mendoza estate, you could earn enough to save your own."

Reynaldo's face was florid with his anger and embarrassment, yet he had no believable denial to offer her.

Avery wagged her head sadly and spoke her sudden decision. "I am sorry, but I will be selling off as many items of value as I can to try and pay Paolo's debts. I do not even know if there is enough to accomplish that, but I will try."

Carlotta let out a moan and fell back onto the couch.

Avery looked up at her brother. "And I will be reducing the household staff within the month, as well. You may want to take that fact into consideration as you plan your return journey."

Reynaldo's knees gave way and his body crumpled to the cushions. Stricken, his skin drained of color as her words impaled his hopes with mortal accuracy.

His dark eyes, mirrors of her own, rose to meet hers. "What shall I do?"

Avery knew she should feel something more than she did—the Galaviz estate was her family's home. Yet she traveled to Madrid at a young age, and grew up alongside Princess Catherine at Alcalá de Henares.

When her father condemned her into the hell of being married to Paolo Pacheco Mendoza, Vizconde de Catalonya, she stopped thinking of him as family. And after nine years with Catherine in England, her once strong attachment to Spain had declined.

"I do not know, Reynaldo. I cannot decide that for you." Avery heaved a shuddered sigh and slid her glance toward Carlotta. Her sister-in-law's sober face displayed a hopeless expression; though as Avery regarded her, she saw a glint of determination begin to grow. She doubted that glint boded well for Reynaldo.

"In spite of my words, you are both welcome to stay here as long as you wish." Avery stood, indicating that she was finished with this interview.

Reynaldo glanced up, and this time stood without being prompted. Clearly he had learned his lesson. Carlotta rose more slowly, her gaze downcast and her features pensive.

Avery escorted the pair to the drawing room door.

"Dinner will be at nine bells this evening. I do not anticipate other guests, so do not make a fuss over your garments. I will not be changing," she added, lest either one believe she still threw barbs in their cumulative direction.

Reynaldo nodded dumbly, and opened the door. Carlotta stepped onto the courtyard balcony first, but then turned around after Reynaldo moved past her, taking one step back into the doorway.

She grabbed both of Avery's hands in hers, staring intently into Avery's eyes. "If you go back to England, Sister, I beg you to take me with you," she whispered.

Avery gave a small shake of her head and answered in kind. "I do not know that I *am* going back."

"But if you do." Carlotta's frantic grip was hurting Avery's fingers. "Please. Do not leave me behind."

Avery opened her mouth to speak, but Carlotta interrupted her. "I will do anything." She leaned closer. "*Anything.* Do you hear me?"

A gush of pity softened Avery's answer. "Yes. I understand."

She though Carlotta was going to cry, so great was her display of relief. "Thank you, Averia. God bless you."

The woman dropped her hands, spun on her silk slipper, and marched past her husband, who stood close enough that he must have heard every word of her secretive request.

Avery looked at her brother. Though she regarded him with sincere regret, she knew her reaction to Carlotta's words was nothing when compared to his personal pain and utter devastation.

Chapter Six

November 24, 1518

Jakob looked up as Percival Bethington strode into his chambers dressed in a dark blue mantle which fell to his hips. It had an intricate gold-embroidered border, about two inches wide, which held a variety of emblems that Jakob did not know the meaning of.

Grinning, Percy spread his arms, splitting the cape open, revealing its white satin lining. He rested his fists on his hips. "What do you think?"

Beneath the mantle he wore a belted robe of crimson velvet. The tubular sleeves and fitted cut of the garment allowed for ease of movement, and the robe's hem fell just above his ankles.

Jakob chuckled. "What on earth are you wearing?"

Percy wagged a finger at him. "Just as I suspected. You have not opened your parcel from the priests."

Jakob felt the blood drain from his face. "No."

"Oh, yes, Sir Jakob Hansen, Knight of the Order of the Golden Fleece." Percy spun on one foot just to goad him, Jakob was certain. "This is what we are to wear when attending all formal activities associated with the esteemed Order."

"Does that include our regular meetings?" *Please say no.*

"No. Only the inaugural meeting on January first. After that we may wear our black mantles—still embroidered, mind you—but apparently we can choose the style and color of our under-apparel."

"Thank the Lord," Jakob muttered.

Percy reached under the cloak and behind his back. "I have saved the best part for last."

The English knight held up a heavy gold collar which Jakob estimated was as wide as the mantle's embroidery. It consisted of alternating gold links: a rectangle piece styled with a cut-out design resembling a sort of fleur-de-lis, and a square piece molded with a sunburst pattern and set with a semiprecious cabochon in its center.

The links met at a right angle in the front, from which point dangled a golden ram, its drooping body suspended by a twisted rope around its middle.

Jakob stood and approached Percy, relieved to see that something of their required dress would demand respect, not only by the impressive size and design, but by its obvious value as well. "What is the stone?"

Percy squinted at it. "Lapis lazuli, I believe. Or perhaps it might be sodalite."

Jakob hefted the jeweled collar in his hand, appreciating the weight. "When do we wear these?"

"Any time we appear in public. Along with the black mantle."

Jakob nodded. "I suppose we are serving in a very—what is the English word? For something not everyone can be a part of?"

Percy shrugged. "Exclusive? Elite?"

"*Eksklusive.* The same as Norsk." Jakob grinned at Percival. "That is a new word for you."

"Another easy one." The English knight grinned. "It's no wonder you learned English so quickly."

Jakob gave a single-shouldered shrug and handed Percy the collar. "As I say, we serve in a very exclusive Order. To dress correctly is important, to ensure we are known."

Percy draped the collar over his head and across his shoulders—the effect was striking, indeed. "I am going to change my clothes and put this away, and then I was thinking we might want to explore Barcelona. Have you an interest?"

Jakob huffed a laugh; his good-humored companion never passed on an opportunity to discover new taverns or other sources of amusement. Showing restraint for the last three days had clearly pushed Bethington to his limit. Besides that, Jakob needed to get outside the palazzo and think about something other than Avery. That path was not taking him anywhere helpful.

"Yes. I would enjoy that."

Bethington bounced a nod, his smile wide. "Good. I'll meet you in the courtyard. Oh—there is one other thing."

Jakob lifted one brow. "What?"

"Wait until you see the hat."

§ § §

"Askel!" Jakob called out, striding into the sleeping chamber. "Have you unpacked the parcel from the priests?"

Askel looked up from the tunic he was cleaning. "Yes, my lord."

"Where did you put the garments?"

The valet set the tunic aside and crossed to a large wooden cabinet. "In here."

Jakob saw the red velvet robe and dark blue mantle—twins of Bethington's—and the more subdued black mantle. "Where is the collar?"

Askel's eyes brightened and he reached behind the clothing. "In this pouch, my lord."

Jakob unfolded the soft, sueded leather to reveal his own version of the golden collar. His, however, had amber in place of the lapis.

He held it up to the light. "I wonder, might that be intentional."

"What, sir?"

Jakob gazed at the younger man. Askel had been in his service for eight years, joining him right after the deadly fire that injured his leg. "Bethington's collar has blue lapis. Mine has Baltic amber."

Askel's features twisted in a sly smile. "King Henry's man did ask me about it."

"Hmph." Jakob rewrapped the collar. Henry the Eighth never ceased to surprise him. "Show me the hat."

Askel pulled a wad of black fabric from a higher shelf. "There are two. This one is for regular usage."

The chaperon consisted of a thick, rolled brim that circled his skull. Bursting from the top, like a fine woolen fountain, pleated fabric imitated a broad feather plume. A narrow swath about three feet in length extended from the left side.

Jakob placed the hat on his head and draped the—what would he call it? A scarf? A veil?—loosely under his chin, and threw the end over his right shoulder. He examined the effect in the silvered glass.

"It is rather fetching, my lord," Askel opined.

Jakob thought he looked passably handsome in the headpiece; it would do. He liked the way his reddish-gold hair looked against the black. "You said there were two?"

Askel nodded. "They are styled alike, but the other is red."

Jakob reached up and removed the chaperon. "When do I wear the red one?"

"Only during the mass of the Virgin." Askel replaced the hat on its shelf.

"That is a relief." Jakob pointed to the second cupboard. "I shall wear the burgundy tunic today. And the high boots. Sir Bethington and I are going exploring."

Askel helped him into the garment—one of King Henry's, acquired for their agreed-upon ruse. Jakob did not offer to return the king's garments when he left England. Considering that he was required to buy himself new clothing as a result of the bargain with Henry, Jakob considered the English king's cast-offs as merely extra compensation.

Jakob thought a moment, and then strapped his sword to his belt. Weapons would not be allowed in the cathedral of course, but at this moment there was nothing about his person to tag him as a knight of the Order. He and Percy were foreigners, still unknown in the city.

He smiled as he went down the back staircase. *A little anonymity never did anyone harm.*

§ § §

There was always a supply of taverns near a church. Jakob didn't know for certain why that was true, only that it had proven so in England, as well as Norway and Denmark. Perhaps for the screwing up of one's courage before going into the confessional. Or for facing the often equally daunting task of completing one's penance when finished. In any case, he and Bethington had their choice of several establishments to pick from once they retraced their steps and returned to the cathedral square.

"Let us have a drink in each," the Englishman suggested. "Find a favorite or two by process of elimination."

Jakob laughed and wagged his head. "You are certainly methodical in your pleasures, my friend."

Percy leaned closer. "I would not want to miss an opportunity by falling lax in my efforts."

Jakob bowed and extended one arm. "Lead on."

The first tavern was entered and exited in quick order. The grubby floor had been covered in straw—an excellent breeding place for vermin of a nasty variety. The smell of unwashed bodies, the sort who never bathed, was rank as well.

"I can accept the smell of sweat on an otherwise clean person," the English knight commented once they were back on the street. "But I find the sort of filth which has actually become part of one's body disagreeable in the extreme."

Jakob agreed, thankful that he was raised to wash himself daily, and bathe whenever the weather was warm enough. "Shall we go into that one?"

Percy read the placard aloud. "*Santos y Pecadores.* Saints and Sinners." He chuckled. "Sounds *perfecto.*"

This establishment was a vast improvement over the first, both in cleanliness and clientele. Jakob noticed a trio of finely dressed men, all wearing the golden collars of the Order. He tapped Percy on the shoulder and tipped his head in their direction.

"Some of our brothers, I believe."

Bethington's gaze followed, and widened a little. "Spaniards, I think. They are talking too fast for me to follow."

"Wait here." Jakob moved through the tavern's patrons toward the bar.

He ordered a pitcher of wine with two goblets and, with his back to the trio, listened to the men's conversation while he waited. They were speaking quite rapidly, but Jakob believed he understood the gist of their conversation.

After paying for the wine, Jakob carried the decanter and glasses back to Percy. "I was able to follow their discussion. If I am not mistaken, they were discussing a celebration of Advent, next Sunday. December first."

Percy startled. "Are we that close to Christmas, then? I have lost track." He counted on his fingers. "Only five more weeks until our mysterious Order convenes."

Jakob handed Percy a goblet of rich red wine. "Shall we introduce ourselves?"

"They seem pleasant enough." The Englishman watched the Spaniards over the rim of his glass as he took a taste of the wine. When he lowered his goblet, he gave Jakob an appreciative look. "This is excellent. What did you ask for?"

"I asked the barkeep what he recommended. This was his choice."

"Ah. Must have been expensive, then." Percy's disappointment was obvious.

Jakob tasted his as well; Percy was right, the wine was very good. He shook his head. "Not at all. It was quite reasonable, especially considering the quality."

Percy swallowed another mouthful of the delectable beverage and glanced at the Spanish knights. "They certainly are well dressed. Why do you believe they are wearing the collars now?"

Jakob had been thinking about that himself. "Two reasons, I believe. First, to gain respect. They are displaying their status quite clearly for everyone to see, even if their observers have no idea what the collar represents."

Bethington dipped his chin in agreement. "And the second reason?"

Jakob met the other man's gaze. "They are our hosts, are they not? We are convening in their country, and in their city. Perhaps they wish for the knights traveling here to recognize that they are part of the Order."

"Ambassadors of a sort?" Percy grinned. "Welcoming respected members as they arrive? I quite like that idea."

Jakob refilled their glasses. "I believe we are about to make new friends," he said in Norsk.

"And I believe you are right," Percy answered in that language. He picked up the decanter. "You will lead, this time."

Jakob did so, standing tall and approaching the trio with confidence. Now was not the time to cower.

"Good evening, gentlemen," he said in Spanish. He indicated their heavy golden collars with the drooping ram. "We are here for the Order also."

Their evaluative looks, which traveled over both him and Bethington, were not as friendly as he would have hoped.

Jakob gave the men a slight bow. "I am Sir Ja—Petter Hansen, representing King Christian the Second of Denmark and Norway."

The eldest man in the group squinted at him. "Japetter?"

Jakob felt his cheeks warming. "My name is Jakob Petter. But I understand Jakob is a difficult name in Spain."

Another evaluative look, this one focusing on his distinctively Nordic features and coloring. "You are not Jewish."

"No, my lord." Jakob offered the usual explanation. "My mother likes the Bible names. And I was meant to be a priest."

To Jakob's relief, Percy stepped into the fray. "And I am Sir Percival Bethington, representing His Royal Highness, King Henry the Eighth of England."

"Welcome to Barcelona, Sir Hansen, Sir Bethington." The knight turned to his companions. "May I present Alvaro de Zuniga y Guzman, Duke of Béjar."

Jakob estimated the man to be about forty years of age. He was slim of physique, sporting a trimmed, gray beard. "I am honored, your Grace."

The elder man continued the introductions. "And this other pup is Pietro Antonio San Severino, Duke of San Marco."

Jakob smiled at the designation; the pup was in his mid-thirties judging by his receding hairline. "My honor as well, your Grace."

"And I," the man paused, turning his body fully toward Jakob. "I am Diego Hurtado de Mendoza, Duke of l'Infantado."

The surname *de Mendoza* zinged through Jakob's frame. He perused the duke's neatly tied grey hair, cloudy brown eyes, and hawkish nose, wondering if Avery's husband might have had a similar look. "Pardon me, your Grace, but on the day we arrived we encountered a funeral procession…"

"My close cousin." The duke did not appear pleased at the connection. "Our fathers were brothers."

"We offer our sorrows," Percy interjected.

"And we are honored to meet you as well, your Grace," Jakob hurried to add. In his surprise at the duke's name, he had neglected that bit of convention.

"Have you been to the priests?" de Zuniga asked.

"Yes, the day we arrived," Jakob answered, indicating the golden collar. "But we did not know we should wear this before the Order."

"It is your choice," de Mendoza said. "But doing so will assure that you receive the proper respect."

"I understand." Jakob placed a hand over his heart. "Thank you."

"Your Spanish is passable, Sir," San Severino complimented. "Where did you learn?"

Jacob shoved aside the pain which the knight's innocent enquiry prompted. He made a motion which included Bethington, still standing by his side. "We had an excellent teacher in England."

"He has taught you well. Your pronunciation rivals a Catalonyan."

"She, your Grace." Jakob halted, wondering how much to reveal. Mendoza knew Paolo, so he must be acquainted with Avery.

Even with that connection, no one in Spain knew where she disappeared to; but Jakob had no idea if she had revealed her whereabouts once she returned. He decided to be vague for the moment.

"Our teacher was a Spanish lady-in-waiting of Queen Catherine's court."

Percival tensed and cut his eyes toward Jakob. His expression shouted, *what are you doing?*

De Zuniga perked up at his words. "So you are acquainted with Catherine of Aragon?"

"Yes." Jakob grasped the opportunity to shift the focus of the conversation. "She is a beautiful woman, and very gracious to aid us in this way."

Before any of the Spanish knights could question him any further, he added, "She is with child again. The babe might be born even now."

Mendoza nodded. "Yes, we had heard that."

Percy lifted his glass. "To a healthy boy!"

Jakob grinned and lifted his glass as well. "A healthy boy!"

The three Spaniards joined in the toast and drank liberally. Then San Severino tilted his head and peered through narrowed eyes at Jakob.

"Has anyone told you that you resemble King Henry?"

§ § §

"What were you thinking?" Percival demanded as he and Jakob made their slightly unsteady way back to the palazzo. The wine was not only delicious, it was strong.

"I do not know." Jakob waved a loose arm. "They were all dukes and they all looked at us like we were *estúpido*."

"Got your Norsk pride up, did it?" Percival poked his arm. "That will get you in trouble, you know."

Jakob grunted. He was well acquainted with that unsettling result since boyhood. "How well do you think Mendoza knows Avery?"

"That is hard to say. He did not look pleased to be connected to his cousin, Paolo, however."

"No, he did not." Jakob took an overly cautious step up a curb. "Do you think anyone knows she was in England?"

Percival copied his action, climbing the treacherous precipice in one try, before continuing to walk beside him. "Do you mean, has she told anyone where she was?"

"Yes. Or is it still a secret."

Percival shrugged. "I guess you would have to ask her."

§ § §

Jakob was not happy about the idea of speaking to Avery again, destroyed as he was by her intentional misdirection concerning her life. Yet on the other hand, he sorely missed her.

Avery's friendship had been the highlight of his five months in

England. Confessing the story to her of how his leg was injured had finally freed him from the heavy guilt under whose shadow he had lived for the last nine years.

Falling in love with her afterward was startling.

Falling out of love with her had not yet been possible.

Should I write her a note?

No. The answer might be too complex for her to explain. In addition to that, she may not want any part of her situation to be written down.

Would she agree to see me?

She would, if she knew why he wished to speak with her. That brought him back to a note. A sealed message for Esteban to hand her in the event she balked.

Should I make an appointment to see her?

No, she could refuse him too easily from a distance. If he was outside her drawing room—with a note—he stood a much better chance of gaining an audience with her.

The note should mention that he had met another knight of the Order: one Diego Hurtado de Mendoza, her cousin-in-law. That should prompt her curiosity at the very least, or her fear at the most extreme.

Either way, she was bound to grant him an interview.

That decided, Jakob turned over and tried to fall asleep, wondering which language he might dream in tonight.

Chapter Seven

November 25, 1518

Avery's hands began to shake when she read Jakob's note. She refolded the missive and gripped it tightly to still the tremors. "Send him in, Esteban."

"Shall I stay with you once again?" His tone evinced his assumption that her answer would be yes.

"That will not be necessary." She gave the majordomo what she hoped he would believe was a confident smile. "I shall be quite safe in the knight's presence."

Esteban pressed his lips together in a most disapproving manner. "As you wish, my lady. But I shall remain close, in case you need any assistance."

Not too close, I hope.

Her impending conversation with Jakob was not one that she wished for anyone to overhear, even her trusted manservant.

Esteban opened the door and stood in the doorway, forcing Jakob to turn sideways to step past him. The Norseman didn't react to the slight, but straightened his shoulders and walked toward her without looking back.

Avery caught Esteban's brief sneer before he exited the room. The majordomo was rather overprotective of her. But better that than lax, she supposed. After all, she had not yet sorted out her friends from her enemies.

And speaking of friends—was Jakob still one of hers? The expression on his handsome face was pleasant enough, though she had hoped for a more emotive greeting. Even anger would show that he cared what she thought of him.

He stopped a few feet in front of her and bowed. The golden collar which he wore over his brown brocade tunic hung in front of his chest, and glimmered when it caught the light. "Good day, Lady Avery."

"Good day, Jakob." She stressed the use of his Christian name while looking pointedly at his chest. "Is that collar for the Order of the Golden Fleece?"

He looked down at the heavy piece of jewelry and lifted the dangling ram in his palm. "Yes. And Henry assured that mine was made with Baltic amber."

That was interesting; the English king clearly must hold Sir Hansen in high esteem to go to that effort. "Please sit."

He chose the closest chair to hers and lowered himself into its curved comfort. "Thank you for seeing me."

Avery put her finger to her lips in a *shushing* gesture, and then motioned for him to move the chair closer. Jakob understood and, rising to his feet, carried the chair to her side so no scraping sounds would betray them.

"What is amiss?" he whispered, concern etching his countenance.

She answered in kind. "I do not wish for our discussion to be heard, and I know that Esteban is waiting near the door."

Jakob's lips twitched. "He does not like me."

"No." She shrugged. "His previous encounter with you was not a happy one."

"Neither was mine with you," he reminded her.

Avery's cheeks caught fire. "I am so very sorry, Jakob. I can only hope that, while you are in Barcelona, you may come to understand how precarious my situation was."

"I am gathering an understanding," he admitted.

"You said I should have trusted you in England and you were right. You have every reason to be angry with me." Avery's heart felt like it had climbed into her throat. "My question now is this: am I able to trust you here? In Spain?"

Jakob leaned back in his chair, his blue eyes dark and brooding. "I think that answer will depend on you, Avery."

Though wary of his response, Avery was forced to ask the question. "What do you want from me, Jakob?"

His gaze dropped and he pulled a long breath, letting it out slowly. When he reclaimed her regard, some of the darkness was gone from his expression.

"I want you to marry me."

Avery's head fell into her hands, muffling her outburst. "I cannot!"

Jakob leaned forward again and spoke in a low, clear tone. "No you cannot. Not yet. But I will be here for months."

Avery peeked at him from between her fingers. "Jakob, please do not—"

He grasped her barricade, and silenced her objection by pulling it down. He wove her fingers between his own.

"Here is what I propose: we both have unknown courses ahead of us. And neither of us knows whom to trust. True?"

Avery nodded. "True."

Jakob stared at her, hard. "Then we shall trust each other. No more secrets between us. Not a one. From this moment forward, we will be completely honest, even if we must cause each other pain."

She nodded, the tiniest blossom of hope sprouting. "I swear to you, Jakob. I will never hide anything from you again, if only you will act as my most trusted advisor."

His expression grew pensive. "I shall do so, Avery, to honor you." He squeezed her hands. "And I will continue to do this, even if I decide, in the end, that I do not wish to marry you after all."

Avery was punched so hard by his words that she couldn't draw a breath. The idea that Jakob might turn her away had not occurred to her; she believed his love to be unshakeable, even when she refused it.

"Thank you," she rasped.

"We shall begin now." Jakob pointed at the note in her lap and whispered, "What does Diego Hurtado de Mendoza know about you?"

Kris Tualla

§ § §

Jakob had not intended to say such a thing to Avery as he had, but he was very satisfied with her reaction to his disquieting words.

Her face drained of color and her barely-discernible pupils widened. As she remained silent, one red splotch blossomed on each cheekbone. And when she spoke, her voice was rough with shock.

He asked the next question quickly, not allowing her time to say or ask anything more.

If she thought he might give up on her, she might take more care with her interactions with him. And hopefully, she would not shoot his arrow back at him and refuse him once and for all.

"Was he at your wedding?" Jakob pressed when Avery didn't speak.

She blinked and caught a breath, her eyes moving side to side. "Yes. Yes, he was."

"Have you seen him since that time?"

"No." She frowned. "I do not think he had much care for Paolo."

"So he did not know you had disappeared, then?"

Avery looked straight at him. "I cannot be sure."

Jakob let go of Avery's hand, unlinking their fingers, and combing his own through his hair. "Have you told anyone where you were?"

She nodded. "My brother and his wife, who arrived this past week."

"Are they trustworthy?"

"Not in the least," Avery huffed. "But they are leaving soon."

Jakob rubbed his face, rasping his beard, and thought about what that information might mean to Avery's situation. His conclusion surprised him. "Then in my opinion, as your trusted advisor, where you spent your years away from this house should no longer be a secret."

"What?" Avery gaped at him.

"The nobility of Barcelona know you were absent from your marriage for nine years, do they not?"

"Well, of course." She snorted her disgust. "And they know

very well what disease my husband died of."

Jakob pointed at her. "And what do you believe they think _you_ were doing all that time?"

Avery slumped in her chair. "I have not thought about that."

"I would wager that serving as highest ranking lady-in-waiting to the Queen of England was not a consideration."

A laugh escaped her. "You are most certainly correct. And now I see your point."

"While Paolo wasted his life with whores, you elevated your station and attended Spain's beloved princess, Catherine of Aragon." Jakob grinned. "That should put any naysayers in their place."

"Yes, it certainly will." Avery gave him a soft smile. "The truth wins out again, Jakob."

"And—it is the easiest path to walk." He rose to his feet. "I will tell Percival that your time in England is to be revealed not hidden."

Avery looked up at him. "Are you leaving?"

There was no place else he needed to be at present. "Was there something else you required?"

Avery hesitated, then shook her head. "Not yet, I suppose."

Jakob sat down and took her hands once more. "What is it, Avery?"

She seemed to turn into herself, as if warding off an attack. "I have been meeting with Paolo's lawyer and accountant. I am afraid the estate is in a bad way."

"How may I help?" he asked, feeling like the proverbial knight rescuing a dame in distress.

"I am not sure," she confessed. "But I do not believe they are being completely honest with me."

"Do you wish for me to be there when you meet with them?" he offered. "My Spanish is not complete, but I can provide a daunting presence."

"And how would I explain your presence without inflaming the gossips?" Avery shook her head. "For now, I shall rest on the assumptions about my financial state made by my soon-to-be revealed connection with Catherine."

"That she rewarded you financially?" Jakob wondered why the queen would not.

"Well, at the least that I have her ear." Avery sighed. "I shall call on you when I have something of import to tell you. Is that acceptable for now?"

Jakob rose to his feet again and pulled her to stand in front of him. He gazed into her nearly-black eyes. "I am your servant, Avery, day or night."

Then he dropped her hands, took a step back, and bowed. Spinning on a heel, he left the room before he lost the will to do so.

§ § §

Avery watched him leave. For a moment, she was afraid he might kiss her; but truthfully she was more afraid of what she might do if he did. As much as she hated to admit it, she was still deeply in love with the Nordic knight—a situation which became painfully clear the day he forced his way into her presence.

One look at him, and she ached to throw everything in her life aside and run into his arms. A woman with less determination might choose to do exactly that and escape with the Norseman, consequences be damned. Avery almost wished she was that sort of woman.

She was not, of course.

Too many impediments stood between her and Jakob, ones which did not require any consideration at all when they were merely dallying in England, and a permanent relationship between them was impossible.

First and foremost was the difference in their class. She was a countess; Jakob was merely a knight, the lowest of all noble stations. After that came the differences in freedom which those ranks provided.

Under normal circumstances, a widowed *vizcondesa* would be financially and personally independent, able to choose her life's path.

Jakob, by contrast, was at the beck and call of his sovereign, dependent on the king for his income. And should he choose to marry without his sovereign's permission, he would be released from the king's service and be left destitute.

In addition to all of that, titled widows in their mid-thirties had responsibilities upon which many people's livelihood depended. Avery was not free to run again, not this time.

The crux of her situation lay in the fact that her husband was dead. She was no longer married. Therefore, any relationship which she encouraged with Jakob could no longer be labeled as adultery. Even if she chose to take him to her bed, fornication seemed a lesser sin than that; at the least she would still remain faithful to one man at a time.

After living a relatively independent life for nine years, Avery felt compelled to ferret out just how much, exactly, remained of her husband's once thriving businesses. And was there any money left? If so, where was it invested?

Once she had those answers, she would decide how—and where—to spend the rest of her life.

And with whom.

Avery crossed the drawing room and pulled the door open. Esteban staggered backwards and nearly fell. "My lady?"

"Esteban, I need to arrange an appointment with Señores Garcia and Montenegro, at their earliest convenience."

The majordomo bowed. "I shall see to that at once."

"I would like them both in attendance—and you as well."

Esteban's surprise altered his normally pleasant expression. "Why, if I might ask?"

"I am going to get to the bottom of Paolo's finances and your knowledge of the household expenses is a very important element in that." Avery gave the servant a steely stare. "And none of you will be excused from my presence until I have all of those answers."

§ § §

After his interview with Avery, Jakob joined Percival at the *Santos y Pecadores* tavern. Since meeting the Spanish knights there, he and Bethington had returned daily for their evening meal, forgoing a supper for two in the palazzo's huge dining room in favor of the chance to know more of their fellow members of the Order. To that end, they always wore their collars so that they might be recognized.

Percival poured him a mug of ale. "How was your audience

Kris Tualla

with the Lady de Mendoza?"

Jakob startled at the name—he still thought of her as Avery Albergar, even though he knew now that never was her name. Jakob answered in Spanish, keeping his words simple for the Englishman's sake.

"Very good. She will not keep her years in England a secret, now. We are to say this to anyone who knows her."

"Did I hear you mention a secret?" Diego Hurtado de Mendoza clapped Jakob on the shoulder and winked conspiratorially. "Do tell."

De Mendoza was exactly the man Jakob hoped might appear. He chuckled. "The point is, it is *not* a secret."

"What is not a secret?" Pietro San Severino set his mug of ale on Jakob and Percy's table. "May we join you gentlemen while you explain?"

Bethington, who had been able to follow the conversation, gave an expansive wave. "Please do, your Graces."

Once the dukes were settled, de Mendoza fixed his brown eyes on Jakob. "Go on, then."

"The story concerns your cousin-under-law, the recently widowed Lady Aver—*ia*, de Mendoza," he stammered.

The duke frowned a bit. He did not look as if he expected anything good to be revealed. "I have not seen her in some years."

Jakob nodded. "That is because she has been absent from Barcelona, and her marriage, for these past nine years."

"I must admit, I cannot blame her." Diego's relief was clear. "And under that circumstance, I assume that she is in good health?"

There was no mistaking the undercurrent of his question. "The lady is in excellent health, your Grace. Rest assured that she was untouched by her husband's unfortunate situation."

De Mendoza lifted his goblet in silent toast before taking a large swallow.

"Do you know where the lady was hiding?" San Severino asked. "Or is that the secret?"

"It was—as long as Paolo de Mendoza was alive." Jakob gave the men a knowing look. "She did not wish to be found and either dragged back to his poxed bed, or publicly divorced on false charges." He added that second part on his own, but it was probably true nonetheless. "Clearly it was the husband's own infidelity that killed him. The lady remained true, even at a distance."

Diego de Mendoza leaned forward, pinning Jakob's gaze with his. "How do you come to know these things?"

Jakob glanced at Percy, relishing the moment. "Do you wish to tell them?"

The English knight shook his head. "You will say it better."

Jakob grinned. "Because Lady, ah, Averia was our Spanish tutor in London. She was the chief lady-in-waiting for Queen Catherine."

"No!" San Severino beamed as his palm hit the tabletop, rattling all their glasses. "That is perfect!"

The elder duke wagged his head. "When she married Paolo we were told she had royal connections, but they were little more than vague rumors."

"Lady Aver-ia—" Soon that name should come more easily to his tongue. "Grew up with Catherine in Madrid and they shared a tutor. When Catherine married Henry the Eighth just over nine years ago, she called the Lady Averia to her court."

"It would seem that the lady seized the opportunity to better her situation, while her husband took a decidedly different path." Diego shrugged. "But how can you be certain she remained faithful to her vows? Royal courts are never known for celibacy, in my experience."

Jakob looked at Percy, whom he caught in mid-swallow. "Tell them what the Lady Averia was called in the Tudor court."

Percy coughed and set down his mug, his face reddening. "Do you mean, um, I do not know the Spanish words."

"Say in English," Diego prompted in that language.

Bethington faced him. "The Ice Maiden."

"*La doncella de hielo?*" the duke translated. Then he began to laugh and continued in Spanish. "Do you gentlemen expect me to believe that such a beautiful and accomplished woman has remained chaste for nine years?"

Percy may not have caught all the words, but he understood the knight's derision. "For one full year, she says no to me. I am told by every man at court, she will say no. Always. And she did."

San Severino slid his bemused gaze to Jakob.

He shrugged. "She refused me as well."

Diego de Mendoza leaned back in his chair, arms crossed over a chest still impressively sturdy for a man of nearing sixty years. "And you found no evidence of any other affaires of the heart?"

"No. None. I do believe her religious convictions concerning adultery kept her strong in the face of temptation." A flicker of Henry's opposing dealings with his own temptations lit Jakob's recollections, but he snuffed it. "She is a devout Catholic, as is the queen."

Pietro San Severino grinned. "I cannot wait to inform my wife of this story. It has the makings of intrigue."

Diego de Mendoza shot Jakob a narrow look. "You say this story is not a secret?"

"No, your Grace. Paolo is dead. The lady is safely returned." Jakob made a dismissive gesture. "When the people discover where she has been, and with whom, any speculation regarding her own reputation can be put to rest."

"I believe her reputation will be elevated as a result," the elder duke posited. "She did quite well for herself, while my cousin languished, a victim of his own debauchery."

Jakob did not disagree with one single word of that appraisal. "As knights of the Order, it may fall to us to protect her in this."

"I agree with you. Yes." De Mendoza nodded. "We must assure that anyone who makes a statement concerning the Lady Averia de Mendoza within our hearing is informed of the truth. This is our chivalrous duty."

Jakob smiled broadly. "Thank you, your Grace."

Chapter Eight

December 1, 1518

Avery sat in the back of Barcelona Cathedral, dressed in the respectfully somber garments of mourning, and tried to pay attention to the Latin religious services on this first Sunday of Advent.

She could not go forward to receive communion today, because she had been negligent about going to confession. She had not confessed, in fact, since Paolo died just over two weeks ago.

Before he passed, she confessed sins such as her anger at her avowed husband who acted in such a way that he was now dying so miserably. Or that she gave in to indolent urges and took a nap, when she should have been doing something useful, but unspecified.

Or that she had impure thoughts—the recipient of those thoughts also remaining distinctly unspecified.

Now that her husband was dead, if she went to confession she would be given wifely opportunities to buy indulgences, light candles, and pray her husband out of purgatory.

Avery had no intention of praying Paolo de Mendoza out of purgatory.

Let his women do it.

The bench on which she sat wobbled and creaked, and the scent of cloves and cedar washed over her. Her soul relaxed in its welcomed presence. She turned her head and smiled up at the tall Norseman who settled beside her.

Of course he would attend church here. When the Order of the Golden Fleece convened one month from today, Jakob would be spending many hours inside these ancient stone walls.

Jakob's shoulder brushed hers and he smiled, but he said nothing.

Avery was suddenly anxious for the service to end so she might ask Jakob what magic he had worked concerning her situation. Since their last talk, whenever she left the palazzo she was accosted by past friends and new acquaintances alike, all offering condolences for her loss.

Other than the frequency, that in itself was not unusual. What ensued however, was.

Question after question about Queen Catherine of Aragon and King Henry the Eighth followed in rapid succession—as if Avery might dissolve away before their curiosity about the charismatic monarchs was sated.

No one acted as if they pitied her any more, as they had done when she first reappeared in her home. Women now regarded her with obvious envy. Men considered her with respect. Invitations to dinners and gatherings increased tenfold, her period of mourning be damned.

In what felt like an overnight occurrence, Lady Averia de Mendoza has been raised from her own death, and had gained a fair amount of noble notice.

"Amen."

Avery made no move to leave, hoping that Jakob would take her hint and remain behind as well. He did.

As men and women filed past the silent pair, their evaluative stares raked over the tall Nordic knight from brow to boots. Jakob wore the Order's collar, as he always did now, and a few of the congregants did seem to know what it stood for.

Others kept their thoughts hidden, though Jakob's expensively tailored velvet tunic and gold-embroidered cloak, combined with the collar, declared him a man of importance.

The smug thought, *and he is standing by* my *side*, skittered through Avery's mind, causing a stab of post-mass guilt.

Forgive me Father, for I have sinned

Again.

"Would you care to see my chair?" Jakob asked when only the priests remained. His deep voice resonated in the stone cathedral, even though he had spoken softly.

Though his question forestalled hers, it did pique Avery's curiosity. "Your chair?"

"For the gathering of the Order." Jakob stepped into the aisle and made way for her. "The members' coats of arms are being painted on the seats in the choir."

Avery frowned and accepted Jakob's proffered arm. "Are they painting over the Saints?"

"So it would seem."

Jakob led her down the aisle to the massive choir at the center of the cathedral. "I was told that the Order's herald, a man named Thomas Isaac, and the Order's treasurer, Jean Micault, were commissioned earlier this year to prepare the church in a manner suitable for the gathering."

Avery had no idea what a momentous occasion this gathering truly was, but when she saw the brilliantly painted coats of arms there could be no doubt. Reds, blues, yellows and greens, liberally gilded with gold leaf, formed elaborate designs on the backs of each of the tall wooden seats.

She stepped up into the choir and walked its length slowly, admiring the intricate work. "Who painted these?"

Jakob answered from the other end. "A man named Joan de Borgonya. Have you heard of him?"

"No." Not that that proved anything about the man. "What does your Christian's coat of arms look like?"

"Like this." Jakob looked at her and grinned, pointing at a chair about one third of the way from the altar.

Avery returned to his side to examine the Danish king's crest. The design showed two bearded men, wearing only appropriately placed leaves and holding large wooden clubs, flanking a shield divided into quadrants by a white cross. One quadrant held four blue lions, growling at the observer. Another held three crowns. In the two bottom quadrants were a dragon and a single lion wielding a scythe.

Sitting atop the coat of arms was a jeweled crown, signifying that this member was a king.

Jakob did a slow turn, examining the other shields. "There it is—Henry's standard. That's where Bethington will sit."

Avery knew Henry the Eighth's coat of arms well, with its red dragon on the left, white hunting dog on the right, and tiny crowned lion, standing on a pearl-crusted crown atop a gold-plated knight's helmet. The design did not evince modesty, any more than the man himself did.

"Though set a bit off, you will face each other." Avery flashed a conspiratorial smile. "That placement will aid in your secretive communications, no doubt."

"Yes." Jakob did not appear to be paying attention to her. "I wonder where de Mendoza will sit."

Avery began to walk away. "Might I ask you something?"

She heard Jakob's booted steps start up behind her. "Of course."

Once she was out of the choir and back on the stone aisle, she turned to face him. "What did you—I mean, how does all of Barcelona already know that I was in England?"

Jakob chuckled. "All of Barcelona?"

"It certainly appears that way." Avery laughed as well. "I have never been such a sought-after dinner guest in my life."

"I merely said that your whereabouts during your absence were no longer a secret." Jakob's expression turned mischievous. "And then the 'secret' became the most important thing to be known."

"Very clever, Sir Hansen." Avery was, in truth, impressed. "I applaud you—and I thank you."

Jakob dipped his chin and offered his arm once more. "I am glad to be at your service, Lady Avery."

The fact that Jakob still called her Avery, instead of Averia, fomented a comforting glow deep in her breast. She and the knight shared her no-longer-secret past, and every time he used her English name he reminded her of their connection.

If only she might hold on to that connection long enough to disentangle herself from Paolo, she would be eternally grateful.

A Nordic Knight of the Golden Fleece

§ § §

Jakob strode home from mass, stretching his right leg as he walked. Already he could tell that the milder Barcelona winter was going to be much easier on his thigh than either the chilling dampness of London or the frigid winters in Denmark.

Warrior needed exercise as much as he did. He hoped that Percy would be amenable to joining him for a long ride and a hunt, but even if the Englishman declined, Jakob would not spend this afternoon inside doors.

Living in the Barcelona was even more restrictive than living in London, because the Spanish town was hemmed in by hills. The ride to find level land where their horses could exercise took the knights far afield—and they only discovered this delta because they asked the Spanish knights for advice.

"Follow the coast south about four or five miles to the river Llobregat." Diego told them. "The land levels out there. Good hunting, as well."

Jakob gave Warrior his head and the stallion broke into a joyous, leg-lengthening gallop. Bethington rode close behind, his whoop of glee nearly blown away in the wind.

The destrier gradually slowed his pace and Jakob took control once more, reining the horse around. Bethington trotted to his side, his broad, ruddy face split with a panting grin.

"Huzzah! That was marvelous!"

Jakob agreed. "We must come out here three times a week. These poor animals cannot be happy in their courtyard any more than we are."

Percy took his bow from his shoulder. "What sort of game do you think might live in those trees?"

Jakob removed his bow as well and pulled an arrow from his quiver. "Let us go and find out."

The copse was about a quarter of a mile upriver. As the men rode forward, rabbits scampered from their path in all directions.

"If nothing else, we'll have rabbits for stew," Percy observed. "As much as I love fish, I do like meat now and again."

Jakob smiled. "Living on the edge of the sea does dictate the menu."

Percy's brow wrinkled. "Denmark is on the sea, is it not?'"

"Yes." Jakob winked. "And we eat a lot of fish."

A rustle in the brush signaled some sort of animal ahead.

"Please let it be a pig or a deer." Percy crossed himself. "Not a wolf or a bear."

Jakob was surprised by his words. "Do wolves and bears live here?"

Percy shrugged. "I do not know. But it does not hurt to pray in any case."

The disturbance proved to be a small herd of deer. Having dogs to flush them into the open would have been helpful, but lacking that the knights were forced to ride into the forest.

As Warrior dodged through the trees, Jakob shot six arrows without hitting his target. The seventh arrow, however, landed true. Warrior skidded to a stop and Jakob slid from the saddle, pulling his hunting knife from his belt. He grasped the small antlers of the struggling buck and slit its throat.

He heard Bethington call out his own success from several yards away. Jakob smiled. They would eat well this season.

Jakob hefted the young buck onto Warrior's back and led the stallion in the direction of Percy's shout, meeting the English knight as he was lifting a small doe onto his horse's back.

"My mouth waters already," Percy said as he tied the carcass to his saddle. He looked at Jakob. "You've torn your tunic. Are you hurt?"

Jakob looked at his arm, surprised. He stuck his fingers into the rip, fished for the wound, and then pulled them out once he explored the damage. His fingers were bloody, but not overly so.

"I suppose the servants at the palazzo might mend both me and my clothing." He shrugged his lack of concern. "Shall we make our way back?"

§ § §

Once again, Avery dressed somberly, though her engagement that evening was of a social nature. While the dinner was intended to celebrate Advent and the nativity season, she felt that to dress in one of her English gowns would go too far beyond commonly held conventions regarding her fresh widowhood.

She had only recently regained a measure of respect in the city, and thankfully was now wholly separated from her dead husband's scandalous misbehaviors. Avery had no desire to risk damaging her repaired reputation before it had a chance to solidify.

Her carriage stopped in front of a palazzo which was close enough to hers that she might have walked the distance in a quarter of an hour—but the Vizcondesa de Catalonya must not stoop to such menial behavior.

Living up to a title was tiring at times, yet it was the only life she had ever known. When she observed how the poor people lived, she thanked God for every convention that must be adhered to; they were an infinitesimal price to pay for her comfort and safety.

A liveried servant stepped forward to hand her down and, with her chin high and shoulders squared, Lady Averia de Mendoza walked into the courtyard of Señor Xavier Medina, Earl of Valencia, her pride at long last intact.

§ § §

The palazzo's resident majordomo, Señor Esparza, made a face when he saw the rip in Jakob's tunic. Clearly he felt that the Norseman had somehow deported himself in an unseemly manner.

"Maria will assist you, my lord. Allow me to escort you." He turned and walked away. Jakob shot Percival a crooked grin before hurrying after the servant.

Maria made a *tsking* sound when she saw the damage. "Are you hurt as well?"

Jakob turned to Señor Esparza and dismissed him. "Thank you. I shall be well cared for."

Once the man was gone, Jakob returned his attention to the little grey bird of a woman whose bright dark eyes were fixed on his. "Yes, but not badly, I do not believe."

Another *tsk*. "I shall judge that, my lord. Please remove your tunic."

Jakob did so, revealing the torn shirt beneath, and the red stain which surrounded the tear. "Shall I remove my shirt?"

Maria used two fingers to spread the fabric and examine the

wound beneath. "Yes. I will need to bandage your arm, but I do not believe it needs stitching."

Jakob complied, pulling the garment over his head. "My valet can repair the shirt. He needs something to occupy his time."

"Askel? Such a nice young man." Maria smiled. "I suppose he knows how to remove bloodstains as well?"

Jakob had never really thought about it, but he nodded anyway.

"Please sit over here by the fire." Maria moved a wooden chair. "The light is better, and warm water is at hand."

Jakob settled his long frame into a chair that was a bit too low for him, causing his knees to rise above his lap.

Maria prodded his arm. "I was wrong, sir. I do believe a stitch or two might do best."

Jakob sighed. No man liked having needles thrust through his skin—but having a wound that did not heal properly was worse, as he well knew.

"Do it then." He looked up at her from his little perch. "But talk to me, so I have something else to concentrate on."

Maria was already preparing her implements. "What shall I say?"

"I have not seen you here at the palazzo," Jakob began. "Have you recently come?"

Maria smiled. "Oh no, I have been here for years. I am the chief lady's maid when ladies are in attendance, and head of the housekeeping staff otherwise."

She washed his wound with warm water, continuing her distracting tale. "And since only you two gentlemen have leased the house, I took a small trip to visit my aging parents. They live in a town called Terrassa, about ten miles to the northwest, over the mountains."

Jakob eyed the steel needle, the light from the fire sliding along its length like shining snakeskin. "And were they well?"

"No, not very, I am afraid. Would you care to look elsewhere?"

Jakob's gaze jumped to hers. "What?"

"I am about to stitch. Do you wish to watch?"

"No." Jakob turned away and looked at the flames. "Where were you employed before you came to work here?"

"I worked for a rather unpleasant man by the name of Paolo de

Mendoza."

Jakob wasn't certain whether he jumped at the stab of the needle or the equally disconcerting stab of the familiar name.

"Hold still, my lord. I shall finish more quickly if you do," Maria chastised.

"I am sorry." Jakob heaved a deep breath. "You were lady's maid for Vizcondesa Averia de Mendoza?"

"Yes. Until she disappeared, of course, and then I was released from that horrid place." Another stab of the needle was followed by the discomfiting slide of silk thread through his skin. "Are you acquainted with the lady?"

Jakob wondered how to answer that—should he confess more than the already revealed truth about Avery's nine-year sanctuary?

"Yes, I am well acquainted with the lady. We met in London, at the court of Henry the Eighth."

Maria's hands stilled. "She went to England? To Catherine?"

"Yes." Jakob looked up at her again. Maria's face had gone pale with the news. "Do you know she has returned?"

Maria slowly eased herself onto a stool, needle in hand and thread extending from Jakob's arm. "No! Why would she go back to him? He is poxed!"

Jakob leaned closer so the thread went slack. "More than that. He is dead."

Maria noticed his movement. "Oh! I had not heard this while I was in Terrassa." She stood carefully and peered at the wound. "One more stitch. And you must tell me about the lady as your distraction."

Jakob chuckled at the irony of her words. Avery was far more to him than a distraction. "I shall start at the beginning, then."

As Jakob described Avery's escape to England, her life there, and how he came to know her, he made the decision to tell Maria his part of the story as well. Something about the slightly older woman inspired his trust—and judging by her questions she had always been very fond of Avery.

"So you still think of her as Avery then?" Maria tied a bandage over his stitches.

"I do," Jakob admitted. "It is special between us."

Maria tilted her head, her hands now folded at her waist. "What else is special between you?"

"I asked her to marry me."

This time Maria fell soundly onto the stool, eyes wide. "What did she say?"

"Nothing. Once she was told Paolo was dying, she fled England without a word to me." Jakob flexed his arm gingerly, testing the limits of its motion. "It was not until I discovered her here in Barcelona, that I found out she was already married."

"Oh, my." Maria stared at the floor as she considered his story. After a several moments, she lifted her eyes to his. "How do things stand with you now?"

Jakob wagged his head. "I still wish to marry her. But there are too many situations which she must sort out first. She has asked for my help, and I have agreed."

Maria nodded. "She has accepted your proposal, then?"

"No." Jakob gave the maid a sly smile. "I told her that once her affairs were set in order, I would decide if I still wanted to marry her."

The woman's jaw dropped and her brow lowered. "Do you love her?" she demanded.

Jakob placed a fist over his heart. "She is the only woman I will ever love. If I do not marry her, then I shall continue my solitary life as a loyal knight of King Christian the Second."

Maria folded her arms over her chest. Clearly she was calculating his worthiness for her beloved Averia. With a slow nod, her decision was made.

"You will help her, sir. And she will be grateful." Maria chewed her lower lip. "And I shall help her understand the happy answer she should give you."

Jakob frowned. "How?"

She leaned forward, smiling, and wordlessly patted his knee.

Chapter Nine

The guests that evening numbered no more than two dozen, by Avery's estimation. Given the small size of the gathering, she was even more surprised to have been counted among them. Accepting a crystal goblet of wine, she let her gaze roam over the rim of her glass, hoping to see at least one familiar face among Señor Xavier Medina's guests.

"Vizcondesa de Mendoza?"

Avery turned toward the voice. A well-dressed gentleman, certainly no older than thirty-five, smiled at her, his even white teeth peeking through a neatly trimmed, white frosted beard.

Interesting grey eyes met hers. "Please allow me, under these intimate circumstances, to introduce myself. I am Señor Gustavo Salazar, and I was acquainted with your husband."

"Good evening, señor." She wondered briefly if Señor Gustavo realized that the stated acquaintance was most definitely not a desired recommendation. "Forgive me, but how, exactly, were you acquainted with the Vizconde?"

"We had some business dealings." He waved a hand. "It was some time ago, obviously. Two years, I believe."

"And what sort of business was that?" Avery pressed.

Señor Salazar looked at her differently of a sudden. "Exports, mostly. Spanish products. Why do you ask?"

Avery drew a bracing breath. "I ask because at the moment I am trying to piece together the far-flung products of my ill husband's irrational decision-making, and am encountering some substantial trouble in doing so."

"I see." The grey eyes narrowed. "Might I be of assistance in any way?"

"You might, yes, if you have any helpful information for me. Otherwise—" Avery finished her wine and handed him the goblet. "Please get me another glass of wine and let us speak of something less dire."

Señor Salazar laughed, a rich baritone staccato which emanated effortlessly from his chest. He accepted the glass with a little bow. "I am off to do your bidding, my lady. I shall return presently."

He did return presently, as promised, and he handed Avery her refilled goblet. "I do, I believe, have information which may be useful to you."

A pinprick of hope focused her attention. "Please tell me."

He shook his head. "Not here. Not tonight."

The wisdom of his caution made her wonder why she had not considered their rather public setting herself. "Of course. I understand."

"This is what I propose." Señor Salazar leaned closer. "Tonight, you allow me to charm and enchant you with my witty banter."

Avery laughed at that. "Yes, I might do so."

"And by the end of the evening, I shall invite you to call me Gustavo."

She lifted one brow. "Am I to suppose that you will wish to call me by my Christian name as well?"

His smile softened. "Averia is a very beautiful name. I love the way it rolls off my tongue."

Avery's jaw slackened. For the moment, she could not think of how to respond.

"And then..." He raised one stiffened finger, silencing any response or objection that she might conjure. "On the morrow I shall call upon you at a reasonable hour, and tell you absolutely everything I know about the business dealings of the departed Vizconde Paolo de Mendoza."

Avery swallowed a gulp of wine. What Señor—*Gustavo* was

offering her now was more information than she had yet received from Señores Garcia and Montenegro.

"I agree to your terms, señor." She accepted his offered arm as the wide doors to the dining room swung open. "But be warned—I do expect a bounteous amount of charm and wit in the coming hours."

Señor Salazar laughed again and Avery smiled. Accepting this dinner invitation was proving quite profitable.

She glanced around the crowd of strangers. "I am becoming quite glad I came this evening, but I must admit, I have no idea why I was invited."

Señor Salazar laid his palm over her hand as they entered the dining room. "You were invited, Lady de Mendoza, because I requested that my friend, the Earl of Valencia, include you in his guest list."

Avery regarded him with a surprised gaze. "Why?"

His cheeks flushed adorably. "Because of my past connection with your husband, I wanted to discern what sort of woman you might be."

That was more than a little disconcerting. "And what sort of woman *might* I be?"

"Surprising." He handed her into a chair, then took the seat besides hers. "I was not expecting a woman so interested in business."

"I must see to my own circumstances," Avery scoffed. "That old scoundrel had no care for my future, I can promise you that."

"And escaping to England assured that you had a future to care for." He gave her a significant look.

Avery glanced around the table; none of the other guests seemed to be paying any attention to her conversation.

Even so, she lowered her voice. "Does everyone believe that Paolo had a hand in his first two wives' demise?"

Señor Salazar shifted, clearly uncomfortable with the question. "I have heard the idea mentioned on several occasions."

To hear those words spoken aloud by a stranger sent a cold shiver of dread up her spine.

"I had wondered if I was verging on lunacy to have those thoughts," she admitted. "And I am not certain whether I am more relieved to have the idea confirmed, or horrified of the exigent possibilities."

"Either way, what is in the past is done with. And this is enough of that unsavory subject." Señor Salazar clapped his hands together and grinned at her. "The time has come for me to commence with the charm and wit."

Avery lifted her wine in silent toast and, finally, relaxed.

December 2, 1518

After providing her with a charming and witty experience the night before, Gustavo kept true to his promise once again. He arrived at the de Mendoza palazzo at one hour before noon, armed with a leather folder filled with a variety of documents. Esteban showed him into the large drawing room where Avery waited.

"Welcome, señor." She extended her hand and he kissed the back of it. "What sort of refreshment would you prefer?"

Gustavo glanced at Esteban. "I am not hungry at the moment, only thirsty. Ale, if you have it."

Esteban bowed and left the room.

"We shall work here." Avery crossed to the largest table. She had paper, a quill, and ink at the ready.

"Excellent." Gustavo laid the folder down and opened it. "I brought everything that I have regarding your husband."

"Dead husband," Avery murmured. "Let's not mistake ourselves that he has anything to say in this."

Gustavo dipped his chin. "I am suitably corrected, my Lady Averia."

Avery settled into her chair and Gustavo sat across from her. The door opened, and Esteban re-entered with a pitcher of ale and a mug.

He frowned when he saw the documents. "Shall I remain with you, my lady?"

Gustavo cut his eyes to hers; their grey darkened and they narrowed ever so slightly.

"No, thank you Esteban." She forced a smile. "I shall call on you if I need you."

The majordomo bowed stiffly, and stalked from the drawing room.

Avery took a chance and acted on what she believed she saw in Gustavo's glance. "Why did you wish him to leave?"

The man shuffled through his papers until he found the one he was searching for. "Because I did not know if you were aware of his business dealings with your—with Paolo."

"Esteban?" Avery's concerned gaze flicked to the closed door and back. "My majordomo was in business with Paolo?"

"Yes." Gustavo slid the contract across the table. "Paolo came to me almost two years ago and asked me to invest with him to build two trade ships."

Avery pulled the contract closer, her gaze moving over it. "Are you still involved?"

"No. As you can see, Paolo never signed the contract."

She frowned at him. "But what has this to do with Esteban?"

Gustavo's expression was kind as he pointed at the document. "I saw these same ships being built about nine months ago, so I enquired as to the owners' names."

Trepidation wrapped around her like a poisonous vine. "Paolo and Esteban?"

"Yes."

Avery shook her head. "That is not possible. For the last year and a half, Paolo was in not of sound enough mind to enter knowingly into—Oh!"

She felt the slam of realization hit like a thick plank across her chest. "Esteban made the contract and forged Paolo's signature."

"So it would seem."

"But with what money—*damn*."

Gustavo's eyes rounded at her profanity. "Lady Averia!"

"Do *not* begrudge me the one single word!" She glared at him. "I assure you, I am exercising a great amount of restraint at this very moment and not loosening a floodgate!"

Gustavo raised both hands and leaned back in surrender.

Avery pounded a fist on the table. "Who owns these ships now?"

"No one, actually. This is where you have some leverage."

She frowned, confused. "What sort of leverage?"

Gustavo leaned forward again. "The ships are being held until final payment is made. Esteban seems to have run out of funds."

"Don't you mean he has run out of *my* funds?" Avery dropped her head onto her arms, folded on the table in front of her.

Her entire world was shaken once again, this time by the revelation that her up-to-this-moment trusted majordomo had used Paolo's money for his own gain. And it was beginning to appear that he bankrupted her in the process.

She had finally received word this morning from Paolo's lawyer and accountant that they would meet with her the day after tomorrow. Perhaps once she saw the figures, she might find a way to salvage the ships.

She lifted her head. "What were you going to export?"

Gustavo blinked, startled by her unanticipated shift. "We planned to carry Merino wool, olive oil, and wine."

"And import?"

"Whatever we find of interest." He laid a hand over Avery's. "I wish to help you, Averia. That is why I wanted to meet with you."

Avery considered the very attractive man across the table. "What will you gain from doing so?"

He blinked again. Obviously he was not accustomed to such blunt questions from a mere woman. "Shall I be honest?"

She sighed, frustrated by his even asking her such a thing. "If you do not intend to always be honest with me, then get up and leave, and do not return. Ever."

Gustavo dipped his chin, his cheeks reddening. "I take your words to heart, my lady."

She rolled her eyes. "Speak."

He laid out one palm. "On the one hand, I retain my desire to partner in these two ships. Trade with the new world is growing, and they have need for what Spain produces."

He laid out the other. "You are a very beautiful woman, Averia, and your life has been complicated by an arranged marriage to a clearly less than desirable sort of man. Now that you are freed from that burden, I would like the chance to win your heart."

That statement mimicked Jakob's challenge in England, the connection unfortunately throwing the Norseman to the forefront of her thoughts.

Yet another man who wanted to *win* her. She was starting to feel like nothing more than a trophy to be put on display.

"Do you have the funds to buy out the ships?"

He blushed. "I—ah—no. Not yet."

No blink that time; perhaps he was beginning to adapt to her forthrightness. "Do you have any plans for how to procure those funds?"

Gustavo smiled then. "You and I might surely figure that out together."

"Along with my royal connections, no doubt." She wondered, then, if she should simply ask Catherine for the money and take ownership of the vessels herself.

"If that is your preference," Gustavo deflected. "But I was thinking of finding investors."

Avery considered the gentleman. Having another ally was a strong enticement. And if Jakob decided he no longer wanted to marry her, then she should not be so hasty as to reject Gustavo. He was handsome and clean, and promised to be honest with her.

Three attributes which her former husband lacked.

"I accept."

Gustavo's smile widened. "Thank you, my lady. How shall we proceed?"

Avery pointed at the untouched remainder of papers in his folder. "What about all of those?"

Gustavo chuckled. "They are merely for effect. It was the contract for the ships that I wished to bring to your attention and discuss with you."

Avery huffed her welcomed release. "I am quite relieved. I was not anticipating a pleasant audience when I saw the bulk of documents which you carried in."

Gustavo folded and tied his packet. He slid an intent gaze in her direction. "I do not believe you should say anything to Esteban as yet."

Of course not. "I did not intend to."

He nodded. "We will also need to ascertain how much capital you have at the moment."

"I have an appointment with Paolo's lawyer and accountant the day after tomorrow. I should have a fair idea by then." That audience would not end so easily as this one, she was certain of that.

Gustavo straightened. "Shall I be present?"

Something in Avery recoiled at the suggestion. She was only just beginning her independent existence and the idea of this man—who was essentially a stranger—being privy to her private finances was repulsive to her.

"No. Thank you. I would rather deal with those men alone." She gave him half a smile to soften her rejection. "In the event that I blurt out anything else unseemly."

Gustavo did laugh at that, in spite of the disappointment etched on his face. "I understand, Averia."

"Are you hungry as yet?" she asked, suddenly aware of her own state. "I believe the midday meal should be served shortly."

His features eased. "Are you inviting me to stay?"

"I am." She gave him a full smile now. "After the news you have brought me, I could use a hefty dose of charm and wit—and I am counting on you to deliver it once again."

§ § §

Avery lay in bed and stared at her canopy. While she managed to enjoy her meal with Gustavo, she tensed every time Esteban entered her presence. She knew she must pretend that nothing was amiss for now and try to figure out a way to claim the ships, which *her* money had built, before she confronted him and released him from her service.

I need to speak with Jakob.

She wanted to get out of bed and go to him immediately—and she might have, if she knew where he lived. How was she going to get a message to him? She would have to send Esteban to ferret out the Nordic knight's location and deliver a missive requesting that he visit her immediately.

With a sigh of frustration, she threw her covers off and walked into the outer chamber of her apartment. By the light of the banked fire, she set out quill and ink, and then lit a candle.

The message should be brief, her urgency only implied.

Avery hated that she thought Esteban might open the note and read it, but the possibility certainly existed. After Señor Salazar left her, the previously trusted majordomo had hovered nearby, as if trying to read her thoughts and discern what she might have learned.

Avery never considered herself to be an actress, though after nine years in the Tudor court she had learned to successfully mask her true thoughts when required. The skill proved helpful this evening, and she would need to call upon it every day until her situation was settled.

Please visit me at your earliest convenience. A.

That should serve her purpose.

Avery folded the paper and sealed it with the de Mendoza crest. Then she crawled back in the bed to resume staring at the canopy.

December 3, 1518

When Jakob received Avery's note, he took it to Maria and asked her opinion of its meaning—to ascertain if hers matched his.

"I would guess that something has happened, but she does not feel it would be safe for her to put that something in writing," the erstwhile lady's maid suggested.

Jakob nodded his silent agreement with that assessment.

Maria handed the missive back to Jakob. "Was the seal broken when you received it?"

"I do not believe so, but I did not examine it closely." Jakob tapped the note against his fingertips. "Is there anyone in her household whom you do not trust?"

Maria shrugged. "Her majordomo, Esteban Gonzalez, assumed more and more of Paolo's duties as the old man sickened. Perhaps he is not pleased to have the Lady Averia returned to stand in his path."

Jakob pondered that thought during his walk to Avery's house. It was quite probable that, because no one in the household knew anything about her whereabouts, they would assume she knew nothing about their actions. And a trusted majordomo would have access to household funds. What might he do with them?

Jakob arrived at the Mendoza palazzo one hour after noon. A servant opened the gate and Jakob entered the courtyard. Esteban waited at the top of the stairs.

Kris Tualla

"How may I be of service, Sir Hansen?" he called down.

Jakob climbed the stairs slowly, but deliberately, ignoring the ever-present stiffness in his right thigh. "The Lady Averia has requested my presence. Will you inform her that I have arrived?" He left off the *por favor* intentionally.

"Wait there." Esteban walked away, disappearing through a doorway.

Jakob topped the stairs and stood on the balcony in the shade of the upper floors. Even in December, the Barcelona sun was strong.

Esteban returned several minutes later. Jakob assumed the delay was intentional on the majordomo's part. Like a chess game, he mused.

And the knight maneuvers in unexpected ways.

"The lady will see you now."

Avery stood behind a tall chair in the same drawing room where she always met with him. Her hands rested on the back of the chair, but her whitened knuckles betrayed her otherwise restful stance. "Thank you Esteban."

Jakob noted that ale and sangria, along with glasses, were already in place. Avery clearly did not wish to be interrupted once their interview began. He turned back to watch the majordomo close the door and did not speak until he heard the latch fall.

Avery stepped around the chair and nearly ran to his side. Jakob forced himself not to extend his arms as if to embrace her, as much as he desperately desired to do so.

She grabbed his forearm. "Thank you for coming so quickly," she whispered. "Please sit with me."

She sank onto a couch, tucking her skirts out of the way to make room for him. "Do you want something to drink?"

Jakob shook his head and took the proffered seat, and then cut to the heart of the matter. "What has happened?"

Avery did not hesitate, clearly unconcerned by the bluntness of his question. "I met a man at an earl's house on Advent Sunday. His name is Gustavo Salazar and he had dealings with Paolo."

Avery's intense expression stopped Jakob from asking any of the myriad of questions which were popping to mind. He dipped a quick nod of acknowledgement and she continued.

"He came to see me yesterday. He had a contract from Paolo to share in the building of two merchant ships. Only Paolo never signed them, and he—Gustavo—thought the ships were never built."

Jakob frowned. "Thought?"

"Yes. He discovered that the ships were actually begun, but not finished, because of monies still owed."

Avery bit her lower lip and pulled a deep breath, her countenance alarmingly dismal. "He went to the dock and asked the shipbuilder whose ships they were, and the names he was given were Paolo de Mendoza and Esteban Gonzalez."

"Your majordomo? Where did he get—Oh!" Jakob knew the answer before he finished the question. "There are two names, but one source of funds."

"Yes. I believe that Esteban expected to finish the ships, and when Paolo died he would leave and become a wealthy trade merchant on his own." Avery waved a hand around her head. "And possibly he expected to take over this very house."

Jakob's earlier supposition was obviously correct. "He did not anticipate your return."

"No. Though I believed it would be quite obvious to everyone that I would come back to Barcelona when my husband died..."

Avery's shoulders slumped and she looked very small and vulnerable. Her eyes lifted to his.

"Please help me, Jakob. I cannot manage this alone."

Chapter Ten

Just having the tall, strong, and unshakeable Norseman by her side eased Avery's growing desperation. Jakob was a calm and logical thinker, and he knew that she understood logic. He would treat her as an equal in this, not as a man swooping in to rescue a helpless woman.

Whatever plan of action they decided on together, would be acted upon together.

Jakob leaned over and poured himself a mug of ale, obviously deciding that the circumstances of this audience required it. "First, you have to know exactly how much of Paolo's money remains."

"Yes. I have an appointment tomorrow afternoon at three on the clock with Señores Garcia and Montenegro, and I shall not allow them to leave my presence until I have obtained that very clear answer." Avery drew a resolute sigh. "I originally asked Esteban to be present as well, but considering what I have learned, I do not believe that would be wise."

"I agree." Jakob sipped his ale.

She gave him a hopeful look. "Might you join us, instead?"

His brow twitched. "I thought you wished to avoid gossip."

"Damn the gossip," she huffed. "There would be plenty of gossip to chew on if my majordomo managed to steal my estate out from under me."

The lady made a profane yet accurate point. "In that case, I shall attend."

Avery looked relieved. "What is the next step? Discover how much is owed on the ships?"

"I would think so, yes." Jakob stroked his short beard. "But that must be discerned carefully, so that Esteban is not alerted."

"And how do you believe that could be best accomplished?"

"An interested party, one with whom Esteban is not acquainted, must make enquiries." Jakob smiled. "Percival Bethington, I think."

Avery's brow shot upward. "Would he agree to do this?"

Jakob nodded. "He is as bored as I am at the moment, waiting for the Order to convene. A diversion would be quite welcome."

"You will not be bored after the first of January," she opined.

"No. And we should not wait to do this." Jakob refilled his mug. "The ship builders will know that Paolo is dead and they will want their payment."

"And if they discover that Esteban is only the majordomo, they will assume that no further payments are coming." Avery blew a breath. "I do hope he lied about that."

Jakob chuckled. "If he wished to be successful in his scheme, then he must have."

"It would be easy work for him to dress finely. To ride in Paolo's carriage. The ruse could be accomplished quite effectively." Avery cast him a sly glance. "As we are both very well aware."

§ § §

"Let me make certain I understand this." Percy planted his feet wide. One arm rested across his chest and he gestured with the other. "I am to go to the shipyard and say that I heard there were two nearly-completed merchant ships available for purchase."

Jakob nodded. "Yes."

Percy's brow furrowed. "Where did I hear it?"

"From… an acquaintance who knew Paolo?" Jakob waved a hand. "Make it a distant connection."

Percy pointed a finger in the air. "A man, who was at the funeral, told my acquaintance that *he* overheard it there. Then my acquaintance told me."

"Good."

Percy rubbed his chin. "And who am I?"

"You have to be wealthy. Why do you not wear your collar and be a knight of the Golden Fleece?" Jakob suggested. "Then, as an outsider, there will be no concerns when no one in Barcelona knows anything about you."

"And yet, as a member of that exalted chivalrous order, I shall be considered trustworthy."

Jakob grunted. "We hope."

Percy's gaze narrowed. "Should I be myself?"

Jakob pondered the ramifications of that idea. Though Esteban had not met Sir Percival Bethington, was he likely to? And if he was given the knight's name, would he connect the Englishman with the Norseman?

Yes, of course he would. The two knights were sharing the leased house. That arrangement had become common knowledge among the servants—especially since the two palazzos were in such close proximity. And as proof of that theory, Maria was familiar with Esteban's situation.

"No, you and I are too closely connected. I believe you should choose another name."

Percy gave him an apologetic look. "I am clearly English, and cannot pretend to be otherwise."

That was true. Too bad. It would have been rather fun to watch Bethington play a Frenchman.

Percy snapped his fingers. "I am the patron for myself."

Jakob cocked one brow. "What?"

He was growing exuberant. "I shall be—give me a name!"

Jakob said the first name that came to mind. "Paul."

Percy made a derogatory face. "Too much like Paolo."

True. "Thomas."

"Thomas, what?" Percy rubbed his hands together. "Windsor?"

Jakob's first instinct was to say no, but he paused. The name sounded like it was connected to English royalty—but not too closely so. "Thomas Windsor. What rank of nobility?"

Percy blew a breath through rounded lips. "The Order is packed with dukes, as it seems. Thomas might need to be a duke as well."

"Perhaps a duke of a more remote part of England?" Jakob

offered.

"Wales." Percy grinned. "I'll be the Duke of Merthyr Tydfil."

Jakob laughed. "Is that an actual place name?"

"Yes!" Percy clapped his hands. "And it must be real, because who would invent such a name as a ruse?"

"Thomas Windsor, Duke of Merthyr Tydfil, Wales." The name and title did sound real enough. "And you will be a patron?"

"Yes. I have traveled to Spain to ensure that King Henry the Eighth's most valuable knight, Sir Percival Bethington, is well situated and cared for." Percy's familiar grin split his ruddy cheeks and his green eyes glowed. "It is perfect."

"Yes. I agree." Jakob poured himself a glass of Percy's ale. "After my audience with Avery and the Señores Garcia and Montenegro on the morrow, we will have more information about the finances to this point."

"And you will tell me everything I need to know."

Jakob dipped his chin and raised his glass in acknowledgement. "And the next day, Thomas Windsor will visit the shipyard."

Percy tapped his chin. "I wonder what he shall wear."

December 4, 1518

Avery sat in the chair and did not move. She stared at the wine glass in her hand, emptied for the third time. Jakob did not refill it, thinking it best that the lady slow down her consumption so that her conversation might remain coherent.

The Mendoza lawyer and accountant were surprised, and not happily so, when they discovered that he was attending the appointment. They objected, of course, but when Avery insisted, there was nothing they could do about it.

The same applied to Esteban, who had been uninvited from the meeting. Avery gave him strict instructions that the quartet was not to be disturbed under any circumstances short of earthquake or fire.

Jakob clenched his jaw to keep from laughing at the comical expressions of desperation which flickered over Esteban's countenance. Yet each time he opened his mouth to speak, Avery quelled his words before they were fully formed.

Unfortunately, her triumph was short-lived, as Paolo's finances were at long last laid out in front of her.

"Might I have more wine, please?" she asked once Señores Garcia and Montenegro departed.

Jakob stood behind Avery and rested his hand on her shoulder.

"Is that wise?"

"I do not care if it is wise," she spat. "And if you will not pour it, I shall get it myself."

Jakob lowered himself into the seat next to hers, his back against the table so he was facing her. Her cheeks were as blanched as limestone, her eyes black as charcoal.

"You will survive this."

"How, Jakob?" she growled. "How is that possible?"

At the moment, he did not have that solution. The short answer to their hours-long meeting was that Esteban had bottomed out all of Paolo's accounts to pay for the ships. He closed all of the investment accounts, withdrawing the principal funds and the accrued interest, so there were no resources there.

And still there were debts. Finishing the ships, of course, was the largest. Jakob thought the smaller ones could be managed by frugality in the palazzo, but until he had that conversation with Avery, he could not be certain.

But that conversation would wait for another day.

Frustrated by his silence, Avery stood and stalked to the sideboard where the sangria waited. She poured the last of it into her goblet.

"It looks like blood," she murmured. "Everything in my life is bleeding." Then she drained the glass.

Jakob was worried about her, afraid that if he left her here, inebriated and alone in this house with Esteban, that she would reveal things which should not yet be spoken. Managing to pull her estate out of the depths to which it had been dragged would require planning, and keeping secrets from the majordomo was key at this point.

And so, the lady must not be left alone. The way he saw it, he had two options.

He could carry her away from the house, and stow her somewhere for the night. Except, he had no carriage. And once the effects of the wine hit her fully, Avery was not going to be in any condition to walk.

If he requested her carriage, Esteban would never allow him to ride off with the intoxicated Lady Mendoza. He would keep her here, and probably pour even more wine into her until she told him everything that transpired during the afternoon.

If I cannot take her away...

Avery had already shown disdain for gossip in the face of the seriousness of her situation. He prayed now that she was sincere in her stance.

Jakob walked to Avery and stood in front of her. She lifted her chin to stare up at him, abject misery carving deep hollows in her cheeks. She let go of the empty glass, whose life was narrowly spared by the carpet underfoot, and gripped his sleeves. Part in grief and part for balance, he guessed.

His decision made, he leaned over and gathered her in his arms, lifting her without effort. Avery did not object, instead, she looped one arm around his neck, and buried her face under his chin.

Jakob crossed to the door, and managed to get it open without dropping her. "Direct me to your chamber, my lady."

§ § §

Avery's head throbbed and her bladder demanded immediate attention. She sat up in bed and realized that she was fully clothed. Not only that, but she had no recollection of how she got there or why she was not in her nightdress. She climbed from the bed, grabbing the canopy poster for balance, and stumbled in the dim light to the chamber pot, wondering why the floor was swaying.

She managed to piss without spilling, and then moved to the table to pour water in the basin and wash her face.

A sudden snore from the outer room made her jump and spin around far too quickly. She fell to her knees, her heart bashing her ribs and her body tingling with fear. Her stomach roiled and she felt as if she might vomit. Who was there?

And why?

Dread suffused her core as she recalled the hours spent earlier that day with men who detailed her complete and utter destruction. She managed to grab the basin in time for her stomach to empty its soured contents in that receptacle and not on the floor.

Between spasms, she heard movement in the outer room. Footsteps approached. She tried to scream between the gut-emptying heaves, but managed no more than strangled squeaks.

In the pale light of a single candle, she saw boots stop beside her. As she panted over the basin, she tried to think rationally without success. "Who—"

Strong hands slid under her arms from behind and lifted her to stand. She put her hands out and leaned on the table for support.

"I'll take care of the mess. Let me help you back to bed."

Jakob.

Relief at the sound of his voice made her want to cry, before the realization that he was sleeping in her chamber zinged through her frame like a well-fueled fire.

Avery turned to face him, albeit more slowly this time. "What are you doing here?" she rasped.

He moved the basin away from their feet and then dipped a towel in the pitcher of cold water. "You were drowning your sorrows in a very large decanter of strong wine. I could not leave you alone."

She glowered. "This is *my* house. I was *not* alone."

Jakob wrung out the cloth and handed it to her. Avery reluctantly accepted the kindness and washed her face. She did feel a little better, but she was still wobbly and needed to sit down.

She staggered to the closest chair and sank into it. Jakob followed. He squatted in front of her, his expression tender.

Avery glared at him. "Explain yourself, sir. Why did you see fit to compromise my reputation this way?"

Jakob's voice was low. "I could not leave you alone with Esteban in your condition. He would have worked every bit of information out of you."

Another shock of realization stabbed her. Nothing about this nightmare was getting better, only much, much worse. She could not breathe of a sudden. Though she gasped for air she could not get enough to satisfy her lungs. The light of the candle grew dim.

She was floating through the air again, and some part of her memory reminded her that she had fainted in front of Jakob before. Her head cleared slowly and she was lying on the couch in her outer room. Flashes of her rooms in England and couches shared with Jakob moved through her awareness like a waking dream.

"Lie still." Jakob left her side and returned with the damp towel. He wiped her face and neck with the cloth. Though she was angry with him and wanted to stop him from tending to her, she had no strength to move any part of her body.

So instead, she began to cry.

Deep, gulping, ugly sobs emanated from her chest. Sorrowful wails, moving up and down in pitch with no discernible pattern, escaped her throat. Her shoulders shook and her belly ached. She rolled on her side and curled into a ball, wishing she could disappear. Or better yet, die.

§ § §

Jakob let Avery cry. That was probably the best thing for her to do at that moment. He went back into the sleeping room and dumped the sour-smelling vomit into the chamber pot, then covered the vessel to contain the stench.

There was scant water left in the pitcher, but he carried it into the outer room anyway. He slid a chair close to the lounging couch, and rewet the towel. He pulled Avery out of her fetal ball and began to wash away her tears.

"Go ahead and cry. Get it all out."

She pressed her fingers over her eyes so she could not look at him, but her sorrow did not slow.

Jakob pushed her hair off her brow. "Tomorrow, we will begin putting our plan to work."

"Wh—what plan?" she gasped between sobs.

In truth, he had no idea. He drifted off to sleep this evening as he played several unsuccessful scenarios to their logical end in his mind. And yet, there were some elements which proved hopeful.

"The important thing is to use what people assume to be true," he offered.

Avery uncovered her eyes. "Wh—what do they assume?"

"Because you are intimate with the Spanish princess, now the queen of England, you have influence. Both in England and here in Spain."

Avery struggled to sit up, but Jakob did not assist her. She needed to start helping herself climb out of this dungeon of despair, and sitting up unaided was a metaphorical beginning.

She gave him a severe look through red-rimmed eyes. "Do I have influence?"

"I am certain that you do, to some extent," he admitted. "And testing that out might be wise at some point. But not until that becomes necessary. And only *if* it becomes necessary."

Avery tried to draw her knees to her chest, but her stiff bodice prevented it.

Jakob set the damp towel aside. "Would you like me to help you dress more comfortably?"

Avery narrowed her eyes. "Are you trying to ruin me?"

Jakob shook his head slowly. "No. I am trying to save you."

"Why?"

He hesitated. "Because we are friends."

The words that he spoke were less than she wanted to hear, he thought, but he would not divert her attentions with an affaire of the heart. Lady Avery needed to find her own way at this time. Only then would she be able to come to him freely, without the weight of her past pinning her helplessly in place.

Jakob gave her a soft smile. "I will help you remove your burning beam, the way you helped me to remove mine."

Avery heaved a constricted sigh, and then turned her back to him. Jakob began to unlace her bodice in shared silence as the church bells rang four times in the near distance.

§ § §

Jakob only left the Mendoza palazzo once he was assured that Avery would be safe there on her own. She ate a little bit of cold supper from the tray which he had ordered much earlier that evening, and her head seemed to clear. As much as he wanted to kiss her mouth when he left, he settled for kissing her hand.

"Thank you, Jakob, for being so kind." Her cheeks pinkened. "I am afraid that I have behaved in a manner of which I am not at all proud."

Jakob gave her a sad smile. "You are faced with a situation far worse than you anticipated. You have every right to grieve in the manner which you did. I am only glad that you invited me here, so that I could protect you and keep you safe."

Her gaze dropped, as did her voice. "I wonder how long it will be before the entire city is claiming that I took you to my bed."

The thought of doing so brought parts of his body to immediate attention. If everyone assumed that he and Avery were lovers, was there anything too horrible about turning the gossip to truth?

Yes. He wanted her as his wife, not his mistress. On this stand, he would not compromise.

Jakob bent in a shallow bow. "I promise that I shall vow that such a liaison never occurred, for whatever good that might do."

"Thank you, again."

He stepped through the door and closed it softly, pausing to say a quick prayer for the lady and her precarious circumstances.

As he turned to leave the palazzo, he saw Esteban, leaning against a wall across the courtyard, watching him. There was nothing to be gained by pretending that he did not notice the majordomo, and something to be gained by acknowledging the man's presence if done right.

Jakob tilted his head and flashed a crooked grin. He saluted Esteban with a flourish and then made his exit with his head high and his back straight.

$\mathcal{C}$hapter Eleven

December 6, 1518

Jakob rode to the docks in the carriage with Percy, but did not get out. Though the afternoon threatened rain, neither man wanted to wait another day to discover what they could about the unfinished trade ships. Jakob was eager, because the sooner Avery had that knowledge, the sooner she could decide how best to move forward.

Percy's motivation was that he found the chance to dress up and play-act enticing and entertaining.

"Be careful what you reveal," Jakob reminded him once again. "Do not say anything that gives the game away."

Percy rolled his bright green eyes. "I understand. Trust me. I am not a fool."

Jakob's gaze raked over Percival Bethington's outrageous apparel, which shouted the converse. "Do not let them think you are."

"Never!" The English knight opened the carriage door and stepped out. Then, with a foppish flip of his wrist, he held an elaborately embroidered kerchief so that it caught the afternoon's damp, gusting breezes. He walked down the pier as if he did not have any urgent business, but was merely curious, his arse swinging like a woman's.

Jakob clapped a hand over his mouth to keep from guffawing and drawing unwanted attention.

The carriage was staying in its place until Percy returned. Making himself comfortable on the bench, Jakob massaged his damp-weather-bothered thigh until he dozed off—a result of yester evening's lack of sleep. He awoke when the English knight climbed inside once more; almost an hour later, he guessed by the angle of cloudy light. As Jakob sat up to make room for his beefy counterpart, the carriage starting moving.

Percival's tunic was spattered with wet spots. "It is raining."

Jakob nodded. "So I see. What did you discover?"

Percy rubbed his newly-shaved jaw. "Their accounting is confusing. They talked about everything in terms of maravedis, but that is like talking about everything in terms of pennies, not pounds."

Jakob nodded. "I experienced that yesterday with Avery's accountant. The numbers are enormous, but the value is low."

"It is good that you know this, so that you can make the calculations sensible."

"What is the balance that is due on the ships?" he pressed.

"Only thirty-five percent. Which is not bad, considering." Percy shrugged. "And if he inflated that for my benefit—"

Jakob threw up a hand. "And we will assume that he did."

"Yes. That means the lady could probably redeem the ships for less."

Jakob leaned forward. "The question now is, how much is that?"

"He offered me the ships individually for one hundred and seventy-five thousand maravedis, or the pair for three hundred and twenty-five."

Jakob required pen and paper to check himself, but he made a guess at the inflated amount. "The lady might be able to procure them for one hundred and twenty-five thousand maravedis each, or thereabouts."

Percy appeared impressed. "Does she have those monies available?"

Jakob snorted. "No. Nothing like that."

"How much does she have?"

Jakob considered how much of Avery's situation to reveal, and landed on as little as possible. "I cannot say for certain."

The Englishman gave a sage nod. "Yes. You are protecting her. I understand, and I approve."

"Thank you for doing this, Bethington." Jakob gave his friend as wry grin. "I could not have done it. And at least we have a target to aim for now."

"It was quite literally my pleasure." Percy shook his head, his expression gone grim. "On the one hand, the shipbuilder stands to make quite a profit if he can re-sell the ships at the higher percentage."

That was evident. "And on the other?"

"I would imagine that very few people have three hundred and twenty-five thousand maravedis at hand. So perhaps the lady does have a bit of time to figure out a solution."

Jakob ran a hand through his hair. "I wonder what that is in pounds sterling?"

"I did ask that, seeing as how I *am* British." Percy winked and cleared his throat. "About thirty-nine thousand pounds."

Jakob blew a whistle. A common laborer generally earned about seven pounds a year; thirty-nine thousand was literally a king's ransom.

He had no idea how Avery was going to raise this much money in the coming months. But he was determined to help her try.

§ § §

Avery slept through breakfast, but she attended the midday meal feeling somewhat restored. She decided to finally have a discussion with Esteban and determine what could be cut from the daily operating expenses in the palazzo. Every little bit that might be saved must be counted at this disastrous point.

She was relieved by Jakob's assertion that people assumed that she had influence, his words proving what she intuited. She needed to think that through more completely at some point and discern how she might use that opinion to her advantage.

Esteban appeared at the dining room door. "You have a visitor, Vizcondesa, but you might wish to greet her in less formal surroundings."

Avery met his eyes and gave him an intentionally blank look, though anger at his betrayal made her pulse surge. "Why? Who is she?"

"A former employee, come to offer her condolences."

The visitor could be one of any number of women, and would probably ask for her job back now that Paolo was dead. There was no point in refusing to see her, however—whoever she was.

"I shall meet her in the small study."

Esteban dipped his chin. "Very good, my lady. I shall escort her there when you are ready."

Avery looked down at the scattered remains of her meal. "Take her there now, Esteban. I have finished."

Avery left the dining room without looking back, her jaw clenched. She entered the small study and settled herself in the largest chair. She drew a steadying breath, folded her hands in a deceptively placid manner, and waited curiously to see who might arrive.

When her former lady's maid, Maria, walked in, Avery let out a little cry and held out her hands. The woman hurried to her and gripped them in her own, her smile bright.

"Lady Averia, welcome home."

Home? *Not in the least bit.* "I am so happy to see you, Maria. Please sit."

The maid lowered herself into the chair facing Avery's. "I am sorry for your loss, my lady." The words, while appropriate, sounded hollow.

Avery was not surprised. "How long after I left did he release you from your position?"

"Three months." Maria gave her a one-shoulder shrug. "I knew you would never return to this city as long as he lived, so I was not surprised."

Avery squeezed the maid's hands. "I am sorry that I did not tell you I was escaping. But I could not risk being found."

"I understand." Maria looked into her eyes. "All of us who were loyal to you knew that you were neither happy nor safe here."

Avery pushed her words past a constricting throat. "But the new maid, Zurina, says that you found other employment."

Maria nodded and her smile brightened once more. "I work at a palazzo not very far from this one."

"And the man leases the house?"

"He does. And a full staff is provided." The maid gave her a shy smile. "I am the chief lady's maid when women are present, and the head of the housekeeping staff at all times."

Avery's shoulders released the tension she was not aware they were holding. "So your situation has improved."

"In many ways, yes. Not only do I have more responsibility and higher wages, but the staff is paid even if the house is vacant."

"Oh!" Avery chuckled. "Does that happen often?"

"During the hottest months, yes." Maria leaned forward a bit. "But we are always serving guests in the winter. Often the same noblemen return, escaping some frigid clime from farther north."

Avery relaxed in her chair. "And do you have a familiar guest this season?"

"No, not at all. In fact, we have only two gentlemen residing." Maria paused, her eyes pinching impishly at the corner. "Members of the Order of the Golden Fleece."

Avery stared at the maid. "No..."

"Oh yes. Two very handsome and delightful knights with whom I believe you are acquainted?" Maria laughed. "And while I can see why you might turn aside the Englishman, I must admit that the Norseman stirs my blood a bit."

"Does he—do *they* know—that we are acquainted?" Avery stammered.

"Sir Hansen does. I do not know if he told Sir Bethington, however."

All sorts of uncomfortable ideas sprouted like springtime weeds in Avery's mind. "Did he send you to talk to me?"

"No, of course not. I am afraid that man does not know *what* he wants." Maria waved a dismissive hand. "And I truly believe that as women, we need to watch out for each other's interests."

Jakob does not know what he wants? Avery's chest tightened. "Is that why you came to see me?"

"In part," Maria admitted. "I wanted to discern how you felt about the gentlemen in question, and to offer my assistance, if you desired."

"Assistance?" Avery's brow lowered. "Exactly what sort are you offering?"

"Well, that depends on whether you wish to repel unwanted advances or attract the man's attention." Maria sat back, smiling, and waited for her answer.

"I—I do not know…" Avery's head was still a bit muzzy from yesterday's unpleasantness, and she was not completely certain she could trust Maria. After all, nine years was a very long time since their previously confidential relationship.

Maria patted her hand. "Well you know where to find me, now, my lady." The maid stood preparing to make her exit.

"Actually, I do not," Avery admitted. "I have sent messages, but have never gone calling on him. *Them*."

"Well, I suppose that we shall need to remedy that situation soon." Maria crossed the small study to the door.

"How?" Avery called after her.

Maria grinned. "You leave that to me."

And then she was gone.

December 7, 1518

Avery spent two full days following Esteban around the palazzo in order to quiz him regarding every employee's task and salary. The majordomo was polite at the beginning, but by yesterday his patience had clearly worn thin. The man was not accustomed to having anyone check up on him. Heaven knows, Paolo was in no condition to do so.

"Juan, tell me what it is you do," Avery said to a boy of about sixteen, who was leaning against a wall in the stable as they approached.

"I told you that he cleans the stalls, Lady Mendoza," Esteban grumbled.

Avery regarded Esteban, her patience at his deflections growing thin as well. "I thought Pedro cleaned the stables."

Esteban's tone was clipped. "Yes. He does."

Avery lifted her skirts and walked down the paved aisle through the center of the stalls. "We have ten stalls, but only four horses. Is that correct?"

"Yes."

Avery turned around to face the majordomo. "What purpose do the horses serve?"

Esteban all but snorted. "They pull the carriage, obviously."

"Two horses pull the carriage, Señor Gonzales," Avery said slowly, as if speaking to a fool. "What use are the second two horses put to?"

Esteban's eyes narrowed. "They are saddle trained. To carry a single rider through town."

Avery nodded slowly. "Well, I have no need for a mount. Neither does Paolo, any longer." She smiled sweetly. "Shall we visit the laundry next?"

Having finally finished today's tour, Avery sat at a desk in her outer chamber to evaluate what she had learned. When her dinner tray arrived, she sniffed it suspiciously, wondering if Esteban might be angry enough to poison her.

At first, the impromptu thought was merely a joke—until she recalled Paolo's first two wives. Was Esteban employed in the palazzo then?

I shall ask Maria.

For now, she ignored her rumbling belly and only ate the bread and cheese, forgoing the stew. She eyed the wine, wondering if she should risk it.

"I cannot live in fear," she resolved. *If I do die, I shall be in Heaven shortly.* And Esteban would be consigned to the pits of Hell for murdering her.

She poured herself a glass and returned to the task at hand.

Avery stared at the list of employees. Twenty-seven mouths to feed, and twenty-seven salaries to pay, and all to care for her and a largely unused house. The clear solution was to cut back as far back as possible.

"But I am supposedly a woman of international influence," she muttered. How might she prop up that façade and save money at the same time?

Avery leaned back in her chair and pondered the possibly fatal goblet of wine in her hand. It seemed that every simple discovery and subsequent decision expanded her already unhappy situation to encompass huge portions of her life.

She sipped the ruby liquid in small bits, trying to discern any unusual flavors in the beverage. Finding none, she poured a second glass, though still eschewing the stew—better to be careful, after all—and gave serious consideration to her parsimonious plan.

It seemed that everything about her life which required reconsideration coalesced into two questions. First, how would she live? And secondly, where?

Avery considered her life here in Barcelona. Now that her economic situation turned out to be so completely different from what she anticipated, only the palazzo and the climate held her here. She spent five miserable years in this city with Paolo before escaping to the Tudor court. Five unhappy years out of the nearly thirty-five of her life had not endeared her to the city.

"What about returning to Madrid?" she asked the wine.

Madrid without any connections, she realized. She moved away from that city at the age of twenty, and Catherine was already in England by then. Her parents had passed years ago, God rest their souls. And her brother Reynaldo, well, he had his hands full with the failing Galaviz estate in Segovia and his ever-so-lovely wife, Carlotta.

Avery wrinkled her nose and swirled the dark liquid in her glass, watching the wine slide around the goblet's walls in translucent burgundy sheets, and wondered if she might consider leaving Spain altogether.

But to leave Spain permanently was not something Avery had ever planned to do. Nine years ago, she escaped a horrid marriage with the knowledge that she must return at some point. Her home in the Tudor court was always a temporary situation. Avery— *Averia*— was a Spaniard. And she would remain a Spaniard for the rest of her days.

"No, I must find my way here." She drained her wineglass. If she was frugal, she should be able to pay the small debts. Then perhaps she could find enough money to make small payments, and secure the shipbuilder's loyalty, while she raised the remainder of the necessary funds.

Avery shoved aside the third question which was jumping up and down in her chest and screaming through her thoughts. Her feelings for Jakob would need to wait.

If she ended up destitute despite her efforts, then forgoing her title and marrying the knight became a possibility. Of course, that would require her to accompany the Norseman to Denmark to obtain his king's permission first—not an assured outcome, at all.

"And then I would have to live in the far north and make do with his income." Avery was not certain she could do either of those things.

There was always Gustavo Salazar. Marrying him would solve her financial situation, and she could remain in Spain.

She would think more about that possibility later, in spite of the sinking feeling it prompted in her mood. Tonight, she must concentrate on the task at hand, and begin to reorder her household.

She pulled out a sheet of paper and resolutely began her list. "I shall need a cook."

Georgette.

"And she will require an assistant, and a scullery maid."

Ana. Enriqueta.

"And I require a lady's maid..."

Zurina.

"And a chamber maid."

Sofia.

"We need someone to drive the carriage and care for the horses."

Antonio. Pedro.

"Laundry."

Maribel.

"A housekeeper."

Jacinda.

"And someone to oversee the staff."

Avery clenched her jaw and scowled as she wrote *Esteban*. She knew she must; she could not tip her hand just yet.

Her staff of twenty-seven could easily be cut to this staff of ten, but that still seemed excessive for one woman. Avery tapped the quill's feather against her lips, thinking.

If she closed down all of the unused rooms, draping the furniture—no, *selling* the furniture!—she could retain just one housekeeper who would also see to her chamber.

She crossed off Sofia.

"I will sell the saddle horses." She crossed off Pedro. Antonio could easily care for two animals and the carriages.

Avery made a heading halfway down her page, *To Sell*. Under that, she wrote *furnishings, two horses, the large carriage*.

A household of nine people should not be difficult to cook for, since Avery had no intentions of entertaining. She crossed off Enriqueta, reasoning that Ana could both help cook and wash dishes. Now they were eight.

"I shall give Esteban extra duties in the meantime." Avery's lips curved in a devious smile. "He will assist any staff member who requires help." *Even in the laundry.*

Avery consulted her notes. Different staff members were paid differing salaries, but when she totaled the cost of the nineteen employees which she would release from her service on the morrow, she would immediately begin saving over a thousand maravedis a week.

"That is over one hundred and twenty pounds sterling, I believe." After nine years in England, she was more comfortable thinking in their system. "Nearly five hundred pounds a month."

That was a very substantial amount of money. Added to the items she would sell meant she should have nearly five thousand pounds in cash only a month from today. That converted to sixty thousand maravedis to pay toward the balance on the ships.

Jakob should have completed his part of the investigation by now. Avery penned a quick note asking if she could visit him on the morrow. She summoned Esteban to have the note delivered—only nine bells had rung this evening, so the hour was not late.

She handed her majordomo the sealed letter. "Please see that this message is delivered to Sir Hansen this evening."

Esteban's heated gaze nearly set the paper aflame. "Of course, Vizcondesa."

He turned to do her bidding, but she continued speaking, her tone making it clear that she had not yet dismissed him. "And on the morrow, I want you to assemble the entire staff in the courtyard at ten on the clock."

Esteban faced her and his brow lowered. "My lady?"

"I have made some rather hard decisions regarding the future of this household, based on the Vizconde's gross mismanagement of his affairs." Avery lifted one brow, daring Esteban to contradict her. "I will need to explain those decisions to the staff, along with their unhappy ramifications."

Esteban's cheeks ruddied violently. "Yes. Of course. I shall see to it."

"Thank you." Avery smiled stiffly. "You may go now."

Chapter Twelve

December 8, 1518

Avery walked into the palazzo's courtyard about two minutes after the church bells rang the tenth hour of the morning, giving everyone on her staff ample chance to gather as she requested. The sky was low and heavily clouded but with no breeze—a fit setting for the news she was about to deliver.

She practiced her speech before going to bed, and again when she arose this morning. She wanted to make certain that the staff all knew that Esteban was largely to blame for her current situation, without saying so outright. And, that she was truly very sorry to have to let so many of them go.

Standing before her assembled staff, Avery flashed a sad smile and let her eyes meet each gaze that was aimed in her direction. Her smile faded, however, when her eyes met Esteban's.

She addressed the gathering with a somber voice. "First of all, I want to thank you all for your service to Paolo Mendoza over the past several years. I, for one, appreciate it greatly."

Avery turned to her left and began a slow pace. "I know that you all are aware of exactly what afflicted my husband. And you can testify to the behaviors which led him to such a gruesome end."

She paused and faced the somber servants.

Kris Tualla

"I was spared the same fate, only because I removed myself from his forceful advances before he was infected."

Avery let that idea hang for a moment, before reversing her direction and resuming her slow pace. "Due to his diseased state, Paolo was not able to make wise decisions regarding the efficient management of his affairs. And because I was in England, I was not informed, nor consulted, about any of the decisions which were made on his behalf."

"My lady, we did not know where you were," Esteban objected.

Avery halted and faced him. "When Paolo Mendoza was finally dying, I was informed, obviously. Had you sincerely tried to reach me, you could have."

Before Esteban could argue that clearly questionable point, Avery returned her regard to the servants, saying, "Unfortunately, some very bad choices were made concerning Paolo's finances, and were completed on his behalf."

Judging by the lowering of brows, several of the servants intuited what was coming. Accusatory glances cut toward Esteban.

Avery walked again, letting her shoulders droop, and clasped her hands in front of her waist. "I am afraid that there is simply not enough money remaining to allow me to run this palazzo in such an elegant manner any longer."

The heads of the gathered crowd pivoted, as if to question if they had heard her correctly. Esteban shifted his weight, but stared straight ahead, not meeting anyone's gaze.

Avery stopped and pulled a kerchief from her sleeve and dabbed her eyes, which were actually tearing up. The situation was truly tragic and it cut her to the core. She drew a deep breath before faced the men and women once more.

"I will be selling most of the furnishings, the two saddle horses, and the large carriage. Once the unused rooms are emptied, they will be closed off."

A low rumble wafted toward her, and Avery wiped her eyes again. "I am so very, very sorry, but I find I am forced to let all but seven of you go—though I will do so with strong letters of reference. This circumstance is not of *your* doing."

Now the object of their collective disdain was very clear. Esteban's jaw tightened, rippling his cheeks. Smudges of burgundy splotched his cheekbones.

"If I call your name, please meet me in the large drawing room in a quarter of an hour. And if I do not, then please return to your quarters and pack your personal belongings. I shall have your reference letters ready in one hour." The small crowd silenced, each countenance drawn and sober, and most blanched with concern.

"Georgette, Ana, Zurina, Antonio, Maribel, Jacinda... and Esteban." When she announced the majordomo's name, Avery thought she heard someone actually growl. "Thank you. You all are dismissed."

Avery turned and quickly climbed the stairs to the main floor before she broke down and cried in front of those whom she had released from her service. She went into the large drawing room and laid out the twenty references, the writing of which kept her up quite late yester evening.

As six of the remaining servants drifted into the room, she thanked each one personally, assuring them how much they were valued. Esteban was the last one to enter, and when he did, Avery began her explanation of the new staff duties.

"I am but one simple person to care for, so your load should not be heavy. Because of my financial situation, I will not be entertaining or hosting overnight guests. And, because most of the rooms will shuttered, they will not require cleaning."

Worried brows began to ease and stances relaxed.

"Georgette, you still have the kitchen and Ana as your assistant. Unfortunately, the scullery duties must be shared between you."

The women nodded and answered in tandem. "Yes, my lady."

"Zurina, you will remain as my lady's maid, in addition to acting as my chamber maid."

The woman gave her a soft, understanding smile.

"Maribel and Jacinda, you will share the housekeeping and laundry duties."

The girls looked at each other and Jacinda clasped Maribel's hand. Clearly both were relieved to still be employed.

"Antonio, the complete care of the two carriage horses now rests on your capable shoulders, as well as maintenance of the small carriage."

He gave a little bow. "Thank you, my lady."

Kris Tualla

Avery faced Esteban, whose sharp stare might have killed her, if mere looks were capable of such a thing.

"Esteban will remain as the staff manager, but with one addition." She paused to increase his discomfort, noting by the whitening of his lips that she had succeeded. "Because he is intimately familiar with each one of your duties, you are to call on his assistance if you ever find yourself falling behind."

"What?" The word exploded from the majordomo. "You expect me to labor in the menial tasks?"

Avery raised her brow, as if surprised by his outburst. "You will continue to receive your superior salary, Esteban. Do not have a care about that. Unless..." She shrugged. "You find these conditions so intolerable that you wish to resign."

He glowered at her, his tightly-pressed lips squirming in barely contained anger.

"I am sorry, but there is nothing else I can do." Avery waved an innocent palm toward the tiny group. "I am trying to avoid being forced to sell the palazzo altogether and releasing everyone from their employment."

All eyes moved to Esteban. The majordomo must know he was trapped, and if he still had any hope of redeeming the ships for himself, he could not separate himself from the Mendoza name.

"No, Vizcondesa" The words sounded like they were being grated off his tongue. "I do not wish to resign."

Avery smiled at him, heaping salt onto his raw dignity. "Thank you for your loyalty, Esteban. I will not ever forget all that you have done."

She did not wait to discern whether he caught the double edge of her words, but dismissed the still-employed servants with the explanation, "I must now meet with those of your comrades who are departing, and give them their references. And you all must begin your new assignments."

Once alone in the drawing room, Avery shook out her trembling hands and poured a hefty cup of ale. The fraught confrontation had gone as well as she could have expected, and she was fairly certain that she had earned the staunch loyalty of the six remaining servants.

Esteban was the antithesis of loyal, and having him in the house did make her uncomfortable. And yet, she could not risk cutting him loose to try and secure funding for the ships on her own.

She determined that she would need to speak to Georgette and Ana regarding the preparation and serving of her food, in the event her suspicions regarding Esteban proved plausible.

§ § §

Jakob, along with Percival, waited in their palazzo's main drawing room. He fidgeted as he wondered how best to tell Avery how much money was required to pay for the ships.

Since Percy's visit to the shipbuilder, Jakob had avoided contacting Avery and spent most of his waking hours trying to come up with a variety of options for her situation. His efforts had fallen woefully short.

When Avery strode into the room, it was immediately apparent by her demeanor that something about her had changed. Jakob and Percival rose to their feet.

Jakob stepped behind a chair. "You look lovely today, Lady Avery. Please, sit. Would you care for any refreshment?"

Avery flashed a brilliant smile before lowering herself into the proffered seat. "No, thank you, Sir Jakob. I do need to remain clear-headed for our discussion."

Jakob declined to make a comment, not wishing to innocently offend, and reclaimed his seat. Percy sat as well. Both men waited for Avery to start the conversation.

She began with, "Were you able to visit the shipbuilder?"

Percy nodded. "Yes, Lady Avery."

"And was your conversation fruitful?"

"Yes. It was," Percy said slowly.

Avery's expression dimmed and she glanced at Jakob. "Shall I assume that the news was not good?"

"And yet, it is not entirely bad," he offered.

Avery groaned and rubbed her forehead with her fingertips. "Please, simply tell me."

"The shipbuilder is asking outside investors for thirty-five percent of the original agreement in order to complete the ships." Jakob waited for her to look at him before he continued. "However,

Percival and I believe that the remaining balance is most likely only twenty-five percent."

"So he will make additional profit if he sells to someone other than me?" Avery shook her head. "That is bad news."

"Actually..." Percy winced and slid his glance to Jakob's. "That was the good news."

"What?" Avery's dark eyes shifted their focus from one man to the other. "How is that good news?"

"Because of the amount of ready money that would be required to meet the thirty-five percent requirement." Jakob waited to see if Avery would come to the obvious conclusion.

She did. "So the twenty-five percent is a very large sum as well."

Jakob put up one hand. "Understand that, unless we can see the original contract, we are only making assumptions and estimates."

"I can get you the original contract. Or at least, the one that Paolo never signed." Avery's dark brows pulled together. "I would expect the numbers to be close, if not the same."

Jakob gave her a kind smile. "That would be helpful."

She pulled a deep breath. "You have not told me your estimate as yet."

Jakob and Percy exchanged a quick look, one which designated Jakob as the bearer of the worsening news. He returned his attention to Avery.

"Two hundred and fifty thousand maravedis should complete the contract." He cleared his throat. "Or about thirty thousand pounds sterling."

Avery's eyes rounded. Her jaw fell slack. Otherwise she did not move.

"If it helps," Percy offered. "Another investor would need to present three hundred and twenty-five thousand maravedis, or about forty-five thousand pounds."

Avery glared at him, but still did not speak.

Jakob knew that Avery's cash at hand was less than fifty thousand maravedis at best, about six thousand pounds. And she still had a household to maintain.

"I thought... I mean, I made some changes..." Avery waved a limp hand. "It is not nearly enough."

Jakob leaned forward. "What changes?"

Avery blinked, and then shifted her gaze to his. "I will have some wine."

Percy stood immediately and moved to do her bidding.

"What changes, Avery?" Jakob repeated his question.

She resettled her stance in the chair, hunching down defensively, as if bracing for an attack. "To begin with, I decided to reduce my household. I am closing most of the rooms and will sell the furnishings."

Jakob nodded. "Go on."

"I am also planning to sell the two saddle horses, and the large carriage." She looked hopeless. "I expect that to raise about ten thousand maravedis, though now it sounds like nothing."

Jakob shook his head. "It is not nothing."

Percy handed her a goblet of wine. "Every amount will help. Sometimes it takes money to earn money."

Avery accepted the glass, her expression skeptical. "And, I reduced my staff to seven servants. That saves me over five hundred maravedis a week."

"That is thirty thousand maravedis by beginning of January." Percy shrugged. "If you make payments toward the remaining costs, you might forestall another buyer."

"Might," Avery repeated. "Or he sells the ships out from under me, and I lose everything."

"You still have the palazzo," Jakob reminded her.

She turned to face him. "It does me no good if I have no income. And if I sell it, then I have no home."

§ § §

Gustavo Salazar was waiting for Avery when she returned. She crossed the drawing room, smiling, truly glad to see him.

"I am so sorry, Señor Salazar." Avery offered her hand. "If I had known to expect you, I would have been at home."

Gustavo kissed the back of her hand. "Please, my lady, you called me Gustavo at our last meeting. Have I done something to cause you to reverse our friendly interaction?"

"No, of course not." Avery sank into a chair and motioned for him to do that same. "You may continue to call me Averia."

His grey eyes met hers, pinched by his smile. "You are looking well, Averia."

While she doubted that was true, considering her harrowing week, Avery appreciated the kindness. "Thank you. As are you, sir."

She, on the other hand, was being completely truthful. For a man in his mid-thirties, Gustavo was lean and fit, the only betrayal of his maturity were the two streaks of white, framing his chin in his neat brown beard.

She noted with satisfaction that Esteban had served Gustavo wine and olives while her guest waited, glad to see the majordomo was not going to start an all-out war with her just yet.

Avery gave the man an encouraging look. "To what do I owe the honor of this visit, Gustavo?"

Gustavo's expression dimmed. "I have news about the trade ships."

Avery forced herself not to react outwardly, though her heart lurched. "What sort of news?"

"I have learned that a gentleman from England, a duke, has made enquiries about the ships."

Her relief was quickly replaced with curious concern. "How do you come to know this, Gustavo?"

"As I told you before, I am still quite interested in the pursuit of trade." The tone of his voice was a bit tentative. "I have asked the shipbuilder to keep me informed of the status of the two ships."

"I see." Avery considered the handsome man beside her.

"After all," he added. "They were originally to be mine."

"So they were." Avery leaned back and wondered if she faced a friend, or an enemy. "What is your plan?"

Gustavo chuckled and his cheeks reddened. "To be honest, Averia, my plans were changed the moment I set eyes on you."

Avery sucked a little gasp. "What does that mean?"

"That means…" Gustavo peered at her from lowered brows. "Do I still have your permission to be completely honest, even though I the risk of offending you?"

"Yes. Please." She leaned forward again, wondering if what

was about to happen, was what she expected.

Gustavo hesitated—gathering his thoughts, if the twitches in his expression were trustworthy. "I am thirty-seven years old. I have never married, and I have no children. Sailing off on a trade ship seemed to be a fine plan for the second half of my life."

Avery nodded.

"When I met you, Averia, I was struck to my very core by your beauty and grace." He gave a little shrug. "I know you have been quite recently widowed, but I also know that your marriage to Paolo was …less than happy."

Avery huffed. "And the reason I absented myself for nine years."

"Precisely. And that is why I am risking offense now, because I believe that you are not a typical widow."

Understanding zinged through Avery's frame as she realized where this conversation was, indeed, headed. "Gustavo…"

He put up a hand. "Please. Averia, allow me to continue."

She nodded, keeping her expression carefully blank.

"You are a woman, of a like age to my own, also with no children. We have much in common in that."

Avery nodded again.

"I have observed that you have a mind for business as well." He gave her a soft smile. "Am I correct?"

"Yes," she admitted.

Gustavo reached for her hand. "I know well that this moment is not the appropriate time for you to make a decision, and I do not expect one until Paolo's affairs are set to rights. But…" He squared his shoulders. "I would like to make you a proposal."

"What sort of proposal?" Avery whispered.

Gustavo gazed into her eyes. "Let us join together, Averia, both in business and in marriage."

Though this was exactly what she expected him to say, once the words were spoken aloud they gained an incredible amount of weight.

"All I ask is that you consider this idea." Gustavo squeezed her hand. "I do believe that we would make a good match."

He was probably right, Avery realized with a start. And if there was no Jakob, she might even accept him this very afternoon.

And yet, while there still was a Jakob, he did say *if I decide I do not wish to marry you after all.* Though she had not lied outright, perhaps the Norseman was so hurt by her lack of honesty that he would not consider her as more than a friend ever again.

If that were true, then Gustavo's proposal was every bit as attractive a suggestion as the man himself.

Avery faced him. "First let me say that I am not offended in any way. In fact, I am quite flattered."

Gustavo grinned his relief. "I am so glad to hear that, Averia."

"Secondly, you are quite correct when you acknowledge that I cannot agree to this proposal today. I am still ferreting out the truth about Paolo's finances."

He nodded. "Of course."

"That said…" Avery gave Gustavo a shy smile. "I shall happily consider your proposal with favor."

Gustavo squeezed her hand again. "Will you dine with me this evening?"

A twinge of panic stopped her. She was in no rush to remarry, and did not wish to give Gustavo the idea she was more ready to move in that direction than she actually was. "I am rather tired this afternoon, Gustavo. Perhaps tomorrow?"

"Yes. Yes, of course." Gustavo rose to his feet and pulled Avery to hers. "You have made me very happy, Averia. Thank you."

He kissed the back of each one of her hands. "Until tomorrow evening, then."

He gave her a little bow and turned to leave, but then stopped and turned back. "Do you prefer a chaperone?"

Avery laughed. "What reputation do I have to preserve at my age?"

Gustavo smiled and shrugged. "I did not wish to presume."

"I have no qualms about being alone with you in your home," she assured him. "In fact, I rather look forward to it."

Another small bow and an impish grin. "As you wish, Averia."

Avery watched him walk away, wondering what course her life was going to take next.

Chapter Thirteen

December 12, 1518

Avery lay in bed, considering the suppers which she had been invited to over the last three evenings, and her resultant time spent with Gustavo. She found all of the experiences surprisingly pleasant and gradually her guard was lowering. The man truly was the charming individual that he claimed to be at their first meeting.

Gustavo lived in a much smaller house than hers, but it was beautifully appointed. Situated on higher ground and further from the sea, from the upper floor he had a lovely view of the water beyond the red Barcelona rooftops.

Supper was always delicious, the wine he served consistently excellent, and conversation flowed easily between the two of them.

And when Gustavo kissed her goodbye, she felt like a candle melting in his arms. Even now, the memory of his thickly-lashed grey eyes and engaging smile warmed her nether parts.

Whenever she thought of Jakob, the first word that came to her mind was *intense*. When she thought of Gustavo, however, the word *temperate* seemed to fit. Quite the opposite response. The two men could not be more different.

She had not seen Jakob since their conversation about the amount of money due for the ships. The idea that he was avoiding her did raise its ugly head, but then common sense bashed it back down. Simply put, unless they were courting, she and the Nordic knight had no shared business. And while Gustavo was most definitely courting her, Jakob most definitely was not.

Avery sighed and snuggled under her bedcovers, not yet ready to face another rainy winter day.

She had made a visit to the knights' palazzo two days ago to speak with Maria about selling her furniture, but sadly the men were out hunting at the time.

Avery tasked Maria with making enquiries about a reputable agent and then bringing Avery her recommendations. Avery didn't trust Esteban to bring her an agent who would give her the best price—and not split an inflated commission with her unscrupulous majordomo. The last pocket she needed to help fill at this time was Esteban's.

She had also entrusted Antonio with the sale of the horses and carriage, after asking Señor Esparza, majordomo at the knight's leased house, what he thought were fair prices. Her plans were moving forward without a hitch at the moment.

At least my economic ones.

Her romantic ones were in a mess.

Avery tossed aside the covers and donned the robe which lay crumbled across the foot of her bed where she tossed it yester eve. She went to her outer chamber door and rang a brass bell in the hallway, summoning breakfast. She refused to feel guilty that the church bells had already chimed the tenth hour. It was not as though anything was pressing for her time at the moment.

When the tray arrived, Avery gave a little cry of joy when she spied the Tudor seal on a thick letter. She snatched it up and carried it to the window where dim light seeped through the clouds. When she read Catherine's opening words, however, tears blurred her vision.

My dearest friend ~

How deeply I long for your sweetest comfort these last dark days. The news I must write to you concerns tragedies of two kinds, and I do not know how I will survive their merciless combination.

The first is the loss of another daughter. My confinement, yet again, did not bring forth life, but only grief. I cannot express the depths of my sorrow in words, and I have spent these last tearful days alone in my chamber, wishing you were by my side to carry me through this dark valley.

She never drew a breath, this little girl. The midwives say that they do not know why. I am most certainly cursed for some unknown transgression, and shall never bear my husband a son. Especially not now.

This is the second tragedy, my dearest Averia. My husband has taken a mistress, one of the maids of honor, the one named Elizabeth Blount. Do you remember her? She was the one so enamored of Sir Hansen, though that knight never paid her any heed.

After I learned of Henry's infatuation with the girl, I never again felt my baby stir in my womb. It was as if his infidelity against me had killed her. And now I grieve both her inability to live, and my husband's inability to be faithful.

Do write to me soon, Averia. I pray every day that your circumstances in Barcelona are settled and that you are contented with your life there, even though I would give anything to have you returned to me.

With greatest affection ~
C

Avery sat beside her breakfast tray; all desire to eat even the smallest bite had dissipated with each of Catherine's words. The letter rested in her lap, her dripping tears leaving wet spots on the ink.

With Jakob gone, Henry's dalliance with Bessie had lost its

disguise. The king, in his lust, was clearly not careful enough to protect Catherine from discovering the truth. And now she had lost yet another baby.

At the least, Jakob's involvement was not revealed, Avery thought selfishly. Because that meant Catherine would not believe Avery knew of the adultery. Or, that Avery had lied to her about it.

Jakob. Avery blotted her tears from the letter with her napkin. *I have to tell him.*

Today.

§ § §

Jakob read the letter in silence, noticing the spots where the ink had started to spread. Avery's tears, he would guess, as she was still shedding them.

He looked up from the missive. "I am so sorry, Avery."

She nodded a little. "It is not your fault that you could not remain at court any longer."

Jakob refolded the thick paper. "I cannot feel guilty about my actions there. It is clear that, by doing Henry's bidding, I *was* protecting the queen."

Avery nodded, still slumped in the chair which she had tumbled into upon her arrival at his chamber door.

"Would you care to join me for dinner?" he asked gently.

Her wet expression was guarded. "What about Percy?"

"He's... somewhere. Else." Jakob waved a hand. "Probably visiting one of the many ladies who have caught his eye."

Avery flashed a crooked smile. "Still the same Percy, I see."

Jakob gestured at his non-existent collar of the Order. "And the ornamentation draws them like flies to a honey tree."

He reached out his hand. "Please come and join me, Avery, even if you do not care to eat, for I am famished."

She took his hand and stood, accepting the letter from him, and tucking it inside her skirt's pocket. Jakob wrapped her arm in his and escorted her to the dining room.

Once they were settled and service had begun, Jakob asked, "What has occupied your time of late?"

"Well..." she dipped her spoon into the fish soup and lifted it slowly. "I gave Antonio the task of selling the large carriage and two horses, after consulting with Señor Esparza regarding a fair price."

That surprised him. "You came here? When?"

"You and Percy were hunting." Avery sipped the soup. "This is delicious."

"Juan is a good cook."

Avery nodded her agreement. "I actually came here that day to talk to Maria about finding an agent to buy my furniture. I do not trust Esteban, and would expect him to fill his own pockets with a commission on the sale if he chose the man."

Jakob smiled. Avery was a wise woman. "That was excellent thinking. Was Maria helpful?"

"I do not know yet. I shall speak with her before I leave today."

Jakob had already finished his soup and was waiting for Avery to finish hers. "What else has filled your days?"

She looked at him, her dark eyes finally brightening and her mouth curling with amusement. "I have a suitor."

Jakob's chest tightened. "What does this mean?"

Avery rolled her eyes. "It means that there is a man interested in my hand."

"In marriage?" Jakob was stunned—he had not considered this as a possibility when he threw down his verbal gauntlet weeks ago.

"No, he simply wants my hand. He has no interest in the rest of me." Avery looked at him like he was the supreme fool in a room of fools. "Yes, in marriage."

Jakob's mind jangled with questions. "Who is he?"

Avery set her spoon down and folded her hands in her lap. "Gustavo Salazar, the man who was supposed to build the ships with Paolo, before Esteban shoved him aside."

Jakob concentrated on pulling information from his memory. "And you met him some weeks ago. At the supper of Xavier Medina, Earl of Valencia."

Avery gave a slow nod. "I am impressed. You *have* been paying attention."

"What else does Salazar want from you?" Jakob knew the question was rude, but he wanted Avery to be honest. Making her angry was one way to assure that.

Kris Tualla

Her eyes narrowed. "*Gustavo* was planning to redeem the ships himself. But once he met me, he decided to include me in his plans."

Jakob snorted. "Because he was smitten."

Avery jumped to her feet like a startled cat, practically hissing her words. "What are you saying? That such a thing as this is not possible?"

"Not at all, Avery. I confess to being quite enamored of your beauty from our very first encounter." Jakob leaned across the table. "But I did not want anything *from* you."

"And you believe *that* is why he has proposed." She crossed her arms over her chest, black fire lighting her eyes. "To use me to acquire the ships."

Jakob rose slowly to his feet. "Avery, you are every bit as wise as you are beautiful. Certainly you must believe this is a possibility."

"Of course it's a possibility!" Her obsidian irises glittered and sparked. "Do you not believe that I can discern the truth?"

Jakob hesitated, uncertain of what to say. During her years at court, Avery earned the nickname Ice Maiden because of her refusal to enter into any romantic dalliances.

Except with me.

The reason, as it turned out, was because she was still married to Paolo.

But not anymore.

The longer he was silent, the angrier she appeared. He must say something to avoid a full-blown explosion. "Forgive me, Avery, but your courting skills have gone long unused."

Her jaw dropped. Then her shoulders followed. "Whatever do you mean by that?"

He kept his tone calm, and his voice low. "All through the years when you were pursued at court, you refused everyone, and for good reason. You were never required to discern the true purpose for any man's expressed interest."

Avery sank back onto her chair, her folded arms still shielding her heart. "I did not need to. All any of them wanted was a physical affaire."

"Are you certain of that?"

She blinked, and her gaze dropped to the tabletop. "I—yes."

"You do not sound certain," Jakob ventured.

Avery glared at him again. "What do you know of it?"

"I know this." Jakob leaned forward, his elbows flanking his empty soup bowl. "If I was trying to salvage a plan like the trade ships, then marrying the widow of a signer on the contract would be the first step."

Avery rolled her eyes away from his gaze, her lips pressed into a thin line.

"And if she was as beautiful and desirable as you are, Avery, then performing such a duty is doubly enticing."

She twisted her neck to face him again. A furious blush crept up her pale neck and colored her cheeks. "If I am so beautiful and desirable as you claim, then his affections might well be quite sincere, would you not agree?"

Jakob sucked a breath. His own strategy had just shot back at him, fatally wounding his argument.

"Yes," he admitted.

Avery sagged like a slackened sail. "You do?"

Jakob clenched his jaw, considering down which path he should lead this discussion: toward Avery's best interest, or his own selfish desires.

In the end, his deep love for Avery demanded that he do what was best for her. "Gustavo may well be sincere in his affections. I only meant to warn you of other motives."

"You did not need to warn me, Jakob," she murmured. "I was aware."

"I should have realized that. You are no fool, Avery." Jakob forced a smile and extended his hand across the table. "And so we are still friends?"

Avery swallowed and Jakob watched her throat ripple. She laid a pale hand in his, but did not return his smile. "Friends."

Jakob wrapped his fingers around hers and squeezed gently, stroking his thumb over her skin. "I cannot help myself, Avery. My need to protect you is as strong in my heart as protecting myself."

Her eyes met his. "I am a grown woman, Jakob. And a widow. I am not Uma."

The mention of his long-dead bride sent a jolt through Jakob's frame. Avery's words, however painful to hear, were nonetheless the truth. "No, you are not. And that is why I love you."

Avery looked away, her brow puckering. "I did not yet agree."

Relief sent him a different sort of jolt. "You did not yet agree?"

Avery still did not meet his eyes. "Gustavo says that he is aware that too little time has passed since Paolo's death for me to make such a decision."

The idea that, in reality, too little time had passed for Gustavo to discern whether or not his plan was feasible skittered through Jakob's thoughts. He dare not express that aloud at this fragile moment.

Instead, he said, "He has the original contract for the ships."

Avery looked at him then, clearly confused by his sudden shift of subject. "Shall I ask to see it again? So that we may know for certain the contracted price for the ships?"

Jakob nodded. "That would be helpful, do you not agree?"

"Yes." Avery pushed her chair away from the table. "I am sorry, but it seems that I am not hungry after all."

Jakob scrambled for a reason to make Avery stay at the palazzo. "Will you speak with Maria, then, while I finish my meal?" he suggested "Then come back and tell me what she suggests. Perhaps I can help."

She cast him a skeptical look. "Yes. I shall do exactly that."

Jakob stood as Avery exited the room before dropping back into his chair. The servant scurried in and Jakob asked for the rest of his meal to be served at once. When the food was placed before him, he ate quickly, needing to fill the demanding void in his core before Avery returned.

§ § §

He loves me?

Avery stomped down the main staircase to Maria's world on the ground floor, flummoxed by Jakob's words. He claimed to be enamored of her beauty, called her as wise as she was beautiful, and said she was desirable enough that any man would want her.

Then he called her 'friend.' Why did he no longer want her if, as he stated, he still loves her?

"Lady Averia, it is good to see you."

Maria's warm greeting pulled Avery's attention from the puzzling Nordic knight. "Thank you, Maria."

Maria invited Avery into her little apartment. "Would you care for anything?"

Avery shook her head. "No, thank you. I had some soup with Sir Hansen."

If Maria thought that was an odd response, she did not show it. "Please make yourself comfortable."

Avery sat on one of the carved wooden chairs, waiting until Maria was settled before she asked, "Have you any news for me?"

"Yes, my lady. Señor Esparza and I discussed several options before we agreed on the best agent for your situation." Maria reached into her pocket and pulled out a small, stiff card. "His name is Lorenzo Mechi, and this is the address."

Avery reached for the card. "May I borrow pen and paper? I would like to send him a message without Esteban knowing."

"Of course." Maria stood. "Come to my desk, my lady."

Avery followed the maid to a little wooden desk and sat on Maria's stool. She penned the note to Señor Mechi, asking him to come to her palazzo at one o'clock on the day after tomorrow, promising him a houseful of furniture to sell.

When she finished, she folded the paper and handed it to Maria. "Will you see this delivered today?"

"Straight away, Lady Avery. Is there anything else I might help you with?"

Avery hesitated, but curiosity pushed the query through her lips before she thought better of it. "What did you mean when you said Sir Hansen does not know what he wants?"

Maria chuckled. "Because that man refuses to claim what he wants, he cannot yet decide what to settle for."

Avery straightened. "What is he refusing to claim?"

Maria crossed the apartment to the door, before turning to address Avery once more.

"Do you truly not know?" She grinned and winked. "I shall see to this delivery immediately."

§ § §

Avery climbed the stairs to the main level of the knight's palazzo with much less enthusiasm than when she descended. She had no idea what she would say to Jakob when she was once again in his presence, but she could not leave his house without saying goodbye, at the least.

A servant met her at the door of the dining room and directed her to the drawing room, explaining that Sir Hansen had finished his dinner and was waiting for her there.

When Avery was ushered into the room, she was disappointed to see Percival there as well, effectively forestalling any attempt to have an intimate discussion with Jakob.

"Lady Avery!" Percy set down his glass and strode across the room to kiss her hand. "Jakob told me you were here. I am so glad to have the chance to greet you."

"Thank you, Sir Percival." Avery shifted her gaze to Jakob who watched her from across the room. "Did he inform you as to why I have come?"

Percy pressed a fist to his heart, and his green eyes saddened. "Yes, my lady. Poor Queen Catherine. My most fervent prayers shall be with her this eventide."

Avery squeezed Percy's hand with the one he still held. "I wish I was with her."

"I know you do. And I wish you could be with her, as well."

Jakob walked toward her. "Has Maria been of assistance?"

Avery nodded, shifting her attention to the Norseman. "She consulted with Señor Esparza and presented me with their recommendation for an agent. I have already written him to come to my house the day after tomorrow."

Jakob addressed Percy. "And because of a fortuitous social connection, the lady will soon be able to examine the original contracts for the ships once again, and this time she shall take note of the costs."

Percy grinned at her. "That is excellent news, my lady!"

"Yes, it is." Avery silently thanked Jakob for not saying more. Before he could, she added, "I must be on my way, now. I have many things to organize before the agent comes to the palazzo."

She turned to Jakob. "Thank you for your kind hospitality."

She left before he could say anything else.

Chapter Fourteen

December 14, 1518

Jakob and Percival sat in their carriage and watched the man they were following, who was identified to them as Gustavo Salazar, enter what they were told was his favorite tavern.

Jakob turned to Percy. "Are you ready?"

Percy touched his forehead in salute. "Thomas Windsor, Duke of Merthyr Tydfil, at your service."

Jakob always chuckled when Percy pronounced that mouthful of Welsh words. "Go on then. I shall return in one hour."

Percy climbed from the carriage with a broad grin; the beefy English knight was definitely enjoying his part in the plan. Their carriage driver, who received his instructions before the men left their palazzo, put the carriage in motion as soon as the door shut.

Before Lady Avery exited his home two days ago, Jakob had concocted a scheme.

"We need to investigate Gustavo Salazar," he told Bethington as soon as she was gone.

Percy's eyes brightened. "Who is he?"

"The man with the contracts, who was originally supposed to have built the ships with Paolo Mendoza." Jakob sniffed his disdain for both men. "He is now pursuing the Lady Avery in a romantic manner."

Bethington had the good sense to look horrified. "He must not succeed!"

Jakob met his friend's eyes and spoke his worst fear. "Unless, he truly does love her, redeems the ships, marries her, and provides for her for the rest of her life."

Percival's jaw fell slack and he stared at Jakob as if snakes were slithering from his ears. "Good God, man! Is that what you have come to believe?"

Jakob's emotions were in pitched battle, like cannons blasting through his chest. On the one hand, if he loved Avery, he would want what was best for her. On the other hand, he believed *he* was best for her.

She was certainly best for him. "I cannot answer that until we investigate the man and discern his situation."

"Right. I see." Percy jerked a nod. "I believe the Welsh duke may need to reappear."

Jakob laughed then, relieved to have such a worthy knight on his side. "Indeed."

Riding in the carriage through the hills north of Barcelona gave Jakob some time to consider his actions. He had not intended to tell Avery he was still in love with her, hoping that she would finally come to him with that same confession first.

Yet when she told him that Salazar was courting her, he was forced to reveal his heart. Even so, he intentionally made his statement casually, as matter of known fact, rather than a heartfelt declaration.

He wanted Avery to accept his love for her as fact; that it was common knowledge his feelings for her had not changed. In doing so, Jakob was staking a prior claim, for whatever weight that claim might hold.

When the hour was gone, Jakob was once again in front of Salazar's favorite tavern. Percy wandered out casually, squinted and looked at the sky, clear as a blue glass bowl, and then glanced up and down the street for his carriage.

Jakob knew it was an act, as Bethington was far too savvy a knight to not have seen the carriage straightaway. He walked toward the conveyance purposefully, but not over-eagerly.

Once inside and facing Jakob, he clapped his hands together. His ruddy cheeks split in a grin. "We have got him!"

Jakob heaved a sigh of relief. "What does that mean?"

"I sat near him and ordered my wine. And, as you know, my Spanish is a bit wobbly."

Jakob smiled at that. "Yes."

"So I asked him if he spoke English, under the guise of needing help with Spanish, hoping that he did for more reasons than one."

"Does he?"

Percy shook his head. "Latin. So we conversed in a mixture of the two."

Jakob wished he could have been there in Bethington's place, but the risk of being connected with Avery was too high. "And?"

"I bought him a drink and then introduced myself. I told him I was in Barcelona as a patron of the English knight who was attending the Order of the Golden Fleece on King Henry the Eighth of England's behalf." Percy's bright green eyes twinkled. "At that point I had his complete attention."

"Do you think he knows about your—the *duke's*—interest in the ships?" Jakob asked.

Bethington nodded. "I would not be surprised. So I asked what occupied his time."

Jakob was impressed. "I never thought to ask that."

"Well you should have. The man is flailing."

Jakob frowned. "Flailing?"

"He has made some investments which are not paying off as well as he hoped." Percival shrugged one shoulder. "So I mentioned that I was looking for investments while I was here."

"And?"

The knight grinned. "And he nearly jumped into my lap! He said he was hoping to invest in a pair of trade ships that were nearly completed. He wanted to know if I might be interested in joining him."

"He met you moments before, he knows that you are only in Spain for a brief time, and he offered to go into business with you?"

Percival pointed a finger at Jakob. "I take that as proof that he knew about me. Or, the Welsh duke, that is."

That was most likely true. "Did you ask him how much of an

investment he was expecting to make?"

"I did. And he deflected the question, saying he was still negotiating with the shipbuilder."

Jakob pounded on the roof of the carriage and it slowed to a halt.

"What are you doing?"

"We are going back to talk to the shipbuilder." Jakob hopped out and gave the new instructions to the driver. When he climbed back in, he said, "You will ask if the price can be negotiated, because you assume that there have been no other interested parties at this time of year."

Percival chuckled. "And then we shall know if Salazar is lying."

Salazar, as it turned out *was* lying. "No other investors have come forward to speak with him," Percy confirmed. "In fact, he came down to one hundred and fifty thousand maravedis each. Three hundred thousand for both."

Jakob slapped his friend's knee. "That might mean less for Avery as well."

Bethington grinned. "So what shall we do next?"

"I would wager that Salazar has no idea how much it will cost to finish the ships." Jakob dragged his fingers through his hair. "And from what you say, I doubt he has enough cash to hand to cover it."

Percival nodded, suddenly solemn. "The perception in Barcelona is that Lady Averia Mendoza is well endowed. No one knows that she is down to her last maravedis."

Jakob narrowed his gaze. "She is selling off her furniture, and word will certainly spread. But I do believe that it is important for her to maintain the façade of wealth."

"So, she is refurbishing the palazzo," Bethington stated. "She is purging Paolo's unhappy presence from within its walls."

Jakob snapped his fingers. "Yes! She might even take bids from various craftsmen for the transformation. That will support the masquerade, while delaying any decisions or contracts."

Percival pointed at Jakob. "And the staff that were released were loyal to Paolo, not her."

"She shall be seen as a strong woman, capable of caring for

herself." Jakob huffed a laugh. "Which, of course, she *is*."

Percival gave him a hesitant look. "I assume you will say nothing to her about Salazar's true situation as yet..."

"No. I cannot." Jakob sighed. "She would see that as spite, and not believe anything I told her."

"I could tell her."

"No, you could not either. You and I are the same person when it comes to something like this." Jakob scuttled his fingers through his hair again. "I will visit her and suggest this today. In the event she needs to borrow funds, the bankers must believe her quite capable of repayment."

"Because her investments are in England. The money is not at hand and readily available."

Jakob gave Percival a look of pure admiration. "You are much wiser than you appear, Bethington, do you know that?"

"Of course I do." The English knight leaned forward with a wink. "It is my greatest weapon."

§ § §

In spite of an unsettled stomach, Avery walked through the palazzo with the selling agent, Señor Mechi, and the hovering Esteban. The majordomo stood just to the side, but never more than two or three yards from her elbow, assuring himself the ability to hear whatever she or the agent said.

Avery thought about sending him away, but realized that doing so might raise Señor Mechi's suspicions. It made more sense for the man who ran the household to be present, in the event Mechi had questions that she could not readily answer.

The agent kept tapping his chin and grunting, but he otherwise did not express his reaction to the large volume of paintings, furniture, lamps, crockery, pewter, silver, linens, or glassware which she was offering for sale.

Luckily, he had not been overly inquisitive about her reason for selling off so much of the palazzo's furnishings, because she did not wish to explain, especially in front of Esteban, lest word of her destitute state become common knowledge.

I shall tell him I am thinking about selling the estate, if he asks.
"Might I take a moment, Lady Mendoza?"

Avery startled at the agent's deep gravelly voice, so suddenly emanating from his wiry frame. "Yes, of course."

Truthfully, she appreciated the chance to sit and apply her lace fan to her face. The disruption in her belly caused a film of sweat over her skin on this otherwise cool day.

As Señor Mechi wandered to the other side of the dining room, Jacinda, her housekeeper, appeared at the door. "My lady, you have a visitor."

Esteban looked like he wished to cut himself in half to be in both places at the same time. "Who is it?"

Jacinda's glance bounced between Avery and the majordomo. With a bare-bones staff, the chain of authority had definite chinks. The housekeeper decided to address Avery. "Sir Hansen."

Esteban drew a breath, but Avery forestalled him. "Show him up please."

"Yes, my lady."

Avery swallowed thickly and turned away from Esteban. She could not risk the servant recognizing her discomfiture at the prospect of seeing Jakob again. If only she was feeling better physically, she might feel more prepared to face the knight.

Since Jakob's casual comment about loving her, he had tormented her thoughts, waking and sleeping. But whatever else was in flux in her life, her one certainty was the importance of maintaining the perception of unity with the Norseman.

Señor Mechi still stood off to one side of the room, making notes, scratching them out, making more notes, and mumbling softly. Avery fanned herself and remained seated. Heart pounding, she waited for the arrival of the one man who meant more to her than any man ever had.

Jakob strode into the room, grinning, and arms outstretched. "Lady Averia, I am very sorry to be delayed."

He bent down as she sat, took both her hands, and kissed the back of each.

"Delayed?" Had she forgotten some prearranged encounter?

Jakob smiled down into her eyes. He squeezed her hands. "You mentioned that you wanted my opinions on the value of your posessions."

"Of course. Yes." What game was he playing? "I am so glad you are here now."

The Norseman let go of her hands and walked toward the agent. "Allow me to introduce myself. I am Sir Petter Hansen, knight of King Christian the Second of Norway and Denmark, and a member of the Order of the Golden Fleece."

Avery noted that the Norseman did not use his first name. Considering the Spanish events of the last three decades, this was probably wise. Though no one would think by looking at the six-foot-four, rusty blond and blue-eyed Norseman that he might be Jewish, avoiding the name also avoided the questions.

Señor Mechi gave a small bow. "I am Señor Lorenzo Mechi, and the agent handling the sale of Lady Mendoza's furnishings."

Jakob clapped his hands together. "Excellent. I am quite happy for the lady."

"Happy?" Avery rose slowly to her feet and approached the men, confused. Esteban was close on her heels. "Why do you say you are happy?"

Jakob dipped his chin in her direction and spoke with authority. "Because, my darling, you were *un*happy for so long, saddled with your unfortunate husband. Emptying the palazzo of his memory will finally free you from his years of deceit and oppression."

Avery did not know which stunned her more: Jakob's public use of the shocking endearment, or the realization of what he was doing.

She gripped a chair back for support; her knees felt as if they were dissolving. "Yes. I—I shall be glad to see it all gone."

"And then, you shall begin anew." Jakob swung one arm wide. "This palazzo will glow once more, this time with *your* most beautiful presence."

Esteban grunted.

Avery swung around to face him, and nearly vomited with the motion. "Did you wish to make a comment, Majordomo?"

Esteban glared at Jakob. "No, my lady."

Avery addressed Señor Mechi, determined not to appear weakened. "Shall we speak of numbers Señor?"

Kris Tualla

§ § §

Jakob had no choice but to wait in the large drawing room for Avery to finish her appointment with Señor Mechi in private. He was worried because Avery appeared ill—her face was colorless and the sheen of a fever caught the light. Yet the woman was stubborn enough to continue with the appointment and try to hide her distress.

Powerlessly impatient, Jakob helped himself to wine from the sideboard and nibbled from the bowl of olives which Jacinda set in front of him.

"What are you about, Hansen?" Esteban challenged as the two men walked toward the drawing room, both of them banished from Lady Avery's presence.

"Protecting the Lady Mendoza's reputation, of course." Jakob's tone was intentionally harsh.

Esteban sneered at him. "By calling her 'darling' in the presence of a mere tradesman?"

"I want all of Barcelona to understand that she is not without protection." Jakob turned his head toward Esteban. "And you?"

The majordomo bristled. "What are you suggesting, sir?"

Jakob gave an unconcerned shrug. "I believe you should be thanking me at this moment."

"Thanking you?" Esteban scoffed. "Whatever for?"

"For presenting an easily explained situation for the sale of her goods, and not subjecting the Lady Averia to the humiliation of the truth." Jakob stopped walking and faced the servant. "Something which *you* had not thought of to do."

Esteban's face blanched, then flooded red. "That is not my place, sir."

"What *is* your place, Esteban?"

The man straightened his tunic. "To run this house as efficiently as possible and see to the lady's comfort."

Jakob leaned down to Esteban's eye level. "And if you had *done* your job, she would not need to dismiss most of her staff, nor be forced to sell the very chairs on which she sat."

"You, sir, are out of line!" he spat.

Jakob straightened and glared at the majordomo. "No, sir. You are." He turned on a heel and strode into the drawing room by himself, shutting the door behind him.

In spite of his concern for Avery, Jakob chuckled at Esteban's outrage. It felt very good to call the man out on his failings, though he had to restrain himself from revealing too much. Avery's knowledge of the majordomo's embezzling and building of the ships was still a secret and must remain so until she was able to redeem them out from under the unscrupulous man.

Jakob heard the door latch behind him and turned from the sideboard to see Avery slip into the room. She leaned back against the door, her expression gaunt.

"I do not know whether I should thank you, or slap your cheek until you bleed," she grumbled. She walked stiffly across the room and poured a glass of sangria, her hands shaking.

Jakob took her elbow for support. "Thank me first. Afterward you may beat me bloody."

He rescued the decanter from her unsteady grip, lifted her glass, and carried it to the low table in front of the couch. Avery pulled a deep breath and followed unsteadily.

She sank onto the couch, and reached for the filled goblet. "What were you thinking, using such an endearment?"

Jakob took his seat beside her. "Esteban asked me the same thing."

Avery grunted. "That weasel."

"Exactly." Jakob leaned forward to catch her sullen gaze. "I wanted him—as well as Señor Mechi—to understand that you have friends who will protect your interests."

"He will believe that we are lovers."

Jakob tilted his head. "Love. Not lovers."

Avery set her goblet down so hard that the wine sloshed over the edge. "Jakob, I do not understand you! You said you no longer wished to marry me!"

He shook his head. "No, I said *even if I decided* I no longer wished to marry you."

Avery stared at him, her cheeks blooming unhealthily. "Do you still wish to marry me, then?"

Jakob hesitated; he knew that her unsettled situation made it too soon to examine that possibility. "Avery, are you unwell?"

Kris Tualla

He saw her throat ripple. "I—I am not certain."

"What is amiss?"

She winced. "My stomach has taken offense at something I ate."

Jakob laid the back of his hand on her forehead; though clammy, there was no sign of fever. "Is this the first time?"

"No. But the other times were fleeting." Avery closed her eyes. "I am afraid I will lose this particular battle."

Jakob jumped up and rang the servants' bell. Jacinda appeared moments later.

"Lady Averia is ill." Jakob lifted Avery from her seat. "I shall carry her to her chambers."

Jacinda nodded and followed after him.

"What did you eat?" he asked Avery.

Avery was limp in his arms. "Smoked fish. Eggs. Orange juice. Toasted bread."

Jakob pressed his lips to her ears. "Esteban?"

Avery groaned. "Do you think...?"

Jakob held her against his chest and named the most likely food to be tampered with, though depending on the poison of choice it might have been any of the victuals. "I think you should avoid orange juice."

Avery's pale face blanched even further. "I am frightened."

Jakob looked down into her wet eyes, ringed in bluish-purple. "I shall have a word with your cook and her assistant. I will insist that they deliver your meals to you themselves, and that no one else has access to your food. Ever."

She swallowed as if she was about to puke and nodded. "I mentioned something to them before. But nothing had happened at that point."

"And I will assure it does not happen again."

Once in her room, Jacinda took over Avery's care. Yet when he turned to leave, Avery stopped him. "Jakob, wait."

While Jacinda slipped out of the room to gather supplies, Jakob approached Avery's bed, wary of what she might say or ask of him.

She gripped his hand. "Thank you for offering to speak with Georgette."

Jakob squeezed hers. "I told you that I will protect you. Was she working here nine years ago?"

"No." Avery rolled her head on her pillow and blinked slowly. "There is something else, Jakob. Your words to the agent have saved me."

"A little bit of smoke to obscure the truth," he offered. "My concern is for you, Avery. I still love you."

Her brow puckered weakly. "You said once that you did not."

Jakob chuckled at that. "No, I said I will not be so foolish as to love anyone *else*, ever again. You really should pay my words more heed." Jakob shook his head and changed the subject to one less fraught. "What did the agent say?"

Avery turned her face away from him. "He was impressed."

"He should have been. The furnishings here are stunning. Did he give you a figure?"

Avery nodded. "I had hoped to raise twenty-five or thirty thousand maravedis, but my valuation was incorrect. I am still not used to converting from pounds sterling."

Jakob's brow lowered. "How much did he offer you?"

Avery faced him again. "Forty-five thousand."

Jakob laughed. "That is marvelous news!"

Her soft voice was colored with sarcasm. "Such marvelous news, that when added to the savings in staff salaries, I will have less than half of the total I need for just one of the ships."

"When you see the original contract, you will know for certain," Jakob reminded her. "Your situation might be better than expected. Did you accept his offer?"

"Not yet. I told him there were two other agents coming."

Jakob touched her cheek with the back of his fingers. "As wise as you are beautiful."

Avery took his hand, turned it over, and kissed the palm as the chamber's outer door opened.

"I shall leave you in Jacinda's capable care." Jakob bowed. "And I shall pray for your restored health, my lady."

When he left the chamber, he went in search of the kitchen.

Chapter Fifteen

December 16, 1518

Jakob received a note from Avery a day later, soon after breaking his fast. *Today is my birthday*, the missive announced, *and I do not wish to sup alone. Will you and Percy please join me at eight this evening?*

Jakob blew a relieved sigh and crossed himself. Thank the Lord above, the lady was recovered. For a moment he wondered if dining in Esteban's lair was wise. Certainly the majordomo would not be stupid enough to poison an entire dinner party. Jakob only had to keep a watchful eye on what was served to Avery and trust that Georgette understood the severity of her mistress's situation.

If he remembered correctly, Avery was thirty-five today, and Queen Catherine was now thirty-three. Chances for Henry to have his male heir were diminishing with his aging wife.

Avery, on the other hand, claimed to be at ease with her childless state. Jakob knew that if he did eventually marry her, he would never have children. Since he never expected to marry again in the first place, remaining childless was not worrisome to him.

As he carried the note to Bethington's chamber, he pressed down his excitement at the thought of seeing Avery again. Playing this waiting game with her was difficult, when all he wished to do was gather her up in his arms and take her to his bed, never to leave.

Avery haunted most of Jakob's dreams, and those dreams were not in any way chaste.

"Have supper with Lady Avery? That sounds... delightful."
Percy's hesitation was marked. "But why am I to be included, I
wonder."

Jakob snorted. "So no one present is tempted, I would wager."

The English knight's eyes rounded. "Do you believe she desires
you once more?"

"Yes." Jakob dragged his fingers through his hair. "But the
time is not right for me to pursue her further as yet."

"Not with the Order convening in two weeks." Percy wagged
his head. "Heaven only knows what that will be like."

Jakob leaned back in his chair. "What *do* you believe it will be
like?"

Percy shrugged. "I would expect that, after Henry's Treaty of
London, there will be heated discussions concerning the Ottomans."

"I expect you are correct." Jacob stretched his legs and rubbed
his aching right thigh. During his months in England, Henry
continually pressed Jakob into a variety of physical challenges
which strained the old injury—sometime to the point where Jakob
required opium to numb the pain.

Thankfully, since arriving in Barcelona, he had not been pushed
to that point. "And there is Cristóbal Columbo's new world to
discuss. The man himself may be gone, but Europe is still picking
over his findings."

"At the least, we will not have to wait much longer to find out.
For now," Percy stood, "we should go to the market and find a gift
for the lady on her birthday."

December 17, 1518

Though Avery waited in the still-furnished drawing room for
Gustavo to arrive, her mind was fixed on Jakob. Yester eve's supper
with the two knights proved very entertaining, especially as Jakob
made Percy regale her with amusing stories of his many female
conquests since arriving in Barcelona.

The more the Englishman insisted he was an innocent recipient
of the ladies' attentions, the harder she laughed. Jakob goaded his
companion until both were red-cheeked and breathless with glee.

Kris Tualla

Avery had never seen Jakob so jovial and she wondered what prompted his unusually happy mood.

When the men arrived, Percy presented her with a bottle of a French white wine. Later, Jakob gave her his gift—a simple braided silver ring. He said it reminded him of the Norse puzzle rings of his home.

Avery stared out the window and spun the ring on her finger. It was neither large, nor expensive, but it was a piece of Jakob. Though he only had the one day to procure it, he still found something of himself for the gift. She was deeply moved by his choice, and was glad that her addition of Percy to the invitation stopped her from expressing her gratitude in a physical manner.

The Englishman's presence also forestalled any discussion of her unexplained illnesses. Once she voided her body of whatever disrupted it and slept for half the day, she was back to feeling strong once more.

Except for the suspicion that Esteban might be trying to do her harm, of course.

This morning Avery went to the kitchen to speak with Georgette and Ana herself. Avery found the cook and her assistant mortified that her food may have been tampered with, and assured Avery that they would personally prepare and deliver all of her meals in the future.

"Sir Hansen made us swear on our crosses," Ana said.

Jakob.

Just thinking of him flooded her frame with a wash of warm desire. It was becoming very clear to Avery that she must decide what to do with her life before the Order finished its business and Jakob left Spain—and her—forever.

And the crux of that decision rested on the trade ships.

As if summoned by that very thought, Esteban led Gustavo into the drawing room. Gustavo took her hands and gave a little bow.

"Lady Avery, it is always a pleasure to enter your presence, and a sorrow to leave it."

Her gaze flicked to the rolled leather pouch tucked under one arm, but she dragged her eyes back to meet Señor Salazar's, forcing herself to be patient.

"And you brighten my day, as always, Gustavo." She kissed his cheek. "Would you care for refreshment?"

"Yes, thank you. Something light."

Avery looked past Gustavo to Esteban. "Will you see to it?"

Esteban gave an irritated nod and left the room. He did not close the door behind him.

"Come to the table," Avery urged, deciding to ignore the open door. "We can take a look at the contract while we wait."

Gustavo complied, unrolling the packet which held the contract. "I am curious as to what you are looking for."

There was no reason to hide her intent. "The original cost of the ships."

"Ah, yes." Gustavo leaned over the document. "Here it is."

As Avery stared at the figure, she felt the blood drain from her cheeks.

"Your refreshments, my lady." Esteban strode into the room with a pitcher of cooled tea and a bowl of olives. "Ana will bring the rest momentarily."

Avery faced the majordomo, forcing her expression to be deceptively unconcerned. "Thank you."

Esteban crossed directly to the table where the contract was displayed. He set the tea and olives beside it.

Avery watched his eyes as they moved over the document. They widened briefly before he covered his surprise. Obviously, he recognized what he was looking at.

"That will be all, Esteban."

The man's gaze met hers over a clenched jaw. He hesitated a moment, then left her presence without observing any of the expected courtesies.

Gustavo's brow lowered. "His behavior is unacceptable, Averia."

Avery tried not to allow her irritation with both men color her tone. "I must keep him close, Gustavo. I cannot risk him redeeming the ships out from under me."

"Under *us*." Gustavo's expression eased. "Of course, you are correct. I was not thinking."

Avery formed what she hoped was a smile, all the while wondering how soon she might be able to send a message to Jakob.

December 18, 1518

Avery was not surprised when Jakob was announced; she had desperately hoped he would come to her straight away after reading her message. When he entered the drawing room, his large familiar frame and slight limp made her feel safe.

He held out a note of his own as he approached her. "Maria asked me to deliver this."

"What is it?"

"The names of two additional agents who might give you bids on your household goods." Jakob stopped in front of her. "How are you feeling today, Avery?"

She looked up into his soothing blue eyes. "I have recovered physically. But I have not been better in my mind and emotions."

Jakob slipped his hand around the back of her neck and the warmth of his palm tingled down her spine. He kissed her forehead.

"We shall solve this situation," he whispered.

Avery's knees felt wobbly of a sudden and she sank to the couch cushion. "Tell me how. I really do need to know."

Jakob sat beside her, his body turned toward hers. "The amount due on the ships has been lowered to one hundred and fifty thousand maravedis, each."

That was odd. "How do you know this?"

"Percy made another visit to the shipbuilder, acting as the duke, to determine whether there were any additional enquiries."

Her heart tripped. "And were there? Other than Gustavo, of course."

A puzzling shadow passed over Jakob's brow. "No."

Avery sighed her relief. "At the least the price will not go higher. But I am surprised that he lowered it, considering that two men are interested."

Jakob stood and crossed to the sideboard. "Did Georgette or Ana deliver the ale?"

"Yes. And Ana said she took it from the cask herself."

Jakob nodded and poured himself a glass. "Would you care for some?"

"No, thank you." Avery bit her lower lip, pondering Jakob's discovery. "The amount due is still substantial. Three hundred thousand maravedis is thirty-six thousand pounds."

Jakob returned to her side, stein in hand. "May I give you my opinion?"

She smiled softly. "Of course, Jakob. You are the only person in Spain whom I trust to give me sound counsel."

He set the mug on the low table. "If I were in your position, I would try and find some way to pay one half of the total. Then I would solicit two or three investors to pay the other half."

"So I retain control over the ships and receive half of the revenue." That made sense.

Jakob met her gaze. "How much cash do you have to hand?"

Avery felt her cheeks warming. "About six thousand pounds. That is the entire extent of the 'fortune' that Paolo and Esteban have left me."

"And how much can you raise with the sale of the furnishings and the savings in salaries?"

"Seven thousand pounds." She lifted one shoulder, and held up the note still in her hand. "Unless one of these men offers more."

Jakob nodded. "You will need to keep some in reserve to run your household, but I believe you can safely invest nine thousand pounds at that point."

His suggestion was safe and sensible. "I believe I can manage that."

"Next, you must write to Catherine and ask her to loan you the other nine thousand pounds, which will pay the balance due for one ship."

Avery's shoulders fell. "Considering her state of mind, I would hate to do that."

Jakob took her hand. "She loves you, Avery, and will loan you the money without question, you know this. And you should be able to pay her back with the first sailings."

She stared at her hand lying in his grip and the vision secured her unsteady emotions. "Is there no other way?"

"Not that I can discern."

Avery nodded, resolved to her situation. "I shall write to her today."

"When the money arrives, you should take Señores Garcia and Montenegro with you to the shipbuilder. They must write up a new contract, listing you as one-half owner of the pair of ships."

"To protect my investment, of course. Then Gustavo might invest the other half." She frowned. "Would Esteban have an opportunity to intervene?"

"Only if he raised the thirty-six thousand pounds before you hear from Catherine." Jakob flashed a derisive expression. "I do not foresee that happening."

"But it could." Avery tapped her chin. "I shall need to divert his attentions."

Jakob sipped his ale, and then asked, "How well do you trust Maria?"

"With my life," Avery stated without hesitating. "Why?"

"Using the servants as a way to spread rumors can be very effective." Jakob leaned forward. "Suppose Maria let it be known that you hoped to redeem the ships, but have no resources at hand."

As embarrassing as the suggestion was, such knowledge would ease Esteban's immediate concerns and buy her the time she needed. "Is there a chance that their employers might hear of this?"

"While there is always that chance, I do doubt it. They would have to be asked directly before speaking of it."

Avery's expression grew firmly resolute. "Then I suppose this is the wise solution."

"I will speak with Maria when I return to the palazzo." Jakob took another gulp from his stein before adding, "There is one other consideration."

"Yes?"

"Señor Salazar."

Avery stiffened. "What about him?"

"How much does he plan to invest?"

She briefly glanced away from Jakob's intense gaze before she answered. "He has not mentioned a figure."

Surprisingly, Jakob appeared to expect that answer. "I do not believe you should discuss the specifics of the ships' finances with him until you have made the payment and procured a new contract."

"Because you do not trust him." Avery narrowed her eyes. "Is that because you are jealous?"

Instead of bristling as she expected, Jakob took her jaw between his strong fingers and kissed her. His lips were warm, his tongue teasing. Avery closed her eyes and relished the unanticipated moment.

The realization of how much she missed any sort of physical intimacy with this man skittered through her frame the way a fuse sizzles toward a rocket; the explosion of emotion which followed nearly dropped her to the ground

When the kiss ended and she opened her eyes, he was staring at her with an intensity that seared her to the bone. "I have no reason to be jealous, Avery."

He words startled her. "Are you that uncaring?"

Jakob chuckled. "Not at all, my love. I am that confident."

This time, she kissed him.

§ § §

December 19, 1518

Dearest friend ~

The news of your loss has cut me to the heart. I, too, wish that I could be at your side, to offer what scant comfort I might at the loss of the babe, and to hold you up under the burden of your husband's infidelity. I shall continue to pray my rosary for you daily and without ceasing. May it be that God will see your pain, and intervene on your behalf.

Speaking of trials, I am afraid my situation here is quite desperate. My majordomo has stolen almost all Paolo's money over the last years, and invested in a pair of trade ships under the guise of being my husband's partner. If I cannot pay the balance due on the ships, he might redeem them out from under me, thus leaving me destitute.

I have cut my household staff to one third, and am selling most of the palazzo's goods and furnishings. Jakob (yes, he has found me out) was good enough to publically claim that I am refurbishing the palazzo in order to remove all traces

of my debauched husband, so that is how Barcelona society considers my circumstances for now. It is only a matter of time before the truth is revealed.

This is the second reason I am writing to you. Would you, dear friend, be willing to make me a loan of nine thousand pounds? Combined with the monies I am raising with my thrift, I would be able to redeem one of the ships, and have the contracts rewritten to protect my investment.

Afterward, I shall search out two additional investors to redeem the second ship, and have contracts drawn up which assure that I retain control. Because of my time spent in your court, I do believe I shall have no trouble accomplishing this. And to rest your mind, I should be able to repay the loan within two sailings.

Please give my love to Mary, though she is so young that I fear she will soon forget who I am. Hold her close to your heart, and know that she is God's gracious blessing to you.

With all my love and affection,
A

§ § §

December 23, 1518
Barcelona, Spain

My Lord and King ~

I am now safely and comfortably ensconced in a palazzo in Barcelona, which I am sharing with King Henry's man, Sir Percival Bethington. Because Sir Bethington and I traveled together from London to Barcelona, I received the added benefit of Henry's generosity, which made the journey unexpectedly pleasant.

The Order of the Golden Fleece will convene in nine days. I have met a few of my fellow knights thus far, as there are many Spanish interests represented in the Order's numbers.

Though we will not know for certain until the time comes, Sir Bethington and I expect that the Ottoman threat will be one of the topics of greatest concern, as well as shipping routes and land claims regarding the New World.
I will attempt to bring the Swedish threat to Denmark forward as well, though I am certain Your Highness will understand if the Ottomans capture the lion's share of the Order's attention. I shall write to Your Grace every fortnight to keep you apprised of all that transpires.

I am finding that the milder climate in Barcelona has eased the ache in my leg considerably. Though I will always suffer a limp, I am not in as frequent or severe pain.

Your humble servant,

Sir Jakob Petter Hansen

Kris Tualla

Chapter Sixteen

February 14, 1519

Jakob sat in his seat during this, the sixth week of the eighteenth Chapter Gathering of the Order of the Golden Fleece, glancing frequently across the aisle at Bethington, and waiting for the shouting to die down.

The heated discussion concerned Ottoman brothers Oruç and Hayreddin. Oruç was killed this past year during his invasion of the Moorish Kingdom of Algiers, just across the narrow western end of the Mediterranean Sea from Spain. Hayreddin succeeded his brother as military commander and had requested the Ottomans' assistance in exchange for a declaration of loyalty.

Because of the violent purging of Muslims from Spain, a retaliatory attack was quite possible if Hayreddin succeeded in securing the Ottomans' presence so close to her borders. As a result, King Ferdinand's ten Spanish representatives were asking for the full support of the members of the Order to repel it.

Jakob had nothing to add to the argument. Denmark and

Norway were so far removed from the conflict as to be useless. And when the issue was first brought before the Order, Percy told him privately that Henry gave him strict instructions not to become embroiled with any skirmishes that did not threaten England's soil directly.

Since the last meeting of the Order in 1516, the Pope ordered that the number of members be increased to fifty-one, and voting those members in was the gathering's first order of business. Jakob found the solemn pageantry quite moving and was honored to be in attendance.

Now, however, he was just bored.

When he caught the English knight's eye he tipped his head toward the back of the church.

Percy gave a tiny nod and stood. He made his way toward the door, as if he needed to relieve himself.

A few moments later, Jakob followed. The men slipped out of the cathedral and walked toward their palazzo, ducking into a tavern to escape a damp wind off the sea.

"I will pay for the ale today. You paid for it last time." Percy strode toward the innkeeper.

Jakob sat at a small wooden table by the window. The sky was trying to rain, but thus far had only succeeded in spitting droplets against the thick glass.

"One would think that being an ambassador of your king, and in the center of creating policies and agreements, would be fascinating," Jakob told Avery at supper last week. "The truth is, each man seems to be overly concerned with protecting his own interests, and not considering what might be best for all involved."

"No one wants to appear weak." Avery gave him a sympathetic look. "Can you excuse yourself without being obvious?"

Jakob snorted. "I am beginning to believe that the reason they painted the coats of arms on the seats was to make note of exactly who is missing."

Avery laughed, her mirth a delightful contrast not only to the long days in the cold and musty cathedral, but also the long hours spent in the taverns afterwards—where much of the bandying about for favors took place and rumors were eagerly shared.

Jakob and Percy's early acquaintances, Diego de Mendoza,

Alvaro de Zuniga, and Pietro San Severino, had individually quizzed Bethington regarding his Welsh patron, Thomas Windsor, Duke of Merthyr Tydfil. To his credit, Percy kept a straight face, answering the men's questions casually and with just enough detail to sound believable.

Though how the Spaniards discovered the fictional duke's existence was a mystery, Jakob and Percy agreed that the questions meant that interest in Avery's trade ships was growing. To date, however, she had not been successful in finding any investors other than the vaguely committed Gustavo Salazar.

Percy set down the pitcher of ale and two mugs. "That Bavarian prince, from the house of Wittelsbach—what is his name?"

"Frederick. The Second." Jakob filled his mug. "Why?"

"He asked me a lot of questions about Denmark." Percy took the seat across the little table from Jakob. "I found his interest, well, interesting."

Jakob frowned. "What sort of questions?"

"What sort of health the king's son is in, for one."

"The boy is barely a year old." Jakob made a derisive noise. "Does he have a daughter he needs to marry off?"

Percy shrugged. "Or an alliance to form, perhaps."

"I am not going to worry about him. Let him come to me." Jakob swallowed a refreshing gulp of the ale. "Have there been recent enquiries about the ships?"

"No." Percy dropped his voice. "Is it time for the Duke of Merthyr Tydfil to visit Salazar?"

Jakob nodded, slowly. "Possibly. Two months have gone by and the man continues to pursue Avery without adequately explaining his plans. It is time to push him a bit, I believe."

Bethington grinned. "Then he shall receive a message today."

§ § §

Avery tried very hard to fall in love with Gustavo Salazar, but thus far, the highest emotion she could conjure for the man was warm and amused friendship. With Jakob holding her at arm's length and yet enticing her to come closer at the same time, she thought falling for a different man would make her life simpler.

The trouble with that plan was that her heart would have none of it. Jakob was stubbornly in residence and would not be displaced.

As she gazed at Gustavo across his supper table, she tried to attend to the story he was telling, but her mind kept wandering to her undefined future.

It was still too soon for any money to arrive from England. In the meantime, her bankers kept Esteban from being able to access the remaining Mendoza funds. Now that the sale of her household goods was complete, she had accrued nearly nine thousand pounds in addition. These funds were also safely stowed out of the majordomo's grasp.

Avery absently drummed her fingers on the table top.

"Am I boring you, Averia?"

Avery straightened. "I am sorry, Gustavo. I think I am unusually tired this evening."

"I can certainly understand that. These last weeks of emptying your palazzo have been quite demanding." He gave her a soft smile, one that squeezed the edges of his interesting grey eyes in a very attractive manner. "Have you decided what to do next?"

"I have begun inviting painters to bid on the interior walls," she lied. "It makes the most sense to repaint the plaster while the rooms are empty."

"Very clear thinking, my lady," Gustavo approved.

Encouraged, Avery continued her prevarication. "After that, I will have the floors repaired and refinished."

His expression shifted, evincing concern. "Are you managing your finances adequately? Do you wish for my help?"

Avery's jaw tightened at his condescending words, but she forced it to relax. "No, thank you. I excelled at figures in my tutoring days."

His expression intensified. "Please remember that I am here and willing to assist you in any manner possible."

She smiled stiffly. "And I do appreciate that, Gustavo."

"In that case..." Gustavo stood and cleared his throat. "There is something I would like to ask you this evening, before you grow too exhausted."

As the man walked around to her side of the table, Avery's heart began to pound her ribcage, as if asking to be let out.

"Gustavo—"

He put up a hand to silence her. "Please, Averia, hear me out."

Avery straightened in her chair, pressed her lips together, and jammed her fists into her lap.

Gustavo turned the chair next to hers to face her, and sat. "Three months have passed since Paolo died."

She nodded. Blood rushed in her ears.

"His behaviors and their resultant cause of death were well known. No one in all of Spain would question you for moving forward with your life in less than a year of mourning." Gustavo peered into her eyes. "Especially considering that you vacated his bed more than nine years ago."

Jakob strode into her thoughts and stood, feet apart and arms crossed over his chest, staring at her.

She blinked him away. "I do believe that to be true as well."

Gustavo gave her a crooked smile. "Do you know what day this is?"

"February fourteenth? Oh!" Avery's face flamed. All doubt about what was about to occur dribbled away like the sporadic rain hitting the windows.

"Saint Valentine's day has become a symbol of love." His face reddened a little. "Romantic love."

Avery was struck speechless, her mind a blank darkness of doubt. The only thought she could grasp was she must not give this man an answer.

Gustavo slid out of his chair and knelt beside her. "Averia Galaviz de Mendoza, will you consent to marry me?"

"I—I cannot answer you."

His brow twitched. "Do you not care for me?"

Avery's eyes widened. "No! I mean, yes. I care for you deeply."

"But you do not love me as yet."

"I—you are a very nice man." Gustavo winced; she was making a mess of this. "But I am so uncertain about my future."

"And I wish to settle that uncertainty." He pulled one fist from her lap and unfolded it. "Together we shall build a new and successful future." He kissed her palm.

Avery had every intention of avoiding the direct question until she received word from Catherine, but Gustavo's sudden proposal made that path unwise. She considered him with an intense gaze of her own.

"Since you have broached the subject of finances," she said carefully, "shall we discuss your investment in the trade ships?"

Gustavo blanched, but recovered quickly. "Of course."

Avery lifted her wine glass, trying to appear calm. "How much are you planning to invest?"

"Well, that depends…"

"On what?" She took a sip of wine, her eyes fixed on his.

He tilted his head and gave her an impish look. "On whether you are my business partner or my wife."

While obvious, that answer did not give Avery the information she was seeking. "Please answer as if we were business partners."

Gustavo's expression darkened and he rose from his knees to reclaim his chair. "If we are to be equal partners, then we should invest equal amounts."

"Of course." Avery set her glass on the table top, and irritation at his continuing deflection sparked. "Did you have an amount in mind, Gustavo, or do you expect me to speak the first number?"

"Well, I…" His voice trailed off.

Avery decided at that moment to trust that her royal friend would come to her aid, and quickly. "One hundred and fifty thousand maravedis."

Gustavo's jaw fell so far open, Avery wondered if she might need to lift it off the table for him. His eyes rounded and the idea they might fall out of his head and go rolling across the table cloth nearly discomposed her. Clearly, the man had no idea of the magnitude of the remaining balance.

Gustavo scrubbed a palm across his mouth, and his facial features retreated to their normal stance. "How much?"

"One hundred and fifty thousand maravedis." Avery leaned one elbow on the table and laced her fingers.

He shook his head. "How much of the contract is still due?"

"Twenty-five percent." She frowned. "How much did you believe was still due?"

"Esteban said—" Gustavo's lips snapped closed.

Avery untangled her hands and slapped her palm on the table, making her dinnerware jangle. "Esteban! When were you discussing this with Esteban?"

Señor Salazar looked like a rat trapped by a cat ready to pounce. "The week that Paolo died."

"Why did you speak with him?" Avery knew her voice sounded shrill, but she was too angry to care.

"He came to me, Averia. Because I was on the original contract, he offered me another chance to invest." Gustavo took a splashing gulp of his wine. "He said that only ten percent remained on each ship."

"Seventy thousand maravedis?" Avery's mind ran through a myriad of possibilities. "For ten percent ownership of one ship?"

He nodded. "That was his offer. So you see, I thought that if you put in seventy thousand to pay off one ship, and I paid that same amount for the other we would own both vessels outright..."

Avery growled under her breath. She gripped the arms of her chair and turned it to face Gustavo head on.

"Except, *sir*, it was my husband's money which paid the other ninety percent." Avery gasped as the realization set in. "However, if we were *married*..."

Gustavo had the decency to blush. "Averia, you are a very beautiful woman who has truly claimed my heart—"

"Stop. Please." Avery drew a deep, calming breath and leaned back in her seat. The ramifications of what she had just learned were galloping through her thoughts at breakneck speed. "Did anyone else invest?"

Gustavo's voice was barely audible. "I honestly do not know."

"Esteban was running out of time and money," Avery thought out loud. "If anyone else had invested, they would have come to me by now. You must have been the first man he approached."

"I suppose so."

Avery sniffed. "I assume that you do not have one hundred and fifty thousand maravedis."

"Not at this precise time, no." Gustavo leaned forward. "But that does not mean that I am unwilling to try to raise those funds on your—*our*—behalf."

Avery stared at Gustavo, wondering what to do. Her friend was handsome, intelligent, and engaging. Even if she declined his proposal, she could certainly do worse for a business partner.

"If you can bring me the remaining one hundred and fifty thousand maravedis, then I will grant you what you will have paid for—twenty-five percent of one ship. Even if we eventually marry, that is still a fair offer."

Gustavo brightened a bit at her words and nodded. "I agree."

She pinned his gaze. "Though you were not immediately forthcoming about Esteban, I do trust you, Gustavo."

Gustavo reached for her hand. "I will not disappoint you."

"Thank you for supper." Avery stood. "It is time for me to go."

Chapter Seventeen

February 19, 1519

Jakob poured Percy a mug of cooled ale as the English knight removed the trappings of wealth, handing the rich garments to his valet, Denys. Bethington was of the same mind as Jakob, meaning he preferred the comfort of his work clothes to the restrictions of formal court attire.

"At the least, our Order robes are comfortable," Jakob said as he handed Percy the ale. "I would hate to sit through all those debates with my neck itching and my sleeves dragging in everything."

Percy lifted the mug in agreement, and then took a seat in an upholstered chair in his apartment's outer chamber. He propped his feet on a low table. "That feels better."

Jakob claimed another upholstered chair. "So what did our man have to say?"

Two days ago, Esteban Gonzalez sent Thomas Windsor, Duke of Merthyr Tydfil, a note requesting a meeting to discuss their shared interest in the Mendoza trade ships. It was obvious that the majordomo kept himself informed of any outside interest in the ships.

It was also obvious that he still hoped to redeem them himself.

Percy met his gaze. "He knows exactly how much is left to repay, with and without the discount."

Jakob froze, his mug suspended half-a-foot shy of his mouth. "Would the shipbuilder give Esteban the discount?"

The Englishman shook his head. "No. And that is why he claims to need another investor. As a mask to pay the lower amount and save the money."

Jakob lowered the stein. "How much did he ask you for?"

"One hundred and fifty thousand maravedis, per ship."

"For what percentage?"

Percy gave him a knowing look. "Thirty-three percent."

Jakob huffed a laugh. "And why not? None of the original investment has come from his pocket. Any amount is profit for him."

"That is true." Percy took a long swallow of his ale.

"Has he approached anyone else?"

The English knight shook his head. "He said I was the first man he approached, because of my expressed interest."

Jakob grunted. "Did he give you a specific deadline to reply?"

"One week."

Jakob gulped his ale, set his mug down, and stood. "Avery needs to know."

§ § §

Avery had not left her house for four days. Her revealing conversation with Gustavo shone a much brighter light on her situation and, while she was not in love with the man, the realization that his pursuit of her was founded in economics rather than love left her feeling oddly defeated.

She spent many hours over the last days trying to decide what to say to him. She would not agree to marry him—having no husband was preferable to having a second one who did not truly love her.

She also tried drawing up the terms of a contract, in the event Gustavo was able to raise the monies needed to redeem one of the ships. Of course, her lawyer and accountant would create the actual legal document, but the investment terms were still her decision.

Kris Tualla

"Lady Averia?" Zurina stood in the doorway. "Sir Hansen is here and he would like to speak with you."

Avery ran a hand over her hair. "Am I presentable?"

Her ladies' maid walked toward her. "Let me just..."

A moment later, adjusted and neatened, Avery sent Zurina off to collect Jakob and bring him to the small drawing room. When he arrived, her heart fluttered just a bit when she looked into his eyes.

She smiled. "It is very nice to see you."

Jakob closed the heavy wooden door and strode toward her. "Where is Esteban?"

"It is very nice to see you as well, Avery," she said in a bright tone. "You look lovely today."

Jakob halted in front of her and coughed a rueful chuckle. "You are more than lovely, Avery. I apologize."

Avery gave the Norseman a chastising look. "Accepted. Now why are you concerned with Esteban?"

Jakob took her hand and led her to the only couch in the room. Once they were settled, he whispered in her ear. "Esteban solicited an investment from the Welsh duke, Thomas Windsor."

Surprised, Avery turned her head to look into his eyes. "From Percy?"

Jakob nodded. "Percy met with him earlier this afternoon."

"How did he—"

"The shipbuilder."

"Of course." Anger surged through her veins. "Damn the man."

"Which—"

"Both of them!" Avery jumped up, too furious to hold still. "So he is still trying to escape with his pirate's plunder. *Damn*."

Jakob remained in his seat. "I assume you have not yet heard from Catherine."

"No." Avery paced. "And I am running out of possibilities."

"What about Salazar?"

Avery stopped as if she hit a wall. "He had no idea how much remained on the contract. Once he was informed, it turns out that he does not have the required funds." She cut her gaze to Jakob's. "He did, however, make me a formal proposal of marriage."

Jakob's expression hardened. "What did you say?"

"I did not give him an answer."

"Why not?"

Avery turned her body to fully face Jakob. "Why do you care?"

Jakob rose to his feet. His blue eyes were dark with anger.

Avery took a step back.

Jakob closed the space between them, even though she kept moving backwards until she was against the wall. Her heart felt as if it was trying to climb out her mouth, and she was having a hard time drawing enough breath. Though she wanted to speak, she had no words.

Jakob rested his hands on the wall, one on either side of her head. He stared down into her eyes, searching for something. And then, he lowered his face, parted his lips, and claimed her mouth with his.

§ § §

Why do I care? Avery's question zinged through his body like a bolt of lightning.

She knew that he loved her and her taunt made him feel like a hunted boar, shot with an arrow and increasing its fury to a frantic level.

Did she believe *she* was hunting *him?*

If she did, Jakob had every intention of making it clear which one of them was the prey. He had been patient with her, watching her from a distance and waiting for the best moment to strike, but his patience was gone, pierced through by the stake of another man's claim.

At first, Avery accepted his kiss, neither pulling away, nor kissing him back. Then her arms slipped around his neck. Her body arched forward. Her tongue played with his.

Jakob pulled away, swooped Avery up in his arms, and carried her to the couch. He was dangerously close to tossing up her skirts and finally bringing an end to all this chastity business.

Avery leaned back, supported by the raised end of the couch. She licked her lips, then caught them in her teeth. Her wide dark eyes met his. Jakob hovered over her, his breath coming in aroused huffs.

He lowered himself over her, and kissed her again.

Her hand moved down his body and gripped him through his hose, in the same way she had in London.

Jakob moaned into her mouth.

His finish was swift, and in his urgency he took no time for her pleasure. Eyes closed, his forehead rested against hers as the world came back into focus, knowing he had lost control of the situation. Perhaps he was the prey after all.

Another surge of anger rippled through him. Without moving his head, he listened in horror to his own words, helpless to hold them back as jealousy shoved them past his tongue.

"Did you do this for him as well?"

With a feral growl, Avery slapped him hard, knocking his head away from hers. "How dare you!"

Jakob struggled to sit up, his cheek stinging and his jaw feeling a little out of place. His eyes met hers. "I apologize, Avery. That was not called for."

Avery scrambled off the couch and stood in front of him, fists clenched and eyes flashing. "How could you say such a thing to me?"

Jakob put up his hands in surrender. "I am sorry. I was wrong."

Avery crumpled to the carpet in a heap of skirts. "How—why would you—" A ragged sob cut her voice.

Jakob slid off the couch and knelt in front of her, ignoring the stinging twinge in his right thigh. "I am so sorry, Avery. You are the last person I would ever wish to hurt."

She sniffed wetly and fished a square of linen from her pocket. She did not look at him.

Jakob knew it was time to stop holding back. "I love you, Avery. And the thought of you with another man is intolerable to me."

Her eyes remained downcast, and her voice was soft. "Do you say that only because you are jealous of Gustavo?"

"No." Jakob lifted her chin so she would look at him. "Will you forgive me?"

Avery looked into his eyes for a long time without speaking, as if she was waiting for something.

"Please, Avery. Forgive me."

She nodded.

Jakob pulled her into his embrace and held her against his chest. "Do not marry him," he whispered.

"I won't," she answered in kind.

Jakob believed he knew what Avery wanted him to say next, but this was not the time for him to propose marriage once again. Not with his hose awkwardly soiled, and her crumpled on the floor in tears.

When her finances were settled, and he asked her once again to marry him, he wanted to do so in a manner which showed her the respect she deserved.

The original reason for his visit prompted him to ask, "Have you had any word from Catherine?"

"No." Avery leaned away from him, her expression somber. "It is too soon, as yet."

Jakob tucked a straying strand of black hair behind Avery's ear. "Esteban gave the duke a week to decide about the investment. Perhaps Percy might delay him further."

"That would be helpful." Avery finally looked into his eyes. "Thank you for your help, Jakob. You and Percy truly are my best friends in Spain."

"I shall remember that and curb my tongue in the future." Jakob kissed her forehead. "I am so sorry to have misbehaved. I promise, I will make it up to you."

§ § §

As Jakob walked back to his home in the dark, his stomach growled repeatedly. Avery had offered him supper, but he knew she was trying to save money; so instead of having her cook draw additional provisions from a carefully distributed supply, he lied and said Percy had invited one of the knights of the Order to dine with them.

Foregoing convention, Jakob walked into the first floor kitchen of the leased palazzo and asked for his supper to be sent up to his chamber.

Percy was actually going out this evening with one of the many Spanish noblewomen who found his attempts at their language equally hilarious and adorable. Jakob's jovial and gregarious

English counterpart seemed to make friends wherever he went, and Jakob did not begrudge him the experience.

"Would you call me jovial?" Jakob asked Maria when she brought his tray.

The housekeeper laughed. "Would you call me a child?" She handed Jakob a sealed letter. "This came for you today."

"Thank you." Jakob's hand trembled when he looked at the seal. It was his father's.

"Is everything well with Lady Averia?"

Jakob dragged his gaze back to Maria's. "Gustavo Salazar asked her to marry him. But she will decline."

Maria flashed a knowing smile. "Of course she will."

At that moment, Jakob decided that more ears and eyes attuned to Esteban's actions could only be helpful. "And Esteban is trying to raise the remaining funds to redeem Lady Averia's ships."

"Oh, dear." Maria clasped her hands in front of her. "Will he succeed?"

"Not if word is spread that he bled Mendoza dry." Jakob held up one finger, realizing the other side of that blade. "And—that the lady is using her own resources to repair the damages."

Maria gave a slow, sage nod. "I shall make certain many ears hear both of those things."

"Thank you, Maria."

The older woman smiled again. "I do this for Averia." She winked. "And for you."

When the door to his chamber was once again closed, Jakob dropped into a chair, his heart hammering. He stared at the letter in his hand, too terrified to know what it contained to break the seal just yet.

Since the day he left his father's home in Arendal, Norway nearly fifteen years ago, to take his place as the king of Denmark and Norway's knight, he had never received any missives from his family.

True, it was his younger brother who was supposed to go, and Jakob was to become a priest. Though the brothers desperately wanted to exchange places, his father refused and the familial argument lasted over a month—until the frustrated Jakob packed up his belongings and left without their father's permission. He boarded a trade ship before dawn, arriving at København Castle in Denmark with a forged letter of commitment.

Once settled in the king's service, Jakob wrote three or four letters a year to his family, keeping them apprised of where he was and what he was doing. He even told them about the fire where he was injured trying to save someone he believed to still be inside the building.

Not once had he received a reply.

Until today.

Jakob heaved a deep breath to calm his pulse and slid his thumb under the seal on the parchment. The wax released its hold with a whispered crack. Jakob unfolded the document.

The handwriting was his mother's.

Dearest Jakob ~

Please forgive me for never answering any of your letters. Your father forbade it. But after he burnt the first one, unopened, I hid the rest from him. And I read them all.

I still keep them hidden away, and when my missing you grows too painful, I take them out and read them again. I am so very proud of you, my brave son. You have done very well in your chosen path, and you have brought honor to our family, even if your father refuses to admit this.

Now I am finally writing to you because your father's health is failing. I am begging you to come home, so that he has the chance to reconcile with you before he dies. I hope to see you again, as well, before my time comes, as it surely must. Will you come? And come soon?

Your loving mother, Bergdis

The letter was dated over four months earlier. It would have followed his recent path, first to København, then to London, and now to Barcelona, traveling with whichever ship or courier could be persuaded to carry it.

Kris Tualla

If he left this week, two months' time would pass before Jakob could reach Arendal. And if his father's health was truly precarious five months ago, Jakob might not make it there before his father passed. In addition, he risked the wrath of King Christian if he left the Order before it adjourned.

Jakob refolded the letter, set it on the small table beside his chair, and stared at it, wondering what in hell he was going to do.

Chapter Eighteen

February 22, 1519

Jakob did nothing about the letter for three days. He did not tell Bethington about it, nor Avery. He pushed it from his mind anytime it popped up. For three days, he pretended it had never been written. Or received.

Jakob and Percival were joining a few of the other knights for supper at the *Santos y Pecadores*—Saints and Sinners—tavern across from Barcelona Cathedral.

"How long is the Order normally convened?" he asked Diego de Mendoza before Percy arrived.

Diego shrugged. "Eight or nine weeks. Maybe ten."

Jakob added in his head. "We have been assembled for fifty-one days. Seven weeks. Are we nearly finished?"

The Spanish knight peered at him over the rim of his raised ale mug. "Are you so eager to forgo our hospitality?"

"Not at all." Jakob sipped his own beverage. "It's only that I received a request from my family to return home."

Diego lowered his mug to the table. "Nothing serious, I hope?"

"What is serious?" Percy dropped into the chair next to Jakob.

Diego's eyes slid to Percy and back, but he said nothing. Tact was an important quality for a knight, and the man obviously understood that this was Jakob's tale to tell, not his.

And, the time to tell it had come.

"I received a letter from my mother concerning my father's health."

Percy twisted in his seat to face Jakob, his expression evincing his surprise. "When?"

"Three days ago." Jakob felt his cheeks warming.

The Englishman looked hurt. "Why did you not say anything?"

Jakob shrugged; how could he explain that he did not want to think about it? That the myriad of emotions which his mother's letter stirred up in his breast were physically painful? He rubbed his right thigh out of habit.

Diego had watched the exchange in silence, but now the Spaniard spoke. "Is your father dying?"

Jakob met the man's gaze. "Yes."

"Why would you not go?" Diego pressed.

"Because neither his father nor his mother has spoken to him since he was seventeen, and left Norway to go into the king's service," Percy blurted. Clearly Bethington had no qualms about revealing another man's tales.

"Interesting." Diego returned his attention to his ale.

Percy looked at Jakob. "When will you leave?"

Jakob frowned. "I have not decided."

"Why do you hesitate?"

"I—"

Why am I?

Fear of traveling all that way, only to have his father refuse to acknowledge him, for one. Anger at his father for not understanding the bent of his sons, for another. And furious that his father's financial failures put him and his brother in this position to begin with.

I wonder if he acknowledges Saxby? That thought had never occurred to him before now.

A sudden surge of desire to see his brothers nearly made Jakob cry. He rubbed his eyes to keep the tears from forming. "I have my king's commission to complete."

Both men nodded at that. A knight's duties were not to be ignored.

"We should finish our business soon," Diego said slowly. "All that remains is the lingering question of who shall come to Spain's aid with regard to the Ottomans."

Jakob lifted his mug and sipped his ale, using the moment to collect his composure. "Denmark and Norway are too far distant for King Christian to be able to raise an army and send it in a timely manner."

"And I am certain he would not wish for you to suggest that he do so." Diego's regard moved to Percy. "Our English friend has remained quite silent on the matter. What about Henry?"

Bethington blushed, his normally rosy cheeks going a blotchy burgundy. "I am under instructions not to commit English soldiers, unless the threat is to English soil."

The Spaniard grunted, his features showing disdain. "It seems we will need to crush them ourselves."

"Under these circumstances, Jakob..." Percy deftly shifted the conversation away from Henry's embarrassing recalcitrance and back to his Nordic friend. "I believe you might leave the Order early, without making Christian angry."

Diego's expression eased a bit. "He might even be relieved that you were able to escape before he was forced into action."

Jakob regarded the two men sitting with him at the table. He respected both of them quite highly and their words made sense. And yet, he was still reluctant to agree. Why?

Avery.

The thought of her punched him in the gut.

He did not want to leave Avery, because if he did, there was no guarantee that he would ever find her again.

"The truth is, my father might die before I could arrive. In fact, he may already be dead." Jakob gave a reluctant shrug and drained his mug.

February 25, 1519

Three days later, Jakob stood in Avery's small drawing room, waiting for her to appear. The church bells rang out ten times. Jakob had been awake since five.

After hours of sleepless agonizing, he realized that he did need to travel home to Arendal, and leave as soon as possible. Even if his father was dead before Jakob arrived, this was his chance to show his willingness to reconcile with his mother and brothers.

The fact that, once his mother's letter finally reached him, he chose to leave the esteemed Order of the Golden Fleece early to be at his father's bedside—or grave—would show his family that he never forgot about them. That his letters to them were sincere.

That the rift was never his doing or his desire.

The other consideration he agonized over involved Avery. As much as he wished it was possible, he could not bring himself to repeat his proposal of marriage at this time.

Avery could not abandon her responsibilities at this pivotal point. Her financial future was at stake—and even if she eventually returned to Catherine and the Tudor court, she needed an income to maintain her status there. New gowns and elegant jewelry were as expensive as they were expected. The queen's chief lady-in-waiting's appearance was a direct reflection on Catherine and Henry.

Jakob knew what he must do, as much as that decision carved a hole in his heart.

When Avery entered the drawing room, Jakob's knees weakened. She was the most beautiful woman he had ever met, and he found it hard to remember that he did not like her much after their first meeting. Now he was completely captivated by her.

This interview was going to be much harder than he realized.

Avery smiled at him and held out her hands as she approached. "I have not seen much of you lately. Has the Order been so demanding of your time?"

Jakob gripped Avery's hands and pulled her into his embrace. He rested his chin on her head and held her close, pressing the full length of his body against hers. His throat had tightened and he was afraid that if he tried to speak, he would sound like an English bullfrog.

Avery's arms squeezed his waist. "What is amiss, Jakob?"

He fished his mother's letter from his pocket without letting go of her. Then he loosened his embrace and handed it to her without a word.

Avery's brow wrinkled as she scanned the seal. "Is this from your king?"

Jakob cleared his throat, hoping his voice worked. "No. My mother."

Avery's dark eyes lifted to his and the frown remained in place. "What does it say?"

Jakob unfolded the parchment and translated the Norsk into English—Spanish was one step too far removed for him to manage at the moment. Though his voice wavered, Avery's gaze did not.

"You must be glad that your family wishes you to return." Avery pivoted and stepped away from him so he could not see her face.

"I am," he admitted. "Though the timing is unfortunate."

"Because of the Order," she said over her shoulder.

"Yes. And..."

"And?" Avery still faced away from him. Her shoulders were tense, her hands in front of her waist.

"And... I love you, Avery. You know this."

She gave a small nod.

"But I must leave. And you—" Jakob cleared his throat again. "You must remain here until your situation is settled."

Avery did not move, nor did she speak.

"I will write to you," he offered.

"I do not know where I will be."

Jakob nodded, though she could not see him. "Catherine will know."

"How long?"

"I do not know."

When Avery turned to face him again, her cheeks were surprisingly dry and her expression resolute. "Will I ever see you again, Jakob?"

He laid a hand of promise over his heart. "I shall do everything I am able to assure that you do."

Her eyes narrowed. "And what then?"

Jakob wanted shout, *I will marry you*—but restraint wisely prevailed. "And then, we shall do whatever we wish to do."

Avery closed the gap between them. "Tomorrow is the one week deadline. Esteban will expect his answer from the duke."

Kris Tualla

Startled by the sudden shift in their conversation, Jakob required a moment to think of what to say. All that came to mind was, "Yes. I suppose he will."

Avery's expression was odd. "Good."

"Good?" That made no sense. "How is that good?"

Avery blinked up at him as if she forgot he was in the room. "Would you excuse me? I have an appointment."

Jakob was completely befuddled by Avery's strange reaction.

"Of course." He bowed from the waist and walked past her, out onto the balcony, and down the palazzo staircase, abruptly feeling the need for predictable male companionship, and several pitchers of very strong wine.

§ § §

Avery crumpled to the carpet as soon as Jakob was gone. Her heart pummeled her ribs and her sweating hands trembled. She had reached an impasse and a decision was required.

Stunned by the solution which exploded in her mind during her exchange with Jakob, Avery needed time to examine it thoroughly. The problem was, she did not have time. In order for the idea to succeed, she must act immediately.

"Is this plan wise?" she whispered. "Or am I the consummate fool for even considering it?"

Avery stared at the carpet, its vibrant colors blurring as she considered losing Jakob forever. Every objection to the path which she was considering faded away when confronted with that possibility.

"Even if this plan fails, and I return to Catherine a pauper and a servant," she murmured to no one, "the possibility of a future with Jakob is worth that risk."

With a deep breath of determination, Avery climbed to her feet. She hurried down to the stables to instruct Antonio to hitch the horse to the carriage, before running up to her room to change clothes. With Zurina's help, she would present herself as the confident business women she prayed that she was.

Her first stop: Señor Garcia, Paolo's lawyer.

§ § §

Three hours later, Avery climbed out of Señor Garcia's carriage and strode down the pier to the shipbuilder's office with the lawyer hurrying behind her. After speaking with an incredulous Señor Garcia, she felt confident that her plan would work. All she required now was the self-possession to carry it off.

The shipbuilder looked up at her, clearly surprised to see an elegantly dressed woman at his door.

"May I help you, my lady?"

Avery stepped forward, her chin high, and extended her gloved hand. "I am Señora Averia Galaviz de Mendoza, Vizcondesa de Catalonya. And you are?"

The man paled. "My name is Señor Juan-Pablo Peña, my lady. It is a pleasure to meet you."

Avery cocked a brow. "Yes, I am quite certain of that. May I present my lawyer, Señor Guillermo Garcia?"

Señor Peña shifted his nervous gaze to the man. "My pleasure."

Avery glanced around the office. "Is there a chair?"

Señor Peña pushed his own seat toward her. "Please take mine."

"Thank you." Avery lowered herself slowly. "I have come to make you an offer for my husband's ships."

The man blinked. "I am sorry for your loss, Condesa. But the ships now belong to Señor Esteban Gonzalez."

Avery pinned the man with the hardest gaze she could muster. "Señor Gonzalez is my majordomo. He forged my ill husband's signature and embezzled from his accounts to pay for the ships."

She gave an unconcerned flip of her wrist. "Thankfully, Paolo died before the scheme could be completed, or I would be left destitute."

Señor Peña's regard moved to Señor Garcia's. "Is this true?"

"So it would seem," the lawyer answered.

The shipbuilder frowned. "And as his lawyer, you had no idea?"

Avery looked pointedly at Garcia. The barrister seemed to wish to sink through the floor and drop into the waters below. "I was not consulted."

Peña made a disgusted sound.

Avery turned back to face him. "We are not here to discuss what has been done, but what will be done. I know that there is a balance of three hundred thousand maravedis required to complete both ships. Am I correct?"

The shipbuilder hesitated. Avery had deliberately quoted the discounted price, hoping that when she made her actual offer, her generosity would prompt the man to accept quickly.

"In truth…" he began.

Avery forestalled his objection. "Señor Garcia, would you please give Señor Peña the document I asked you to draw up."

The lawyer handed him the contract.

"What is this?" Peña asked, squinting at the parchment.

"The deed to the Mendoza palazzo."

The shipbuilder's confused gaze lifted from the document to Avery. "What has this to do with me?"

"I will deed it to you." Avery flashed a cunning smile. "In exchange for both ships."

The man's jaw fell slack. He glanced, wide-eyed, at Señor Garcia as if expecting the lawyer to object.

"As I am sure you are aware, the palazzo is worth quite a bit more than the balance on the two ships," Avery continued.

"Yes, my lady." Señor Peña's eyes shifted back to her, before returning to the lawyer's. "Is this offer legitimate?"

Garcia nodded. "Yes."

Avery stood. "So. Will you accept?"

Señor Peña's features split into a wide smile. "Without hesitation, Vizcondesa! Yes! The ships are yours!"

§ § §

Avery stood in Gustavo's drawing room, Señor Garcia still close by her side. One obstacle had been bested; the second—albeit simpler—obstacle was in front of her.

"Lady Averia." Gustavo walked carefully into the room, his eyes flicking to the lawyer and back to her. "To what do I owe the pleasure of your visit?"

"Señor Gustavo Salazar, may I present Señor Guillermo Garcia,

Paolo Mendoza's lawyer." Avery smiled. "May we sit?"

"Yes—yes of course. May I offer refreshment?" The startled Gustavo was already pulling a bell for service.

"Thank you." Avery settled into a padded chair. Señor Garcia did the same.

Gustavo returned to their seats and claimed one of his own.

Avery spoke first. "I have a proposition for you, Gustavo. While it differs from the one you gave me, I do believe you will be pleased."

His brow lowered. "Go on."

"I have traded my palazzo for the pair of ships. I own them wholly now."

"You did?" Gustavo appeared as stunned as the shipbuilder had. "You do?"

"Yes. Unfortunately, I know nothing about running a trade business." She waited for Gustavo to presume her next statement.

He did. And he looked a bit offended. "Are you offering me the job of running it for you?"

"No, not exactly. I am offering you a partnership." Avery grinned. "You shall pay me sixty-five percent of the profits, until I earn back the three hundred thousand maravedis."

Gustavo's eyes narrowed. "And then?"

"And then I will give you forty-nine percent ownership of the vessels, and sixty percent of the profits."

Gustavo turned to the lawyer, just as the shipbuilder had. "Will there be a legal contract?"

"There already is." Señor Garcia pulled it from his leather pouch and set in on the table in front of their chairs. "All that is required is your signature."

Gustavo picked up the document and stared at it in disbelief.

Avery reached over and laid her hand on Gustavo's forearm. "There is one other consideration, Gustavo. I am expecting about one hundred thousand maravedis in funding from Queen Catherine. I shall give you what you need to hire a crew and purchase the first shipment."

Gustavo's gaze shot to hers. "Will I be required to pay that back as well?"

Avery shook her head. "No. I will make my own arrangements

Kris Tualla

with the queen."

A servant entered with a tray of olives, cheeses, and smoked fish, plus a large decanter of wine. Gustavo waited silently while their glasses were filled and the servant exited, closing the door behind him.

His gray eyes were wary as he considered Avery. When he spoke, his voice was soft. "And what about my marriage proposal, Averia?"

She gave him an apologetic look. "I am respectfully declining your offer of marriage, Gustavo. But I do believe that my counter proposal gives you what you truly desired."

"You underestimate yourself, my love." Gustavo pressed his hand to his heart, unfortunately imitating Jakob's parting gesture. "I would have been a good husband to you."

"I have no doubt of that." *But I am in love with another man.* Avery gave herself a mental shake. "Will you accept these terms?"

Gustavo's shoulders slumped before he drew a breath and straightened in his chair. He lifted his wine glass, smiling with both defeat and triumph in his expression.

"I do accept. Shall we toast to our new partnership?"

Avery raised her glass and touched it to his. "And to our shared future successes."

After they drank from their goblets, Gustavo signed the contracts. When they were finished and the signatures witnessed, Señor Garcia took his leave, now that the legal aspects of Avery's plan were accomplished. Though she had no home at the moment, she had secured the ships and therefore an income.

"I shall open an account in Barcelona for you to deposit my shares into," Avery said. "And you will be expected to show your balance sheets to my accountant and send me a copy of them every quarter."

"You have thought this out rather well." Gustavo looked askance at her. "How long have you been planning this?"

Avery laughed. "About six hours."

Gustavo recoiled. "Six hours? What prompted this sudden decision?"

Avery slipped a large olive into her mouth to give herself time to construct a suitable answer. Her respect for Gustavo required honesty; she only needed to offer it kindly, so as not to hurt him further.

"I discovered this morning that I was about to lose something very precious to me. Someone, actually."

A wash of understanding smoothed Gustavo's brow. He huffed a wry chuckle. "Well I hope he deserves you, whomever he is."

And I hope he wants me.

"Thank you, Gustavo." Avery finished her wine. "Might I have another glass before I go?"

Chapter Nineteen

Avery climbed out of her carriage, using her groom Antonio's hand to steady herself. It wasn't the wine that made her wobbly—it was fear.

Everything she had accomplished today was intended to make what she was about to do possible. The only factor which she could not control was Jakob. His reaction was as unpredictable as the path of a butterfly, and that knowledge was what made her so apprehensive now.

When she conceived this plan after he left her this morning— was it really only this morning?—she knew that whatever Jakob said or did, she would survive. Whether she would survive happily was yet to be seen.

Avery took the stairs slowly, forcing herself to breathe deeply in an attempt to slow her heart. When she reached the first floor of the palazzo, she followed a servant girl to the dining room.

"Is Sir Hansen dining early this evening?" Avery asked, surprised by the choice of room.

The girl gave her a puzzled look. "No, my lady."

Avery looked at the dark purple sky; the sunset had only recently faded. "What time is it?"

"A quarter hour past eight bells."

Avery's stomach grumbled. With a start, she realized she had never taken the time for a midday meal. "Thank you. I was not aware."

The girl opened the door.

Avery hesitated. Then she squared her shoulders, lifted her chin, and entered the room.

§ § §

Jakob was surprised when Avery appeared just as he was enjoying the first course of his solitary supper. She was dressed quite differently than she had been this morning. Then, her hair was loosely tied and her gown serviceable. Now, she stood in his dining room in her full and formal countess glory.

Jakob rose to his feet, glad to still be clad in a velvet tunic, and not only his shirt. "Welcome Avery. I was not expecting you."

"I did not realize the hour." She looked stricken. "I can come back when you have finished."

Her eyes dropped to his soup and he heard her belly rumble. Suppressing a smile, he gestured toward Percy's empty seat. "I would be happy for you to join me. As you can see, I am dining alone this evening."

She looked up at him. "I do not wish to impose."

Jakob walked around the end of the table and pulled out Percy's chair. "Please sit, Avery. My soup is growing cold."

She gave a brief smile and took the place offered to her. Jakob motioned to a servant, before reclaiming his chair. The man quickly ladled out another bowl of the fish stew and set it in front of Avery. Her stomach rumbled again.

Jakob could not help asking, "Have you not eaten today?"

Avery blushed. "Not since breaking my fast. I had a rather busy day."

"Please eat." Jakob chuckled. "We can talk when your belly no longer interrupts."

Avery's blush deepened, but she lifted her spoon and made quick work of the soup. The next courses followed, served at a nearly silent table. Though Jakob made a few attempts at starting light conversation, he gave up when Avery gave no more that single word answers or non-committal shrugs.

He did notice that her hands shook a bit.

When she set her implements down beside her nearly cleaned plate, he pushed his own plate aside. He refilled her glass, and his own, before making another attempt at conversation.

"Are you ready to tell me what occupied your day?"

Avery grasped the goblet and swallowed a draught before answering him. "Yes."

Jakob casually leaned back in his chair. "I am quite curious, I must admit. I have seldom seen you in such a state."

"That is because I made some decisions this morning, after you left." She lifted her glass in a toast to herself. "And then, I made everything happen."

Jakob tried not to let his consternation show. "What did you make happen, Avery?"

She gave him a satisfied look. "I redeemed the ships. Both of them."

Jakob straightened. "Did you receive funds from Catherine?"

Avery shook her head. "No. Not yet."

"Then how?"

Avery sucked a breath as if to bolster her courage against any dissent. "I traded the deed for Paolo's palazzo for both finished ships."

Jakob's jaw fell slack.

"I had Paolo's lawyer, Señor Garcia, draw up the contract before I visited Señor Peña—"

"Who?"

"The shipbuilder."

Jakob nodded and motioned for her to continue.

Avery shot him an irritated look before doing so. "I introduced myself, explained that Esteban had forged the contracts and stolen the money."

"I assume he had no idea?"

"None." One side of Avery's mouth lifted. "And when I mentioned the discounted price, he became truly worried."

Jakob snorted. "I wager he did."

"So when I offered the deed to the palazzo, he was more than happy to accept."

"Does Esteban know?"

Avery lifted her wine goblet with an impish grin. "Not yet."

Jakob laughed. "I would pay to see that conversation."

"I won't charge you." Avery sipped her wine, still grinning. "But there is more to tell."

Jakob folded his arms. "I am already very impressed by your decision, Avery. That took quite a bit of courage."

"Thank you. And, yes it did. However—" She pointed her glass at him. "It left me with two new situations to contend with. The first being, I know absolutely nothing about running a trade business."

The solution smacked Jakob solidly in the chest. "But Señor Salazar does."

"He does. And when I declined his marriage proposal, and offered him a strictly business partnership, he eventually accepted." She held up a quelling hand. "And before you ask, I will receive a two-thirds percentage of the profits until the three hundred thousand maravedis are repaid to me."

Jakob was impressed once more. "And then, I assume, the partnership becomes equitable."

Avery nodded. "Essentially, yes. And he is required to show his logs to my accountant and deposit the funds every quarter into my bank here in Barcelona."

Her expression brightened and she wagged a finger in the air. "Oh—and I used a portion of the money I saved to pay off all of the smaller debts. The remainder, plus the money from Catherine, will be used to hire a crew and purchase the first shipment to be sold."

Jakob stared at Avery, stunned by her keen business acumen. "When did you figure all of these things out?"

She blushed again and her demeanor sobered. Her gaze dropped to her unfinished food. "After you announced that you were leaving Spain."

"This morning."

"Yes."

§ § §

Avery lifted her gaze back to Jakob's. What she saw in his expression could only be called esteemed awe. "I assume you approve thus far?" she ventured.

"Approve?" Jakob chuffed. "I know very few men who could have thought this through so quickly." He leaned closer. "You continue to amaze me, Avery. Every day."

Avery realized he was going to kiss her. She leaned forward as well, and their mouths met over the scattered debris of their supper. Only one piece of the puzzle remained—and it was the most harrowing.

With a sigh, she broke away from their wine-flavored kiss and looked into Jakob's beautiful blue eyes. "I said there were two situations to contend with."

"Yes. You no longer have a home." Jakob's expression was unreadable. "Will you return to Catherine's court in England, then?"

Here it was, the pivotal moment. Avery took another fortifying gulp of her wine.

"I might. But that depends on the answer to my next question."

Jakob's eyes narrowed. "What question, Avery?"

She reached for one of his large hands, finding it warm and heavy. Her pulse roared in her ears and her chest was tight. She looked into his eyes, surprised to find unashamed encouragement there.

He knew what she was going to ask him.

She began to cry, sudden sobs making it hard for her to speak.

Jakob squeezed her hand. "Go on, my love."

His countenance was blurry through her tears. "Why are you making *me* ask?" she croaked.

"Because I only ask once." He grinned. "Now, it is your turn."

Avery punched his arm with her free hand. "Are you going to marry me, Jakob Hansen, or not?"

He laughed. "Ask me nicely."

Avery glared at him. "Jakob Petter Hansen, would you do me the honor of becoming my husband?" she ground out.

Jakob rose to his feet and pulled her to hers. Then he laid one hand on each of her wet cheeks and tilted her face up to his.

"Lady Averia Galaviz de Mendoza, I did not believe you would ever ask me."

She still needed his answer. "Is that a yes?"

Jakob looked at her as if she was a spectre from a dream, now come to life. "Yes, Avery. I will marry you. And I will be very glad to do so."

Then he kissed her for so long, and so well, that Avery nearly forgot how to breathe.

February 26, 1519

Avery climbed into her bed after the third bell of the morning was long past. She and Jakob had talked, kissed, and touched for hours, until she must either fall asleep in his arms, or return to her own bed. Truthfully, if she did not have Esteban to confront, she might have stayed the night with her future husband, all convention thrown aside.

"Dress me well, Zurina," she said. "I have important business once again."

"Yes, my lady." Zurina tied Avery's underskirts over her panier.

Avery caught the maid's expression in the silvered glass. "Do not worry, Zurina. All will be well."

The woman did not appear to be convinced. "As you say, my lady."

Once suitably attired and coiffed, Avery collected yesterday's signed contracts. "Please ask Esteban to join me in the small drawing room immediately. And then inform the rest of the staff that I wish to see them there one half of an hour later."

"Of course." Zurina dipped a small curtsy and went to do as asked.

Jacinda stepped into the doorway. "Sir Hansen has arrived, my lady."

"Thank you, Jacinda." Just the mention of his name made Avery's heart stutter with joy. "Please have him join me in the small drawing room."

Once she was alone, Avery took a moment to recheck her appearance and review how she planned to present her news to her staff. She had managed to do the best for them that she could. All but one of them, of course.

Satisfied that she was fully prepared, Avery walked past the remnants of her breakfast and out of her chambers, anticipation over her interview with Esteban lightening her step. She could not wait to see his face when she told him what she had done.

And then she would swiftly send him packing.

When she entered the drawing room, Jakob turned toward her and smiled the biggest smile she had ever witnessed on the stoic Nordic knight. She grinned so widely in return, that her cheeks hurt.

He held out a hand. "Are you real, Avery? Or do I imagine such beauty?"

"Sir Hansen, you are a shameless seducer of women." Avery took his hand. She allowed him to pull her close and gave him a comparatively chaste kiss.

"Woman," he corrected, looking down into her eyes. "Only one has truly claimed my heart."

Avery stepped away and handed Jakob the contracts. "We should be prepared for Esteban. Remember, I will inform him of what has transpired."

"And I am here as your witness and protector." Jakob gave a small bow. "It is my great honor, my love."

Avery wagged a warning finger. "None of that language. Not yet."

Footsteps on the tiles outside heralded Esteban's arrival. When he saw that Jakob was present, his expression darkened.

"You wished to see me?" He did not acknowledge the knight's presence.

"Yes, Esteban. I have some important news to tell you." Avery waved at a chair. "You might want to sit down."

"I prefer to stand."

"As you wish." Avery sat in the largest chair. Jakob stood several feet to her right, his gaze pinned on the majordomo.

Avery lifted her chin, relishing the moment. "The first thing I need to tell you, is that I no longer own this palazzo."

A flicker of surprise moved over Esteban's brow. "You have sold the house? To whom?"

"Not sold exactly. Traded." Without moving her eyes from Esteban, Avery extended her right arm, and Jakob handed her the ship builder's contract.

She handed it off to the majordomo. "I believe you are quite well acquainted with Señor Juan-Pablo Peña, are you not?"

Esteban paled and reached for the contract. "What have you done?"

Avery pointed at the document. "It is all there. I simply traded the palazzo for the two trade ships, which my husband's money has funded."

Esteban glared at her. "This is not legal. Paolo died, leaving me the sole owner."

Avery lifted one brow "So, you admit what you have done?"

"We invested together," Esteban declared.

"Is that so?" Avery glanced at Jakob; the Norseman was clearly enjoying the fraught scene. "And how much of the money was yours, Esteban?"

"My contribution was managerial. I was to operate the trade business." He jabbed a finger in her direction. "I have a contract, as well!"

"Yes, I know." Avery waved a dismissive hand. "I also know how far short you fell in completing the payment. Were you not aware that Señor Peña was trying to find buyers for the ships?"

Esteban's expression shifted to one of disdain. "Of course. That is why I am soliciting investors."

"Such as Thomas Windsor, the Welsh duke?"

The majordomo was clearly not expecting that. "A—among others."

Avery looked at Jakob. "Tell him."

"With pleasure, my lady." Jakob's glee was barely contained. "Thomas Windsor, the Welsh duke, is in actuality Sir Percival Bethington, knight of King Henry the Eighth, his representative at the Order of the Golden Fleece, and my traveling companion and housemate."

Esteban's gaze bounced between the two. "Why did he—"

Avery enjoyed watching the man squirm. "Because once I discovered what you had done, I needed someone to adequately discern the situation. What better ruse than an interested buyer?"

The majordomo's face flushed alarmingly. "You will not succeed at this. Señor Garcia will put a stop to this."

Avery pointed at the contract. "Señor Garcia wrote that contract, accompanied me yesterday when I visited Señor Peña, and witnessed the legal signatures. I am afraid I have already succeeded."

"Those ships are mine!" he shouted.

Avery leapt to her feet, finally free to express her fury. "You paid for them with *my* husband's money! And once Señor Peña was informed that you were *only* the majordomo, and had embezzled the money from your ill employer, he was quite happy to make this trade."

Esteban blanched, silent for the moment and shaking visibly.

"Not only that," Avery pointed at the contract, "but he plans to lease this house and will keep the staff employed for now."

Avery thought Esteban seemed relieved, and she enjoyed the moment before delivering the final blow. "All except for one member, of course."

Esteban's eyes fell to the document and began frantically scanning it.

Avery saved him the trouble. "It seems he does not wish to have a thief in his employ."

Esteban threw the contract on the ground and stepped toward her. Jakob was between them in a blink.

"Step back." His threatening tone left no doubt that he would use force if necessary.

The majordomo hesitated, sneering up at the knight before conceding.

"You have one hour to pack your belongings and leave this house." Avery nodded toward Jakob. "Sir Hansen will assist you."

"I do not require assistance," Esteban growled.

Avery shrugged. "Truly there is not much left to steal. But even so, Sir Hansen will assure that nothing of mine accidently ends up in your trunks."

Esteban spat on the carpet.

Jakob smashed his fist deep into the man's belly.

Esteban dropped to his knees and doubled over, gasping for breath.

Jakob squatted beside the wheezing man. "Do not show such disrespect again."

He stood, grabbed the back of Esteban's tunic, and yanked him upright. "You now have fifty-eight minutes."

Jakob gave Avery an encouraging glance, and shoved the

former servant toward the door. She picked up the contract and followed.

The six remaining servants waited outside, staring in shock as Jakob manhandled their superior out of their sight. They turned as one to face Avery, wide-eyed and concerned.

"Please come in." Avery returned to her chair, but this time she remained standing. Once the six stood in a semi-circle in front of her, she smiled reassuringly.

"This is what has transpired: Esteban stole hundreds of thousands of maravedis from Paolo Mendoza and forged his signature on a contract, making himself a full partner in the building of two trade ships. However, Paolo died before the ships were completely paid for."

Unsettled glances bounced among the servants.

For simplicity's sake Avery intentionally shortened her story. "Once I discovered this, I met with the shipbuilder, explained the situation, and offered him the deed to this palazzo in exchange for the ships. He agreed."

Someone groaned softly. The cook's assistant Ana began to cry.

Avery held up a hand. "You are not being released. He intends to lease the house, with a staff in place."

"So we may stay?" Antonio asked.

"You may." Avery grinned and tipped her head toward the door. "All but one of you, of course."

Maribel the laundress snickered. "I never did like him."

Avery looked at her lady's maid. "Zurina, because it is likely that anyone who leases this property will have their own lady's maid, I would like you to assume Esteban's position for now."

The woman was clearly surprised—and pleased. "Thank you, my lady. But, if I may ask…"

"Where am I going?" Avery's pensive gaze moved to the door. "I do not know where, Zurina. I only know with whom."

Chapter Twenty

Jakob laid two necklaces and a pair of earrings on the table. "Are these yours?"

"This necklace is not." Avery fingered the fresh-water pearls. "But considering all that Esteban took from me, I have no qualms about taking this from him."

Jakob kissed her forehead. "He is waiting outside the gate. I shall inform him that he is free to go. And, I shall instruct Antonio to secure a locksmith and have the gate lock changed today."

"Thank you, Jakob. I appreciate your help."

Avery watched his back as he left, wondering when and where they would marry. Preferably here, in Barcelona, before beginning their journey.

"The banns must be posted for three weeks," Jakob pointed out when she broached the subject over their midday meal. "We could not be married before that."

She set her spoon down. "Are you worried about your father dying before you arrive?"

Jakob shook his head. "If God wants my father to talk to me, He will not take him beforehand. Either that, or he has already passed, in which case three weeks will not make a difference."

"I am glad to hear you say that, because I would hate to send you off before me."

Jakob gave her a puzzled look. "Why would you remain behind?"

"The money from Catherine. I need to be here to accept it and pay Gustavo."

Jakob took a considering sip of ale. "Then this is what I believe we shall do..." He raised one finger. "Visit the priest today and have the banns posted."

A second finger joined the first. "We shall set our wedding for three weeks from today."

A third finger rose. "And, we will begin our travels two days later. The Order will certainly have adjourned by then, if what I have been told proves true."

"And the money?"

Jakob took hold of her hand. "If the money has not arrived from Catherine by then, it is likely not coming."

Sadly, Avery had to agree. "I must give Gustavo all the money I have left, so he can pay for the crew and merchandise."

Jakob dipped his chin in approval. "And we will return to London to settle our finances, before going on to Arendal."

Avery considered the knight. "Will you go to København?"

"Yes. After we visit my family." Jakob shrugged. "But I have been writing King Christian regularly, so the man is informed of what transpired at the Order. I shall write him now and tell him that I am going to Arendal when I leave Spain, and why."

Avery's chest tightened. "Will you ask permission to marry this time?"

Jakob considered her through narrowed eyes. "No. I do not believe I will. At my age I have no desire to wait for an answer."

"What will come of your position?"

Jakob huffed a sardonic laugh. "We shall see."

February 27, 1519

Percy wiped his eyes, his face flushed with laughter. "Hansen you are not funny often, but when you are, your humor is priceless!"

Jakob leaned his backside against a tall table in Percy's outer chamber, arms crossed over his chest, and gave his friend a crooked grin. "*Takk du*. But this is not a joke."

Percy paused in mid-wipe, his hand hovering in front of his face. "I apologize, Jakob. Did I misunderstand you?" The hand dropped to his lap and his expression grew less jovial. "When I asked what you accomplished yesterday, I thought you said that you met with the priest about reading the banns for your marriage."

Jakob chuckled. "You heard correctly."

Percy's brow twisted in disbelief. "Whom are you marrying?"

Jakob threw his arms wide. "Whom would you expect? Lady Avery, of course!"

"No!" Percy jumped to his feet. "Does *she* know?"

Now it was Jakob's turn to laugh. "Of course!" he wheezed. "Can you imagine her reaction if I tried to ambush her?"

Percy whooped at that. "She would remove your stones, tie them around your neck, and drown you with them!"

"Yes. And rightly so." Jakob laughed, pointing a finger at Percy. "I want you as my second."

"I will be honored." Percy bowed at the waist. When he straightened, all his amusement was gone. "In all seriousness, Jakob, has Avery accepted your proposal?"

"No, she turned me down, as you know." Jakob gave a little shrug. "But this time she asked me. And *I* accepted."

Percy wagged his head, admiration sculpting his features. "Not only did you melt the Ice Maiden, but she proposed to you. I am in the presence of a master."

Jakob waved away the comment. "She and I understand each other. That is all."

"So you will wed in three weeks?" Percy frowned. "What about her finances?"

Jakob straightened and turned around. He poured two steins of the cooled ale waiting on the table which he had been leaning against and handed one to Bethington. Then he recounted one-by-one the lady's unmatched activities of the previous day.

"Avery is a startlingly intelligent woman," Percy said. "And she has substantial courage to make all of those arrangements and not be certain of your answer."

Jakob dipped his chin. "I believe she had a fairly good idea of my response."

Percy drained his cup. "We should leave. You can tell me the rest on the way to the cathedral."

§ § §

"Congratulation, Hansen!" Diego de Mendoza pounded Jakob's back as his deep voice bounced off the cathedral's soaring stone walls. "The lady deserves to be happy after her unfortunate marriage to my cousin."

Jakob accepted the congratulations from his brothers in the Order, waiting until the hubbub died down before broaching the subject foremost in his mind. "We will be married on March the nineteenth. Will the Order be adjourned by that time?"

Glances bounced around the gathered group of knights, each one seemingly questioning the others.

Pietro San Severino spoke up first. "I believe we should be done in less than a fortnight. Do you gentlemen agree?"

Alvaro de Zuniga nodded. "The moment France agrees to come to Spain's aid, we can adjourn."

"And they agreed to do so once they signed Henry of England's treaty, did they not?" Diego de Mendoza directed his comment toward the nearby French knight, Laurent de Gorrevod, Comte de Pont de Vaux.

The Frenchman stepped forward, chest puffed out to accept the challenge. "Have you read the treaty, Señor Mendoza?"

"I admit that I have not," he replied.

"If you had," one haughty brow lifted, "then you would know what it states."

Jakob glanced at Bethington—who remained determinedly tight-lipped—before jumping into the fray himself and bringing the issue out in the open.

"If I recall from my time in England," he ventured. "The treaty says that those who sign agree to come to each other's aid, if any come under attack."

"*Exactement!*" Gorrevod pointed a finger at Mendoza. "And Spain is not under attack."

"Our enemies are at our door!" Zuniga blurted.

"They are across the sea." Gorrevod threw up his hands. "If they sail, and if they make landfall, then call on us and we will respond. Until then…"

With a shrug, the Frenchman returned to his seat.

"We are going to have to settle this or no one will ever get out of here alive." San Severino turned to face Jakob. "In the meantime, I believe you should recuse yourself, tell your king you did so to avoid having to choose between the Spanish and the French, and get yourself married."

Jakob laughed and then coughed to disguise his reaction when several scowling countenances turned in his direction. "That is very sage advice, my friend. And I believe that I shall take it."

§ § §

Zurina stared at Avery, blinking back tears. "I am so happy for you, my lady!"

"Thank you, Zurina." Avery had not stopped smiling for the past twelve hours or so, and was convinced she had smiled through the night as well. "We have quite a lot of work to do, I am afraid. Señor Peña will allow me to remain here until Sir Hansen and I depart in three weeks, but what I am taking with me must be packed up before then."

"And it shall be accomplished, do not have a moment's concern about that." Zurina wiped her eyes and looked around the room. "What shall you wear for your wedding?"

"I do not care," Avery admitted. "You choose for me. I would be willing to parade through the streets of Barcelona in a nightdress, if that meant our marriage was legally and quickly performed."

The maid chuckled. "I would never allow that. Your reputation aside, my reputation as a lady's maid would be completely destroyed."

Avery considered her simple chambers; everything of value had been sold and only the bare necessities remained. "I wonder where we shall spend our wedding night."

"If you choose to spend it here, rest assured I shall make it perfect," Zurina assured her.

Considering the many hours she spent in Jakob's arms on a

simple couch, Avery was not overly concerned. Her first full night with him as her husband would be wonderful wherever they lay down together.

"My lady?"

Feeling a blush warm her cheeks, Avery pulled her attention back to her maid. "I am certain you will. Thank you, Zurina."

March 16, 1519

Only three more days.

Jakob walked to Avery's palazzo in the bright midday, having left his final meeting at Barcelona Cathedral. He gave his official leave to the Order of the Golden Fleece this morning, on the grounds that his king requested him to do so.

It was not the truth, exactly, though Jakob had written to Christian and explained the situation. With the members from both France and Spain pressuring the others to take a side in their debate, he wrote, it was better for Jakob to take his leave before Denmark and Norway made a powerful enemy with either side.

He was certain that Christian would agree. But if Christian did not, by the time his letter reached København, and the king responded, it would be too late in any case. The Order would certainly have adjourned by then.

With the majordomo no longer in residence, housekeeper Jacinda greeted him at the gate and took him to the small drawing room to meet with Avery. Though Jakob thought the palazzo looked empty after Avery sold the majority of the furnishings, the house was positively denuded now.

In the last weeks since he accepted her proposal, Avery had packed or sold nearly every bit of the contents on the first and second floors. She only left the servants' quarters on the ground floor intact, as those men and women would remain in residence here, eventually serving under the leadership of a new majordomo of Señor Peña's choosing.

Jakob's mouth twitched as he recalled Esteban's impotent anger at his abrupt dismissal, once the scheming weasel was out-maneuvered by Avery. The man received far less than he ultimately deserved, but at the least he was finally gone.

Avery swept into the room, her eyes twinkling once they landed on his.

Jakob grinned. "*Du er for vakker til å være ekte.*"

"I am very glad you think I am beautiful." Avery reached out her hands. "And I assure you that I am quite real. The ache in my aging back reminds me of this fact."

Jakob clasped her hands and pulled her into a lingering kiss. "I will love away all of your aches and pains," he teased.

"And I will let you," she teased back. "Are you hungry?"

He nodded. "Come have lunch with me."

Avery gave him a chastising look. "I do have food here, Jakob. I am not destitute."

Jakob looked around the sparse room with exaggerated skepticism. "Forgive me if I do not believe you."

Avery pulled her hands free, punched him in the chest, and went to ring for food. "Did you extricate yourself from the Order?"

Jakob pulled a deep breath through his nose. "I did."

Avery turned back to face him, her brow furrowed. "And in just three more days, Christian will have *two* reasons to remove you from his service."

"I do not care."

"Are you certain?" Avery slipped her arms around his waist. "You say so now, but this is a very unusual choice for any knight to make."

Jakob held her close. "With the income from your ships, we shall be fine. And, I am willing to return to England if necessary, and ask to enter Henry's service. He owes me his life, if you will recall."

"As long as he does," Avery huffed.

"My lady?" Jacinda stood in the doorway. "You have another visitor."

Avery pulled away from him and faced the housekeeper. "Who is it?"

"He says he comes from Queen Catherine."

"He is English? Show him up!"

Jacinda nodded and disappeared from sight.

Avery beamed up at him. "Jakob, the money!"

A sense of relief suffused his core, chasing away the apprehension of uncertainty which the queen's long silence had fomented. Though the money was no longer critical, it would still be extremely helpful in Avery's transition.

He grinned. "It must be. Why send a servant otherwise?"

The man who appeared was stout, middle-aged, and dressed in full beefeater regalia. When he spied Avery, he bowed.

"Good day, Lady Avery. I come with greetings from Her Royal Highness, Queen Catherine of Aragon."

"Thank you, good sir. Please come in."

As he approached her, the courier's eyes moved in wide-eyed surprise around the empty room.

"Your arrival is perfectly timed, good sir," Avery said. "I am vacating Barcelona in a matter of days, as you can see."

The man's shoulders relaxed at her words. "Yes, my lady."

"Have you something for me?"

"Yes, my lady. Please follow me."

Avery and Jakob followed the beefeater onto the balcony. In the courtyard below was a wagon with three padlocked wooden trunks on its bed. Two large draft horses chuffed and stomped their hooves on the tiled patio.

"I was charged to hand this into your hands only. As you can imagine, the queen did not trust any other method of delivery."

"Yes, indeed." Avery glanced at Jakob with a stunned expression. "How much is there?"

"Nine hundred pounds sterling. Three hundred in coinage in each trunk." He reached into his tunic and withdrew a leather pouch. "I also have a signed and sealed bank debit from the queen, allowing the holder to withdraw up to an additional eight thousand and one hundred pounds from the royal treasury within one year from today."

The beefeater handed the folded parchment to Avery. Jakob perused it over her shoulder. With black and red ink, plus gold leaf, an elaborate signature, and a wax seal trailing three short ribbons in the Tudor colors, the document was obviously meant to impress.

"Ten percent in coin, plus signed and documented surety for the remainder," Jakob said. "The queen was very wise in handling the loan this way."

Avery gave him a thoughtful smile. "If the remainder is not claimed in full within the year, then my repayment is diminished."

Jakob nodded. "And, with the funds you were able to save, it may not need to be."

Avery heaved a sigh. "I am so relieved, you cannot imagine."

"Though this is only a portion of the total, I believe you should deliver it to the bankers immediately," Jakob cautioned. "You have a largely female staff here and no defenses."

The beefeater slid Jakob an approving look. "I agree, sir. My lady, if you will direct me?"

"I will ride with him," Jakob declared. "Have Antonio follow with you in the carriage."

§ § §

"If I might ask you sir," Jakob ventured once the silver-and-copper coins were safely deposited in Avery's account at the bank. "Are you now returning to London?"

"Yes, Sir Hansen." The beefeater, whose name also turned out to be Henry, waved toward the nearly-emptied wagon and its driver, waiting on the side of the sunny street. "We were instructed to return straightaway and give a report concerning the Lady Avery's situation to Her Highness."

"I assume you will return along the same path as you came?"

"Yes, sir."

"And what was that path?"

Henry shaded his eyes, obviously unperturbed by Jakob's odd track of questions. "We sailed from London to Bilbao, and drove to Barcelona from there."

"How much time did that journey require?" Jakob continued.

"Just over one month."

Avery looked up at Jakob, her expression inscrutable. "What are you thinking?"

Jakob met her gaze, his plan solidifying as he did. "I suggest that Henry and his companion rest here in Barcelona for the next five days."

Henry frowned. "My lord—"

Jakob held up a hand to interrupt the man's objection. "Hear me out, Henry. The Lady Avery and I are to be married in three days."

The beefeater's jaw dropped. "Are you? Does the queen know?"

"Not yet," Avery admitted.

Jakob continued before the conversation could veer again. "Two days after that, if the lady has no objection, we shall accompany you back to London."

Avery's face brightened. "Jakob, that is brilliant."

Henry's uncertain glance shifted to the driver and back. "But what—"

"In the meantime, you shall both relax in the palazzo which I share with Sir Percival Bethington, and enjoy our generous hospitality." Jakob grinned. "What do you say?"

"The queen don't know what day we arrived," the driver said to Henry, his expression hopeful. "Five days ain't a concern."

"Gentlemen." Avery stepped forward and gave the pair a reassuring smile. "If you return to the court with Sir Hansen and myself in your company, any delay will be promptly forgiven, I assure you."

Henry's face smoothed. The responsibility for this decision was now in the Lady Avery's noble hands.

He bowed. "Under that circumstance, I agree, my lady. And we gratefully accept both your generous offer of hospitality, Sir Hansen, and your noble companionship, Lady Avery, on our journey home."

The grateful look Avery gave Jakob warmed his core, before corralling that heat and sending it straight to his groin. He gave Avery a wicked smile.

Three more days.

Ϙhapter Ꞇwenty-One

Avery's heart stuttered in her chest as Antonio handed her down from her carriage. Zurina had spent the morning fussing over her hair and her gown, finally declaring the end result complete less than one half of an hour before her scheduled noon wedding mass. Luckily, her home was less than half a mile from the cathedral and the midday bell had not yet rung.

Avery walked up the steps to the cathedral's patio alone and moved over the smooth stones as if in a dream. She barely had the chance to adjust to all of the changes in her life over the past weeks and now this pivotal day was already half gone.

While she was marrying for a second time, this was the first time she was marrying for love.

Yet her husband-to-be was from a country and culture she had never given a previous thought to; now that it mattered, she knew she had much more to learn about the Norseman.

Adding to her situation was the fact that both of them were flying in the face of convention, marrying without permission of their respective sovereigns. While the results of that made no difference in Avery's case, the decision was most definitely going to affect Jakob's future circumstances.

Father God, please protect us.

The thick wooden doors under the pointed Gothic arch of Barcelona's Cathedral de Eulalia stood open, welcoming faithful worshippers on this mild spring day. Avery stepped through the doors, halting as her eyes adjusted to the dimness inside.

She glanced around, looking for Jakob, hearing only the shouted discussion coming from the sanctuary.

"Vizcondesa Mendoza?"

Avery turned toward the voice.

"Padre James!" She dipped in a small, respectful curtsy before reaching out her hands.

The elder priest took her hands in his, his skin thin and mapped with blue veins. "I am so very happy for you, my lady. When I sent word of your husband's imminent death, I had no idea what sort of miracle God was working on your behalf."

Avery's cheeks warmed. "Do you believe Sir Hansen is a miracle?"

The priest smiled. "Do you not?" He tucked her hand into his elbow. "Come, child. Let us join the groom."

Padre James led her toward a chapel on one side of the transept. "The Order of the Golden Fleece is still in session, I am afraid, so our noon masses are held in the Chapel of the Virgin."

When they rounded the corner, Avery stopped walking, the vision of her nearly-husband claiming her ability to breathe.

Jakob turned to face her. He wore her favorite blue velvet and pearl-pleated tunic under the black cape of the Order. His hose were dark gray, and his tall black boots gleamed with polish.

His red-gold hair was combed back from his face, revealing his broad brow, high cheekbones, and eyes that matched the blue of his garment. The Order's heavy golden collar glinted in the cathedral's ever-present candlelight.

Askel had completed his valet's job to perfection.

Jakob's deep voice was soft, but it still made her body tremble. *"Min dame, du er fantastisk."* My lady, you are stunning.

Avery opened her fan and demurely covered the bottom half of her face. *"Takk, min herre."* Thank you, my lord.

Padre James walked her forward. "Sit here, my lady, until you are called up to participate."

Avery sat on the bench on the left side of the aisle. Jakob sat on the bench on the right. Only then did she notice Percival and the other handful of knights scattered across the front two benches. Askel sat a row behind them next to Denys, and grinning like a fool.

A warm voice tickled her ear. "You look beautiful, my lady. God bless you."

Avery turned around and met Maria's eyes. "Thank you."

Then her gaze shifted and blurred. The remaining household staff from her stripped estate entered and sat behind her in the chapel.

"How did you all—"

"Sir Hansen, of course," Maria chastised. "He said that you must have people here who care for you, not only for him."

Avery looked at Jakob, beaming at her across the aisle.

"*Jeg elsker deg,*" she whispered. I love you.

"*Jeg elsker deg, også,*" he replied in kind.

§ § §

Jakob stared at the priest, but he did not hear a single word of the mass. He hoped that he did not miss his moment—certainly the priest would not allow him to—but he was completely unable to corral his thoughts. He had never seen Avery look so beautiful and, considering the lady's multitude of attributes, this was quite an accomplishment, indeed.

Today she wore a deep red brocaded gown with a black-and-red silk head covering shot through with gold threads. Three strands of multi-colored pearls twisted through her hair, echoing the dark, narrow braids which were looped and pinned behind her ear.

The black Spanish lace fan was a perfect veil.

Lord Father, how did You manage to bless me so?

This wedding was a miracle, that much was clear. Jakob never expected his commission to visit London before proceeding to the Order to result in either his reprieve from past guilt or the discovery of new love.

While his first reaction to the assignment was disappointment, he now thanked God every night that King Christian tapped him for the unusual task.

Diego de Mendoza, sitting on Jakob's right, leaned toward him. "You are a lucky man, Hansen. I hope you understand this."

Jakob slid his gaze to Diego's. "I owe your cousin a debt of gratitude," he whispered. "If he had ever made her the least bit happy, she would not become mine today."

Diego chuckled and cleared his throat, giving the presiding priest a solemn nod.

"Sir Hansen." The priest's tone was stern as he repeated the previously unheard summons.

Jakob rose to his feet, noting that Avery was already standing. He offered her his arm and then the couple stepped forward. Percival materialized by his right elbow.

The priest continued the mass with Jakob and Avery doing their part. When he reached the section where they were to make their vows, Jakob repeated the priest's words while he slid the braided silver ring back onto Avery's finger.

Though he offered to buy her a new ring for the wedding, she declined.

"You may do so on our first anniversary," she stated. "Assuming we are not homeless and destitute, of course."

The mass continued until, finally, Jakob and Avery were declared married in the sight of God and the Church. He looked down into her nearly-black eyes, wanting to sweep her up in his arms and carry her to straight to his bed, the wedding dinner forgone.

For now, he must be satisfied with a chaste kiss.

The Spanish knights Diego Hurtado de Mendoza, Alvaro de Zuniga y Guzman, and Pietro Antonio San Severino were joining Jakob and Percival back at their leased palazzo for the celebratory meal though, of course, neither Askel nor any of Avery's servants would be joining them at the table.

"I only wish Catherine could have been here." Avery's voice was breathless between their no-longer-chaste kisses in the carriage. She sat across his lap and Jakob knew by the way she wiggled her bottom that she felt his desire rise beneath her, even through her layers of skirts and underskirts.

She bit his earlobe. "Soon, my love."

Jakob groaned. "I hope I live that long."

§ § §

The midday meal was served in seven long courses for Jakob, Avery, Percival, and the three Spanish knights. Avery ate lightly—her stomach was jumpy enough in anticipation of bedding Jakob for the first time.

She wondered if she would still remember what to do in the marital bed a decade after refusing her first husband... But then, that man never was a good lover. Perhaps she should forget those unhappy experiences and start her lessons anew.

Jakob, Avery was convinced, would be a very good lover if their sport in London was an indication.

The knights rose to their feet as one.

"We shall take our leave, Vizcondesa Averia de Hansen," Diego stated. "Thank you for a wonderful meal, and congratulations once again in your marriage."

Avery startled at the name, then recovered her scant composure. "Thank Señor Mendoza. Your words mean quite a lot to me."

Percival circled around the end of the table and lifted her hand to his lips. "The best man has won, my lady. I concede graciously."

Avery laughed. "It is high time for that, good sir."

Percy looked at Jakob. "I will make my exit as well, and return two days hence to see you off."

Jakob was clearly surprised. "Where are you going?"

"I am leaving the palazzo to give you and your bride some well-deserved privacy. And—" Percival placed a palm over his heart. "I am afraid my broken heart must be mended."

Jakob chuckled. "I assume you have a candidate in mind to assist with the repairs?"

"Several." Percy winked. "Do not worry about me."

Avery felt a rush of relief. While she never had feelings for the English knight, the idea of him sleeping in the same house on her and Jakob's wedding night definitely felt awkward.

Jakob nuzzled her ear. "We are alone, wife."

Avery turned into his embrace.

§ § §

Jakob lay on his back, panting, his limbs thrown wide and his groin still throbbing with fading pleasure. The sun painted the sky outside his bedroom chamber in brilliant yellows and oranges, the gathering clouds responding in reds and purples. Even the heavens were celebrating with them.

Thank you, Father. Again.

Avery snuggled close, her breasts pressed to his side, and her knee resting between his thighs. Every time she exhaled, a soft moan escaped with her breaths.

"I was afraid I had forgotten how…" she murmured.

Jakob would have laughed if he had any strength left.

"That is why the second time was important," he said with false solemnity. "To confirm that we both remembered the process adequately."

Avery reached up and turned his face toward hers. "If you remembered any more *adequately*, you might be a widower once again."

Jakob did chuckle at that. "Swived to death on your wedding day? That would certainly assure my reputation with the ladies."

Avery pinched his freshly shaved jaw. "I have been married once to a man who had a reputation with the ladies. I have no care for another."

Jakob shifted onto his side to face her. "You are the only lady I will ever love, or lay with, for the rest of my life, Avery."

She gave him a sultry smile. "And I with you as well, Jakob."

Though they had exchanged similar vows in the mass, these statements made now, tangled in his sheets, naked and floating in post-coital bliss, solidified their marriage in his soul.

"I love you. More than I can say in words, my wife."

Avery kissed him softly, her lips still swollen and smudged with their play. "Your body said it quite eloquently, husband. Both times."

Jakob grinned at her, his core still quivering. "Then this is the language I will continue to use."

Avery rolled onto her back and ran her palms over her body in invitation. "And you always said you were good with languages…"

March 21, 1519

The dawn approached slowly, a fact that Avery was quite grateful for. She slept very well these last two nights—once the time for sleep was finally reached.

Neither she nor Jakob anticipated the overwhelming intensity of their desires for each other, as both admitted that they had determinedly tamped those longings down for many years under their previous circumstances.

Now married, and freed from their respective pasts, all of those denied yearnings erupted like a volcano. Since their wedding forty hours ago, Avery estimated that they had spent less than eight of those hours outside of Jakob's chambers.

Today she and Jakob were closing the door on Barcelona, her widowhood, and the Order of the Golden Fleece, and beginning their month-long journey to London.

The first of three cities which they needed to visit, Avery was surprised to realize that returning to England would actually feel like going home to her. She was also anxious to see Catherine again and determine how her friend was recovering from her duet of devastations.

"We will not stay in London for long, will we, husband," she said drowsily, stretching languorously before leaving their cozy linen cocoon.

"Not this time." Jakob's voice was rough with remnants of sleep. He sat up and swung his legs over the edge of the bed. "I want to get to Arendal and finish my duties there as quickly as possible."

Avery sat up as well and hugged her sheet-shrouded knees, reluctant to end their newly-wedded intimacy and reenter the world at large. "Perhaps you will find the situation less fraught than you expect."

Jakob cast a bleary gaze over his shoulder. "If my mother is the only member of my family who wishes to see me, then my brothers and father—if he is still alive—will assure that we are made miserable while we reside there."

Avery lifted one resolute brow. "If that is the case, we shall simply leave. And then, you will no longer have reason to feel guilty for leaving them in the first place."

Jakob twisted to face fully her. "How do you know I feel guilty?"

"You went against your father's wishes and caused a rift in your family." Avery straightened her legs. The sheet fell to her lap, exposing her breasts. Jakob's gaze dropped briefly and his lips twitched.

Avery continued when he looked up at her eyes once more. "And though you were correct in your point, and tried as best you could to keep the rift from forming, it grew nonetheless. You cannot help but feel responsible."

"You are a very wise woman." His lips twitched again. "Perhaps I should marry you."

Avery laughed. "I am sorry, sir, but at the moment I am quite happily espoused."

Jakob leaned closer. "If he ever mistreats you in any way, or worse, ignores you, you must inform me immediately."

Avery dipped her chin. "And what will you do, Sir Knight?"

"I shall thrash him within an inch of his life, so that as long as he lives, he treats you the way you deserve to be treated."

Jakob's lips landed on hers and claimed them thoroughly. After a sound kissing, he groaned and pulled away. "We must be off now, wife. Or we shall never leave."

§ § §

Avery and Zurina—who would return to Spain once the couple reached London—sat in the wagon on a bench made of trunks and covered with blankets. Beefeater Henry had shown enough forethought to procure a canopy, so that the women were protected from too much sun, or any light rains they might encounter.

Jakob rode Warrior, whose prancing behavior made it clear that the stallion was anxious to leave the confines of city life. Askel followed behind, riding a spare draft horse.

"We shall make good distances, sir," Henry told Jakob once the journey began. "The coins and trunks were over seven hundred pounds all told, so our load is lightened by half."

"How long will it take to reach Bilbao?"

"It's almost four hundred miles. While we might make forty miles a day at this pace, I would plan on about twelve days."

Jakob nodded his acknowledgement and grinned at Avery. He was uncertain how she would react to leaving Barcelona, and was surprised by how unaffected she appeared.

After hugging Maria goodbye, Avery climbed into the wagon dry-eyed and smiling.

"I only lived in Barcelona for five miserable years," she reminded him when he asked. "In truth, I was more tearful when I was forced to return, than either time I have left."

"And what about leaving Spain?" he pressed.

Avery thought about that a moment. Jakob noted a variety of emotions flicker through her expression.

"I am not sorrowful, I must admit this. But then, I am leaving for a much happier reason this time." She smiled up at him and he felt as if he was drowning in the dark pools of her exotic eyes. "I am not escaping a life with a terrible husband. I am joining my life with a cherished one."

Jakob reached for her hand. "*Jeg elsker deg.*"

She squeezed his in return. "*Jeg elsker deg også.*"

Chapter Twenty-Two

April 19, 1519
London, England

The last time Jakob sailed up the Thames, he had nothing but questions about his future. How odd and unexpected that future was turning out to be.

Avery smiled at him and pointed. "I can see the Tower. It will not be long now."

Jakob was also glad to note the white stone landmark rising above the horizon. He hated sailing and, even with a lusty wife in his bed, he found scant comfort on a ship.

"I shall revel in resting on a bed which rocks only from our motions, and not from the sea's," he whispered in her ear.

Avery's cheeks pinkened endearingly. At thirty-five years of age, she seemed almost girlish in her response to their bedsport.

"What is the date?" he asked, a sudden realization prodding him.

Her brow wrinkled. "If I am counting correctly, today should be the nineteenth of April. Why?"

Jakob chuckled. "Because if you *are* correct, then I am thirty-three years old today."

Avery spun to face him. "Why did you not tell me earlier?"

"I forgot," he answered honestly. "I was not thinking about it when we left Barcelona, and since that day I have had other thoughts occupying my mind."

Avery blushed again, glancing around for ears that might overhear him. "Are you nervous about seeing Henry again?"

Jakob looked down into her eyes. "Should I be?"

"I am not certain how he will react to our marriage." Avery bit her lower lip.

"I may be mistaken," Jakob said slowly, "but I believe you have more to worry about than I do. I am not English, so I am not Henry's subject."

Avery lifted one shoulder. "I am not English either, so I am not actually subject to his rulings. But I did live here under his protection."

Jakob understood the delicate balance. "And on this day we shall enter the court and announce that, as friends of the king and queen, we wish to share with them the good news of our marriage."

"On your birthday," Avery added.

Jakob pointed a finger at her. "Yes. Today is my birthday. That will be our distraction."

Avery laid a hand on his chest. "I am sorry that I do not have a gift for you."

"You can give me the only gift I truly wish for later this night." Jakob grinned. "In a long bed that does not move."

§ § §

Avery wanted to run into Catherine's presence and if the queen was in her chambers she would have done so; but on this balmy afternoon Henry and Catherine were undertaking their royal duties in the throne room. Normally, she and Jakob would need to be announced.

However, Jakob had a different plan.

Beefeater Henry was announced. Once his audience commenced, he assured the queen that Lady Avery was in excellent health and doing very well. Jakob and Avery waited outside the door, listening for the perfect moment to make their surprise appearance.

"Are you quite certain, sir? You saw her and spoke with her?" Catherine's voice was heavy with concern.

"Go on," Jakob whispered, his eyes twinkling with mischief. "I shall join you in a moment."

Avery dipped a quick nod, stepped through the doorway, and walked past the bemused herald.

"My queen, why would you doubt this fine gentleman's word?" she asked, beaming and striding forward. "He has proved quite trustworthy thus far."

"*Averia!*" Catherine jumped from her throne without any regard for either king or crowd, and hurried through the room to meet her. "My dearest friend!"

Catherine gathered Avery into a tight, sobbing hug. "I cannot believe you are here. I have missed you so."

Avery tried to speak past her own tears, but Catherine's emotional reaction was much more extreme than she expected.

"I am so sorry I was not here, Cathy," she whispered.

"It was not your fault." Catherine sniffed wetly. "None of it was." After another moment, the queen loosened her grip and stepped back, wiping her eyes. "Have you returned to stay?"

Avery wished at that moment that there had been no letter from Arendal—and yet it was that crucial letter that put her life-changing events into motion. Events which resulted in her standing here, married, in the Tudor court today.

"Not just yet, I am sorry to say." Avery's heart started to pound with anticipation, sending blood rushing in her ears. "I must go to Norway first."

Catherine shook her head in confusion. "Why? Has something happened to Sir Hansen?"

Avery grasped that question as the perfect introduction to her news. "Yes. I am afraid it has."

"What has happened to Hansen?" King Henry had come forward from his throne and now stood behind the queen's shoulder.

Avery tried not to give too much away with her expression, all the while hoping Jakob would catch her cue to enter the room. "I am afraid he has succumbed…"

Catherine's eyes rounded. "To what?"

Jakob's deep voice sounded from behind her. "To marriage,

your Highnesses."

Avery's relieved grin returned as the royal couple stared past her toward Jakob in stunned surprise.

"Marriage to whom?" Henry demanded as Jakob approached.

Avery turned her brief regard to her husband. The Nordic knight was smiling like a lunatic.

She faced the king again and curtsied. "To me, your Graces."

Catherine gasped. "Do you speak truly, *Averia?* You have married the Norseman?"

"I have. We were married in Barcelona Cathedral two days before joining this man—" Avery gestured toward the other Henry in the room, "—on his journey back to you."

Jakob bowed to the pair of sovereigns. "We believed that appearing before you was the best way to assure both your Graces of the lady's good health and well-being."

Avery grabbed Catherine's hands, deciding to broach her concern forthwith. "Are you angry with me?"

Catherine shook her head as fresh tears filled her eyes. "As you have reminded me many times, you are not my subject. On the contrary, I could not be happier."

Avery kissed Catherine's damp cheek. "Thank you, your Highness."

King Henry extended his hand to Jakob. "Congratulations are in order, Hansen."

As Jakob bowed again and the men shook hands, Avery was reminded once more of the striking similarity in their looks.

"There is another reason to celebrate," she said. "Today is Jakob's thirty-third birthday."

Henry laughed and clapped his hands together. "It would seem that our supper tonight shall be a triple celebration! The marriage, the birthday, and the return of our friends to our bosom."

Avery raised her relieved gaze to Jakob's happy countenance.

He winked.

§ § §

"I shall never eat again," Jakob moaned. He was stretched out on the large bed in Avery's restored chamber. "And as much as I desired to make passionate love with you this evening, I find myself immobilized by the king's generous and forced hospitality."

Avery sat on the bed beside him, brushing her dark brown hair; Jakob watched the candlelight slither up and down its glossy length. He reached out to comb his fingers through the thick strands, loving the silken way they felt against his skin.

"I must admit, husband, that I am overdone as well." Avery yawned. "And I anticipate sleeping for so many hours, that I may not wake until noon."

Jakob chuckled. "Even so, I may not eat again until supper."

Avery set her brush on the table near the bed. "Make room for me, please. Your length has claimed all corners of the bed."

"The luxury of so much room has made me selfish, I admit it." Jakob withdrew his limbs and slid to the far side. "After weeks in a ship's bunk shorter than I by half a foot, I covet the ability to lie down without bending my legs."

Avery snuggled next to him, and he rested his cheek against her head. Her hair smelled of roses.

"Our first obstacle has been met and conquered," he murmured.

"Um hm."

"How long must we politely remain in England?"

He felt Avery tense against him. "We only arrived this very afternoon."

"I do not suggest that we leave on the morrow." He gave her scalp a conciliatory kiss. "But I do not wish to dally more than a week."

His wife's body relaxed a little. "Will we sail from London?"

Jakob wondered about that himself. Henry originally said he might be willing to transport Jakob to England's northernmost port, so that his ship's voyage to Denmark might be shortened. But now Jakob had Avery's comfort to consider as well.

He countered with, "What is the northernmost port in England?"

Avery pondered that for a moment. "Newcastle-Upon-Tyne."

"How far is that?"

"Four days' journey, I believe."

Jakob sighed. "I will look at a map tomorrow, but I do not believe those four days across land will not save us as much time as

Kris Tualla

I had originally hoped."

Avery tilted her head to look at him, her dark eyes glittering in the pale candlelight. "So you believe that sailing from London directly to Arendal to be the quickest way to travel?"

"It seems that may be so." Jakob draped his arm over Avery, holding her close. "Let us get some sleep, in the event Henry's celebratory mood continues on the morrow."

Avery kissed his hand. "Happy birthday, husband."

Jakob smiled.

Facing his family with this beautiful Spanish noblewoman on his arm as his wife was certainly going to soften the impact of anything they might throw at him.

Chapter Twenty-Two

April 20, 1519

Henry sat in his private meeting room with Charles Brandon, the Duke of Suffolk, and offered Jakob a glass of wine.

"Yes. Thank you, your Grace." Jakob felt safe in this interview because he owed King Henry nothing.

In fact, the opposite was true.

A servant poured goblets of wine for the three men before backing through the door and closing it. Jakob turned curious attention toward the two highest ranking men in England.

Brandon spoke first. "I assume you know what has transpired with the queen since we saw you last."

Jakob dipped his chin. "My wife allowed me to read the letter, which the queen wrote to her. I offer my deepest condolences, your Highness."

Henry took a long draught of his wine before acknowledging Jakob's words. "You were not here to play your part. I suppose the discovery was inevitable."

A shock jolted Jakob. His gaze shot from Henry to Brandon and back. "You do not hold *me* accountable for the miscarriage..."

"No. Of course not." The Duke injected, gesturing with his goblet. "You do have your own king to serve."

"And yet, I served King Henry quite well when I was here, your Grace." Jakob plunged forward, not wishing to lose ground. "I even saved his life, when my own was put at mortal risk."

Brandon nodded. "You did dispose of the assassin in a quick and quiet manner, and for that the king is very grateful."

Henry pinned Jakob's gaze. "Bessie is with child. My child. She will deliver in two months."

Jakob's mouth fell open, though he was unsure whether congratulations were appropriate. "Will—will you claim the babe?"

"If it is a boy." Henry sipped his wine before continuing. "That is what I promised Bessie, in exchange for her silence on the other matter."

"Bastard girls are not important," Jakob observed. "They have no claim or power."

"No, they do not." Henry drained his cup and held it toward Brandon. The duke refilled the chalice and returned it to the king.

Henry took another drink before asking, "Please explain to me why did Sir Bethington not travel back to court with you."

Jakob relaxed. This was an easy question. "Because the Order was still in session when I left Barcelona."

Henry stared at him from under a lowered brow. "And why did you leave the Order before it adjourned?"

Jakob felt a punch in the gut at saying the words aloud once more. He pulled a steadying breath. "I received word that my father is dying. My mother asked that I return home."

Henry nodded slowly. "And Christian granted your request?"

This was going to be tricky. Jakob needed to be honest, while still explaining his decision in a logical and complimentary light.

"I did not ask him, your Grace. It was my best judgment that I remove myself—and as a result, my king—from the current discussion at the Order. So I sent him an explanation of my actions before I left."

Henry leaned forward in his chair. "And what discussion was that?"

Jakob was on solid ground once more. "France and Spain were in disagreement and pressing for every delegate to align with one or the other of them concerning the Ottoman question."

He spread his hands helplessly. "Being so far distant, Denmark and Norway cannot help. For that reason, I did not believe it wise for me to make enemies with either king on Christian's behalf. So, I explained to him that my father is dying and I could leave without my absence reflecting poorly on him."

Henry's eyes narrowed. "What about Bethington?"

Jakob threw Percy the credit for his own observation. "He quoted your Treaty of London, your Highness. Because Spain was not yet invaded, France was not yet bound to provide an army."

"He is a good man." The king leaned back, relieved. "I chose well, it would seem."

Jakob gave a hint of a smile. "Yes, your Grace."

"But your father is truly dying?" Brandon asked.

"Or he is already dead. Yes." Jakob felt an unexpected surge of regret. Perhaps because he was heading toward Arendal, the guard on his emotions was lowering. "My mother's letter was sent over six months ago, now. Even though I left Barcelona less than one month after I received it, I do not know what I shall find once I arrive in Arendal."

Henry crossed himself. "My condolences, Hansen."

"Why did you not leave immediately?" Brandon's mouth quirked; Jakob guessed the duke had intuited the reason.

Jakob grinned at him, glad for yet another shift in their conversation. "Banns must be read for three weeks."

"About that…" Henry slapped his own thigh in disbelief. "How did you manage to win the lady? She was untouchable."

Jakob wondered if Henry knew as much about Avery as Catherine did. No matter, all was out in the open now. He waggled a finger at the king and his duke.

"She *was* untouchable—until her husband in Barcelona finally died of syphilis."

The surprised reactions of both men proved Catherine's careful protection of Avery's secret. "She was *married?*" they exclaimed in tandem.

"The day I arrived in Barcelona, the man was being buried."

"Barcelona?" Henry frowned at Brandon. "I thought she was from Toledo."

Over more glasses of wine, Jakob regaled the men with the tale of Avery's unhappy circumstances in Barcelona and the explanation of her assumed identity in London.

"The queen was instrumental in saving Lady Avery's life, you see," Jakob offered, hoping that King Henry truly did. "By offering her sanctuary, Avery was removed from the abuses of her husband, retaliation for not providing him an heir, and the mortal results of his careless life."

Henry paled. Of a sudden, Jakob realized the similarities between Avery and Catherine's situations. His mouth went dry.

"And how *did* she escape?" the young king growled.

Jakob swallowed a gulp of wine, wondering how to extricate himself from the awkward blunder. "She outlined her circumstances to Catherine, who invited her to court. A priest in Barcelona helped her escape, and he kept her secret until it was time for her to return."

"Was she able to salvage anything of the estate?" Brandon was clearly redirecting the discussion.

Jakob would thank him later. "Yes." He then outlined, in distracting detail, Avery's brilliant handling of her situation so that she was finally free to remarry and leave Spain.

When he was finished, Henry shook his head. "In addition to leaving the order early, you did not ask your king for permission to marry, either?"

Jakob flashed a contrite expression. "No, your Grace."

"What do you expect him to do when you return to København?" Brandon's brow wrinkled. "You *are* planning to return to København, are you not?"

"Yes, your Grace. After I am finished in Arendal." Jakob shrugged. "I do not know what his highness will do with me. But he has every reason to dismiss me."

"Yes, he does." The duke rose to his feet, signaling the end of the interview. "Thank you for your time."

Jakob stood as well.

"Thank you, your Graces." He bowed and backed away the appropriate distance before straightening to leave. He gave once last glance in Henry's direction.

Henry was staring at him, his expression hard as marble.

§ § §

"I do not know why I still cry." Catherine dabbed her eyes. "Five months have passed since I lost the babe."

"When we were last together, we were anticipating the happy arrival of a son." Avery handed the queen a cup of wine. "It is because I am returned that your grief is freshened. I am so very sorry for that."

Catherine shook her head slowly. "No, *Averia*. Do not be sorry. It is a great comfort to me that you are here now."

Avery winced. "I only wish that I could stay longer."

Catherine's hand stilled, the wine cup not yet to her lips. "How long will you bide here?"

"We must be gone in a week." Avery heaved a shaky sigh. "My husband's mother hopes he will arrive before his father passes."

Catherine frowned. "Might he have passed already?"

"Yes. But there is no way to know."

"Your husband." One side of the queen's mouth lifted under her sad eyes. "Hearing you say such a thing, and to be happy about it, lifts my spirits. And God Himself knows how much I need that."

As Catherine drank deeply from her cup, Avery asked, "Is there another matter that troubles you?"

Catherin lowered the goblet and stared at its blood-red contents. When she finally spoke her voice was so low, that it took Avery a moment to fully understand what the queen had said.

"Bessie is with child."

Avery gasped. "Oh, Cathy!"

Catherine's eyes lifted to hers. "She is seven months gone. The king is understandably thrilled."

"Is she still at court?" Avery could not imagine what a daily horror that would be for her friend.

"Heavens, no! I removed that trollop the moment I knew." Catherine made a disgusted moue. "But Henry objected, and only agreed to have her live elsewhere, and not be completely dishonored."

"Is he... are they..." Avery could not finish the question, but Catherine's stricken expression gave her the answer.

"Yes, he visits her regularly. And though I am certain she pleasures him, I doubt that he lays with her. He still believes it may hurt the child, no matter who the mother is." Catherine took another long draught of wine, then handed the empty cup to Avery.

Avery walked to the sideboard and refilled the goblet. She had no words with which to comfort Catherine. Henry was the king and he would selfishly do what he pleased, without regard for any mere woman's feelings—whether the woman in question was a queen or trollop. His drive to father a male child consumed him.

When she gave the glass back to Catherine, the queen grabbed her hand. "Pray for my darling Mary, Avery. I am thirty-three years old. I know I will never bear another child. She must become queen after her father."

Avery lifted Catherine's hand to her lips and kissed it. "May God hear the cries of your heart, my dearest friend, and heed them."

"Thank you, my friend." The queen dried her cheeks and straightened her shoulders. "Now, tell me what happened with your ships."

§ § §

Avery and Jakob entered the dining room to an entirely different response than the previous night. Yester eve, their presence alone was enough of a surprise, let alone the fact that the Ice Maiden of the Tudor court had married.

Not only that, but after spurning every nobleman who had attempted to win her throughout her nine years in court, Avery had chosen an unknown foreigner over all of them. To further fan the flames of gossip, the man did not even own a respectable title, but was a mere knight and far below her station.

Avery's true name and title, Señora Averia Galaviz de Mendoza, Vizcondesa de Catalonya, sent waves of auditory shock through yester eve's assemblage, as stares ricocheted, heads touched, and questions were murmured.

As much as they could, she and Jakob explained what had occurred, and the reason for Avery's deceptions. Thankfully, King Henry's desire to be the center of attention kept pulling the crowd's apparent attention back to him. But Avery saw the continual glances and whispers.

Tonight, after the members of the court had a full day to discuss, form opinions, and conjure more questions, Avery and

Jakob's reception was less shocked and more curious.

And, judging by the expressions on the gathered faces, that curiosity was of a much more friendly nature than last night's attention. Perhaps it even held a touch of admiration.

Jakob flashed a crooked smile at Avery as he answered a young woman's enquiry. "Sir Bethington will return soon, I am certain. The death of my father necessitated my leaving Barcelona before the Order adjourned."

Though Jakob truncated his story, Avery approved. The true explanation of his exit was complicated enough, that to repeat it throughout the evening would quickly grow tiresome.

"Oh! My condolences, sir." The pretty blonde curtsied before moving away.

Avery rose on her toes to speak in Jakob's ear. "Percy will return as an unmarried man, will he not?"

Jakob chuckled. "I believe Percy will die in his dotage as an unmarried man."

"Sir Hansen!"

Avery and Jakob turned toward the voice.

John de Vere, the Earl of Oxford was working his way through the crowd. "Or should I call you your Lordship, now that you have married so well?" he asked when he reached them. He winked and extended his hand. "Congratulations."

Jakob shook the man's hand. "Many thanks, my lord." He turned and addressed Avery. "What do you say to that?"

Avery gave an apologetic shrug. "Both in Spain and in England, titles pass from men to women, but not in the other direction, I am afraid."

"So I am saved," Jakob teased. "I am freed from convention and may remain as I am."

De Vere wagged his head. "I do not know how you won the lady, good sir, but you have the admiration of the entire court, titled or not!"

Two ornately attired men and a heavily bejeweled woman, none of whom Avery recognized, now stood close enough to overhear the conversation. One of the men directed his attention toward Jakob.

"Is it true, Sir Hansen, that you have gone into the shipping business?"

Jakob rested his hand on Avery's lower back. "You have been misinformed, I am afraid. That would be my wife."

The trio regarded Avery, brows spiking in either surprise or disapproval. Until someone spoke, it was impossible to discern their collective mood.

"Lady Avery?" the man blurted.

Jakob straightened and glared down his nose at the man. "Yes. The lady has made several wise decisions concerning her dead husband's estate, assuring herself additional income for life."

"I do not believe we have been introduced," Avery interjected.

With a furious blush, the man bowed. "Forgive me, Lady Avery. I am James Winthrop, Baron of Wingate. May I present my brother, Robert and his wife, Margaret."

Avery gave them each a barely polite smile. "My pleasure. Now if you will excuse us, I believe supper is about to be served."

Jakob immediately offered his elbow, which Avery accepted. As they moved toward the opening doorway she muttered under her breath, "Pompous ass."

Jakob coughed a hearty laugh.

April 26, 1519

Zurina curtsied, her eyes pooling with tears. "I shall miss you, my lady," she said in Spanish. "It has been my honor to serve you these past few months."

Avery grabbed the maid's hands and answered in kind. "Your service was invaluable to me, Zurina. I do not know how I might have survived without your loyalty and your compassionate assistance."

She wiped her eyes. "Thank you for your kind words."

Avery squeezed her hands before letting go. "Safe journey."

Zurina turned away and climbed the ramp to the ship.

Emily stepped up beside Avery. "She may be sorry to lose you, my lady, but I am very glad to have you returned to us."

Avery regarded the English ladies' maid who had served her for so many years. "And I am glad to be returned, even for this short time."

Emily regarded her with wide eyes. "What will Norway be like?"

Avery shrugged, a twinge of apprehension snaking through her gut. "I cannot answer that, I am afraid. But we leave on the morrow, and soon we shall discover that for ourselves."

Chapter Twenty-Three

May 20, 1519
Arendal, Norway

The last time Jakob saw Arendal, he was barely seventeen and escaping his father's dictum. That was sixteen years ago and Jakob wondered if anything about the small seaside village might have changed.

Their ship sailed past scattered rocky islands, inhabited only by gulls and other seabirds, which crowded Arendal's outlet to the North Sea. Near to the pier, a cluster of buildings gradually grew visible in the hazy morning. They surrounded a tall stave church made of piled logs, which anchored the town.

When Jakob made his furtive exit at dawn, he did not look back as the ship glided away toward the open waters. Now, watching his childhood home slowly appear through the fog, he felt as if this was one more of the many dreams—nightmares?—which haunted him on nights he took the opium for pain.

This time it felt real and yet not real at the same time.

Avery's hand slipped into his. "How are you faring, husband?"

Jakob tipped his face down to look into her eyes. "I am not certain."

She nodded. "I understand. I felt odd when I returned to

Barcelona."

"The question I struggle with, is how should I feel?" Jakob returned his gaze to the rapidly approaching town. "Should I feel joy at returning? Or apprehensive about my reception?"

"Both, I would imagine." She gave his hand a little squeeze. "At the least, you are assured that your mother will be glad to see you."

He wagged his head. "But will my older brother Johan be glad? This I cannot know. And will my younger brother Saxby be here— or did he become a priest after all?"

Avery bit her lower lip, her eyes fixed on the town. Of course, she had far fewer answers as a foreigner than he would as a returning resident.

Jakob sighed and turned his regard in the same direction. "The question which looms largest, of course, is whether my father still lives."

Avery squeezed his hand again, remaining motionless by his side as the ship eased against the pier. A small crew of deckhands grabbed ropes from the ship and tied them to the iron moorings. Soon after, the planked walkway was pushed over the edge of the ship, hooked onto the ship's deck railing and resting on the dock below.

Jakob remained rooted in his spot, ignoring the flurry of pier activity, and examined the town for changes. He saw none which were immediately apparent. Arendal appeared as it always had: a neat, secure fishing village tucked onto Norway's southern coast. A mere ninety miles over the sea to Denmark.

The thought of Denmark brought another flood of considerations to Jakob's mind. He pushed them into a mental cupboard for now and locked the door.

First his family. Then the king.

"I am going to see to Warrior," he said of a sudden. "I shall meet you on the dock."

Avery nodded, her brow pinched in concern as he walked away from her.

A portion of the deck was being opened like horizontal shutters, allowing the larger items—and animals—to be raised in slings from the hold below. Jakob and Askel made certain that Warrior was made as safe and comfortable as possible during their voyages. Askel was with the stallion even now, helping to harness and blindfold the horse for his airborne transport to solid ground.

His destrier turned out to be an easier sailor than Jakob, thankfully, and was unperturbed by the rocking of the ship. The horse did grow anxious as he was lifted by the sling, however, but that ordeal was a humanely brief one.

Jakob hurried down the planks to comfort the destrier when his hooves hit the wooden dock.

"There you are, my strong boy," Jakob cooed as he removed the blindfold. "You are on solid ground once more, my friend."

Warrior tossed his head and shook his mane, snorting his irritation with the indignity of his recent treatment. Jakob offered a little apple he had stored in his pocket and Warrior snatched it from his palm. The horse examined his new surroundings with interest as he chewed.

Jakob patted the animal's neck. "We shall ride into an unknown battle today, my friend. I hope you are prepared."

Warrior head-butted him in response.

§ § §

Avery and Emily stood on the pier and watched as their trunks were loaded onto a rented wagon. Askel scurried around the dock, assuring that not one of their last worldly possessions went missing.

Jakob waited with Warrior, who only wore a bridle. He planned to ride the stallion bare-backed, and lead the way to Hansen Hall.

Avery looked toward the bluff which lay just west of the village center. Jakob had pointed out the barely visible stone structure on its apex as they sailed inward, but Avery could not see any of it clearly. She trusted his explanation that the path to the ancient homestead was about a mile in length, and uphill most of the way.

After three-quarters of an hour, Avery and Emily were handed into a small carriage. Askel gave Jakob a leg up to mount his huge destrier, before settling himself onto the seat of the wagon beside the driver. When Jakob gave the nod to start moving, Avery saw the grim set of his jaw and his eyes narrowed in the pale gray day.

The little parade—knight, carriage, and wagon—made its

unheralded way to Jakob's family estate. All the way, Avery prayed silently for her husband, pleading with God to protect him and his secretly tender heart from unkind actions on the part of his family members.

And please let Jakob be kind as well.

Avery knew her husband's guard was up and internally fortified. Accustomed to being prepared for the worst, she hoped he would not be so overly wary as to misunderstand any attempts at reconciliation, no matter how awkward those attempts might prove to be.

She wondered what sort of woman his mother would be. Bergdis was strong enough to defy her husband in secret; but if Fafnir still lived, how would she react once she presented the defiant son at his father's bedside?

Hansen Hall was suddenly in front of them. Dominated by a round tower built of rough stones, its turreted top stood three stories over the road, and five over the empty moat that dipped around it. There were no windows in the tower, only the vertical slits which allowed archers to defend the inhabitants.

Extending off one side of the tower was a two-story structure, built a bit more recently of quarried stone. This addition had glass windows, leaded in a multitude of small diamond-shaped panes. Peeking over the flat roof of the medieval façade were several tall chimneys.

Through the carriage's open windows, Avery breathed in the damp tang of the North Sea. Over the cries of single-minded gulls, she could hear waves splashing softly below, and wondered how far down the water was.

"Shall we go on, my lord?" Askel prompted after the group had halted for several minutes.

Jakob startled, turning dark eyes toward the valet. "Yes. Of course,"

Their horses' hooves crunched up the drive made of crushed white stone and shells. The main entrance was centered in the medieval section, in an arched alcove at the end of the moat bridge. A heavy wooden door stood under a carved "H" which had, on either side, sculpted friezes. With Thor on one side, and Christ on the other, they proved that Christianity had reached Norway several centuries earlier.

Jakob swung his leg over the stallion and dismounted. Askel hopped down from the wagon and hurried to take the animal by the reins. The carriage door opened, and Avery was handed down by the driver.

Jakob stepped to her side and she looped her arm through his. Together, they climbed the steps to the massive portal. Avery noticed that the stones were starting to wear down in the middle, the strongest proof that this was indeed an ancient homestead. Jakob grabbed the round iron knocker and thrust it against the plank, the deep sound echoing beyond.

§ § §

Jakob did not recognize the man that opened the door. His gaze slid past Jakob to the assemblage in the courtyard, widened under a furrowed brow, then returned to his.

"May I help you?"

Jakob had settled into his imposing knight's stance before he knocked on the door. Now he looked down his nose at the shorter man and said the only thing which made sense.

"I am Jakob Petter Hansen. Is my mother at home?"

The man blanched. "A moment please."

And he shut the door.

Jakob snorted a chuckle. What else might he do?

"There is no sign of a house in mourning," Avery offered. "Perhaps we have arrived in time."

"Either that—" Jakob coughed and cleared his throat, trying to dislodge his heart from its unfortunate new location. "—or my father has already been dead these six months."

The door flew open once more, and Jakob stared down into his mother's eyes. Their fading blue was ringed in white, and her once-red hair heavily streaked with white, but her astonished smile was still the same.

"Jakob!" she sobbed.

Jakob enveloped her in his arms, surprised at how much smaller she was than he remembered. "I came home, Mother," he murmured. "Just as you asked."

For several minutes Jakob was only aware of his mother's relief, so strong that it suffused his core with momentary peace. If only this was the end of their visit and not the beginning, he could be wholly happy to have made the journey.

As her sobs and her grasp eased, Jakob took a small step back. His heart pounded with renewed concern as he asked, "And Father?"

Bergdis wiped her nose on a small square of linen. "He lives. Barely. He has not spoken for three days, so the end is very near."

Jakob nodded, glad that he arrived before his father passed, even if he could not converse with the man. "I came as soon as I was able. But I was in Barcelona, in Spain, on the king's business when your letter found me."

Bergdis gaped up at him. "What were you doing there?"

Jakob smiled a little and extended his hand to Avery, who stood behind him. "Getting married, for one."

As his Spanish wife stepped forward, his mother gasped. "You are married at last? Your wife is so beautiful!"

Avery blushed. "Thank you, Lady Hansen. And now I see how Jakob is so beautiful, also," she managed in Norsk.

Silenced for a moment by Avery's statement, Bergdis blinked. "You speak Norsk?"

She grinned. "A very little."

Behind them the wagon master cleared his throat. Obviously the man had other things to do with his time besides witness this extended introduction.

"Shall I see to the luggage, my lord?" Askel asked.

Snapped back into her role by the valet's question, Bergdis Hansen began to bark orders. She herded Jakob and Avery inside and turned them toward the large gathering room. She directed her manservant where to settle the couple and put Emily and Askel into his care.

"And bring refreshments," she called after him.

Jakob escorted Avery to a cushioned bench he knew well, standing in the same spot, near the massive hearth, where it had rested when he left. He waited until his mother's attention was returned to them before enquiring about his brothers.

"Johan is meeting with a merchant this morning, but I expect him to return after midday." Bergdis sat on a wooden chair, which she slid closer to her son.

"Is he married?"

His mother sobered. "He was. He lost her after the birth of their third child, Torgild, who is now eight. But he also has a fourteen-year-old son and heir named Ragnar, and a twelve-year-old daughter named Birgit, who has just joined Saxby in the service of the church."

Jakob smiled at that. "So Saxby did become a priest, just as he wished to?"

Bergdis nodded. "After you disappeared, your father gave way. After all, he had promised God one of his sons and Saxby was the only son remaining."

"I am sorry, Mother." Jakob looked at the clean stone floor beneath his boots. "I was still a boy and I did not know what else to do."

"I forgave you, Jakob. And long before I forgave your father, I am afraid." She sighed. "If he had not been so stubborn, I would not have lost you."

He looked up at her again. "But one of us needed to go to Denmark. Father's situation demanded it."

"And yet, I could have written to you. You might have been allowed to visit. And once the debt was satisfied, you might have come back."

Jakob knew in his heart that he never would have returned to Arendal to stay—there was no place for him here, other than acting as chamberlain to Johan. Yet the wistful tone in his mother's voice twisted his core.

"I am here now, Mamma. Let us enjoy this visit. I do not know when I will be able to return after this."

§ § §

Avery watched the exchange between Jakob and his mother, understanding enough of their words to follow their tender conversation. She tried to imagine what Bergdis' life had been like these last sixteen years, unable to communicate with her adored son, and blaming her own husband for causing the rift. The letters Jakob sent her were secreted away somewhere in this house, a treasured connection to a boy who was lost to her.

And now returned.

"Please say again, slowly," Avery replied to a question she only half heard.

Bergdis smiled softly. "Jakob says he met you in London. But you are from Spain?"

"Yes. I served Queen Catherine. She is my dear friend from we were children." Avery waved her hand and corrected herself, "From *when* we were children."

"Your Norsk is not bad," Bergdis complimented. "How did you learn?"

Avery grinned. "I teach Jakob Spanish for Barcelona, and he makes me learn Norsk."

Bergdis addressed Jakob. "Why were you in Barcelona?"

Avery felt Jakob straighten with pride beside her. "I am King Christian's most trusted knight, and so I was sent as his representative to the gathering there of the Order of the Golden Fleece."

A servant girl entered the room with a tray of cheeses and a pitcher of ale. Avery shooed her away and then served Jakob and Bergdis without trying to follow their quickly-spoken conversation. She caught enough words to be able to follow the gist of Jakob's narrative and Bergdis' questions, to know what the son was telling the mother.

Only when the story reached her handling of the ships, did their sentences slow and their gazes move to her.

"So now you are a merchant yourself?" Bergdis sounded impressed, though her expression evinced her doubts.

"Yes." Avery's tone held no apology. "I saved some dignity, and some hope, from the men who try to take all from me."

Jakob grinned at her. "I cannot think of another woman who could think and act so quickly and be so correct in her decisions."

Bergdis stared at her son. "So you married three weeks later, and then sailed immediately for Arendal?"

"We traveled immediately to London first," Jakob corrected. "And after a few days we sailed to Arendal from there."

"We are glad to arrive in time, Lady Hansen," Avery offered.

Bergdis reached out a hand and laid it over Avery's. Her skin was cool and dry. "Please, call me Bergdis. May I call you Avery?"

"Of course." Avery flashed a quick smile. "Or daughter."

Bergdis' hand flew to her mouth, then moved to her throat. "May I? I have no daughters now and no hope for any more."

"I would be honored, Bergdis." Then Avery asked the question that Jakob had not yet voiced. "When will my husband be able to see his father?"

§ § §

Jakob could not decide whether to chastise Avery for asking the question, or fall to his knees and thank her. Both reactions held equal merit.

His mother rose slowly to her feet, rubbing her hands in a nervous response which he recognized with a shock of recollection.

"I do not suppose anything will be gained by postponing that moment." Her eyes darted around the room as if searching for an excuse. "That is the reason you have come."

Jakob stood and pulled one of his mother's frantic hands from its nervous task and clasped it between his. He waited until she calmed herself somewhat and looked up at him, before he spoke.

"We came because you asked us to, Mamma," he said gently. "We were not certain Father would still be alive, and even so, we both left our duties and traveled two months to see you."

Something about his demeanor seemed to ease his mother. Jakob let go of her hands and reached for Avery's. "Go on. We will follow right behind you."

Jakob watched his mother's back as she resolutely climbed the stone steps to the second floor. "How long has he been ill?"

Her answer tumbled back at him. "More than a year, I think. I was not sure for the first several months. Until his cough did not improve, no matter what we tried."

Jakob felt Avery's hand on his arm. Its warm, steady pressure seemed to anchor him as he imagined what his father used to look like—and prepared himself for what the man might look like now.

Even so, his dire preparations fell woefully short.

Fafnir Hansen was nothing more than a skin-covered skull

topping a pile of blankets, which showed little evidence of a body beneath.

Jakob stared, watching for a sign of life. "How is he alive?"

Bergdis crossed the room where his father lay—the outer room of his parents' apartment—and touched his forehead. "There is still warmth."

Jakob stumbled forward and dropped to his knees beside the cot. "Is he aware of anything?"

"I cannot know. But I will tell you this." She rested a trembling hand on Jakob's shoulder. "When he took his worst turn, I finally told him that I wrote to you and asked you to come."

Jakob did not take his eyes from his father, watching the man's chest rise and fall in slow, miniscule breaths. "Was he angry?"

"Yes," she admitted. "But I think he was angry with himself."

Jakob looked up at his mother. "Why do you say that?"

Her brow twitched. "Because he has not yet died, though I cannot imagine how he survives."

Avery knelt beside him. "Does she believe he willed himself to remain alive until you arrived?" she asked him in English.

Jakob translated the question for his mother.

Bergdis lifted one shoulder in a sad shrug. "Perhaps."

"Talk to him, Jakob," Avery urged. Her dark eyes met his in wide-eyed intensity. "Take ahold of his hand and say all of the things you need to say."

Jakob felt his cheeks flush, and he glanced at his mother before returning his regard to his wife. "I don't..."

"Say it in English. Or in Spanish. Your mother will not understand you." She laid a hand on his thigh. "This is your chance to forgive him. He has waited for you."

Jakob looked at his father's paper-thin eyelids and sparse fringe of white lashes. All of the man's veins were blue, as if his blood had already run cold. "I do not think he can hear me."

Avery squeezed his thigh. "Does that matter?"

No. I do not suppose it does.

Jakob slid his hand under the blanket and linked his fingers between his father's cold and bony ones. He spoke in a mixture of languages, saying the first word that came to his mind for each of the ideas he wanted to express.

"I am sorry, Pappa, but I had to leave. You were too stubborn to see what was best for your own sons, for Saxby and me. But I forgave you this, and I tried for years to make you understand that."

Jakob glanced at his mother. Tears streamed down her pale cheeks as she stood rooted in her spot. The pressure of Avery's warm hand on his injured thigh encouraged him to continue. He stared again at his father's waxy face.

"And even though you never read my letters, Pappa, I want you to know that I always strove to make you proud. To bring you honor, as your son."

Jakob sniffed and wiped his eyes on his sleeve. "And I succeeded very well, Pappa. I succeeded *very* well. I only wish you could have shared my successes with me. This is my life's single greatest regret."

With a jolt, Jakob realized that was true; this regret was much deeper than Uma and the fire ever could be. And when her parents turned away from her, he now realized, their rejection mimicked his father's rejection of him, and that was why it affected him so deeply.

But that other rejection ended with the death of their daughter. Their relationship could never, ever be restored, and that was a foundational component of his own pain and guilt.

Why had he not seen that?

Because I never understood the truth of my own loss until now.

Jakob lifted his father's hand off the mattress and pulled it out from under the blankets. He pressed those chilled, knobby fingers against his lips and kissed them.

"I love you, Pappa," he whispered in Norsk. "I always have, and I always will."

Without warning, his father convulsed, his chest expanding in a sudden intake of air. A quick whoosh of expulsion was followed by a long, slow wheeze.

Fafnir Hansen did not breathe again.

Chapter Twenty-Four

Neither Bergdis, Jakob, nor Avery moved. The only sound in the room was a chorus of wet sniffles, muted by either a sleeve, or crumpled squares of damp linen.

Bergdis crossed herself. "I do not know what you said to him, son. But it is clear to me that, whatever it was, he waited to hear it."

Avery lifted teary eyes to Jakob's mother. "I am sorry for your loss, Bergdis."

The older woman wiped her eyes. "It is a blessing to see him finally go. He has been that miserable for these many months."

Avery leaned forward and looked at Jakob's wet, ruddy face. "Shall I leave you alone for a time?"

He closed his eyes and nodded.

Avery climbed to her feet and took Bergdis by the hand. "Do you need to prepare for to bury?" she managed in Norsk.

Bergdis turned toward the doorway. "No, my dear. All the details have been arranged long ago. I only need to notify the priest."

Avery glanced over her shoulder. "Did he have last rites?"

"Several times." Bergdis led her into the hallway. "And unless he was still capable of having impure thoughts, he has not sinned since any of them."

The women walked to the stairs and descended side-by-side.

Avery felt a shift in her new mother-in-law's mood. Her step was lighter and the lines which webbed her face moments ago were easing.

"I will send my man, Karsten, for the priest and the *begravelsesbyrå*," Bergdis said as she led Avery toward the back of the house. "Would you care for more ale? Wine perhaps?"

"No, thank you. I am well. What is *begravelsesbyrå?*"

"The man who makes the casket and digs the grave." Bergdis waved one hand. "The casket is waiting, of course, but the grave is not yet dug in the churchyard."

Avery followed Bergdis into the kitchen and waited while she gave Karsten her instructions. Then the older woman lit a small lamp and faced Avery again.

Her mouth curved in a sad and wistful smile. "Come with me, Avery. I want to show you something."

As Bergdis led her down a windowless passage on the ground floor, Avery noticed that once inside the manor the transition from the ninth-century tower to the fourteenth-century hall was not as disjointed as it was on the exterior.

Bergdis stopped outside an unusual door. Set deep into the wall, there were carvings around it depicting Christ and the Stations of the Cross. Bergdis turned the handle, the clank of its latch echoing down the hallway.

Beyond the door was a small chapel. The faintest smell of rot underlay the cold, damp odor of stone. Wooden benches sat in perpetual formation; faithful, waiting.

"You have a church," Avery whispered.

Bergdis carried the lamp to the front of the little chapel and pointed at the gravestones set in the floor by the altar. "He built it."

"Rydar Martin Petter-Edvard Hansen, born 1324, died 1401," Avery read out loud.

"He came home from Greenland after the Black Death," Bergdis explained. "No one from his family survived, so he reclaimed the land and reestablished the family."

Avery read the inscription on the stone set alongside his. "Belovd Wyfe, Grier MacInnes Hansen, born 1328, Scotland, died 1401."

Though the floor was paved with gravestones, these two were

the oldest graves in the chapel.

"They had seven children, five that survived infancy." Bergdis lifted the lamp and pointed to engraved stones along the outer wall. "Four sons and a daughter. They are all there, along with their wives."

Avery gestured at the other engraved markers. "All are the Hansens who lived here after?"

"Yes. But as you can see, this is not a very large room. Now my husband's family must either pave the hallway, or bury their dead in the churchyard." Bergdis set the lamp on the carved marble altarpiece, stepped behind it, and squatted down. "But I thought this would be the perfect hiding place."

Avery leaned over to watch as her mother-in-law reached inside the nook which would normally hold the Host and pulled out a wooden box. She looked up at Avery and smiled.

"Do you know what I have in here?"

Avery's heart lurched. "Jakob's letters?"

"Yes." Bergdis handed the surprisingly heavy box to Avery before grasping the altar for support to regain her feet. "We shall take this to the great hall, where the light is good."

Avery carried the box and followed Bergdis. The chapel door was closed and latched behind them before Bergdis dampened the lamp.

"Thank you, you show me this," Avery said, pointing at the chapel door.

Bergdis waved one hand. "This house will never be Jakob's, but he is a Hansen, and so are you, now. I hope you will always feel welcomed here, and that this house will hold no more secrets."

In the hall, Avery set the box on the low table near the hearth, then reclaimed the same seat as earlier. Bergdis sat as well and pulled a key from her pocket. She held it up for Avery to see.

"He burned the first letter, you see. I had to be so very careful after that."

Avery nodded. "I know this. Jakob reads me your letter."

Bergdis unlocked the box. Jammed in tight vertical formation were more letters than Avery expected, though she realized of a sudden that they represented sixteen years' worth of communications from a distant son to his estranged and silent parents.

"When was last one?" she asked.

"From København, just before he left for the Order." Bergdis wagged her head sadly. "He did not write again, so my letter was sent to the palace, even though I knew he was no longer there."

"The palace sends letter to London, where Jakob is with King Henry Eight," Avery explained in her most valiant Norsk. "And London sends letter to Spain, to Barcelona Cathedral. Jakob owns it after."

Bergdis looked surprised. "All that way?"

"Yes. I think God wants Jakob here." Avery gave a little shrug. "And so Jakob is here."

The front door of the manor creaked open and heavy boot heels resounded in the entry hall. Male voices engaged in an exchange which Avery could not understand.

"Johan is returned." Bergdis turned in her chair to face the doorway. "I must tell him about Fafnir."

A tall man strode into the room. Though his hair was more blond that Jakob's and his frame was much leaner, their familial resemblance could not be mistaken. He stopped of a sudden when he spied Avery.

"I did not realize we had a guest." Johan bowed politely. "Madam."

Avery rose to her feet, unsure what the custom was in this land. She dipped her chin and said, "Good sir."

Bergdis pushed herself to her feet. "Johan, this is Lady Avery Hansen. Avery, this is my eldest son, Johan Fafnir Hansen."

Johan's gaze swept over Avery's obviously foreign style, pausing pointedly on her black hair and dark eyes. His brows rose and twisted with doubt. "Hansen?"

Bergdis nodded. "Yes. She is Jakob's wife."

Johan gaped stupidly at his mother. "Jakob? Which Jakob?"

"Your *brother*, of course," she scoffed.

"How—when—I..." Johan strode forward. "Is Jakob *here?*"

"He is."

"Where?" Johan spread his arms wide. "And why?"

"I wrote to him and asked him to come and attend your father's deathbed." Bergdis' mood sobered. "He arrived in time to see your father pass."

Johan straightened, his cheeks draining of color. "Father passed, finally? When?"

Bergdis wiped away fresh tears and glanced at the clock. "About one half hour ago."

Avery watched the ensuing discussion between Bergdis and her son, not catching every word of their rapid exchange, but picking up every nuance of the emotions within.

Poor Johan had walked into the house and was immediately hit with news of his long-lost brother's unanticipated return—with a foreign wife in tow—and his father's death, all in a matter of seconds.

No wonder he was gob-smacked.

"Come and sit, Johan," his mother urged. "Have a glass of ale to recover yourself."

Johan approached slowly and his incredulous expression fell to the open wooden box. He pointed an accusing finger at its contents.

"What are those?"

In the face of Johan's anger, Avery sank slowly into her chair, believing it was best that she minimize her presence in the room, lest she become an unwitting target of his wrath simply by being a present stranger.

"What *are* those, Mother?" he asked again.

Bergdis sighed. "Letters, Johan."

Johan halted his advance when he reached the low table. "Letters from *whom?*"

"Jakob."

"What game have you played?" he shouted, his arms swinging wildly. "There must be fifty letters there!"

"Lower your voice! What will your new sister think of you?" Bergdis lifted her chin in defiance of her son's anger. "And so you know, there are sixty-two letters here."

Johan glanced at Avery and visibly pulled back his reaction. "Sixty *two?*"

"Yes." Bergdis sniffed wetly and crossed her arms. "There would have been sixty-three, but your father burned the first one."

Johan's cheeks sank and his shoulders fell as the barrage of information overwhelmed him. He dropped into the nearest seat and stared at the floor, murmuring, "Good God."

Bergdis was now the only one standing. "God is good, indeed, Johan. He has restored your brother to us in time for your father to rest peacefully."

Johan looked at his mother again. "Am I to understand, that for all those years Jakob wrote you these letters, and Saxby and I never knew about them?"

Bergdis lowered into her chair. "Yes. And I am very sorry about that. But if your father ever found out, they all would have been destroyed."

Johan scrubbed his hands over his face. The words, "Good God..." emerged again from behind them, the sound hollowed by his palms.

"I thought I heard some crazed berserker barge in." Jakob stood inside the room's wide doorway. His eyes were red-rimmed, but he was grinning. "Will you not welcome your own brother?"

§ § §

Johan stood and turned to face Jakob. He stared at Jakob as if he was seeing a spectre. "Jakob? Is it really you?"

Jakob snorted. "Do I look so different?"

"You look so old!"

As did Johan, truth be told; the difference between a lad of nineteen and a man of thirty-five was significant. "That may be, but I am still younger than you!"

Johan approached him warily. "Did you write letters to Mamma?"

Jakob glanced toward his mother and saw the wooden box stuffed with evidence on the table. He returned his gaze to his elder brother, and nodded. "Yes. Three or four times a year."

His brother's eyes narrowed. "Did she ever answer you?"

Jakob could not look at his mother; his emotions were too fragile to shoulder her regret at that moment. "No."

"Never?"

"No."

Johan threw his arm in the direction of the box. "And yet you kept writing? Why?"

"I hoped…" Jakob's vision blurred and he quickly swiped the moisture away. "I *always* hoped that someone kept reading."

Bergdis appeared at Johan's side and rested her hand on his arm. "Jakob was never at fault, Johan, and now the truth can be known. Your father was the one who kept him away from us."

A range of confused emotions scuttled over Johan's face. "Pappa is truly dead now… And though he pretended Jakob was dead, my brother is now resurrected." He stared at his mother. "Have I got that sorted correctly?"

Jakob crossed his arms over his chest. "Yes, I believe so."

Johan turned on his heel, directing his attention toward Avery. She sat primly on her seat, her dark eyes wide and mouth pressed shut. A splotch of red rode high on each of her cheeks.

"And you have a wife." Johan shot his attention back to Jakob. "Is this your first one?"

Jakob coughed his surprise at the question. Of course a man of his age might have been married more than once, what with the fragility of the fairer sex. But even so the question caught him off his guard.

"Why do you ask that?" Avery jumped up, eyes sparking dangerously. "I am sorry. But I think is rude."

"I—uh—well you are of an age," Johan sputtered. "Perhaps I should have asked *how long* you have been married."

Avery's deflection gave Jakob a welcomed moment to regain his composure; he resolved to thank her quite vigorously in their bed later.

"Two months," he stated. "And no, she is not my first. She is my second, and my last."

"My husband has much to tell. You have much to listen." Avery closed the space between them. Her pointed finger moved from one to the other and back. "I think Jakob and Johan must come together. Be brothers. *Now.*"

Jakob chuckled softly. "She does not have much Norsk."

Johan's demeanor eased. "But she has enough." He held out his hand.

Jakob grabbed Johan's arm and pulled him into a back-pounding embrace. "I have missed you, brother."

"And I have missed you as well."

Avery pulled her wadded linen from her pocket and wiped her eyes once again. This time, however, she was smiling.

§ § §

Bergdis insisted that all other narrations wait until the eventide meal and shuffled Jakob and Avery off to settle into their quarters. The *begravelsesbyrå* brought the casket, and what remained of Fafnir Hansen was washed, dressed, and laid out inside, before the body was placed in the hall for the next day's visiting mourners.

Avery slipped into the room to examine her husband's father alone. Though wasted by disease—consumption was the accepted diagnosis—he had been a tall man, as proved by the length of the casket. Avery searched his features and found the foundation for both Johan and Jakob's high cheekbones and broad brows.

Fafnir's hair was a faded, pale yellow, almost white. He would have been a blond in his youth. Bergdis had light red hair at one time and the combination created Jakob's copper-and-brass locks.

"Johan is blond," she whispered to herself. "I wonder about Saxby?"

"He cannot hear you, you realize." Jakob stepped behind Avery and slid his hands around her waist. His lips descended on her neck, sending a quiver of delight over her shoulders.

"I was not speaking to him," Avery countered, tilting her head to make room for Jakob's pleasant attentions. "I was only wondering aloud what color of hair your younger brother has."

"Embarrassingly bright red, I am afraid." Jakob stopped nuzzling her neck and rested his chin on top of her head. "Yet another reason not to be a soldier. That flaming head is a target."

"Will I meet him, do you think?"

"Perhaps. But I do not yet know where he is."

A timid voice floated toward them. "Sir Jakob?"

Jakob backed away from Avery and they both turned toward the doorway to see a blushing servant girl. "Yes?"

She dipped a quick curtsy. "I am very sorry to disturb you, Sir, but Lady Bergdis has announced supper."

§ § §

Jakob sat Avery next to him. "Forgive me if I must translate at times. My wife does understand more than she can speak, but would appreciate clear and slow conversation."

"What languages does she speak?" Johan asked, settling himself at the head of the table.

"I speak English, Spanish, and Latin, of course. Jakob does as well," Avery answered for herself. "Now I learn Norsk."

Johan had the decency to appear contrite. "I apologize, Lady Avery. I did not mean to ignore you."

Avery leaned forward. "Please, Johan, call me Avery. We are family."

As the food was set before them, Jakob pointed out the pickled herring. "You have herring in England, but ours is made to last longer."

"Is harder to fish in ice, yes?" Avery offered. "I understand."

Jakob squeezed Avery's thigh under the table. He was so proud of his wife at that moment.

Johan considered Jakob with a concerned expression. "Were you limping when you came in just now?"

Jakob looked at Avery, wondering how much to say.

"You already told them you were married once before," she said in English. "There is no reason not to continue with your honesty."

Jakob nodded and returned his regard to Johan. "Yes. This is a sad story."

Thus resolved, Jakob told his mother and brother about Uma, their secret wedding, and the fire which claimed her life. He did not leave out any details, even including some he had not mentioned to Avery.

"You lost Uma at about the same time I lost Gunhilda." Johan heaved a deep sigh. "How odd life is."

Bergdis' motherly expression was sympathetic. "And your leg still pains you?"

"At times." Jakob gestured toward the ceiling with his spoon. "I spent that much time kneeling on the floor today, beside Pappa. It was hard on the muscle."

"Can I give you something to help the pain?"

Ever the mother, no matter how old the son. "No, thank you

Mamma. Askel is well skilled, as is Avery."

Bergdis turned to her daughter-in-law. "Were you married before, as well?" she asked kindly.

"Yes." Avery reached for Jakob's hand. "But he is not good man. I go far away from him for many years."

"Oh!" Bergdis looked stricken. "I am so sorry."

Johan shifted in his seat and refilled his wineglass. "Where did you go?"

"Avery grew up with Catherine of Aragon," Jakob stepped in to ease the telling. "So when Avery's arranged marriage turned out to be dangerous, she escaped to London."

Avery nodded. "I am lady-in-waiting for the Spanish queen of England."

"The chief lady-in-waiting for the wife of King Henry the Eighth," Jakob clarified. "But she hid her true identity from everyone, to keep her husband from finding her."

"My name is—*was*—Señora Averia Galaviz de Mendoza, Vizcondesa de Catalonya." Avery smiled shyly at Jakob. "Now I am happy to be Lady Avery Galaviz de Hansen."

Johan cast an impressed glance in Jakob's direction. "So how did you meet my brother?"

Now it was Jakob's turn to explain the Order of the Golden Fleece, his part in it, and the time he spent in London before going on to Spain.

Well, not everything about London, of course.

By the time he finished describing his discovery of Avery in the funeral procession, both his mother and Johan had stopped eating, focusing completely on his and Avery's shared narrative.

"Are you a Viscount, now?" Johan asked Jakob.

He shook his head. "While my wife retains her title, it does not pass to her husband."

"I only use in England or Spain." Avery shrugged. "No other place is important."

Jakob gave Avery a conspiratorial grin. "Shall I tell them about the ships?"

"Ships?" Johan straightened. "What ships?"

Avery waved her permission for Jakob to explain that whole debacle—along with her unique and brilliant solution.

For a moment, Johan seemed unable to speak. He inhaled, and his mouth moved, but whatever thoughts battled for domination had not yet declared a winner.

"Trade with us!" he blurted.

"What?" Avery looked at Jakob and asked in English, "What products are there to trade here?"

Jakob translated the question into Norsk and allowed Johan to answer it.

"Norway has many resources. Arctic salmon—dried or smoked, for one. Cod, herring. Various animal pelts, thick and warm. Wool..." His brother's mouth twitched. "Even ice. We do have an abundance."

Chapter Twenty-Five

May 21, 1519

The stream of visitors started at mid-morning and continued throughout the day. Fafnir might not have always been the wisest business man, and his stubborn pride clearly caused the rift in his family, but he was widely known.

By the warm way Johan was greeted and conversed with, however, much of the visitation today was based in the respect he had earned since taking over the Hansen estate and businesses from his father. Jakob was very glad to see that the Hansen name was once more highly respected.

For himself, Jakob decided that he and Avery would put themselves on regal display. "That will be the easiest way to announce to Arendal that, whatever my father may have said about my disappearance, I brought him great honor in my absence."

Avery looked a little skeptical. "Will you offend Johan by doing so?"

"By being who I am?" Jakob shook his head. "If I do less, then I disrespect my father."

In the end, she agreed, appearing in the same burgundy gown and pearls in which she married him, much to her maid Emily's delight.

For his part, Askel dressed Jakob in full Order regalia, from the satin-lined velvet cape to the heavy gold collar, only forgoing the hat.

"King Henry himself ordered the Baltic amber," Jakob explained to anyone who asked about the ornament. "He wished to bring honor to our King Christian, in whose service I acted."

Whether provably true or not, the explanation clearly impressed those who heard it.

As the day drew to an end, Johan sidled up next to Avery. With an impish glint in his eyes, he leaned over and spoke softly in her ear. "This particular gathering has been anticipated for many months, as you know."

She nodded.

"So, when the opportunity arose, I spoke to some gentlemen who are in attendance about trading with Spain and England."

Avery pinned her lips between her teeth to keep from smiling. Johan was, indeed, the sort of businessman who would set his father's accounts to rights. She nodded again.

"Let us draw up some contracts before you and my brother leave Arendal, shall we?"

She nodded for a third time and allowed some of the repressed smile to smooth her brow and light up her eyes.

Johan frowned a little. "Do you know how long you will bide here?"

Avery glanced toward her tall, handsome, and impressive husband. "No. We have not talked this."

"Tomorrow, then." With a small bow from the waist, Johan returned to the last remaining pair of visitors.

Jakob crossed to her side. He looked pleased. "I was just told that Saxby is expected to arrive for the burial."

"Where is he?"

"His monastery is in Tønsberg, about seventy miles towards Áslo. But Saxby met Johan in Kragero so that he could accompany Birgit the rest of the way to the nunnery there." Jakob looked down and straightened the heavy golden collar. "As it turned out, Saxby planned to remain in Kragero for another week, visiting the family of an official."

"I still do not understand…"

"Kragero is only about forty miles distant. The *begravelsesbyrå* heard of this and took it upon himself to send a swift rider to fetch my brother." Jakob glanced in that man's direction. "I must suspect that he hopes for substantial additional compensation as a result."

Avery gave him a crooked smile. "Dare I say, if he succeeds, he will deserve it?"

Jakob chuckled. "I must agree. But as a result, the burial will be postponed a day or two."

Avery wrinkled her nose. "How long before it becomes unbearable?"

Jakob shrugged. "Thankfully my father has scant flesh left. And we will be certain to burn plenty of candles around the casket."

Avery turned her attention to Johan. "I suppose Birgit will come with him, since Saxby is her guardian, and the deceased is her grandfather." She faced Jakob again. "How long will we remain in Arendal?"

"Are you eager to leave so soon?" Jakob felt a stab of irritation at that thought.

"No, not at all." Avery lowered her voice. "Johan has spoken with several men and wishes to draw up contracts for trade, using my ships."

Jakob straightened and looked down at his wife. "Is this true?"

"Unless he is a known liar," she quipped. "But he does not seem to be."

Jakob snorted, incredulous at this news. He never considered Arendal as a port of trade for Avery's ships, though now it was obvious to him that he should have.

He lifted Avery's hand and kissed the back of it. "Clearly, I have married well. Your keen industry will carry me through my dotage."

She smiled and winked. "*Our* dotage. I am older than you, remember?"

May 23, 1519

Saxby arrived two days later, with twelve-year-old Birgit at his side. Though Johan explained that it was his daughter's choice to join the nuns and take the religious vows, the lanky adolescent girl was clearly glad to have the unexpected chance to see her family one last time. And meeting her unknown Uncle Jakob was an additional blessing to arise from Fafnir's death.

The burial mass took place the same day Saxby and Birgit arrived. Of course, the Catholic service was in Latin, so Avery understood all that was said.

Once at the graveside, however, Norsk took over and she struggled to catch as many words as she could. If spoken slowly, she could match some of the unfamiliar words to English, just as Jakob had done when he arrived in England.

A year ago.

Avery sat in Hansen Hall afterward, pondering how her life had changed so completely in that short amount of time. Not only was she finally free of her horrid first husband, she had found another much more desirable one. In addition to that, she was now an independent woman of business, with what looked to become a profitable trade industry. With Norway.

She smiled into her wine glass. *Thank you, Father.*

Across the room from her, the Hansen brothers sat in front of the hearth, babbling in Norsk far too rapid—and too broken with tears and laughter—for her to begin to follow.

Saxby was the youngest brother at thirty years of age. He turned out to be as tall as the other two, and his hair was indeed a ridiculous shade of red. Dressed in his priest's robes, he was imposing and engaging at the same time. Avery imagined that his flock in Tønsberg adored him.

Even in the company of the other two, Johan was still reserved, and while she assumed that was simply part of his nature, the stress of the last few days had disappeared from his brow. Even so, he listened more than he spoke, as the brothers reacquainted themselves.

Jakob was the biggest surprise.

When Avery first met him in the Tudor court, he was struggling to learn English, acting on a commission which had unclear parameters, and living under a many-years-old guilty burden of his own. Today in this hall the language was his, his role in the family was restored, and the burdens of the past were lifted.

If Avery found him attractive before, watching him cry, laugh, and tease so joyfully with his brothers made him positively glorious. Her heart swelled impossibly in her chest. She had never loved anyone so well as she loved her husband at that moment.

Bergdis approached and Avery slid over to make room for her mother-in-law on the bench.

"I suspect they will be at it for hours." Bergdis held up a small crockery pitcher and offered Avery more ale.

Avery lifted her glass. "Thank you."

Bergdis also seemed to have relaxed. Avery understood quite well how the final passing of someone long ill could provide more relief than grief. And, of course, Bergdis now had her lost son back in her home for the first time in sixteen years.

Bergdis poured the last splash of ale into her own cup. "Supper will be served soon."

Avery laid a hand over her mother-in-law's. "I know you are happy and sad today."

Bergdis sighed. "This truly is a day of so many differing emotions. I have buried my husband of thirty seven years and will spend the rest of my life alone. For this I am sad. How could I not be?"

The older woman's tearing eyes shifted to the boisterous trio of big men across the room. "But I have all of my sons, together again at last. And I see so clearly what Fafnir would not."

"What is that?" Avery asked, though she believed she knew.

Bergdis returned her gaze to Avery. "That Jakob was correct. He was not suited to be a priest, but was the better choice to go to Denmark."

Avery spoke slowly, searching for the Norsk words she knew. "I do not know him long, but I think Saxby is very good priest."

Bergdis nodded and dabbed her eyes with a linen square. "He truly is. He loves serving God, and never complains about any of the hardships of serving his congregation as well."

Avery squeezed the woman's hand. "Both sons do what they are made for."

"Yes." Bergdis heaved another sigh. "And I believe Fafnir did come to realize this in the end. When I told him I asked Jakob to come home, I could see that he was relieved. I wish he could have spoken to Jakob, though."

"Hm." Avery took a little sip of ale. "I do not know, but I think this is better."

Bergdis regarded her with surprise. "Why?"

"If Fafnir has pride, he will want to keep it. Do you understand?" Avery attempted. "He will say words that do not help."

"Oh, my!" Bergdis huffed and flashed a crooked smile. "I do believe you are right!"

"This time, Jakob says his words and Fafnir cannot argument."

"No, he could not *argue*." Bergdis looked at Avery as if figuring something out about her new daughter. "You are a wise woman, Avery."

She felt her cheeks warming. "Hard things make wisdom, yes?"

"Yes. Yes they do. "Bergdis leaned closer. "May I ask you a personal question?"

Avery nodded. "Of course."

"You have no children. Are you barren?"

Now her cheeks were on fire. "Perhaps. Or my husband was."

"Do you expect to have children with Jakob?"

Avery wagged her head. "No. Not with my age. I have thirty five years."

"I assume you and he have talked about this."

"We have. And we agree children are not..." her words failed her and she shrugged.

"Important?" Bergdis guessed.

Avery nodded. "Yes. Important. Thank you."

Bergdis stood, her expression unreadable. "I shall see to supper."

As his mother walked out of the room, Jakob shot Avery a curious look. She smiled her reassurance, lifted her glass in a silent toast, and wondered what Bergdis was really thinking.

§ § §

Jakob could not eat another bite; not if he wanted to love his wife tonight, which he most definitely did. He apologized to her several times for the quick verbal exchanges between the occupants at the table, and translated when he could, but the cause was lost before it began.

He put up one hand, declining a third serving of reindeer, and spoke to Saxby. "How long will you bide?"

His younger brother glanced at Birgit who, as a young woman about to begin her vocation, had joined the adults for the evening meal. "I believe I might justify a week's absence, under the circumstances. And I can certainly explain the delay to the Mother at the convent in Tønsberg."

Birgit lowered her eyes, her lips pressed in a shy smile.

"What about you, Jakob?" Johan asked. "When are you expected to return to København?"

Jakob glanced at Avery, whose expression was carefully blank. "I am not certain."

"No? Why not?" Johan pressed.

Jakob returned his gaze to his older brother. "I wrote to the king when I left the Order to come here, but of course there was no time for him to respond."

"Might he write to you here?" Bergdis asked.

Jakob had not considered that. "I suppose it is possible."

Saxby waved a hand of benediction. "Between your marriage, and the death of your father, certainly a few weeks are reasonable."

"Yes. About that." Jakob cleared his throat. "I did not inform the king about my marriage."

Shocked glances ricocheted between the table's occupants.

"There was no time." Jakob shifted in his seat, the creak of the chair chastising him. "Not if I was to come here before Pappa passed."

"What will the king do?" Bergdis asked softly.

"I do not know," Jakob answered truthfully. "He had not bothered to arrange any marriages for me in Denmark, so there are no promises that have been broken."

"But you married, *again* I must add, without your sovereign's permission." Johan looked pointedly at Avery.

"Again?" Saxby blurted.

Jakob gave his brother a hastily truncated explanation, before addressing what he thought Johan had in mind. "I asked Avery to marry *me* when we were in England. She declined, because she was already married. Even in Barcelona, she did not press the point. This was *my* choice and *my* decision."

Bergdis was clearly worried. "So what will you do, Jakob, if King Christian releases you from your position?"

"Would you expect to live here?" The tone of Johan's voice made it quite clear that this was not his brother's preference.

"No. Not at all." When he saw his mother's face fall, he added, "Not that returning to the bosom of my family would not be comforting…"

Avery shot him a warning look.

"…but there is no place for me here."

Saxby pointed a spoon at him. "If there is no place for you in København or in Arendal, would you go to back to Spain? To Avery's home?"

Jakob shook his head. "Avery has no home in Spain. Her brother inherited the Galaviz family estate, and she has dissolved her dead husband's remaining assets."

"She will go back to Catherine."

All eyes turned toward Birgit. Though she had not yet spoken, clearly the girl had been listening to the conversations. Her pale blue eyes widened as she faced Avery.

"Will you not, Auntie? Return to serve your dearest friend?"

Avery smiled at the adolescent. "You are very smart, Birgit. Yes. This is what we do."

Johan frowned at Jakob. "If your wife is a lady-in-waiting for the queen of England, how will you spend your days?"

"I believe King Henry might take me into his service as one of his knights." Jakob's lips twitched. "He owes me a favor."

Now the glances which bounced around the table were clearly skeptical.

"The esteemed King Henry the Eighth of England owes *you* a favor?" Johan chuckled. "Brother, I cannot imagine what you have done to create such an impossible situation."

No, you cannot.

"I am making an assumption, of course," Jakob began, dragging out the answer to enhance its impact. "But most men, no matter what their station in society, appreciate it greatly when someone saves their life."

§ § §

Avery laughed as Jakob tumbled, naked, into their bed. "I thought Johan was going to suffer an apoplexy when you said you saved Henry's life!"

Grinning, he stretched his frame along hers as his hand began to explore her body. "My brothers have no idea how I have spent these years away."

Avery gasped when he found her most responsive spot. She shifted to give him room.

"And so," he continued, "I wanted to let them know that my absence has not been wasted."

Avery grabbed his head and pulled his mouth to hers. Little moans of pleasure escaped her.

He broke away from the kiss and rested his forehead against hers. "I thank God every day that I found you, Avery."

"As do I," she breathed.

"I love you, more than I can say."

She sighed and pressed his hand against her. "Then stop talking and show me."

He did.

Chapter Twenty-Six

June 17, 1519

In all, Jakob and Avery remained in Arendal just over three weeks. Jakob would have enjoyed a bit more time, but he felt the urgency of resolving his situation grow more strongly with each passing sunrise.

Though the northern tip of Denmark was only ninety miles across the North Sea, København lay south another hundred and sixty miles or so. The journey would require five or six days, depending on the sea winds.

Jakob blew a sigh as he leaned over the edge of the ship's railing and watched sea gulls fight over the remains of his midday meal floating on the undulating waters below.

Avery rubbed his back. "Today is the third day. You are usually better on the fourth, are you not?"

Jakob wiped his mouth with the damp linen she handed him. "Yes," he growled. "And with this damned wind, we should land by the evening of the fifth."

Avery chuckled. "Long soft journey, or quick and brisk. I do not think you can win either way."

Jakob swiped his brow. "God willing, I will have no more than one voyage left in my lifetime."

Avery folded her arms and leaned her back against the railing, peering up into his eyes. "London? Or Arendal?"

Jakob sniffed and spat into the water. "Two voyages, then."

"Be honest with me husband. What do you think Christian will do with you?"

Jakob had an idea, but he would not bet on it. "I cannot presume to guess, my love."

Avery stared out at the endless water. "I am quite pleased with the trade contracts."

Jakob suspected his wife was changing the subject to take his mind off his belly and he appreciated the effort. Sometimes her distractions worked quite well, though the most effective ones generally took place in their bed.

"It was obvious to me that Johan was quite pleased."

Avery returned her gaze to his. "Do you believe he will ever remarry?"

Jakob shrugged. "He could if he wanted to. But I cannot discern if he wants to."

"Perhaps our marriage will encourage him."

"Perhaps it will."

Avery turned around again and leaned her elbows on the railing. The wind tugged wisps of her hair from her headpiece and she kept trying to lock them behind her ears with little success.

"At any rate, Gustavo should receive the letters in another six weeks."

Jakob attempted to help with the flailing bits of black hair. "I am very proud of you, wife. You have the sort of mind for business that most women do not possess."

Avery snorted. "Do not sell my gender short, husband. Many a household would be bankrupt, if it were not for the economic skills of the lady."

"Even so." He gave up on her hair and ran a fingertip down her cheek. "Should anyone comment on your abilities, I shall set them straight."

Avery gave him a sly smile, one that reminded him of her skills at distraction. "And I shall reward my knight well for rectifying his lady's reputation."

Jakob straightened. "I believe I shall go to the cabin and lie down for a bit."

Avery slipped her arm through his. "Let me see to your comfort, husband. It is the least I can do."

June 19, 1519
København, Denmark

Jakob led Avery to his apartments in an outer wing of the royal residence as the church bells in the square rang seven times.

"Askel will show Emily where everything goes and help her get you settled. We have but an hour before supper is served, so I am afraid we shall have to appear as we are."

Avery noted the sparse elegance of the residence as they walked through its myriad of halls. Obviously, this structure was not as old as either the Tower of London or Windsor Castle.

"As long as I can wash my face, and Emily can fix my hair, I shall be satisfied." Avery looked up at Jakob when he stopped in front of a door. "This has been your home for all these years?"

"Only since I was made a knight at twenty-two. Before that, I resided at a different location." Jakob opened the door. The furnishings were draped with linens and the air was stale. "I should open the window."

Jakob disappeared through the door to the sleeping chamber while Avery examined the outer room of the apartment. Just as his rooms were in London, this chamber was orderly and neat with little ornamentation. In a moment, she felt the summer breeze whoosh through the space, freshening the air.

Askel entered through the outer door, laden with Jakob's satchels. A wide-eyed Emily followed behind him and a phalanx of porters followed her. In less than five minutes, Jakob and Avery's trunks and boxes had turned the outer room into an obstacle course.

Jakob stood with his hands on his hips, surveying the disarray. "Askel?"

The valet straightened, holding a hat box. "Yes, sir?"

"This can wait a bit. I would like you to inform the king that I have returned, so that my appearance at supper is not a surprise to him."

"Yes, my lord." Askel looked around and set the hat box on a table. Then with a bow of his head, he left.

Emily stepped forward. "Shall I begin to sort this out, my lady?"

"Have you been shown to your room?"

"Yes, my lady." She gave a little smile. "I shall be quite comfortable.

"Good." Avery looked at Jakob. "It is my understanding that I shall only have time to wash my face and have my hair repaired before we must go to supper."

Jakob nodded, frowning and feeling his beard. "And I believe I shall have a shave."

§ § §

Once the couple was coifed and clean-jawed, Jakob entered the dining room with Avery gripping his arm. Heads swerved and eyes widened. Jakob had never attended supper with any woman on his arm before, much less a dark-eyed Spanish beauty, and murmured speculation bubbled up around them.

"Jakob! You have returned at last!" Hans Andersen's eyes were fixed on Avery. "And what delightful treat have you brought home?"

Jakob turned sideways to face his friend. "Sir Andersen, may I present my wife, Lady Avery Galaviz Hansen."

The other knight's jaw dropped. "Wife you say?"

"Indeed." Jakob grinned and addressed Avery in slow Norsk. "Hans and I became knights at the same time."

Avery smiled softly. "I am pleased to meet you."

Hans' brow furrowed. "Did the king send his permission while you were in Spain?"

Jakob clapped his friend on the shoulder. "In truth, I did not ask him."

Hans recoiled, his expression carrying a warning. "In that case, it has been a pleasure to serve beside you."

"Sir Hansen!"

Jakob turned slowly and gave King Christian his best courtly bow. "Your Grace."

When he straightened, the king asked, "And who is this lovely creature at your side?"

"Your Highness, may I introduce Lady Averia Galaviz de Hansen, Countess of Catalonya?"

"I am honored, your Grace." Avery curtsied deeply.

"Hansen?" Christian barked. "Do not tell me you discovered some long-lost relative in Spain?"

Jakob relaxed his shoulders and clasped his hands in front of him. "No, my lord."

The king's eyes narrowed. "Have you presumed to marry without my permission?"

"I am afraid that the desperate situation in which the lady found herself, did not allow the months required for that correspondence to take place. I was forced to act quickly to save her honor." Jakob realized too late what sort of *situation* that sounded like.

Christian's gaze swept over a furiously blushing Avery—even with her limited Norsk, she caught the unintended double meaning—before he arched one brow. "Are you to be a father?"

Jakob coughed. "No, your Grace. The situation was *financial*. The result of an unsavory first husband, now deceased."

Christian's lips twisted. "The lady made an unsavory marriage? That sounds rather foolish."

This conversation was not improving. Avery looked to be suppressing an angry retort, obliging Jakob to speak quickly. "Lady Avery was only twenty when her father agreed to what appeared to be a financially advantageous marriage."

"And?"

Jakob now had the opportunity to steer the subject in a more complementary direction. "And once the true nature of the man was known, the lady escaped to England, where she has served for nine years as chief lady-in-waiting for her lifelong friend, Queen Catherine of Aragon—the wife of King Henry the Eighth."

Christian's demeanor shifted. "And that is where you became acquainted."

Jakob dipped his chin. "Yes, your Grace."

The king pressed his lips together and his eyes narrowed. "I do not wish to keep everyone waiting any longer for their supper, but this discussion is most assuredly not finished."

Jakob waited, heart thumping steadily against his ribs like a death knell.

"I shall expect you in my chamber one half hour after the meal is concluded, Sir Hansen." Christian turned and spoke loudly enough for anyone within twenty feet to hear. "There are consequences for such rash behavior by a formerly trusted knight."

Jakob bent in a grim bow. "I understand, your Grace."

When he straightened, he looped Avery's arm through his and walked stiffly into the dining hall with only the hint of a limp.

§ § §

Avery tried to focus on Emily's labors as the maid helped her prepare for bed. "Go on to bed, Emily, and do not worry about unpacking anything else until tomorrow. It may be that we will not be staying long."

Emily curtsied. "Yes, my lady."

Askel still waited in the outer room, but Avery did not feel she should dismiss him; he was Jakob's loyal valet and would wait for his master even if she tried to send him to bed.

Avery sat on the edge of the mattress, wondering how much more time she would need to waste before her husband returned. One little table in the bedchamber held a small stack of books; Avery walked over to see if any of them might be in a language she understood.

Finding a Latin book on philosophy, she carried it back to the bed, turned up the lamp, and tried to concentrate on the words on the page rather than the dread in her heart. She was not very successful.

And the sound of Jakob's deep voice and lilting Norsk on the other side of the door, Avery tossed the book aside. She gathered her knees under her and stared at the bedchamber door, willing it to open quickly.

When it did, she faced a somber husband.

"Are you released from service?" she blurted, disinclined to wait for that answer,

"Not entirely. Not yet." Jakob began to unfasten his tunic. "Will you help me? I sent Askel to bed so we could talk privately before I explain it to him."

Avery clambered from the bed and helped her husband undress, laying the garments over the chairs in the room. Askel would sort them in the morning.

She poured fresh water into the basin and handed him a cloth. "I suppose you should start at the beginning."

Jakob wet the cloth and began to wash under his arms. "Obviously, the king was displeased."

"Obviously. We knew he would be."

"Yes." Jakob rinsed the cloth and continued his ablutions. "He made a point of telling me that to allow a knight—any knight—to flaunt convention without consequence would make his king appear foolish and weak."

Avery sank into the remaining chair not adorned with Jakob's clothes. "He makes a point, I am afraid."

"He does indeed." Jakob reached for his nightshirt, which Askel had laid across the foot of the bed. "And yet, in light of my long service, he did not wish to dismiss me outright."

"What does he wish to do?"

"Humiliate me." Jakob's head disappeared under the loose linen shirt, and reappeared through the neck opening. "He wishes to make an example of me."

Avery's indignant rage began to burn in her core. "And you will allow him to?"

"I have no choice."

"Why not?" She jumped to her feet. "Why not merely leave?"

He sighed and gave her a patient look. "It is not so simple as that."

She crossed her arms in front of her, chin jutting. "Then please, explain it to me."

Jakob held out his hand, beckoning her to him. "Let's go into the front room, have a glass of wine, and discuss it."

Avery stalked through the bedchamber door and claimed a spot on the couch. Jakob followed, and went to the sideboard to fill their cups. He handed Avery hers, then sat beside her.

"First of all, I acted wrongly. We must remember this."

Avery reluctantly agreed. "Did you explain the circumstances?"

"Yes, of course." Jakob sipped his wine. "I also reminded him

Kris Tualla

of your influence in King Henry's court."

Avery's shoulders drooped. "Yet even so, he feels he must assert his sovereignty over you."

"As is his right."

Avery stared at the wine in her cup. It was amber in color and sweeter than the red wines she was accustomed to. "So what form is this humiliation to take?"

Displeasure tightened Jakob's features. "Starting immediately I—well, *we*—are banned from court appearances."

"No more suppers. No competitions. No festivities." Since she did not know these people, and was unable to follow their rapid conversations, this censure would mainly impact Jakob.

"Correct." He took another drink.

Avery waved a hand, indicating the apartment. "What about our living quarters?"

One corner of Jakob's mouth quirked. "How could I be humiliated, if my exclusion from these things could not be observed by everyone?"

"So we will live here, clearly visible under everyone's noses, and then your banishment from the king's side will be obvious?" Avery snorted. "How mature of him."

Jakob shrugged. "We have a home. We can take meals in our rooms if we choose to, or we can go about the city. Our time is ours for the most part."

Avery tried to tamp down her irritation for Jakob's sake. "How long must we remain here in København under these constraints?"

"I am not certain."

"Make a conjecture."

Jakob blew a breath through pursed lips. "I would guess perhaps three months."

"Until mid-September or so." Avery leaned toward Jakob and looked him hard in the eye. "And then what?"

"And then, once my punishment ends, I am free to do as I wish, and with all of my Danish investments intact," Jakob explained. "If I left now, I would lose everything I have accrued."

"King Christian would simply take it."

He gave her an apologetic look. "He has invested in me for sixteen years and would see it as his legal repayment."

Avery heaved a sigh. "So you would be made penniless and have no income."

"Yes." Jakob chuckled. "And I am afraid that my manly pride will not allow me to live off of my wife's charity for the remainder of my days."

Avery nodded. She understood his mindset clearly; if he thought differently, however, he would not be the man she fell in love with. "Have you decided if you will remain in his service after that?"

"No. I believe we shall make that decision together." He reached out and took her hand. "If you do not grow to love Denmark, then I will take you back to England."

Avery's irritation with their situation evaporated in the light of her husband's selfless generosity. "I love you, Jakob."

His thumb stroked the back of her hand. "And I love you, Avery. I would do anything for you."

"And in exchange, I do promise to try and love Denmark." She smiled seductively and pushed her nightdress off her shoulder. "Shall we begin that process now?"

§ § §

Jakob curled around his wife in complete post-coital bliss, thrums of pleasure still trilling through his frame. For the last half of an hour, their passionate bedsport pushed aside all considerations of his situation with his king.

He had not been completely honest with Avery about Christian's demands, but told her enough for her to understand how they would live. What he held back from her was how precarious his situation truly was.

Denmark was now openly at war with Sweden and, though the war was mostly fought at sea, the threat on land was real as well. With Christian hobbling him so publically, Jakob could be in danger.

Yet he could not, in good conscience, leave behind a king he had respected and served for so long. Nor could he abandon a decent income of his own making. To live off of Avery's trade business would be a constant thorn, pricking him until he was consumed by that pain, and the rot of the wound would poison his love for her.

He meant it when he told her he would take her back to England. After spending several months there, Jakob believed he would adjust to living in that country far better than Avery would adjust to living in this one.

He only had to survive the next three or four months, and his destiny would once more be in his own hands.

Chapter Twenty-Seven

June 25, 1519

Jakob and Avery spent the next week settling into Jakob's apartments in the royal residence. Besides breaking their fast, they took one additional meal a day in their rooms, and the other—either midday or supper—in some establishment which Jakob knew in the city.

The problem with that, as far as Avery was concerned, was that Jakob did not always join her for the second meal and she was left to dine in their apartment alone.

"I cannot slink off like a recalcitrant pup," Jakob stated when she broached the subject after breakfast. "After my absence, I must reestablish my alliances, so that when I am reinstated I will not have lost my influences."

After spending years in a royal court, Avery understood exactly to what her husband referred. That did not ease her loneliness, however.

"If only I could find a companion," she said. "Someone who speaks English or even Latin. Perhaps someone to help me with Danish and Norsk."

Jakob pulled her close. "Would it help if I arranged for a carriage to be available whenever you wished?"

Avery looped her arms around his neck. "I suppose. It might be nice to get some fresh air every day."

"Then consider it done. I shall make the arrangements this morning." Jakob kissed her tenderly, his mouth tasting of smoked salmon and soft cheese.

Avery sighed and leaned into him. Since arriving in København, their lovemaking had been particularly intense. She would believe that to be a good thing, if it were not controverted by the deepening lines of stress around Jakob's mouth and a wariness in his eyes. Christian's punitive actions were clearly harder on Jakob than he admitted.

When the kiss ended, he rested his forehead against hers. "Remember to smile when you are in public. The best way to survive this stricture is to appear unconcerned with the outcome."

He made a good point. The wisdom of Solomon stated that showing kindness to an enemy was like heaping burning coals on that enemy's head.

Avery brushed a piece of lint from Jakob's chest. "Yes, husband. I promise. I shall be positively giddy."

Jakob slid a knuckle under her chin and lifted her face to his. "And I promise you, Avery, all will be right in the end."

She gave him what she hoped was a reassuring smile. "Go, now, and conquer Denmark."

He gave her another quick kiss before striding out of the room, leaving her to fill another day with her own devices.

§ § §

Hans Andersen waited in the prearranged spot, a small chapel inside the red brick and gothic-arched *Vor Frue Kirke*—Church of Our Lady—next to the *Universitet* of København.

"I am sorry if I am late." Jakob dropped onto the bench beside him. "Avery had some concerns which I needed to address before I left."

Hans turned worried brown eyes on his. "What sort of concerns?"

Jakob waved a hand. "She is bored and lonely, as you might well understand. I arranged for her to have a carriage and driver at her disposal, so that while I am not with her, she can get out from under Christian's roof and do as she pleases."

Hans nodded slowly. "The king's retribution is hard on both of you."

"It is." Jakob looked up at a massive scaffold rising at the entrance of the cathedral, and the myriad of workmen scaling it. "What is being done here?"

Hans gave a little snort. "Christian has decided to commemorate himself by building a great tower. From what I have seen of the plans—of which he is very proud, I must add—the tower is to be as high as the church is long."

Jakob frowned and returned his regard to Hans. "That is an odd sort of proportion, is it not?"

The other knight shrugged. "You, out of all of us, know how prideful the king is. I can only assume he wishes to tell the world what a magnificent ruler he is."

"And because of all the activity here, no one will mark our conversation." Jakob nodded his approval. "So what have you brought me here to discuss?"

"Our not-so-magnificent ruler." Hans twisted on the bench so that he faced the entrance to the chapel. "Are you aware of his plans to invade Sweden?"

"No." Jakob flashed a rueful smile. "He does not confide in me these days."

Hans shook his head. "It will be a disaster. The Swedes only want to secede from the Kalmar Union and get out from under Danish rule, but Christian continues to fight them."

"The Swedes have always been troublesome," Jakob observed. "Why not simply let them go?"

Hans waved a hand toward the construction. "Ask the man who is commemorating himself with an over-sized tower."

Jakob chuckled. "I see your point. But what does this have to do with me?"

The knight folded his hands. "Why are you still here?"

Jakob chuckled again. "What do you mean by that?"

"I mean, once Christian lowered his decree, why did you not simply leave Denmark?" Hans shrugged. "You have a Spanish wife who is friends with the English queen. So I ask again, why are you still here?"

Jakob's mood sobered. "I do have some pride of my own, Hans. I cannot bear to live on my wife's charity."

"How does remaining in København prevent that?"

Jakob heaved a resigned sigh. "I have substantial investments here, which will continue to provide me with an income if Christian releases me after all of this nonsense."

"I guessed as much. And if you leave, the money remains here?" Hans pressed.

Jakob nodded. "He has given the banks orders not to allow me to withdraw my funds. In addition, the king has placed a guard in the stable and on the dock. If I, or my wife, try to leave København, we will be stopped and searched."

"He really does want to make an example of you," Hans sympathized. "Why, do you suppose?"

Jakob waved his hand toward the scaffold. "Ask the man who is commemorating himself with an over-sized tower."

Hans laughed, and ran a hand though his pale blond hair. "Now I see *your* point."

"Is that all you wished to ask me?" Jakob stretched out his leg and rubbed his thigh. "If so, perhaps a tavern might be our next stop."

"No, there was something else." Hans lowered his voice. "How much money would it require to replace what you lost if you left?"

Jakob gave the knight a confused look. "What do you mean?"

"I mean..." Hans' gaze shifted to the opening to the chapel, then back to Jakob. "There are men who wish to secure Sweden's secession from the Union. Wealthy men."

Jakob leaned back and folded his arms over his chest. This conversation had just taken a very dangerous turn and his response must be well measured. "I would never do the king harm."

"You would not be asked to."

"What, then?"

Hans' eyes locked onto Jakob's. "We are speaking about quite a large sum of money. Can I trust your discretion?"

"Can you trust me?" Jakob countered. "How long have you known me?"

Hans' eyes narrowed. "I have known you since you were

seventeen Jakob. And because you have always behaved in an honorable and trustworthy manner, I personally put your name and your situation forward to the men involved."

Jakob said nothing, but waited for Hans to continue. He did not want to be accused of encouraging this conversation, should it be discovered later.

"The king has put you and your wife in a very unsatisfactory position, Jakob. He actions are not worthy of you. And I am empowered to offer you enough money to leave Denmark comfortably." Hans lifted one unconcerned shoulder. "And the task is simple. You would leave immediately upon completing it."

Jakob pondered his next words carefully. "Who are these men?"

"I cannot say."

"Then I cannot believe you."

Hans frowned. "What do you need to know?"

"I would like to meet them and judge their character for myself."

"Impossible!" Hans blurted.

"Then we are finished." Jakob stood and stretched, grinning at his friend. "Would you care to get lunch?"

The knight rose to his feet as well, looking as if he was about to lose a very large fish from a very trusted net. "I will ask, Jakob. But I cannot promise anything."

"That is fair." He turned as if to leave, then turned back. "How much money are we talking about?"

Hans relaxed a little. "A large amount."

"A large amount to a pauper? Or to a king?" Jakob wagged his head. "Can you be more specific?"

"Fifty thousand krone."

Jakob did the conversion his mind; that amount was about five thousand in English pounds. "Seventy-five thousand and I will think about it."

Hans recoiled. "Are you mad?"

"That is only seventy-five hundred in pounds sterling, and I am a young man yet, with refined tastes." Jakob pointed a stiff finger at Hans. "You ask me, a knight sworn to the king's service, to commit some sort of treason. Considering that, I believe it is a bargain."

Hans had lost much of his bravado, but clearly not his hope.

"Because you are so trusted, I believe they might comply with your requests. I will ask."

Jakob assumed that the other knight would be paid as well, if he succeeded in this negotiation, but he needed to make the other man work for his portion. "Good. Now let's eat. I have worked up an appetite."

§ § §

Jakob paused in the hallway, realigning his composure before facing Avery. He had hidden much of what he revealed to Hans about their imprisoned station from his wife and he needed to appear unconcerned in her presence.

Then, of course, Hans' startling scheme must remain undisclosed as well. Jakob hoped he had not demanded too much, and scuttled the proposition altogether. Yet he did not wish to appear too eager to accept, thereby raising the men's suspicions as to his motives.

There was a very fine line to walk in situations like these, and he prayed he had not strayed from it.

Avery greeted him with a bright smile when he finally opened the door. "Welcome back, husband. Was your day profitable?"

Her choice of words, while quite common, threw him for a moment. "We shall see," he said casually. "And was yours?"

"Oh, yes!" She stood and approached him. "Why did you not tell me there was a university here?"

"Because women cannot attend," he replied, wondering what her point was.

"No, but they can peruse the library, if they smile sweetly enough." Avery laughed. "And flummox the librarian with a barrage of languages he does not understand."

Jakob had to laugh as well. "You snuck into the university library? What next? Lecturing to a class?"

Avery smacked his chest with the back of her hand. "Someday women will lecture, I would wager. Our gender does not prevent us from having keen minds."

"As you have clearly proven, my dearest love." Jakob patted his belly. "I had a very large midday meal and feel the need for exercise. Will you walk with me?"

Avery reached for a hat. "If you will buy me chocolate. My midday meal was not so grand."

"Agreed." Jakob smiled at Avery. Walking never alerted a guard and they were free to stroll through the streets unmolested—especially when he was attired in his knight's finery.

His wife never appeared anything but noble.

"Perhaps we might dine near the water this evening," he suggested. "The weather is quite mild."

§ § §

Jakob was definitely up to something.

Avery watched his eyes constantly drift aside to stare at nothing during their supper, before he returned his attention to her and asked her to repeat what she just said. Perhaps their odd banishment was wearing on him more than she realized.

"There is a church beside the university," she began.

Jakob's blue eyes shot to hers. "Yes?"

Odd. "And it appears to be under some sort of construction."

Jakob nodded. "Christian is building an enormous tower as a tribute to himself."

"Your king rivals Henry with his confidence, I think."

"Yes."

Avery gave up trying to engage her husband after a while and their walk back to the royal residence was a quiet one. Whatever he had done that day was weighing on him, and as yet he had not chosen to tell her what that was.

When they reached their apartment, Askel handed Jakob a note. He opened it, read it, and then tossed it in the fire.

"Was that anything important?" Avery asked.

Jakob shook his head, smiling. "Hans wants to meet with me and hear about my time in the Order, is all."

"So I shall miss you again during the day."

"Supper, actually." He kissed her forehead. "He wants to take me to some duke's home, so I might be put on display."

"Politics?" she ventured.

Jakob stroked her cheek. "What else do powerful men play at?"

Avery tried to hide her disappointment at his coming absence, and resolved to breach the university library's barricade once more in recompense. A woman needed some sort of distraction, after all.

June 26, 1519

Jakob climbed into the carriage, which met him in front of the *Vor Frue Kirke*, and took the seat facing Hans Andersen. "You work quickly, Hans."

He shrugged. "The men involved wish for this situation to be resolved quickly."

Though the church bells had just rung seven times, the sun was hours from setting this close to the solstice. A warm breeze freshened the inside of the carriage and Jakob turned his face toward the clean air. What he was about to do felt very dirty.

"So the men have agreed to meet with me. That is something."

"Man," Hans corrected. "We are meeting secretly with Nygaard Wold, Duke of Holstein."

Jakob continued to watch out the window. "What about the money?"

"You will need to discuss that with His Grace."

Jakob nodded and said no more until they reached a small manor surrounded by trees, about half an hour outside of København. He let Hans disembark first and then followed, all of his senses on alert.

A gray-haired gentleman, who had clearly never missed a meal in the last decade, waited in a small room off to the right of the entry hall. "Welcome Sir Andersen, Sir Hansen, to our clandestine gathering."

As Jakob approached, he recognized the man from his scattered appearances at Christian's court. "Your Grace."

"Please have a seat. May I offer you sherry?"

Jakob declined, not caring for the sweet wine. Hans, however, accepted.

"Thank you for meeting with me, your Grace," Jakob offered.

"Thank you for considering your involvement," he countered. "I doubt Christian was thinking clearly when he set up his most trusted knight to be disgraced."

"Formerly most trusted. By his own public statement," Jakob corrected.

"Yes, well. Not everyone is wise enough to watch his words. Especially a young king who believes himself to be invincible." Wold sneered. "Have you seen the monstrosity he is building?"

"The cathedral tower?" Jakob allowed a crooked smile. "Perhaps the king is compensating for some sort of physical disappointment."

The duke blinked, and then burst into raucous laughter. "Very good, Sir Hansen! I believe I shall repeat that jest myself."

Jakob waited for the duke to compose himself; eagerness would not serve him well tonight.

Wold wiped his eyes. "Has Sir Andersen explained what it is that we want you to do?"

"Not yet."

The flamboyant duke nodded. "We want access to Christian, away from the city."

Jakob gestured out the window. "Someplace like this?"

"Precisely."

He shifted in his chair. "And what will you do with him, once you have him?"

Wold put up two fleshy hands. "We only want to speak with him, convince him to see our side, and come to a trade agreement."

Next you will tell me that the sun will rise in the west and I will believe that just as strongly.

Jakob smiled at the man. "All you require of me is to get him alone in a carriage and bring him here."

Wold chuckled. "I knew you had a quick mind."

"And while you have your discussion, I will return immediately to København, board a ship, and be gone before the king returns."

"Exactly."

"You guarantee my safe passage, in exchange for my silence and absence."

The duke nodded. "We do."

Jakob folded his arms over his chest. "You realize that I must take my own steps to assure my safety."

Hans, who had been sipping his sherry in silence, sat forward.

"What sort of steps?"

"I will document all that has transpired thus far, and with whom, including the payment amount." Jakob shrugged. "If I do not return safely and board the ship with the payment intact, then all will be revealed."

"Now see here—" Hans blustered.

Wold cut him off. "I agree."

"But—"

The Duke of Holstein was clearly annoyed. "Oh for God's sake, Andersen. This is the best way to assure that all goes well. We are asking the man to trust us with his life and his future. Of course he needs to take precautions. I admire him for it."

Jakob heaved a satisfied sigh. "All that remains now, your Grace, is to agree on the payment. How far are you gentlemen willing to go to secure your lives and your futures?"

Chapter Twenty-Eight

July 9, 1519

For two weeks Jakob had been impatiently waiting for a private audience with Christian. Unfortunately, some of his frustration had spilled over onto Avery, who was frustrated in her own right.

"I have nothing to do, and no one to talk to," she said yesterday. "And while I was sorry when you were not with me, these last days with you snapping at me over nothing have been far worse."

"What will you have me do?" he growled. "I am no happier than you about our circumstances."

"We should leave the city," Avery suggested. "Go to the countryside and stay in a little inn somewhere, take long walks, and enjoy the change."

Jakob drew a deep breath. "We cannot."

"Why not? Is it money?" Avery began to fumble in her pocket.

"No. It is not money." Jakob dragged his fingers through his hair. "The king will not allow us to leave."

"What?" Her brow plunged. "When did this begin?"

"It was this way from the start. I did not tell you because I knew you would be angry." Jakob rested his hands on his hips. "And he has guards on the docks as well."

She snorted. "Are you so important that he goes to these

lengths?"

"There is more going on than you know, Avery."

"Tell me."

"I cannot." Jakob closed the space between them and lifted her hands. "I need you to trust me. For your safety and for mine. Will you do this?"

She gave him a skeptical look. "And how long must I trust you in this silence?"

"A week. Two weeks. I am not certain. But I promise you that all of our troubles will be over quickly."

She gazed into his eyes, hers too dark to see her pupils. "Do you love me?"

Jakob's knees nearly buckled. "More than I love myself. You are everything to me."

"Then I shall do as you say." She pulled her hands from his and dropped onto a chair. "We are truly prisoners, then?"

His heart broke for her. "Yes. For now."

Today Jakob was granted an audience, albeit not a private one. Even so, the ability to speak with his sovereign at long last was a huge relief. The sooner this business was concluded, the sooner he and Avery could depart København. He said a silent prayer, asking for God's provenance.

Christian sat in his informal throne, in the large room where he met with his subjects. Jakob gave his best courtly bow.

"Rise before your leg gives way," Christian barked. "What say you, Sir Hansen?"

Jakob knew his request would sound strange, and he had struggled for the last two week with how to phrase it. "Your Grace, I have a favor to ask of you."

Christian cocked a brow. "You ask a favor when your status is so precarious?"

"Yes, your Grace."

The king gestured impatiently. "Well? What is it?"

"My wife wishes to purchase some property south of København. I was hoping your Highness might be willing to ride out with me and give your permission."

Christian straightened. "How far south?"

"Three or four miles." Jakob cleared his suddenly dry throat.

"About one half of an hour."

"Will she go with us?"

"No. Your Grace and I shall travel alone, and not make a fuss over it." Jakob glanced at one of the scowling noblemen who attended the king and knew he needed to say more. "If you approve, I will make the purchase on her behalf, as she is not only a woman, but also a foreigner."

One of the king's brows lifted. "When did you wish to make this little journey?"

"At your earliest convenience, your Highness." Jakob bowed again, but not as deeply. "I am your most humble servant."

Christian stared at Jakob through narrowed eyes. Jakob met his gaze and respectfully dipped his chin.

The king sat back in his seat. "I believe we shall journey on the morrow, after the midday meal. Meet me under the portico at two bells."

A surge of relief flooded Jakob's frame and he felt weak afterward. "Gladly, your Grace. Thank you."

Jakob backed away and turned to leave.

"Hansen!"

He turned back. "Your Grace?"

Christian's intensity trembled in the air between them. "I still expect you to perform your duties."

Jakob began to tremble. "Without fail, your highness."

Once away from the king, Jakob crumpled on the staircase, and sat with his head between his knees. Anyone who saw him there would assume his leg pained him, and such an assumption would buy him time to think.

After the king agreed to go with him, he believed the hardest part of his covert commission to be completed. He did not expect the king to remind him of his knightly duties.

Jakob was not comfortable with intrigue, now that he was married. To risk his own life was one thing; to imperil his wife was another thing entirely. And the war with Sweden had broken out while he was gone—he had no idea what he was returning to.

Several minutes passed before Jakob felt recovered enough to face his wife.

He climbed the steps slowly, making a mental inventory of

what must go with him on the morrow. There was scant time to prepare, but prepare they must.

July 10, 1519

Jakob kissed Avery so sweetly that she pulled away. Her dark eyes examined his face intently, obviously not misinterpreting his heartfelt affections. "What is happening, Jakob?"

He swallowed thickly. "Everything, my love."

She gasped softly. "What shall I do?"

"Pray for me, wife. If all goes well, our banishment shall come to an end."

He kissed her again to keep her from asking any more questions, and then strode from the room. Askel waited in the hallway as instructed and handed Jakob his sword and knife.

"God be with you, my lord."

He patted the valet's shoulder. "He will be, Askel."

Jakob tucked his knife inside his boot and descended the stairs quickly as he could. When he exited the door of the residence, the king's carriage was in place. He gave a map with directions to the driver, before the footman opened the door and Jakob climbed in.

How many more carriage rides with a king and a secret purpose must I endure in this lifetime?

Christian's gaze dropped to the sword at Jakob's side. "I see you heeded my expectations."

"Yes, your Grace."

The king motioned out the window of the cab and the carriage began to move.

Once more, Jakob's senses were on high, as he listened for the sounds of hooves and tack, proof that this meeting was not between only a few men. His heart thumped in his chest, hard but steady. His hand rested on the hilt of his sword. He shifted his foot and felt the pressure of the knife against his calf.

He could not be more ready.

The house came into view, visible in vertical stripes between the sheltering trees. "We have arrived, your Grace."

Christian banged on the roof of the carriage and the driver

slowed the horses. They approached the house at a walk.

"Get down and stay down, your Grace!" Jakob instructed Christian once their progress halted, and hove himself from the conveyance.

He stood outside the carriage, waiting.

The door of the house opened and Nygaard Wold appeared. "Have you brought what we requested?"

"I have."

Wold barked a command and several armed men ran around the corners of the house.

"What is this, Wold?" Jakob shouted. "You said you only wanted to talk!"

Wold chuckled and called out, "Honest men are the easiest to fool."

He gave a signal and the men slowly approached the carriage, weapons at the ready.

As the men moved forward, a trumpet sounded in the woods. Before a single arrow was loosed in in Jakob's direction, the king's guard emerged from the forest on horseback, swarming the brigands from every point on the compass.

Jakob spun and pulled himself up next to the carriage driver. He retrieved his bow and quiver from under the seat. His task was to keep anyone from actually reaching the king.

He shot one man in the neck, and nearly removed another's arm with his sword.

"Bring the traitors to the carriage!" Jakob bellowed over the fighting. "And bring them alive!"

The frantic and bloody confrontation did not last more than five minutes, as out-manned as the treasonous rebels were. When the uneven battle was over, two dozen men lay on the ground, dead or dying. Not one of the fallen wore the king's colors, Jakob was pleased to note.

Five disheveled Danish noblemen had been trussed. Some were bleeding or bruised, and all were prodded toward the carriage to face their king.

Jakob climbed down as King Christian stepped out of the conveyance, his sword still at the ready in the event one of the noblemen acted even more foolishly than they already had.

"What have we here?" Christian walked a slow circle around the men. "I see the houses of Orlamünde, Regenstein, Gleichen and Everstein are all represented. And I expect your leader to be the esteemed Duke. Am I correct?"

Nygaard Wold lifted his multiply-layered chin and sniffed. "We five are but the top of a very large iceberg. Sweden will triumph gloriously over Denmark in the end."

King Christian looked at the officers and soldiers surrounding them. "I accuse these five gentlemen of treason against their king and against their country. Has anyone any dissenting evidence?"

Of course, no one spoke; Wold's words had already condemned them.

Christian motioned to his captain and the man dismounted, along with two lieutenants. "Kill them. Then load the bodies in the wagon."

Two of the men—both of them still in their twenties—began to cry. One middle-aged man tried to charge the king, but Jakob's sword stopped his progress. The man stared stupidly at the hilt protruding from his chest before dropping lifeless to the ground.

Jakob rested a boot on his shoulder and removed his sword. He wiped the blood on the man's tunic.

The captain and each lieutenant slit the throats of the two sobbing men, and another man who seemed to not understand what was happening. The only man left standing was the duke.

Christian stepped in front of him. "Should I say I am surprised, Nygaard?"

His brow twitched. "Are you?"

Christian made a disgusted face. "Not in the least," he sneered before taking three large steps back. "Sir Hansen?"

Jakob planted his boots at shoulder's width and gripped his sword with both arms. Nygaard Wold stared at him, his faced twisted in fury.

Jakob met the man's gaze. "Dishonest men believe themselves invincible."

He swung his sword with all his strength, neatly removing Wold's head from his body. Jakob looked down at the detached face. The man's eyes rolled wildly for an instant, before the pupils dilated, sightless.

The king clapped him on the back. "You have redeemed yourself this day."

Jakob whirled and knelt in front of his sovereign, careful not to put his knee in a bloody puddle and ruin his hose. "It was my honor, your Grace."

"Rise, Sir Hansen, and accept the accolades which are due you."

When he rose, King Christian was smiling at him.

§ § §

Avery vomited her lunch, too nervous and frightened to keep it down. Emily offered her a wet cloth and a cup of tea, stroking her hair in a soothing manner. A dull headache threatened in spite of the maid attempts to calm her.

Whatever was Jakob about? She prayed through her rosary over and over again, each time adding a plea for Jakob.

Please, Father, keep him safe. Do not allow him to do anything foolish.

Askel was of no help—he had no idea what his master had been up to these past weeks.

The church bells in the distance rang four times. Avery's nerves were shredded like boiled meat and she could not concentrate on anything productive. Instead, she paced the length of the apartment, from the hall door to the bedchamber window and back, rosary beads dribbling through her fingers.

When she believed she must truly lose her sanity, Askel threw the door open. "Sir Hansen has returned!"

Avery ran into the hallway and collided with her husband.

He pushed her away and held her at arm's length. "Have a care. I am blood stained." When he saw her shocked expression, he added, "It is not my blood!"

"Wh—whose blood is it?" she stammered.

"A traitor, whose band King Christian has rightly had put to death."

Avery rubbed her forehead, shoving the ache away. "I do not understand, Jakob. Where were you and what were you doing?"

Instead of answering, he turned to Askel. "I need to wash, and my wife needs a hot bath."

"Yes, sir!" The valet sprinted away.

"Emily?"

The maid's voice was close behind her. "Yes, sir?"

"Once she is refreshed, you will need to dress Lady Avery in her best finery for supper in royal dining hall."

Avery's hand fell to the side and she stared at Jakob. "You are forgiven?"

"I assure you, I earned it well." He tilted his head. "Shall we retire to our chamber so that I may remove another man's blood?"

"Of course." Avery spun on her heel and marched back inside.

Jakob and Emily followed.

Emily held out her hands. "Give me your tunic, Sir. I will start cleaning it."

Avery helped Jakob out of the gruesome garment. Emily took it without flinching and headed toward the laundry. Though there was blood on his hose, Jakob would wait for Askel before handing them off.

"Please tell me what has transpired—before I expire from trepidation!" Avery pleaded.

Jakob poured a cup of wine and handed it to her. "You should sit." He looked down. "Forgive me if I do not."

Avery accepted the cup, sat, and took a long draught of the amber liquid.

"Let me begin by asking your forgiveness, Avery—I have not told you the entire truth before now."

She looked up at him. "I assume there was good reason."

Jakob nodded. "Christian asked me to play a dangerous role and the utmost secrecy was required for it to succeed."

He took a gulp of wine and continued. "Christian suggested that if his enemies believed me to be in a position where betraying him would free me, they might approach me with an offer."

Avery's eyes rounded. "So he was never angry?"

Jakob huffed. "Oh, no. He was most definitely angry. And he used that anger to convince me to agree."

Of course. "And then you *were* approached."

"The traitors—four noblemen led by a duke—offered me seventy thousand krone to lead Christian into their trap."

"How much—"

"Seven thousand pounds sterling."

"Oh, my."

"Yes." Jakob drained his cup and refilled it. "The only part of the plan of which I was uncertain was Christian's refusal to meet with me privately when the plan was culminating."

Avery frowned. "What were his reasons?"

Jakob gestured with his wine glass. "If anyone in his court was involved, and knew that he met with me alone, he was afraid that knowledge might scare them off and ruin the plan."

She reluctantly agreed. "I believe he had a valid point."

"He did. And luckily, when I appeared in his court yesterday, he understood what I was telling him."

"So this afternoon, you and the king turned the trap on them."

"We did." Jakob looked quite pleased.

"And the blood…" she left the sentence dangling in the air between them.

"The rebels are dead to a man."

The door opened, and a large copper tub was brought in, followed by three servants carrying buckets of hot water. Askel followed with towels.

Jakob grinned at her. "Your bath, my lady."

§ § §

The hot water did wonders for her mood, and by the time she was dressed and coiffed—and Jakob washed and shaved—Avery felt invincible. She rested her arm in his as they approached the dining hall, head high, and proud to near bursting of her husband.

When they entered the hall, a herald stepped to their side. "The king has requested that you sit near him. Please follow me."

As they did so, Avery glanced up Jakob. His brow was once again smooth and the only visible creases emanated from the corners of his bright blue eyes.

"Here you are, Sir. Madam." The herald held a chair for Avery.

She took her seat—to the right of the king and queen's head table—and Jakob dropped into the chair on her left. He tilted his head close to hers.

"We have certainly elevated our place in the court," he whispered.

"You have," she replied in kind. "I am still a foreigner who does not speak Norsk or Danish."

Jakob leaned back and considered her, his expression pensive. "We have not been here long."

"No we have not," she conceded. "And we have been 'undesirables' for all of that time. Until now, of course."

"Give it a chance, Avery." He squeezed her thigh under the table. "No final decisions have to be made as yet."

Avery smiled at Jakob, though she was having a very difficult time liking Denmark. Hopefully her experience would be different from here on out. If it was not, she would need to ask Jakob to consider returning to England before the weather turned.

It is only July. You still have almost three months.

The chatter around them hushed of a sudden as King Christian stood. He lifted a gilded cup and proceeded to make some sort of speech.

Avery caught Jakob's name, something about thanking him, a growling reference to someone named Nygaard Wold. His narrative ended with, "*Skåle!*"

"*Skåle!*" the crowd echoed, raising their cups as well.

Jakob rose to his feet and bowed at the waist. "Thank you. It is my pleasure to serve our King and Queen."

He reclaimed his seat and squeezed her thigh once again.

Avery took the cue, beamed at him, and lifted her cup to honor him.

"*Jeg elsker deg, min mann,*" she whispered.

"*Jeg elsker deg også, min kone.*" The glint in his eyes clearly indicated that he planned to show her just how much he loved her once they were alone again.

As the meal progressed, more of the table's occupants engaged Jakob in conversation. He tried to include Avery when he could, and translated when he felt something was important for her to understand, but she still struggled.

"If only they would speak more slowly," she said once the meal was concluded. The couple strolled casually toward their apartment. "Then I might be able to connect the words with ones I understand—or intuit the meanings of those I do not."

Jakob gave her a sympathetic nod. "The men I spoke with in England were kind enough to do so. And you were an excellent tutor for Spanish. I am sorry that your experience here has, thus far, been less helpful."

Avery sighed and flashed a rueful grin. "I shall give it time, as you requested."

Their progress was interrupted by a middle-aged couple who fawned embarrassingly over Jakob. He blushed and tried to deflect their commendations, but to no avail. After several minutes, they left, having only given Avery the most cursory attention.

A thought had occurred to her as she stood beside her husband, seething, but with a determinedly polite smile pasted on her face.

"Where is Hans Andersen?" she asked once the couple departed.

Jakob's expression sobered of a sudden. "He will hang in the morning."

Avery's jaw fell slack. "Not your friend!"

"He was the one who approached me." Jakob grimaced. "He actually recommended me to the duke as the candidate who was close enough, and angry enough, to do the king harm."

"I am so sorry, Jakob."

"As am I."

She laid her hand over his. "Will you attend the hanging?"

He nodded. "I want him to see me there. I will try to let him know that I am not angry with him."

Avery scowled. "Are you not?"

Jakob stopped walking and looked around, before answering her. "He made a mistake, Avery. He was seduced by money and power. But he was a good and loyal knight at one time."

She understood. "You want him to go to the gallows with that reminder."

"I do."

Avery started walking again. "If only every man and woman in København was as considerate as you."

Jakob kissed her forehead and repeated her words. "Do give it time."

Chapter Twenty-Nine

August 15, 1519

Jakob knew Avery was unhappy. Though more than a month had passed since his reinstatement to court and the king's favor, the women in the royal residence continued to give her no more than polite attention.

It did not help that Avery was still struggling with the language. That was undeniably his fault, since he spoke English to her for the most part, only slipping into Norsk when others were present. Or Spanish in bed.

Her maid Emily also spoke only English, managing to communicate with Askel when she needed assistance in completing her duties.

While Askel was eager to help the admittedly pretty maid, something about her demeanor revealed her belief that her time in Denmark was temporary. Rather than try to fit in with the multitude of servants, she was merely biding her time until Avery announced their return to the Tudor court.

Jakob sighed and reined Warrior around to begin their return to the royal residence. He really hoped that a long ride in the countryside would soothe his mind. In actuality, the more he considered their circumstances, the more obvious it was becoming that returning to England was the best choice.

Jakob had considered that option from the start—but as an alternative, should Christian send him away. Not merely as a ruse to capture traitors, but if the king actually revoked Jakob's knighthood.

Jakob had been able to slip back into his duties without effort, but that only made Avery's struggles more obvious.

"What say you, Warrior?" Jakob patted the stallion's massive neck. "Can you survive one more voyage?"

The destrier shook his mane and snorted.

Jakob chuckled. "If I can, then you can."

Was the decision made, then?

Jakob was unwilling to say the words aloud just yet. Once made, the decision would be irreversible.

He was not a man who wished to bounce between countries, a fact that these past fifteen months had clearly proved. While his ideas about what constituted a home had changed, the desire for a permanent one had become more firmly set.

"I am thirty-three, and my wife is thirty-five," he explained to Warrior. "It is time for us to settle somewhere and live out our lives in peace."

He was surprised to realize that returning to København no longer felt like returning home. Perhaps that was because he had finally returned to Arendal after sixteen years and his relationship with his family was repaired at last.

Even so, he had no desire to live in Arendal because there was no place for him there.

So how did he feel about England?

An unanticipated warmth bloomed in his chest. England was where he met Avery. It was where he was released from eight years of bondage to a guilt that was not his to carry. And it was where he fell in love—real love—for the first time.

Jakob smiled. Perhaps England truly was his home now.

The thought came to him that Avery had also bounced between countries. And all the while she was in England, she had been hiding from the truth and living a lie. Though she said she had no reason to return to Spain, could she call England her home and be sincere about it?

"It is time to answer that question." He rubbed the stallion's ears. "Ready yourself, War. We might be sailing once again."

Jakob kicked the stallion's sides, and the huge horse leapt into a ground-swallowing gallop back toward the city.

§ § §

When he walked into the apartment, he took a hard look at Avery, the first objective one in weeks. Her cheeks were pale and even her lips seemed to have lost color. He could not remember the last time he heard her laugh.

Jakob dropped to his knees in front of her. "Will you forgive me, Avery, for being so blind?"

Avery's brows drew together. "How are you blind?"

"I had been hoping for something, and not seeing that it was not the right thing for you." He gave an apologetic shrug. "Today I realized, as it turns out, it is not right for me, either."

Avery's eyes widened. "Were you hoping for a child?"

A shock zinged through Jakob's core. "A child—what?—no— are you?"

Avery shook her head soberly. "No."

Jakob rocked back on his heels. "Good."

"Good?" Avery blurted. "Why is that good?"

Jakob threw up his hands. "It is not good, it is not bad. But that is not what I was speaking about."

"Then what *were* you speaking about?"

Jakob rested his palms on his thighs. "I am speaking about our home."

She winced. "Here?"

Jakob wagged his head. "No. København is the place that I escaped to, when my own home no longer offered me an acceptable path."

Avery heaved a relieved sigh. "Much in the same manner as when I escaped to London."

"Yes." Jakob expressed a newly sprouted idea. "And while I have always considered Norway my home, I have no desire to live there."

Avery's eyes pinched at the corners, though she was not smiling. "I have always considered Spain to be my home, but I also have no desire to live there."

"I came to København and remained for eight years."

"I went to London and remained for nine."

Here was the pivotal moment. Jakob drew a deep breath. "København has never been my home."

Avery stilled, as if afraid to breathe.

"Was London ever your home?" Jakob asked softly.

Avery's eyes welled with unspilt tears. "Not when I lived there, but…"

"But?" Jakob prompted.

"When we left Barcelona together, I was not thinking about any particular place as being my home." She wiped her cheeks, her tears having topped their dam. "And yet, when I spied the White Tower upon our return, my first thought was—"

"We are almost home?" Jakob finished the sentence.

"Yes," she whispered.

Jakob reached for her hands. "Where is home for you now, Avery?"

She looked stricken by the query. Clearly she thought Jakob wanted her to say Denmark. "Be honest with me, Avery. I need to know."

"I don't—"

"Tell me."

Her gaze fell to the floor. "England. London."

And there it was.

Jakob closed his eyes and pictured the Tower, Windsor Castle, the Thames, and the countryside around York Place. The mental images evoked pleasant feelings—for the most part. If they returned there to live, however, he would need to have a hard conversation with King Henry the Eighth.

Not if.

When.

Jakob opened his eyes to see Avery's dark orbs fixed on his. He smiled at her. "Then we shall go home."

"For how long?" Avery hedged.

"For the rest of our lives, I expect."

Avery recoiled. "Do not tease me, Jakob. I cannot bear it."

He spread his palms. "Why do you believe me a tease?"

"Because—" A sob severed her reply.

Jakob pulled Avery from her chair and into his lap. "I should have realized it sooner. Denmark was never my home, so how could it ever be yours?"

"Oh Jakob..." She circled his torso with her arms. "Are we truly returning to England to live?"

"We are, my love."

"And are you truly satisfied with this decision?"

Jakob laughed. "I am. Although I will need to have a very serious discussion with Henry. Our previous arrangement is no longer acceptable."

Avery leaned away. "When shall we leave?"

"As soon as we can make arrangements." Jakob kissed her soundly. "I shall speak with Christian. *After* I have collected all of my investments, that is."

Avery's delighted laugh was the most beautiful sound he had ever heard.

August 22, 1519

"Leaving?" King Christian frowned. "I am not sending you anywhere."

"No, your Grace." Jakob stood in the same place, and in the same stance, as he had when Christian first told him about the role he would play at Order of the Golden Fleece. "But I am taking my wife back to England. Back to King Henry's court."

"Can she not travel alone?"

"Of course she is capable, your Highness, that is not the point."

Christian was growing increasingly irritated. "Then what is the point?"

"I will not be returning to København."

The king stared at Jakob, as if the top of his head had just flopped open and bubbles were spilling out. "You do not have my permission to leave, Hansen."

Jakob changed his approach. "That is why I have requested this audience. To ask your permission."

"And if I say no?"

"Then I must resign as your knight, and leave København carrying away nothing more than I arrived with."

And my accrued investments, of course.

Those funds were already safely stowed on the waiting ship, along with everyone he loved and everything else he owned.

"You are a singularly ungrateful man, Hansen, do you know that?" Christian growled.

"An ungrateful man, who risked his very life to save your kingdom—and succeeded." Jakob bowed. "Once again, it was my honor to serve you."

The king's gaze ricocheted around the room, landing on several of the waiting nobility. Clearly he was measuring Jakob's reply and his pending response against their loyalties.

"Get out."

"Thank you, your Grace." Jakob backed away from the throne, turned at the door, and sprinted toward freedom.

September 29, 1519

Avery stood on the London dock and wagged her head at the enormous pile of trunks, crates, boxes, tack, and satchels which comprised the worldly possessions and lives of her, Jakob, Emily, Askel—and Warrior.

"I do not know where all of this will go." She shaded her eyes against the late afternoon sun. "We will require different accommodations than our last stay. Now that we will be permanent residents, we cannot sleep either on the ladies' floor or the men's."

"Well, we cannot leave everything sitting here." Jakob looked down the pier. "I will hire a wagon. Once our possessions are inside the Tower walls, we can secure a guard for them until we know where we shall reside."

A wagon procured and loaded, Jakob and Avery walked behind it to the gate of the Tower. "I wonder if Higgins will be on duty," she mused. "It will be nice to see him again."

Jakob grinned. "It is nice to see all of this again."

Avery laughed. Joy bubbled up inside her as she and her beloved husband approached the fortress which they had come to

Kris Tualla

think of as their permanent home.

She strained to see if the Tudor standard was flying from the turrets. "Do you think Henry and Catherine are in attendance?"

A gust of wind answered her question, snapping the blue, red, and gold flags with sudden enthusiasm.

"I wonder if Bessie successfully birthed her child." Jakob glanced at Avery, whose mood was dampened by the comment.

"I cannot wish her or the child harm," she said. "But if she and the babe survived, I do pray it was a girl."

"A girl would not present a complication, that is true," Jakob observed. "And Henry would not need to claim it."

"Higgins!" Avery ran forward and grabbed the hands of the guard. "We have come home at last."

The Beefeater beamed, his ruddy face shining with joy. "Aye, and it is good to welcome ye, Lady Avery." He turned to Jakob. "Good day, Sir Hansen. Ye are looking quite braw."

"Thank you, Higgins." Jakob waved a hand toward the laden wagon. "We shall need a spot to unload all of this, and an overnight guard to see our belongings safe."

"Until we see the queen, we have no idea where we will bide," Avery explained.

The guard appeared hopeful. "Are ye remaining with us this time, Lady?"

"That is our hope, Higgins. I expect to return to my post as Catherine's chief lady-in-waiting."

He shifted his gaze to Jakob. "And yon knight?"

"Sir Hansen has resigned his post in Denmark." Avery smiled at her husband. "He will offer his services to King Henry."

Higgins nodded. "Best of luck to ye, Sir."

"Thank you, again."

The wagon was pulled into the courtyard, and unloaded into one of the Tower's many store rooms—one with a lock, thankfully. The satchels which held their immediate needs were left in Askel's care, while Emily went to the kitchen to announce their return.

Avery knew word of their presence would spread through the servants like a wild fire, so her first priority was to speak with Catherine.

"What will you do while you are waiting for me?" she asked

Jakob. "Try to speak with Henry?"

"No, I believe that conversation should wait until your status with Catherine is confirmed," he replied. "If she reinstates you, and Henry does not wish to retain me, then I can offer my services to the queen in his stead."

Avery gave him an approving grin. "You have thought of everything, it seems."

Jakob winked at her. "That is part of my trade and my training, my lady."

Avery sighed happily. "Where shall I find you after my audience with Catherine, then?"

Jakob combed his fingers through his hair. "I believe I shall search out Bethington. He has certainly returned by now and I am curious about how the Order ended."

"Would he still reside here?" Avery wondered. "He had his own residence before Henry brought him in to become acquainted with you."

"I shall soon discover that answer." Jakob kissed her forehead. "Go see your friend. We shall meet again at seven bells, in the royal hallway."

§ § §

Avery asked to be announced to the queen, and the herald was grinning as he did so. Catherine came forward to greet her and the two women hugged each other tightly.

"These months of silence have been so painfully long, Averia." Catherine loosened her grip and stepped back, still holding Avery's hands. "We have so much to talk about."

"My absence was well spent, your Grace." Because of the other women on the room, Avery used the formal address; but she smiled so widely at her friend that her cheeks ached. "For I have come home to you, unencumbered at last."

Catherine's eyes widened. "You are here to stay?"

Avery dipped a curtsy. "If you will have me, your Highness."

"If I will have you!" The queen laughed. "This has been my daily prayer since I saw you last!"

"I am very glad." Avery glanced at the young woman standing

closest to Catherine. "In what position shall I serve you?"

Catherine let her shoulders fall. "You shall once again be my chief lady-in-waiting, of course. Anne has known since I elevated her that, if you were ever to return to court, you would reclaim your station."

"It is quite acceptable to me, Lady Avery," the girl assured her. "You are her highness's dearest friend, and we all understand that."

"Thank you," Avery murmured.

Catherine squeezed Avery's hands. "And now everyone knows of your troubles and your marriage. You did not abandon me, nor the court, on a whim."

"I am grateful, your Grace." Avery curtsied again. "And so very glad to have come home to you."

"And is Sir Hansen well?"

Avery was startled to realize she had not mentioned her own husband. "He is, your Grace. And I have much to tell you about his experiences as well."

"He is here, with you?" Catherine confirmed.

"Yes, of course." Avery decided to go on and broach the first awkward subject. "But that raises a question..."

Catherine's brow wrinkled. "What question is that?"

"Where shall we reside?"

The queen laughed. "Of course! Now that you and your Nordic husband have come to stay, you will want your own residence." She let go of Avery's hands and waved the herald over. "Would you find out which of the houses inside the wall might be available?"

He bowed. "Yes, my Queen."

"And find out how soon one might be prepared for Lady Avery and Sir Hansen."

"With pleasure, your Highness."

Catherine returned her attention to Avery. "As you did on your last visit, you and your husband may occupy your apartments in the meantime."

Avery smiled her relief. "Thank you."

Catherine instructed Anne to see that the rooms of that apartment were freshened immediately, then she shooed all the ladies away. Once the door closed behind them, Catherine led Avery to a pair of upholstered chairs.

"I wanted to speak with you freely and in private, my dearest friend. I, too, have much to say."

Avery sat down after the queen did, her heart suddenly heavy. "What has transpired, Cathy?"

Catherine's demeanor shifted and the queen seemed to age ten years in that moment. "Bessie birthed a boy."

Avery gasped. "Oh, no! When?"

"Three months ago."

"And is he—" Avery did not know which question would be less painful, but settled on, "Healthy?"

Catherine heaved a shuddering sigh. "He is positively robust."

Avery scrambled for any encouraging word for her friend, but came up short. "What about Henry?"

"Do you want wine?" Catherine rose to her feet. "I do."

Avery stood as well. "I will pour, Cathy. You sit."

The queen sank back into her chair. Avery crossed to the sideboard and poured two glasses, moving back into her role seamlessly, and glad that the wine was a familiar red. She returned to their chairs, handed Catherine one goblet, and then reclaimed her own seat.

Catherine stared at the burgundy liquid, her voice low. "Henry claimed the bastard. Named him Henry Fitzroy."

"Henry, son of royalty?" Avery shook her head, aghast. "I assume, then, that he is certain of Bessie's fidelity."

Catherine huffed and took a large drink of the wine. "I would not trust the wanton if she swore that the sun rises in the east. But the child looks like Henry, so it was his seed that sprouted."

Avery slumped in her chair. "I am so very sorry, my dear friend."

Catherine shot her a fierce look. "Henry may have claimed the bastard, but my Mary will be queen. I swear this on my own life."

Chapter Thirty

Jakob found Bethington in the same apartment in which he resided before the pair of knights departed for Barcelona. When his valet, Denys, responded to Jakob's pounding on the door, a wide grin split the man's cheeks.

Jakob put a finger against his lips to forestall Denys's greeting. "Is Sir Bethington in?" he whispered.

Denys nodded, pulled the door open wider, and stepped out of Jakob's way.

"Who is it?" Percival called from the other room.

"A father whose daughter you have defiled!" Jakob shouted.

Percival bolted through the door. "Sir, I assure you—" He stopped dead. "You bastard!"

Jakob laughed. "Is that the way you greet your long-missed companion?"

Percival strode toward the door, green eyes twinkling over his ruddy cheeks. He clasped Jakob's outstretched arm. "What are you doing here? I thought you and Lady Avery went to Norway!"

"We did. And then we went to Denmark."

"But was your father still alive when you arrived?"

Jakob put up his free hand. "I have much to ask and much to tell. Where do you wish to talk?"

The tavern crowd was thinning as common Londoners went

home to their early suppers. Jakob selected a table by the window while Percival bought a pitcher of ale.

The English knight poured a stein for each of them, then plopped, grinning, into the seat across from Jakob. "Tell me everything."

Jakob took a fortifying gulp of ale and then told Percy about his visit to his family, his last words to his father, and the man's last breath.

Bethington reached across the small table and gave Jakob's arm a solid pat. "Condolences, my friend. I am glad you were able to say what you did."

"As am I," Jakob admitted. "I feel as if a door has been closed, and that part of my life will no longer haunt my thoughts."

Percy refilled his stein. "What happened when you went to Denmark? Was Christian accepting of your marriage?"

Jakob chuckled. "No. And he dragged me through quite a mess as punishment."

Bethington's jaw fell slack as he listened to Jakob's tale of international intrigue and his secret role in the king's plan. This time, he smacked Jakob's arm hard.

"Is this your new calling? Saving kings' lives?"

Jakob froze. He racked his brain, trying to remember how the death of the groom who mistook him for King Henry had been explained, but he could not recall any sort of story. Perhaps the incident never was clarified, and the truth was buried with the man's body.

He waved his hand dismissively. "Even so, I needed to collect my investments before telling Christian that I was leaving. He was quite angry then, as well."

Bethington frowned. "But he did give you permission to leave his service?"

"Begrudgingly." Jakob sipped his ale. "But Avery, Askel, Emily, and Warrior were already safely aboard the ship when I asked him. Or told him, rather."

"Was he aware of that?"

"No. The guards were removed after the business with the traitors was completed."

Percival nodded his approval. "Good plan."

"Yes." Jakob gestured toward Percy with his ale. "When did you return?"

"Around mid-June."

That was surprising. "Did the meeting of the Order go so long?"

"No, we adjourned two weeks after you left." Bethington chuckled. "We all grew wearily tired of the constant bickering between France and Spain. So, I quoted the Treaty of London once again, we voted for France to do as they wished, and hastily wrapped up the rest of our meager business in a neat package."

"If the Order was finished by the first of April or so, why did it take you so long to travel back to London?" Jakob asked.

"I did not depart immediately." The Englishman's lips twisted in a sly smile. "I remained for another month."

Though he guessed the reason, Jakob still asked, "What held you there?"

"The weather was so beautiful. Much warmer and sunnier than here." He tipped his head toward the gray evening sky. "I wanted to enjoy the climate as long as I was able."

Jakob was skeptical of that explanation. "So you stayed in Barcelona for the weather?"

"Well, to be truthful, other aspects were quite warm as well."

"Ah—there it is." Jakob grinned. "What was her name?"

Percy's expression turned wistful. "Their names were Anna, Eucilia, and Carmen."

Jakob's head fell back and he laughed. "Still the same Percival."

"Admit it—you would have worried about me if I was not."

Jakob nodded. "This is true."

"During your travels, did you hear anything about Spain's triumph?" Bethington asked, his joviality dimmed.

"No." The shift made Jakob nervous. "What occurred?"

"The Spanish retook the city of Algiers by themselves."

"And the Ottomans?"

"Never arrived."

"So the threat was not as severe as we were led to believe?" Jakob wagged his head. "I am glad we did not force France to be involved.

Percival regarded him over the rim of his raised stein. "And now you are back in London. What will you do?" He took a sip.

Jakob refilled his own cup. "My wife expects to serve the queen once more. And I—" He stopped, realizing once again that he could not mention that he had saved Henry's life. His actions of more than a year ago would always remain a strictly guarded secret. "I will offer my services to King Henry first."

"And if he declines?"

"Then I will offer them to Queen Catherine."

Bethington peered at him. "And if she declines?"

Jakob did not have a third plan, because he truly did not believe he needed one. "I suppose I will live off my investments and find some other industry to occupy my time."

Percival nodded. "How much did you escape with, if you do not mind me asking?

"I do not mind, because I will need advice as to whom I should invest it with in London." Jakob leaned closer. "I have what amounts to about four thousand pounds sterling."

Percy's brows shot upward toward his unruly hairline. "That will support you for the next twenty years—and in a courtly manner—even without interest!"

Jakob nodded. "And Avery has her shipping business, remember. In fact, her first contract is with my older brother."

Bethington slapped the table but kept his voice low. "You two will become rich as royalty!"

That thought turned Jakob's mood to a more serious vein. "But we will not have children to pass our wealth to."

Percy frowned. "Are you certain of that?"

"Avery is thirty-five and I am thirty-three. We are too old to start raising a family."

I hope.

The English knight made a sign of blessing. "In that case, my good sir, you shall become a philanthropist extraordinaire and better our society when you take your leave of it."

"Perhaps you shall be right." Jakob laughed and drained his stein.

§ § §

When Jakob and Percival returned to the Tower, he was directed to Avery's previously occupied chambers. Arriving at the apartment, he discovered that Askel had unpacked his satchel and made him every bit as comfortable as he had been on their last visit, several months earlier.

"Catherine is procuring us a house within the Tower walls," Avery chirped happily as she arranged her things. "We should be able to move into it within a fortnight."

This was good news. Obviously it meant that Avery was reinstated as the queen's chief lady-in-waiting. "How was your visit with Catherine otherwise?"

Avery stopped her activity and whirled to face him. "Bessie birthed a boy."

Jakob heaved a heavy sigh. The answer to his next question would speak volumes. "And did Henry claim it?"

She nodded. "He named the boy Henry Fitzroy."

Jakob snorted. "I do not suppose he could be any clearer than that."

"Catherine is devastated."

"Of course she is." Perhaps he would bypass Henry and offer his loyalty directly to the queen. At the least his ruse had successfully remained a secret. "And now Henry will be informed of our return."

"Yes. He should not be surprised at supper." She returned to her puttering. "A surprised Henry is not always a pleasant Henry, I am afraid."

The clock in the hallway chimed. Jakob brushed his hands over his tunic and hose. "We should go."

Bethington met them at the bottom of the stairs. "My Lady Avery, you are as strikingly beautiful as ever."

"And you are as charming, good sir." Avery smiled at the knight. "It is good to see you again, Percy. I want to thank you again for all of your help in Barcelona."

"Do not for a moment believe that any of it was a hardship," Jakob interjected. "He was as happy as a cat in a dairy the entire time."

"Perhaps so, but Thomas Windsor, Duke of Merthyr Tydfil's skillful assistance was crucial nonetheless." Percy offered Avery his arm. "Let us leave this ingrate behind, shall we?"

Avery laughed and accepted his elbow, but she looped her other arm through Jakob's. "I shall enter on both of your arms, and thereby be the envy of all the ladies at court."

Judging by the looks cast in her direction, she was not wrong.

Avery took her seat between Jakob and Percival. Her unannounced reappearance, with the foreign husband still in attendance, was clearly wearing on some of the newer court members.

Those who were part of the Tudor court when Jakob arrived, and had the chance to know him, were for the most part pleased to see Lady Avery happily married at last. And Avery assured Jakob that the lady-in-waiting whom she supplanted by her return insisted she held no animosity toward his wife.

"It is not an easy position to manage," Avery reminded him before they descend the stairs for supper. "Pleasing a queen is not a task to be taken lightly."

"And so, it is a great advantage to have been her lifelong confidant," he replied.

Avery smiled up at him. "Not everyone is so blessed."

Henry was sitting in his chair in the center of the raised dais in the front of the dining hall. Catherine was by his side. Both royals conversed with the occupants of the chairs beside them, but not with each other. If that kept up, there would be no hope for another heir.

Henry's gaze moved to Jakob and he motioned for the Norseman to approach.

Jakob did so and bowed in front of the king. "Good eventide, your Grace."

"Welcome, once again, to my court, Sir Hansen. I understand your wife has returned to her post as the queen's chief lady-in-waiting."

"Yes, your Grace." Jakob smiled politely. "And she is very happy to regain her position."

Henry's gaze narrowed. "What are your plans?"

Jakob shifted his expression to one of supplication. "If I may, I would like to request an audience with your Highness to glean your advice on this matter."

"A private audience?"

Jakob understood what Henry was asking. "I have no objections to the Duke of Suffolk joining us. In fact, I would welcome his wisdom as well."

Henry nodded slowly. "Come to the throne room on the morrow at ten in the morning. I shall make time for you at some point."

"Thank you, your Grace." Jakob backed away and returned to his seat.

"What did Henry say?" Avery murmured.

"He granted me an audience on the morrow, to discuss my plans." Jakob sighed. "I shall covet your prayers, dearest wife."

September 30, 1519

Jakob arrived before ten and waited over two hours to be admitted into the king's presence. Henry knew he was there; making him wait was a statement of who held the power. That Henry felt he needed to do so, gave Jakob hope.

Either he remembers that he owes me his life, or he wants to make a request of me.

Whichever situation turned out to be true did not matter to Jakob. Through his conversation with Bethington—which he repeated to Avery before they went to bed—he realized that he did not need the king's favor, he only desired it.

In truth, Jakob held the power this time.

When he was ushered in, the steward closed the door, leaving Jakob alone with King Henry and Charles Brandon, Duke of Suffolk.

He faced the king and bowed. "Your Highness, thank you for granting me a private audience."

Brandon strode forward, smiling and with his hand extended. "Welcome back, Hansen. I am sorry to have missed your triumphal return yester eve."

Jakob clasped the duke's arm. "Thank you, your Grace. I am truthful when I say that I am very glad to be back."

Brandon indicated a chair facing the king and took his seat on Henry's right. Jakob sat and faced the king.

Henry pinned him with a narrowed gaze. "I believe we are to discuss your future, are we not?"

Jakob dipped his chin. "Yes, your Grace."

"I wish to discuss your past, first. How was your time in Norway?"

Jakob related his tale about his father's death, his reuniting with his family, and Avery's contract with his elder brother.

Henry stared at Jakob for quiet moment. "What occurred when you returned to Denmark?"

Jakob began the second portion of his story. "While King Christian was glad to have avoided being put in that difficult political position by my vacating the Order, he was very displeased about my marrying without his permission."

He continued the telling, including his subterfuge in aborting the coup, and the subsequent saving of King Christian's life.

Henry snorted. "So your new vocation consists of subverting plots and saving kings' lives."

Jakob cleared his throat to stifle the laugh that hearing a statement so similar to Bethington's prompted. He did not know what sort of response was expected, so he said, "A knight's vocation is always defined by protecting the king he is serving, your Grace."

"Well said, Hansen." Henry's expression eased. "And now you have returned to my court, having been banished from Christian's."

Jakob risked Henry's displeasure by correcting him, but he did not wish to be viewed as desperate in any way. "In truth, I chose to leave."

Henry folded his arms over his chest. "Why would a knight—one who was obviously respected and trusted by his sovereign—chose to leave that man's service?"

Jakob drew a breath. "My wife was miserable."

That was obviously not the response that the king expected to her. "Your wife was miserable?" he repeated, incredulous. "You left a secure and coveted position because your *wife* was miserable?"

"Yes, your Grace." Jakob straightened in his seat. "I did."

"And what were your expectations?" Brandon asked.

Jakob directed his answer to the duke. "I expected my wife to be able to resume serving Queen Catherine, whom she has loved since they were girls together in Alcalá de Henares."

"What expectations do you hold for yourself?" Henry demanded.

Jakob faced the powerful young King of England. "I am offering myself, a respected and trusted knight, into your service, your Highness."

Henry leaned back, rubbing a finger over his upper lip, and staring at Jakob. Jakob could not discern whether the sovereign expected that offer or not. Either way, he could do nothing but wait for Henry to speak.

"What will you do if I decline?"

Jakob gave the hint of a shrug. "With your permission, I may offer my services to the queen. Or I might live off of my investments, and find another way to occupy my days."

This response was clearly not anticipated. Henry turned to look at Brandon. "What have you to say?"

Brandon hesitated before replying. Jakob saw the shadow of several emotions flicker over the duke's visage. "Will you wish for Sir Hansen to resume his previous activities?"

Jakob's gut clenched. He was ready to decline, and forcefully if necessary.

Henry returned his regard to Jakob. "I had considered that possibility, though the queen is not currently with child."

Jakob dipped his chin, speaking in the most deferential tone he could conjure. "With all respect due to you, your Grace, I am not willing to resume our ruse."

"What if I made that a condition of accepting your offer?"

"Then I would withdraw it."

Henry frowned. "And if I banished you from my court?"

Jakob's pulse surged. This game of cat and mouse was growing dangerous, but he could not back down. "I would live with my wife outside of the Tower walls."

"And if I banished you from England?" Henry growled.

Jakob slid from the chair to kneel in front of the volatile young sovereign. "Then I would ask why you disliked your own wife so strongly."

The Duke of Suffolk stepped into the confrontation, speaking quickly to shield Jakob from Henry's anger. "He means because the queen is so much happier and compliant when the Lady Avery is by her side, your Grace. Her depressed state over the loss of her last child might be ameliorated, and surely another child will be conceived quickly as a result."

Henry huffed and glared at Jakob, kneeling on the rug in front of him. "I shall need to give the matter some thought."

"Of course, your Grace," Jakob placated. "I did not expect your Highness to make such a decision during our audience."

"You are dismissed."

"Thank you, your Grace." Jakob rose stiffly to his feet and briefly rubbed his thigh. "Might I ask one more question of the duke?"

Scowling, Henry gave a permissive wave. Jakob faced Brandon, choosing his words carefully. "You will recall the groom I killed, the one who mistook me for the king."

"Yes, of course." The duke narrowed his eyes. "What about him?"

"Since returning this time, I realized that do not know how his death was explained." Jakob spread his palms in supplication, but he slid a hard look toward Henry. "It would be helpful in keeping my role in saving the king's life a secret, if I was able to put forth the same story."

Brandon understood Jakob's intent perfectly. "I will discuss this matter with the king and have an answer for you soon."

Jakob bowed deeply. "Thank you, your Graces."

He backed away, turned, and let himself out of the room. Though his heart was pounding and his hands shaking, he could no longer suppress his grin.

Ợhapter Ţhirty-Øne

October 3, 1519

Henry waited three days before revealing his decision to Jakob. During that time, Jakob kept his mind and his hands occupied by lending his assistance to the preparations taking place in the house he and Avery would soon occupy.

Jakob believed in his heart that he would not be banished from the Tudor court, so the efforts he put forth would not be wasted.

Charles Brandon had a clear head, and as much influence as any man was able to have with regards to King Henry the Eighth. Brandon knew what Jakob was doing by ending their audience with the reminder that the king owed his life to the Nordic knight, and he promised an answer.

And once again, he stepped in to protect me from Henry.

Perhaps serving as a knight for the King of England was not a wise path, considering Jakob's habitually blunt manner. He found that he was becoming less tolerant of royal fits and moods as he grew older, and he did not foresee Henry becoming any less arrogant.

When the day aged and he returned to the apartment which he and Avery shared, the missive with a royal seal waited on a table. Jakob decided to wash and change for supper before he opened it.

He had achieved a clean shirt and hose when Avery hurried into their rooms. "I only have half of an hour to wash and change," she moaned. "Emily!"

The maid was at her side in an instant and began helping her out of her gown. Askel was wiping the last bits of soap from Jakob's cleanly shaven jaw.

Avery spied the letter on the table and her eyes rounded. "Is that a note from Henry at last?"

"I believe so." Jakob stood and stuck his hands through the armholes of his tunic. "I will open it once we are ready to go to supper."

Avery spoke over her shoulder as Emily tied the lacings on her bodice. "Why are you waiting?"

"In part, so you could be with me when I read it," he admitted as he fastened the tunic. "And because I do not wish to have time to stew over it, if the message is displeasing."

"Curiosity is consuming me." Avery's voice was muffled by the heavy skirt over her head. When she emerged, coif unscathed, her next words were quite clear. "But I do wonder about the wisdom of you serving Henry."

Jakob chuckled. He had not expressed his own concerns to his wife—she was simply that observant. "As do I, I must admit."

Once her skirt was secured, Avery stepped to the table and lifted the note. She handed it to Jakob. "Open it."

Jakob noticed Askel and Emily both occupying themselves with mundane tasks, obviously unwilling to leave the room before his fate—and theirs by extension—was revealed.

He slid his thumb under the seal, which released its grip in the thick paper with a complaining crack. He unfolded the note and recognized Brandon's handwriting.

"Brandon wrote this," he said before reading it aloud. "The king greatly appreciates your generous offer of service. However—"

"Oh, no!" Avery groaned.

Jakob put up a reassuring hand. "It is his esteemed opinion that your particular skills might be better suited for serving the Queen in his stead."

Avery's expression brightened. "That is good, is it not?"

"Allow me to finish," Jakob chastised lightly, then continued to read aloud. "I have spoken with Queen Catherine, and she will expect your answer this evening."

Avery scowled. "She did not say anything to me about this."

"Perhaps she did not wish to force you to encourage me to accept the king's disrespect." Jakob handed her the note.

Avery reread the letter. "I suppose you are right, for his dismissal of your offer, and successive handing you off to the queen, would be insulting to most men in your position."

"And yet, it is a relief to me." Jakob gazed into Avery's eyes. "And I believe it is a relief to you as well."

She smiled softly. "I confess that it is. Now we shall serve the same sovereign side-by-side. And a much less precarious one, if I might be so truthful as to add that opinion."

Jakob laughed. "I agree."

Avery laid the letter on the table and Jakob offered his wife his arm. "Let us adjourn to our supper, where I shall inform Charles Brandon that I shall serve Queen Catherine gladly."

Avery stood on her toes, eyes twinkling like obsidian, and kissed him. "And later, dearest husband, perhaps we can celebrate."

Jakob led her from the apartment, more content with his life at that moment than he ever believed he could be.

A Nordic Knight of the Golden Fleece

Postscript:

The Order of the Golden Fleece was first created to have a grand master and twenty-three knights, but membership was increased to fifty-one in 1519. The Order was founded to defend the Roman Catholic religion, to uphold the usages of chivalry, and to settle disputes between its knights and members, who had the right to trial by their fellow members on charges of rebellion, treason, or heresy.

Diego Hurtado de Mendoza, Third Duke of l'Infantado, Alvaro de Zuniga y Guzman, Second Duke of Béjar, Pietro Antonio San Severino, Duke of San Marco, and Laurent de Gorrevod, Comte de Pont de Vaux were all living knights of the Order.

Nygaard Wold, Duke of Holstein, is fictional, as was the attempted Danish coup in 1519. In 1520, however, Christian II invaded Sweden in a battle known as the Stockholm Bloodbath. His cruelty led to his being deposed in 1523, at the age of 42.

Henry VIII continued his affaire with Bessie Blount long enough to get her with child a second time. A daughter, Elizabeth Tailboys, was born in the spring of 1520 and surnamed for Gilbert Tailboys, Bessie's official fiancé.

As for Henry Fitzroy, for the first time since the 12th Century, an illegitimate son was elevated to peerage, becoming the Duke of Richmond and Somerset. However, the young Duke's career came to an end, when the flawed Tudor genes intervened, and he succumbed to consumption in July 1536 at the age of twenty-seven.

In 1535 at the age of fifty-three, the Bavarian prince Frederick II, Elector Palatine and member of the 1519 gathering of the Order of the Golden Fleece, married the oldest daughter of King Christian II of Denmark and Norway. Dorothea was just fifteen at the time. In 1536 and 1537, the prince was involved in two unsuccessful coup attempts against King Christian III of Denmark-Norway.

Thomas Windsor, Duke of Merthyr Tydfil, is purely fictional.

An Unexpected Viking

A Paranormal
Romantic Suspense Trilogy
in The Hansen Series

An Unexpected Viking

Chapter One

Hollis McKenna walked into the hotel foyer and spotted him across the space, leaning casually against the wall. His eyes flicked back and forth, examining the largely female crowd with unexpected seriousness. She assumed he must be one of the cover models, dressed as he was in costume—though fur and leather were unfortunate choices on this roasting summer evening in Phoenix.

"Thank God for air-conditioning," she murmured into her chilled glass of complementary Chardonnay. Even with the cooling system blasting, the gathered attendees made the ballroom foyer uncomfortably warm.

Hollis was attending this convention alone at the urging of her boss, who insisted she needed the break from work. The museum's unexpected bequest of several thousand European artifacts made the hiring of an additional collections manager necessary—and was the only reason Hollis was in Arizona. As far as she was concerned, work was the point. Not some stupid romance novel event.

Her boss insisted, however, claiming that a weekend spent with a bunch of fun authors and hunky young guys was just the thing Hollis needed. Admittedly, because she had been working such long hours, she hadn't had time to make many friends here. While it did limit her social options, and Hollis was okay with that, she finally gave in rather than waste any more time or energy arguing about it.

Besides, Miranda paid for her non-refundable ticket.

What she really needed, she grudgingly admitted to herself, was a break from the monotony of what her life had become now that she was thirty. This was one reason she accepted this job and moved halfway across the country. The other reason was Matt.

After spending a decade of loving and living with her college boyfriend, Matt ended their relationship over a year ago. Said he wanted time to 'rediscover' himself. Become 'a better man' for her. What he discovered, however, was a sudden fiancé and quick, yet enormous, wedding.

And he never even left Milwaukee.

Realizing she had been a fool, Hollis's life soon became an endless round of alarm clocks, premade dinners from the deli, and online dating failures. She seemed destined to be alone and was seriously contemplating adopting several feral cats to seal that fate.

Speaking of alone, Mr. Fur-and-Leather remained rooted in his spot, completely ignored by the otherwise friendly and enthusiastic crowd. The sound bouncing around her was impressive: two hundred women and a handful of men, all talking at once in a happy cacophony of excitement and reconnection. As she watched him, his skittish gaze eventually landed on hers.

Hollis sucked a quick breath and held it. His eyes were an ocean-clear blue, but no less penetrating than if they had been solid black. As he watched her, watching him, his eyes widened and he straightened, eschewing the wall's support. His hands rolled into fists.

What should I do now?

Hollis looked away, but could not stop herself from looking back. He still stared at her, his expression somber.

She took the first step without thinking about it. As she approached him—eyes fixed on each other's—the ladies in her path stepped aside with crooked smiles and puzzled expressions. She didn't pay attention to them—she was being pulled toward the handsome stranger as if he had caught her on a hook and was reeling her in. She stopped in front of him and looked up into his eyes. He was well over six feet tall with dark blond hair hanging below his shoulders.

Hollis spoke first. "Hello."

His gaze shot around the foyer before returning to hers. "Do you have one of those shiny rectangles to press to your ear?"

She made a skeptical face, reached into her hip pocket, and pulled out her phone. "Do you mean this?"

"Yes." He wagged a finger, indicating that she should lift the phone to her ear. "Hold it up while we speak."

Hollis complied with the strange request because she was too curious not to. "Are you one of the models?"

He frowned. "No. What is a model?"

"The Men of Our Dreams contestants." Hollis noticed an accent which she could not place. "If you aren't one of them, then why are you wearing a costume?"

His hands stroked the laced leather vest over his linen shirt and then his palms slid down the sides of his leather pants. "These are my clothes."

"But it's over a hundred degrees outside." She waved a hand at the surrounding glass walls. "Aren't you hot?"

He looked a little embarrassed. "I do not feel heat. Or cold, anymore."

Her hand sagged away from my ear, incredulous at his claim, and he gestured urgently for her to put it back in place. "Keep your shiny thing there."

Frustrated, Hollis held the phone in front of his unshaven face instead. "Why?"

"I don't mean to interrupt, but... are you okay?"

Hollis turned to her right to face a woman wearing a purple cowboy hat made of straw, and one of the surprisingly cute event t-shirts that came free with registration. The woman's concern for Hollis, however, was much more obvious than the reason for it.

"Yes. I'm fine. I'm just talking to this guy." She gestured with the hand holding her phone.

The other woman's eyes flicked to the phone. "Oh, I'm sorry." She flashed an embarrassed smile and backed away, waving her hands in a *go on* sort of motion. "Sorry."

Hollis returned her attention to Mr. Hunky Fur-and-Leather, who now had a first name. "As I was just saying—"

He flicked his finger. "Shiny thing. Now."

She grunted and smacked her phone against her ear.

Ouch. She should have worn smaller earrings. "Why do I need to have my phone against my ear for you to talk to me?"

He leaned close enough that his hair should have ticked her

cheek. "Because you are the only one who can see me."

Hollis's eyes rounded and she whirled around to face the gathered attendees, sloshing wine on the carpeted floor. Her sudden movement garnered brief flashes of friendly attention, before the participants shot odd looks in her direction, and then returned to their momentarily interrupted conversations. Not a single one of them so much as glanced at the tall, leather-clad stranger by her side.

"How is this possible?" Her head felt woozy, like it might float off her shoulders and go bouncing against the ornate ceiling.

She raised her phone to her ear once more—more slowly this time—but it felt as heavy as her battered college-graduation briefcase. She turned back to stare at the tall man. "Are you a ghost?"

He shrugged. "Perhaps."

"Perhaps?" Hollis squeaked, her anger growing. "*Perhaps?*"

He looked inexplicably stricken. "To be honest, I am not sure what I am."

"Well if you don't know, then what am I to think?" she shouted. "Have I gone crazy?"

His gaze lifted over her head and his brow lowered. "Do you have a private chamber?"

"I have a suite in the hotel, if that's what you mean." Hollis recoiled, shocked. "Certainly you don't expect—"

"My lady, you are garnishing an overabundance of unwanted attention." He moved to take her elbow and she imagined that she felt his touch. "I do suggest that we retire to a private setting to continue this discussion, if only for the benefit of your own repute."

Hollis blew an exasperated sigh, slammed her wine glass on a marble side table hard enough that she was relieved the stem didn't shatter, and strode through the foyer, past the crowded bar, toward the elevators to the suites. She didn't dare look behind her. She could feel the weight of inquisitive stares on her back and wondered if she might be better off spending the rest of the weekend in her suite, watching cable and ordering in copious amounts of Chinese food.

When the elevator doors opened, Hollis stepped inside and pressed the button for the second floor. She moved to stand against the back wall, as is correct in polite society. She was alone in the car.

"Of course, I'm alone," she muttered. What did she expect?

Obviously Miranda was right. Hollis had been working too hard, to the point of hallucinating after a couple glasses of wine. *Okay, three.* What the heck—they were free.

When the elevator doors opened, she gasped, sucking the air from the car. Her mysterious man waited on the landing.

"How did you do that?"

"I do not know." He extended a hand. "Come out before the panels slide closed."

Hollis rolled her eyes, stomped out of the elevator and turned right, then right again. Her suite was halfway down the hall and had a very lovely view of the swimming pool below and golf course beyond. If she made the cable and Chinese food decision, at least the weekend's scenery would be enticing.

She fumbled for the room key, hands shaking, and slid the card into the electronic lock the wrong way.

"Damn."

She flipped it over and inserted it again, receiving a condescending beep for the effort. Hollis pressed the handle down and shouldered her way into the room. She let the heavy door fall shut behind her, reasoning that a ghost wouldn't be affected by a mere steel portal. Stopping in the middle of the living room, she turned to face the—whatever he was.

His gaze roamed around the room, taking in details. "It is very clean."

"Yes. The maids come every day."

He nodded. "You must be very wealthy."

Hollis laughed at that. "If I was wealthy, I'd be staying at the Phoenician."

His brow wrinkled. "In Egypt?"

She waved his question away; that answer was far too long and pointless. "Who are you?"

He pressed a fist to his heart and bowed at the waist. "My name is Sveyn Hansen. I come from the home of my father and my father's father, Arendal."

Though the name sounded vaguely familiar, she shook her head. "Where is that?"

Sveyn straightened. "On the southern coast of Norway."

Her jaw dropped. "Are you a Viking?"

"Not any longer." He motioned toward the sleeper sofa. "Will you sit?"

Hollis sank onto the sofa, kicked off her sandals, and tucked her legs under her. She grabbed a throw pillow and clutched it to her chest for protection.

Against a ghost?

She grunted and tossed the pillow back in place. "Okay. Tell me your story."

Sveyn paced back and forth, his long legs eating up the carpeted space with ease. "It was the year ten-seventy. The new religion had come to Norway, and the old religionists were fighting against it."

"New religion?" Hollis interrupted to be certain.

Sveyn paused. "Christianity."

She nodded and waved for him to continue.

"Young Magnus Haraldsson had just died, and his youngest brother, Olaf Haraldsson took his place as king. He was the one who decreed that Norway was now a Christian country." Sveyn stopped his pacing and regarded her with an intense blue gaze. "The *viking*—raiding—must stop. Do you understand?"

Hollis was admittedly entranced, as impossible as this tale was. "Yes. Viking is a verb."

He waved an approving finger in her direction. "But not everyone agrees. When the pagan halls are converted to churches, there are fights between the men. Battles, with strong beliefs on both sides."

"Were you killed?" *What the hell am I asking?*

Sveyn Hansen squatted in front of her. He looked so impossibly real, so enticingly solid, and so unbelievably handsome with his dark blond hair, icy blue eyes, and strong jaw line.

"I was impaled by a long sword through my gut. I was lying in the cold snow, my hot blood running from my body." His eyes pinned hers as his hand moved to the bloodied gash in his vest, which she had been too stunned to notice before he pointed it out.

Hollis felt the unexpected prickle of tears. "And?" she whispered.

"The priest has my head." Sveyn mimed his narrative. "And Old Eric has my feet."

"Old Eric?" Hollis shrugged; her knowledge of Viking lore was limited, because up until very recently this evening she hadn't been that interested. "Who is he?"

"Tunrida? Loki?"

Her blank expression spoke volumes.

Sveyn leaned forward. "The devil himself."

"Oh! Like a tug-of-war?"

Now his expression went blank.

"Each one had hold of you, and they were trying to pull you to their own side. Am I right?"

He nodded, his frighteningly intense expression pulling her in. "There was a sudden flash of light so bright I was blinded, and a roar of thunder that rattled my bones. When everything faded away, I was like this."

Hollis stared at him, wondering if she dared to believe him. "What does 'like this' mean?"

Sveyn would have sighed, she thought, if he was breathing. "I am not dead, and I am not alive."

She unfolded her legs and leaned toward him. "You want me to believe that you are caught in between?"

His shoulders slumped. "I have no other explanation."

Hollis's scientific training kicked into gear. "How extensively can you interact with the three dimensional world?"

Sveyn blinked, but understood her question in spite of his claimed antiquity. "I can see and hear. I cannot taste or smell."

"What about touch?" She lifted her hand. "Can you feel this?"

Hollis pressed her palm against his chest. His form was soft, like pressing into whipped cream—it's there, but only barely.

With a grunt, Sveyn jerked backwards as if she had burned him and scrambled to his feet. He rubbed his chest. His eyes rounded under a startled brow. "My God! I felt that!"

Hollis stood, incredulous and trembling. When her hand moved against the Viking, she definitely felt something. Whatever sort of being he was, or had become, he was definitely *here*.

"Wha—what does this mean?" she stammered.

He reached toward her and tried to grab her hands, but his fingers passed through hers with an ephemeral chill. She jerked her hands back, her pulse surging with adrenaline.

Disappointment pulled his body downward in defeat. "I

thought... I hoped..."

He peered down into her eyes. Hollis clearly saw his soul then: tortured, tired, lonely. So very lonely. Even more lonely and heartbroken than she was.

His voice rumbled in her chest like a looming monsoon storm. "What now?"

Coming in 2015

THE HANSEN FAMILY TREE

Sveyn Hansen* (b. 1035 ~ Arendal, Norway)

***

Rydar Hansen (b. 1324 ~ Arendal, Norway)
Grier MacInnes (b. 1328 ~ Durness, Scotland)

Eryndal Bell Hansen (b. 1327 ~ Bedford, England)
Andrew Drummond (b. 1325 ~ Falkirk, Scotland)

***

Jakob Petter Hansen (b. 1485 ~ Arendal, Norway)
Avery Galaviz de Mendoza (b. 1483 ~ Madrid, Spain)

***

Brander Hansen (b. 1689 ~ Arendal, Norway)
Regin Kildahl (b. 1693 ~ Hamar, Norway)

***

Martin Hansen (b. 1721 ~ Arendal, Norway)
Dagne Sivertsen (b. 1725 ~ Ljan, Norway)

Reidar Hansen (b. 1750 ~ Boston, Massachusetts)
Kristen Sven (b. 1754 ~ Philadelphia, Pennsylvania)

Nicolas Hansen (b. 1787 ~ Cheltenham, Missouri Territory)
Siobhan Sydney Bell (b. 1789 ~ Shelbyville, Kentucky)

Stefan Hansen (b. 1813 ~ Cheltenham, Missouri)
Kirsten Hansen (b. 1820 ~ Cheltenham, Missouri)
Leif Fredericksen Hansen (b. 1809 ~ Christiania, Norway)

***

*Hollis McKenna Hansen (b. Sparta, Wisconsin)

Kris Tualla is a dynamic, award-winning, and internationally published author of historical romance and suspense. She started in 2006 with nothing but a nugget of a character in mind, and has created a dynasty with The Hansen Series, and its spin-off, The Discreet Gentleman Series. Find out more at: www.KrisTualla.com

Kris is an active PAN member of Romance Writers of America, the Historical Novel Society, and Sisters in Crime, and was invited to be a guest instructor at the Piper Writing Center at Arizona State University. An enthusiastic speaker and teacher, Kris co-created **The Dreams Convention**—combining Arizona's only romance reader event: ArizonaDreaminEvent.com and its author-focused companion: BuildintheDream.com.

*"In the Historical Romance genre, there have been countless kilted warrior stories told. I say it's time for a new breed of heroes. Come along with me and find out why: **Norway IS the new Scotland!**"*

Made in the USA
Charleston, SC
20 March 2016